The FOOTBALL WHISPERER

MEL A ROWE

Also by MEL A ROWE

Avoiding the Pity Party

Unplanned Party

Winter's Walk

THE ELSIE CREEK SERIES

The ART of DUST

DIAMOND in the DUST

CAKED in DUST

Xmas DUST

Copyright

The Following Is Written In Australian English

PROLOGUE

The MCG
(Melbourne Cricket Ground),
A U S T R A L I A .

No matter what, Ward wasn't going to let Sheldon win—not today. His palms curled into fists as Ward ignored Sheldon's side-smirk and focused on the prize.

Amid the deafening roar of over ninety thousand spectators, men battled like fighters in a modern-day Colosseum. The crowd's passion reverberated through Ward's body, energising him.

He shouldered into position amongst the mash of uniforms, getting elbowed by other players while striving for possession of their talisman, the Sherrin. Slick with sweat, Ward stole the red leather ball from another man's hands. He burst through the scuffle, bounced the ball against the manicured turf, and with an almighty boom of thunder that echoed from his boot to ball, it sailed through sombre skies.

Ward trailed its projection as players jostled for the

best position. Open palms begged to receive the gift, but it was captured in a vice-like grip by his tall-timber teammate, Nick.

Ward pulled up his Saints' game-day socks, glancing at the rest of his teammates. He led the arrow-head wave of warring males back into position, as they regained their breaths ready to battle the Magpies as soon as the ball broke free.

Two teams. Eighteen men on-field, while four waited like chained fighting dogs ready to pounce from the bench, all bearing the battle-weight upon their shoulders. They would do this. For their teammates, for the club, for the fans, and for the dream of becoming Australia's finest.

Scents of rain and mashed grasses mixed with meat pies, beer, and wet wool, filtered down from the over-full stands. Thunder rolled like a wooden whiskey barrel across a stone floor, spilling rain in bucket loads that drenched cowering crowds. An icy wind whipped through the stadium, but nothing would disrupt the Grand Final replay.

The ball slippery. The ground an ice rink, and visibility was reduced. But the warriors remained and fought amongst the sweat, tears, and mud.

Again, there was the rush into the mud-pit to gain possession as they soldiered on, thrashing it out for the umpire's centre bounce of the ball. The ruck-men punched at the Sherrin that ricocheted higher and further along the field.

Ward leaped onto a team player's back for elevation as his stretched fingertips grazed the leathered jewel twirling in the rain.

Sheldon mirrored Ward's action, clambering over another player, vying for the ball.

Ward's human step ladder slipped in the sludge and the floor beneath Ward was gone. He pushed off, gaining for leverage while still reaching for that ball. All that mattered was getting possession of that damned ball. Blinded by tunnel vision, he didn't see it coming.

Ward and Sheldon collided, spearing into each other mid-air. Head to head. Shoulder to shoulder. The pain blinded Ward as gravity pushed him crown first to earth.

And there his world stopped.

Knocked unconscious, his body twitched as if lying on a watery bed of electrified grass. Then he finally stilled beside Sheldon.

The ball bounced twice, then rolled to a stop in the puddle between the two players.

Nobody moved. A collective gasp came from the crowd. Everyone waited for a sign of life from either of the motionless men sprawled across the grass beneath the pouring rain…

Because it looked like they'd broken their necks!

One

'Home sweet whatever.' Hunched in pain, Ward shuffled through his front door like a ninety-year-old fart, with his parents following. His housemates were at practice, which is where Ward would rather be. Yet, being home was better than that crummy hospital room. Especially since he'd been forced to share with Sheldon because that's how the *Spinal Care Unit* was set up—it was worse than torture. Not the bed, not the pain, but dealing with Sheldon!

Somehow, Sheldon's war story got bigger every time he spoke to the constant parade of women fawning over him. Ward wanted a bucket to hurl in, if he could only lift his head to do it.

At least Ward's teammates visited, even if they sat and gawked at Sheldon's never-ending parade of women. *How did the wanker do it?* The only way the prick slept straight from all his lies was because he'd been bound up tight into a full body brace, they were forced to surrender to.

Amazingly, they'd suffered the same injury. Both strapped in for safety, waiting for the swelling to reduce along the spine, with their own specialised nurse watching over them. Or Ward would've gotten out of bed and thumped Sheldon's big mouth shut.

Thankfully, he no longer had to deal with that side-smirking-snob at home.

Ward shucked off his shoes, tugged off his jacket, then attempted to toss it onto the coat hook. Instead, it dropped to the floor. Ward leaned over but straightened again as the chunky brace pinched his neck. He tugged at his restrictive, hot and itchy neck brace, poking a finger down the side to let some air in.

'I'll get it.' Brian dropped Ward's bag to the side and scooped up the jacket. 'Where does this go?'

'Anywhere, Dad.' Ward didn't care, focusing on his most sacred spot in the world—his chair.

'Here we are, dear.' Shirley placed a pillow on the nearest of the three leather recliners in the lounge room.

'Not my chair, Mum.' Ward limped to the middle reclining chair and prepared himself to sit. Back turned, hands gripped the armrests, and, as if bearing weights, his bum found the seat…slowly.

There was no plonking with the TV's remote control in hand. No flicking the handle to put his feet up in one swift well-practised move. Nope, now it was slow and steady, to avoid a whole new world of hurt.

But he was home. Front and centre of the TV. In his favourite chair, allowing his spine to curve into the cool leather. *Now this was living.*

'Forgot you've got your own chairs,' said Shirley, tucking the pillow behind him.

'Every man should have a favourite chair.' Brian dropped into the spare seat on the left, flicked the handle back, crossed his loafers at the ankles on the footrest and began to rock. 'Reckon one like this would do me.'

'I should get you one and call it a Father's Day gift for the next ten years,' Ward said, struggling to shift his simple feather pillow into position.

'And I'll have a beer fridge for Christmas.' Brian patted the small bar fridge identical to the other two sitting beside each recliner.

'We're not having a beer fridge in the lounge room.' Shirley then turned to her son and said, 'Now, are you sure you don't want to come home, dear?'

'I'm fine, Mum.' If Ward didn't move fast, he'd avoid the literal pain in the neck.

But what bothered him most was the damned constant tingling ache in his fingers and toes. It was like growing pains in the body, with a droning dentist-drill in his head that didn't switch off, no matter how many drugs they'd given him.

'What did the surgeon say?' Shirley asked, wringing her together, so tight her knuckles went white.

'Um...' Ward didn't want to worry his mother who'd aged overnight where there was grey in her auburn hair. Her lips pressed into a line that accentuated ex-smoker's lines, while concerned creases deepened around her hazel eyes.

'I'll be okay, Mum. Promise.' He had to believe it.

'*Helloooooo, everyone,*' hollered Tina, bursting through the open door. Her many layers of clothing rustled as her jewellery jangled.

'Who left the door open?' Ward wanted to run but couldn't. Not when he'd just sat down and didn't know how long it'd take to get up again.

'Hi, Mum.' Tina kissed Shirley's cheek. 'Hey, Dad.' Her smile disappeared as she looked down her nose. 'Ward.'

Ward winced up at his older sister, wearing an entire rainbow of colours in layers and lace. Her wrists were wrapped in assorted beads, with bells on her anklets. Reeking of Dragon's Blood, or Unicorn Turds, or whatever incense she'd rolled in. Tina, his new-age cosmic-loving sister didn't suit the décor of his place. She clashed with the dark tones of timber and leather. She even clashed with the Saint's team colours on the giant flag pinned to the wall. Tina was just too bright for this room.

Worse, her latest boyfriend, *What's-his-name*, strolled in behind her. Was Ward still suffering memory loss from the unremembered fall to not remember What's-his-name? Not that it mattered, his sister's men never stuck around long enough to remember their names.

Tina stood in front of her brother cradling a casserole dish. 'I brought you some stew.'

'Beef?' Ward silently prayed.

'You did take a whack to the head. It's my famous mung-bean and tofu stew, of course.'

'Ugh.' He hated that mud and his sister's many odd vegetarian diet-of-the-day-dishes. Ward wanted meat, where veggies were only there to decorate the plate. His fruit and veg requirements for the day got blended into one drink. Simple. Not tofu and mung-bean-muck that smelt like peppered baked dirt.

But they weren't allowed to tell Tina that, looking to his mum for help.

'Thank you, Tina, that's so thoughtful. I'll put it in the kitchen for the boys to eat later,' said Shirley, taking the dish away.

'You remember Ron, don't you, Dad?' Tina said, stroking What's-his-name who was short, with big hands that looked like they had some strength in the grip 'The jockey.'

Ward tried to suppress the smirk, he knew his dad didn't remember Ron either. *Did Ron shop in the kids' section for clothes?*

'Err...' Brian's leather chair squelched as he shifted forward to shake hands with the small man. 'How's the world of racing, Ron?'

Ron nodded. 'Good.'

'Oh honey, tell them or I will. I'm not shy.' Tina put her arm around her boyfriend's shoulders as Ward and his dad rolled eyes at each other.

Tina shy? Nope—never. Tina was the relative who

embarrassed you in public. As her brother, Ward always walked twenty paces behind her to not be associated with his hippy-magic-mung-bean-loving-nightmare of a sister.

'Ron's going into his first race this weekend.' Tina wrapped her arm tighter around Ron, stroking his brown hair like the doll she used to drag down the corridor as a kid.

'Horse race?' Shirley asked, returning from the kitchen.

'Yeah, race twelve. Can't wait,' said Ron.

'It's so great, isn't it? Ron's off his drug charges and he's now free to ride again. I'm so proud of you, honey.' Tina kissed Ron's cheek, then sighed and smiled at him.

Ron cleared his throat and tugged at his shirt's collar. 'So, ah, what did the Doc say about your neck, Ward?'

'Yeah, what did they say? How come you're still wearing a neck brace at home?'

Ward winced as his sister's chalkboard-grating voice echoed with the ache squirrelling down his spine. He didn't want to answer Tina's questions. He didn't even want her in his house.

Tina's skirts rustled as she turned towards Shirley. 'Mum, what did the doctors say?'

'Well, the surgeon told your brother to rest up for a week and then he goes back for more tests.'

'*Surgeon? Noooooo, you can't let 'em cut you up?*' Tina's voice bounced off the walls forcing the TV screen to shudder.

'Mum didn't say that.' Trust his sister to bark out what he didn't want to hear, and no doubt most of the suburb had heard her too.

'*I heard surgeon.*' Tina slapped palms on her generous hips, generous from the layers of clothing twenty gypsies could wear. 'You know anaesthetic gives you cancer. They reckon you lose ten years off your life when you're put under, that's *if* you wake up again. And then you'll suffer from arthritis. And then—'

'*Shut up.* I don't need to hear that!' Why was she here tormenting him?

Tina stepped back as if slapped in the face, with mouth moving but silent.

'Your brother doesn't need to hear that, dear. Not when he's just gotten out of hospital,' said Shirley.

At least the hospital had saved him from his sister for a little while. She'd been too scared she'd catch some tropical limb-dropping-disease from walking inside the main doors. Which, thankfully, kept her voice from echoing down the corridors that'd trigger an entire maternity ward of babies to scream.

'But *Muuuuum,*' whined Tina.

'I know you care, dear, but they're waiting to see if your brother's body will sort itself out.'

'No doubt, with enough chemical drugs to rot your insides.' Tina pointed to the pile of pill bottles on the bar fridge next to her brother. 'What are you? Footy Neanderthals with your housemates in matching reclining chairs, worshipping the idols on the big screen. Don't you know what a coffee table is, instead of using your matching bar fridge tops to show off all your pills? You Footballers are a breed of your own, living together, dressing the same, eating the same—'

'They're vitamins, Club-supplied and Coach-approved.' Ward hadn't unpacked his pill packets from the hospital yet.

Brian picked up one of the pill bottles and checked out the label. 'Multi-vitamins, huh?'

'All part of our health and training regime.' The club had a team of dietician's, physicians, physios, and almost everything else but a neuro-surgeon.

'You'd get all the proper nutrients your body needs by eating fruits and vegetables and drinking water, instead of sports drinks that are full of sugar and salts,' said Tina in another one of her know-it-all tirades.

'Mum?' Ward looked to his mother for help, unable to kick his sister out because he couldn't lift a leg if he tried.

How the hell was he going to kick a football again?

Ward's heart rate spiked as if stabbed with shards of ice. He licked his lips and gasped for breath. *I'm okay. I'm okay.* Mentally repeating the mantra he'd replayed since the accident.

Inhaling deep through the nose, filling his diaphragm. He exhaled slowly through the mouth, trying to relax the fear gripping his entire body, as the armrest's leather creaked beneath his grip.

Shirley stepped in between her adult children. 'Tina, we know you're only looking out for your brother, but he's got a large team of people behind him.'

'So where are they now, huh?' Tina waved at the team flag that was the only piece of art on the wall. It hung alongside the bookcase filled with trophies and medals instead of books.

'The physio will be here after team practice.' Where Ward wished he was instead of suffering this conversation.

'What recovery programme have they got you doing?' Ron asked, peeking over Tina's bulky, lace-covered shoulder.

'Daily physio and stretching exercises, hoping to manipulate the nerve back into place.'

'And if it doesn't?' Ron asked.

Ward frowned and swallowed the lump. 'I'll go and see the specialist.' Nope, he wasn't saying surgeon. 'Until then, I'll do what I'm told by the professionals.' He was well trained to follow orders, especially when it came to taking care of his body to play the game he lived for.

'Is it a pinched nerve?' Ron asked.

'Yeah.' It sucked that Ward couldn't nod.

'You had that, didn't you, honey,' said Tina.

'Uh-huh. I'd pinched a nerve in my shoulder from a fall during a practice race,' said Ron. 'It gave me a dead-arm for ages.'

'Long way to fall,' murmured Brian. 'I mean, those racehorses are big.'

'Those thoroughbreds are *huge*, Dad,' said Tina with wide eyes.

Shirley asked, 'How did you un-pinch your shoulder nerve, Ron?'

'They had me doing the same as Ward. Rest up in hope the body worked itself out. Mind you, I didn't have no physio visiting me at home. And…'

'And what else, dear?' Shirley asked.

'Nah, you'll think I'm nuts.'

Tina stroked Ron's arm. 'No, they won't, honey.'

Ron rubbed his shoulder as if reliving the pain. 'I tried physio to manipulate that sucker.'

'Did it work?' Ward asked.

'No, and they'd scheduled me in for surgery.'

'*Nooo…*' Tina palm-slapped her mouth as the widescreen rattled behind her.

Ron reached out and stopped the TV shaking on the wall. 'Loose connection?'

'Voice-quake,' mumbled Ward. He was about to complain about his sister, but his mum stopped him with one of her peacekeeper-looks.

'Go on, Ron,' said Shirley.

'The day before I was scheduled for surgery, I was at the track to get my pay. And, well, they had this…' Ron shoved his hands into his jeans' pockets, raising his shoulders to his ears. 'That's when I saw the horse whisperer.'

His dad stopped rocking in his chair. His sister didn't

shift her many layers. His mum rubbed her lips together. And for the first time since Ward had arrived home, it was silent. 'The what-whisperer?'

'Does she talk to animals?' Shirley's head tilted almost sideways. Ward was surprised at how much neck movement his mother possessed.

'Like that movie we saw?' Brian shook his head side to side, resuming his rocking-chair-ride.

'Well, she isn't, but she is.' Ron rubbed the back of his neck and rolled his shoulder.

'So, what is she, honey?' Tina asked with her head nodding up and down, up and down.

Tugging at his itchy neck brace, Ward didn't know what was worse, this stupid conversation, or that they were all showing off their full range of neck movement.

'She's a horse healer,' replied Ron.

Tina's eyes widened as did her mouthy smile. 'Like with crystals, and ointments, and incense?

'I never saw any, and I thought it was hocus-pocus-crap too. But she heals horses through massage. I've seen it. She works with the stables' vets as a legit master of something. Swear it.'

Shirley rubbed her lips together as if to formulate another one of her ever-tactful responses. Tina blinked trying to process impossible possibilities. And, as per usual, Brian screwed up his nose and said nothing. Would it be rude for Ward to ask his family to have this conversation of nonsense elsewhere?

'How?' Shirley asked.

'I dunno, she just did.' Ron rolled his whole shoulder and arm in the air.

Show off. 'What did she do to fix your shoulder?' Ward was already over this whole horse-healing tangent.

'Well, she was working on one of the horses when my mate asked if she worked on humans too.'

'And did she?' Tina asked.

'Nah, she doesn't touch people, only horses. Reckons they don't talk back or complain. She's cheeky.' Ron chuckled as Tina frowned, rubbing her lips like her mother.

'She must've helped you,' said Brian, mid-chair rock.

'She did,' said Ron. 'She worked out from the way I was carrying myself that I'd pinched a nerve before I'd even explained it to her. Then she walks up, puts her hands under my jacket and fixed it. Just like that.' Ron faced the family, who looked at him unconvinced. 'I dunno how to explain it. I felt this heat, then this vibration, and then she tugged on my upper arm and I felt it give. Before that, I'd had this constant tingling ache in my arm since I fell. Then it was gone, just like that. Swear it.'

No one in Ward's family moved or nodded. Not that Ward could, nor wanted to. He just didn't believe any of this horse-nonsense.

'Hey, as much as Tina tries to do her new age stuff, this woman did it like magic. It's the truth.'

'I believe you, honey,' said Tina.

'You would,' mumbled Ward.

Tina scowled at her brother, and then in the blink of an eye, she smiled down at her boyfriend. 'Ron, how much did she charge you?'

'A carton of beer.'

'What?' Chorused the father and son.

'Yep,' said Ron with a grin, 'she told me to leave the carton on the counter as her fee. She even bet me another carton of beer that they'd cancel my surgery, which is what happened the next day. So yeah, it cost me two cartons of beer.'

'Horse-shit.' After being forced to share a room with Sheldon's bull, now Ward had to suffer in his own home too. *Not gonna happen.*

Tina glared at her brother. '*Muuum.*'

Again, the TV shuddered on the wall.

Ron reached out and steadied it, then pointed at Ward. 'I agree, I was just like you. But by that stage, I was willing to try anything because I couldn't sleep from that continuous dull ache in my arm. I couldn't get comfortable and I'd tried everything everyone was telling me to do. But then this woman, in not even five minutes flat, healed me in the corridor by the stables and walked away.'

'Has this horse lady done this to anyone else?' Brian asked, while he shrugged at Ward arching his eyebrow.

'It's rare, she's only done a few of the blokes down the track. She doesn't advertise it because horses are her specialty. It's why we call her the Horse Whisperer, coz we've seen 'em cranky adrenalin-filled thoroughbreds bow down to her. She's got this calming effect over 'em when she massages them.'

'So, it's like a holistic massage? *That's what you need, Ward.*' Tina's booming voice forced Ward and Brian to lean back into their seats. Again, Ron gripped the corner of the shuddering television, glancing at Tina, then back at the TV.

'I'm not having some voodoo-whatever touching me.' Not when Ward had a trained medical team behind him, skilled in proven science.

'She'd tell you the same,' said Ron, chuckling.

'Ron, can you find out what this lady does, please?' Shirley asked.

Ward glared at the mother he loved. 'Not happening, Mum. I'll only do what the Club tells me to do.' No way was he having some old hag covered in horsehair, touching him with hands as hard as hoofs, and chipped yellow nails strong enough to pick off a horseshoe straight from the hoof.

'Shirl, our boy's right. He's got the physio visiting soon, and we all know the Club will look out for him. They always do.' Brian reached over and patted his son's shoulder.

Ward winced against the spearing pain as if his skin would splinter like glass. It sucked being so weak and helpless like this overnight. *I'm okay. I'm okay.*

'There's no harm in asking before Ward has surgery, dear. He's only got a week to recover, and there's nothing wrong with trying alternatives.'

Now his parents were talking over him like he was still in primary school. Why did he check out of the hospital? How many steps would it take to get to his room? How long would it take to get out of his favourite chair?

'I guess you're right, Shirl.'

Ward stared at his dad in disbelief. Was he still tripping on some wonder drugs and having a delayed reaction? Or was he still in his hospital bed about to wake up for a sponge bath?

Brian rested his elbows on his knees and lowered himself to face his son. 'It wouldn't hurt to ask, Ward. Acupuncture cured your Uncle Tom of smoking.'

'And there's Aunt Annabelle and your cousin who saw that naturopath for their allergies too, dear,' said Shirley.

Tina's many skirt layers rustled louder than a dozen kids screwing up a ream of paper as she shifted towards her brother. 'I'm always into alternative medicines first,' Tina said, 'it's healthier and more natural, you know.'

Ward groaned. He couldn't lower his chin any further against the neck brace. Couldn't leave because he'd just got here, and lived here, and it was an effort to walk. 'I've got the Club's medics looking after me and I only listen to them, so leave it.' He wished they'd all leave, unsure which was worse, his family's homecoming, or sharing a hospital room with Sheldon?

Two

A week later, Ward was snappy. His prime physical condition was slipping away, now reduced to the status of an old man. With a continuous stiff neck, grinding his teeth against the pain, tasting sweat and assorted antiseptics, Ward shuffled along the wide corridor to see the specialist—still refusing to call the man a surgeon.

'Oh man,' whined Sam.

'What?' Ward gave his housemate a sideways glance. He gripped the railing and hauled himself along the corridor. *This sucked.* Two weeks ago, he would've slid down this corridor in his socks, just for the hell of it. But now, he walked around like a hunchback with an iron rod rammed up his spine and a stinky neck brace.

'Sheldon's in the waiting room.'

'For real?' Why did they insist on keeping them together since the game's accident? Sure, they were both players, but they weren't twins. They weren't even friends. Yet, the way the spinal unit was set up, there was no one-on-one with the doctors because they'd miraculously suffered the same injuries.

'But it's his women, mate.' Sam sucked his bottom lip

loud like slurping through a straw.

'Whatever.' Ward was not in the mood for female company, especially Sheldon's cast-offs. All Ward wanted was the nearest seat.

Ward gripped the hard, plastic armrests and with bent knees, he gently lowered his body weight. He leaned back even slower, then revelled in the glory of the humble chair.

Sam plonked into the seat beside Ward, and said, 'Sheldon's got twins, dude. Blondes with enough cleavage to drown in.'

'No way.' Ward looked up as high as his body allowed and his jaw dropped as far as the neck brace let him. Were they centrefold models? *How did the prick do that?*

'Sheldon.' Ward's voice dropped in a gravelly pitch as he coldly eyed Sheldon with a woman on either side. Sheldon in his designer jeans, the polished boots, the bad boy leather jacket, and that neck brace. Even wounded, that BS-artist oozed rock star appeal that had those women pawing at Sheldon like he was some prized mink coat.

'Ward.' Sheldon's tone was silky-smooth with his lips twisting as he squinted at Ward. 'Any change?'

No smug side-smirk from Sheldon—*now that was a first.*

'Nah. You?' *Dammit,* why was he engaging with the enemy? Why were they even in the same enclosed breathing space?

Sheldon's chest rose in a huff. 'No change.'

'*Sheldon and Ward,*' called the nurse.

Both men, with their aides, were helped to stand.

'Sorry, you'll have to share the room as there's been an emergency and your consultations have been pushed together. Unless you want to reschedule?' The nurse asked by the open doorway.

'*No,*' both men chorused.

Ward didn't want to come back, he was here to be healed!

'Well then, gentlemen, through there and into the gowns please.' The nurse pointed to the examination room that seemed a hundred metres too far away.

'I'll be right, Sam.' Ward didn't need his housemate to hold his hand. If he had twin models to help, like Sheldon, it might be different.

'You girls stay,' said Sheldon as he hobbled forward.

Both men shunted across the shiny linoleum floor and separated to the opposite sides of the corridor where they gripped the handrail to propel them towards the open doorway. Amongst the grunts, groans, hand slides and boot shuffles, it was a race to see who got to the finish line first.

Ward stopped. *What was this crap?* It was a hospital, not the bloody football field. 'After you.'

He let Sheldon shuffle past, noticing they walked the same. Sheldon had the dark rings under the eyes, stiff shoulders, hunched back, the neck brace and lack of arm movement. Just like Ward.

So how come Ward didn't have twin models doting over him?

No, he had to suffer with his mung-bean-mud-making-big-sister who was on his case, while his housemates fled for the front door leaving Ward at the mercy of his family.

Inside the room made of two examination beds that was as clinically bare as any footy changeroom found in the many stadiums he'd visited across the country.

Ward slipped off his shirt, grateful he went for slap-happy-comfort in clothing, unlike Sheldon, struggling out of his belted jeans and boots. *Yep, when a man's in pain you dress for no bastard—or blonde busty twins.* 'So, no changes, huh?' Ward asked, dumping his shirt onto the examination bed.

'Can't sleep. Can't get comfortable, no matter what the girls do for me.'

Ward refused to conjure what the women were doing to Sheldon—that'd be the stuff of nightmares. 'Everything ticking you off lately?'

'Yes. You?'

'Oh, yeah.' Ward slid on the hospital gown, wishing he could reach around to tie up the back. Why change wardrobe when the specialist was only checking his neck?

'I'm doing physio twice a day, but nothing's working. You?'

'Yeah, same,' replied Ward. 'Hey, you've got the best in the business, how come you aren't any better?' Sheldon worked for the team that had the money, and the creep was loaded in family money too.

'Wish I was. I'm so over it. I can't walk straight or look up.'

'Have you got that tingling in the fingers and toes, with the constant ache shooting down the arm too?'

'That's the worst, I can't switch that off.'

'Yeah, I hear you.' Ward sighed. The hospital gown slid off his shoulders and crumbled into his lap as he sat on the edge of the examination bed staring at the floor. He wanted nothing in common with Sheldon. He didn't even want to be in this room, suffering from an injury that was taking too long to heal.

'So…' The specialist leaned against the door jamb watching the two men, with charts tucked under his arm as his spectacles swung in his other hand. 'I hear you both.' The specialist pushed off the frame, as the nurse shut the door behind them, and he faced the pair of sportsmen. 'And I can see you both. So, any changes?'

'No,' replied Sheldon with a scowl.

'Ditto,' said Ward, 'and over it!'

The specialist slipped on his glasses and started his examination on Sheldon with a series of *Mm's*. He ticked and flicked the chart, then shifted onto Ward.

Ward licked his lips, tasting the sterile air as the doctor conducted his examination. 'And?' Ward wanted answers, not silence, not pain. He wanted a cure.

The specialist clicked his pen and scribbled on the

chart. 'I'm going to schedule you both in for more tests as part of our preparation strategy for surgery.'

'Hey, hold on a second.' Ward tried to stand tall and face this high-priced medicine-man. 'Isn't there anything else you can do first?' His body was his golden ticket and he could hear his sister's irritating chalkboard-grating-screech going off in his head. He knew surgery in the neck was dangerous territory. One small slip meant he'd never walk again. After all, his sister had shoved a printed list of faults for this type of operation in his face only yesterday.

Sheldon winced as he tried to stand straight and said, 'I agree with Ward. Aren't there any other alternatives available?'

Ward blinked at Sheldon. It'd have to be the first time Sheldon agreed with him in a long time. How much pain was Sheldon in, to not share some smart-arse comeback?

'I'll be doing more tests to pinpoint the exact locations of pain and to check for improvement comparisons against the first set of tests. If none, then it's a matter of getting in there and releasing the pressure. I'll discuss it further with your Club's physicians. You may try for manipulation but be aware of the risks.'

'Are you talking about using a chiropractor? The Club's chiro won't do it, he said it might make it worse,' said Sheldon.

'Really?' Ward hadn't tried that yet.

'Your chiropractor's right,' said the specialist. 'Any harsh, forceful, or even sudden movement could pinch it more, or cut it off completely while in that state. I've read your physio reports and they've both been administering the treatment I've recommended. I'll write you up a script for sleeping pills.'

'Doc, is that medication AFL approved and not on the banned drug register?' Ward asked.

'Do you want to sleep or not?'

'*I want to play again.*' Ward clenched his teeth, frowning at the complete stranger who now controlled his entire world. 'I'll do whatever you or the Club tells me to do, as long you can fix it and get me back on that field.'

'I'll schedule the tests. In the meantime, keep up with the physio treatments and rest.'

'What about acupuncture, or deep tissue massage?' Sheldon asked.

The specialist peered over his spectacles with his pen paused over the charts. 'Gentlemen, you both have pinched nerves. If it stays in that position any longer than necessary, it could cause permanent damage.'

'Shiiit.' Ward leaned against the bed's edge and sighed, defeated. 'Fine, book me in.'

'Only thing permanent on my body is my ink-work, so sign me up too,' said Sheldon.

The specialist tucked the charts under his arm, took off his glasses and faced the pair. 'We'll schedule you in for preparations. Stick with the programme and, hopefully, we'll have you playing by next year.'

'NEXT YEAR!' Sheldon and Ward chorused.

The specialist headed for the door opened by the waiting nurse. 'Just work on today first, gentlemen.'

Ward's hospital gown fell to the floor as he clutched the pain in his chest, unable to breathe.

No football for a year?

Football was his job.

More than his job.

It was his life!

To have a year off was impossible. It wasn't going to happen. No way.

'*This is all your fault, Ward.*' Sheldon snarled, pointing his finger at Ward like a spear's tip.

Ward stepped into Sheldon's finger, nose to nose, toe to toe. Even if his body was screaming in pain, right now he was so angry he could walk through fire and not feel it. '*You did this to the both of us.*'

The nurse backed out the doorway. '*Security?*'

'I knew it,' said Sam, bursting into the room. 'All right fellas, calm down.' Sam pulled Ward back while pressing a palm against Sheldon's chest and wedged between the pair. 'Do you wanna get banned from this hospital too?'

'Damn it.' Ward stepped back, slid into his unlaced shoes and snatched his shirt and jacket from Sam. 'Let's go.' No such thing as a fast getaway as he shunted out the door, half-dressed, and into a blast of wintry air.

Even the icy wind couldn't cool his anger, not when he was on the edge of hell's abyss of eternal pain. He'd been at the top of his game—would he ever reach that level again?

His sister's voice niggled in the back of his mind forcing that trickle of fear to trail down his spine—would he even survive the surgery?

Three

'Surgery? Man, that's deep,' muttered Sam, seated beside Ward in their matching recliners, where the television played in the background.

Nick, seated on the other side of Ward, said, 'No one likes surgery or recovery time.'

'A year. A whole season, gone.' Ward gripped his chair's armrests. 'The worst part is, I've got Sheldon along for the ride, except he's got models.'

'Twins.' Sam grinned as he sat forward. 'Should've seen them, Nick. They had—'

'*Hullllooooo,*' hollered Tina, bursting through the front door.

Nick screwed up his nose as if the air had been fouled. 'How did your sister get inside?'

'Because Sam left the door unlocked,' replied Ward.

'My bad,' mumbled Sam, sinking into his seat.

'Hello, boys,' said Shirley, following Tina to stand before the three men. 'Well, what did the doctor say?'

Ward didn't want to upset his mother, he didn't want his sister here. And he didn't want to share his news with Tina present, because he had a bad feeling it was about to get worse.

'Tell us straight,' demanded Tina, towering over him.

'No lectures from you.' Ward winced at his sister's clothes where the swirling tie-dye pattern were making him dizzy.

'Oh god, that means bloody surgery.' Tina wailed with hands in the air.

'What's wrong with the TV?' Nick asked, leaping from his seat to steady the shuddering screen.

'Voice-quake.' It was a shoulder-shrugging moment, yet Ward couldn't shrug because of the neck brace.

'Wow, it's true.' Sam's eyes widened at the wide-screen then at Tina.

'We should get my Dad in to check the connections he put on this wall, ' Nick said, peering behind the screen.

'I know how to fix it so it never happens again.' Ward glared at his sister and prepared for the final eviction.

'Now, Tina,' said Shirley, putting her arm around her daughter's shoulders. 'Remember to be gentle with your brother.'

Damn it. His mum gave him her peacekeeper's look, reducing his speech to a death-glare. He hadn't seen his sister for months, yet here she was terrorising him on a daily basis.

'*Mum, Ward can't have surgery.*' With a rustle of her many layers, Tina swivelled to face her brother. 'Ward, that's the neck. The spinal cord. Nerves. You could end up living in a wheelchair—'

'Your brother doesn't need to hear that, dear.'

'Mum doesn't need to hear that, Tina.' Ward was dangerously close to the fiery edge that still simmered from his confrontation with Sheldon. But the worry in his mother's face bothered him more.

'Surgery is the last resort when *you haven't tried all avenues*,' said Tina, leaning in closer and smothering Ward with her pungent incense cloud.

Ward's leather chair creaked from his grip as his knuckles went white. If his sister got any closer, she'd be entering his swinging zone. 'If they don't do something soon it might become permanent.'

'Or they'll permanently damage your spinal cord! *I'm calling Ron for that horse whisperer.*' Tina reached into the folds of her many skirts and whipped out her mobile.

'The what?' Nick asked, leaning against the wall still holding the corner of the TV.

'The horse whisperer,' replied Tina, scrolling through her phone's screen. 'She fixed Ron's shoulder the day before surgery.'

'Not happening, Tina,' said Ward. 'I'm not letting any voodoo horse doctor touch me.'

Tina swiped the air flippantly at Ward as she headed to the kitchen, talking on the phone. 'Ron, honey…'

Nick returned to his seat from holding the TV, saying, 'Horse whisperer? That's new.'

'Let's hope she can help you, dear,' said Shirley, taking a seat next to Nick on the massive man-couch.

'Mum, she works on horses. How do we know she's not another one of Tina's groupie-cultist-of-the-day weirdos?'

'I tried acupuncture for my calf when it kept cramping. It worked for me,' said Nick. 'Have you tried that?'

'Ron's at the track,' said Tina, bustling through from the kitchen. 'He said she's in town for today's race-meet, so I'm going to see this woman now.'

Shirley shoved off the couch and shouldered her handbag. 'I'm going too.'

'Mum, no,' said Ward.

'Listen, I'll see if she's normal for you.' Shirley kissed her son's cheek. 'You know if your sister goes, she'll scare her off.'

'Good.'

'There's no harm in trying, dear.'

'*Come on, Mum, we don't want to miss her.*' Tina slid on her sunglasses and opened the front door.

'Why won't they listen?' Ward wanted to punch something. But it hurt to punch. Now reduced to tapping his fists on the armrests, leaving a dent in the leather—ruining his chair.

'I say try it,' said Sam, jumping to his feet to lock the front door. 'Horse whisperer, wasn't that a movie?'

'We'll get you a saddle.' Nick chuckled, patting Ward's arm.

'Nick off.' Inch by inch, Ward rose from his chair

wishing for a quick pain-free exit.

'Just teasin', man,' said Nick. 'Why not try it? You've got nothing to lose.'

'I'm not having some god-knows-what working on me when they only work on animals. I'm not a dog.'

'No, but you're snappy as a snake with a bloody sore head, mate,' said Sam, sliding back into his seat.

'Damn.' Ward stopped at the doorway to his room and shunted around to face his housemates' concerned expressions as the guilt gripped his chest. 'I'm sorry. I don't mean to take this out on you guys.'

'We know you don't. You're usually laid back about everything,' said Nick.

'Except during game time, then there's no stopping you,' said Sam. 'Mate, we can see it's ticking you off, not being able to sleep, sit, walk, stand, nothing. We get it.'

'I...um...' Great, a minute ago Ward wanted to tear his sister's head off, and now he wanted to man-hug his best mates for understanding. This rollercoaster ride of emotions was crap. The only time he ever got emotional was when it came to the game—a game he couldn't play for a year.

Ward gripped his heart as it once again speared ice into his chest. Gone from the game for a year and he'd lose his spot on the team. He'd lose his room in this house. His wages. His lifestyle. Everything.

'I reckon you should try it, Ward. That way we can get rid of your sister and save our TV from her voice-quake,' Nick said, waving at their wide-screen.

Ward faced the muted game on the TV. When would he play again? 'A Tina-free zone, now that'd be a bonus.'

'Yeah, with none of that dirt smelling stew,' called out Sam.

'If Tina gets this woman here, I'll never hear the end of it.'

'But can you imagine if it worked?' Nick said.

'Why me?' Ward shuffled from the room. He didn't want to get trapped by a horse-toothed, grey-haired horse-tail-plaited woman, who'd smell of horse dung, swatting at her personal swarm of horse flies. Why wasn't anyone listening to him?

Four

BANG. BANG. BANG. Tina's fists pummelled against the front door. 'I know you're home, Brendan.'

'*Go Away.*' Ward sat in his chair and raised the remote to turn up the TV.

'Mum's here.'

'Oh, man.' He couldn't leave his mother outside. 'Hold on.' Ward heaved, huffed and puffed getting out of the chair. With his slow shoe-shuffle, he panted as if he'd run a marathon to the front door. How unfit had he become?

'Thank you.' Tina walked in with head held high accompanied by the rustle of her many skirts.

'Boys not home?' Shirley asked, following.

'No, they're at a club function.' Which is where he'd love to be, or anywhere else instead of being housebound.

'Here, let me help you.' Shirley put her arm through her son's and guided him towards his chair.

'Thanks, Mum. You can stay, but Tina can go.'

'*I'm not leaving yet.* I'm waiting for Ron.' Tina crossed her arms and tapped her foot, making her bell covered anklet jingle.

'Why is Ron coming here?'

'To bring that silly horse whisperer.'

Ward stood hunched before his chair, scowling sideways at his sister. 'I. Said. *No.*'

'You know what? I'm thinking the same thing. We should've left her at the racetrack, Mum.'

'Why the sudden change, Tina?' Yet, the faster his sister toe-tapped her jingling bell-tune, the redder her face got, he expected steam to scream from her ears any second now.

'She told me to piss off.'

Ward grinned. He couldn't help it. 'To your face?'

'She said I was spooking the horses.'

'Well you were being loud and rude, dear,' said Shirley.

'Let me guess,' said Ward, 'Tina barged in and did her usual of demanding her crap be done yesterday. Hope you didn't start a stampede, I heard racehorses can run, you know.' Her ankle bells were irritating. 'Do you sleep with those bells on?'

'What?' Tina raised her skirts to peek at her ankles.

At least that stopped the bells. 'So, she's not coming?'

'No, she's coming.' Tina dropped her skirts with a shoulder-sagging sigh.

'Why, if she told you to piss off?' Ward wished he'd been there to see that.

'Mum and Ron talked her into it. Ron's showing her the way after her last patient. And I'm here to make sure *this bitch doesn't do the wrong thing.'*

'So, I'm a bitch now?' A female voice asked with a laugh.

Ward froze with his back to the door. That wasn't an old hag's laugh.

'Sorry, Zara, my daughter gets a little hot-headed in her protectiveness of family,' said Shirley at the door. 'Please come inside. You too, Ron.'

'Thank you. Whoa, now this is a man-cave! Don't lose me here, Ron.' Zara said to the jockey.

'It's cool, the boys at the track would clobber me if I did.' Ron went and stood beside Tina in front of the TV. 'Tina, be nice. This is part of my working world, okay?'

Tina rolled her eyes. 'Okay.'

'How are you, Ward?' Ron asked.

Ward stood by the chair he was dying to sit in. 'Ron.' He couldn't nod at the jockey in his riding breeches, long boots and shirt.

'Ward, this is Zara,' introduced Ron.

Ward braced himself as he turned to face the door. Confused, because her voice was young, soft and feminine, and her laughter was unexpected. He raised his eyes, and they widened, as his jaw dropped as far as the neck brace allowed him.

'Hi,' Zara said, wearing tall riding boots like Ron, showing off shapely legs in tight long pants, topped by a grey hoodie and a black, sleeveless, puff vest. She ripped off her black beanie, brushing fingers over her hair and smiled.

'Um...' Ward gripped the back of his chair to steady himself. It was as if the world stopped, then tilted.

Her butterscotch blonde hair was worn in a soft plait that reminded him of summer. She swept her fringe to the right, tucking it behind her dainty ear to reveal her ice-blue eyes that were like a clear winter's sky. His heart thumped as she smiled to reveal dimples.

'You poor bugger.'

'What?' He rubbed his eyes as if waking from a dream.

Zara walked around him as her eyes scanned his body.

He inhaled her aroma of apricot nectar and gardenias, reminding him of cool summer night breezes and fresh-clipped lawns with that promising tin-tasting tang of rain in the air. 'You're not the horse whisperer-thingy, are you?'

'No.' Zara laughed as she looked him over.

'That's what we call you at the track, Zara,' said Ron.

'I wish you guys wouldn't. People think up lots of crazy stuff when you say that, and the way Ward is looking at me, I'm right.'

'Sorry.' How could he have thought such horrid things about her? Yet, he searched for her hands. They were small, soft, with no yellow nails strong enough to pick off horseshoes. Was he hallucinating? 'What are you then?'

Tina's toe-tapping started the bell jingle all over

again.

'Ugh, those bells.' Ward groaned in pain. How could he have his daydream while the nightmare of his sister was still in the room?

Zara stepped towards Ward and asked, 'You've got a pinched nerve, huh?'

'Yeah.' He wanted to nod. Yet, he'd never been more exposed or helpless as a man in his entire life—until now.

'Your mother was telling me you're looking at surgery, huh?'

'Yeah,' Ward croaked. It was as if he'd lost his voice and his brain had switched off.

Should he hide in his room in shame? He looked like crap. Hadn't shaved in days, where showering was a mission. Wearing whatever he could slip on because he hadn't expected to be presented to a woman.

Yet, her shirt was untucked at the bottom of her hoodie. She wore no jewellery or makeup. She brushed aside stray strands of hair that feathered around her cheekbones, looking so soft and silky. Zara's natural beauty was breathtaking.

Zara rubbed her palms together. 'May I?'

Was he clean enough for this woman to touch him? Did he have time for a shower?

'I'll be gentle.' As gentle as her voice, she placed her hand on his shoulder blades as her warm fingertips found their way under his brace. Her eyes watched him. He couldn't, and didn't want to look away.

'*He's got —*' as Tina started, Ron grabbed the corner of the TV to stop its shuddering. Ward stepped back as if woken from a daydream, and Zara's hand fell, suddenly cold away from her touch.

'Was I talking to you?' Zara asked, staring at Tina who said nothing. Zara then returned her attention to Ward. 'Your sister, huh?' Her grin exposed her dimples.

'Yeah. You want her you can have her.'

'No thanks. At least you still have your sense of humour.' Zara giggled, and for the first time since the fall, Ward wanted to smile with her.

Tina's skirts rustled as she stepped towards them. '*How rude are you?*'

Zara turned and faced Tina. 'Look, no offence, Tina, but you don't have to shout when you speak.'

'I do not shout when I speak.'

'You do,' said Zara, 'and if you don't realise that I suggest you have a hearing test. I bet that's why you're so pushy, you think no one can hear you.'

Tina gasped with eyes and mouth wide open.

Ward grinned at his loud and overbearing sister rendered speechless.

'Ron, take your girlfriend home, I can't work if she's here with her negativity crowding our space,' said Zara.

'Good idea,' said Shirley. Tina, be a dear and go home with Ron, please.'

'Thanks for this, Zara, I'll see you trackside tomorrow for that coffee I owe you.' Ron grabbed Tina's hand. 'Maybe you should get a hearing test, Tina,' Ron said as he closed the door behind them.

'You might be right about Tina's hearing,' Shirley said to Zara. 'My sister had hearing problems for years and we never even noticed.'

'My dad's the same. He used to have the television on so loud and refused to use a mobile because he couldn't hear. I had to make the appointment myself and then trick him to come with me.'

'Did he have a hearing problem?' Shirley asked.

'Yep. He's got a hearing aid now, so I can't sneak into the house anymore and raid his rum like I used to.' Zara laughed lightly as she removed her jacket and tossed it over Sam's chair. Pushing up her sleeves she faced Ward. 'Okay, this is the deal, I can't and won't promise anything. I want no complaints, no biting, kicking, or back scratching,' she said with a grin. 'There'll be no back-chatting or bullshitting and we'll get on just fine. And, if you're lucky, I might even feed you a carrot.'

'Oh man.' Ward couldn't help himself but chuckle. After a week of hell, this woman had him smiling. But the best part was, Zara had kicked his sister out. He'd happy dance if he could.

'Can I get you anything, Zara?' Shirley asked.

'If this is a bachelor's pad, I doubt they'd have any tea?'

'I keep a stash for when I visit my boy. Care for a cuppa?'

'That'd be great. Thanks, Shirley.' Zara grabbed the cushions and blanket off the oversized couch and started arranging them on the carpet.

Ward stood unsure. 'What do you want me to do?'

'Nothing. Your job is to relax and, hopefully, you'll get some sleep.' Zara stood in front of him and held out her palms. 'Come on, I won't bite. Do you?'

'No.' He put his palms in hers, they were so soft and small compared to his. He cringed with guilt for having all those bad thoughts about her.

'I'll help you down to the floor where you'll lay face down in the centre of these cushions I've set up. Put your weight on me and lower yourself to your knees. I've got you.' All the way to the carpet she never broke eye contact until he found himself on his knees. 'I'm guessing you're doing this against your will, huh?'

'Yeah, sorry.' He was now the world's greatest buffoon with his naked butt blowing in the wind for all to see.

'Don't be. All I'm going to do is massage that area to try and give you some relief first. Then, I'll see if there is anything I can do. So please, don't get your hopes up.'

'No offence, I won't.'

'Good. I like defiance in my sceptical clients.' She smiled, showing her dimples.

He just had to smile back.

Zara knelt down before him, still holding his hand, and with the other she reached for his shoulder. A surge of electrified warmth travelled through his skin to his heart.

Zara snatched her hands back and blinked at her palms. 'Are we getting static from the carpet?'

She'd felt that too?

'Might take my boots off, while you remove your shirt.' She jumped to her feet, kicked them off by the door, then walked back in her mismatched, brightly coloured socks.

His slid off his shirt letting it drop to the side, and grinned. 'You're wearing odd socks?'

'Huh?' Her toes wriggled in her socks. The left was lemon, the right a cherry red. 'I got dressed in the dark this morning, running late,' she said with a shrug, and again pushed up the sleeves of her hoodie.

'No way.' He'd never met a woman like her. Even in this house of men, they looked twice in the mirror before they walked out the door. Except for his sister, who mustn't own a wardrobe to hang her clothes in because she wore it all at once.

Kneeling before him, Zara shared a soft smile and explained, 'Our mission is to get you to lie down on your side first, then we'll roll you onto your stomach.'

'But, my neck.' Ward clutched his neck brace like it'd become his security blanket.

'I've got the cushions down for support, trust me, okay?'

'But we've only just met.'

'I know, you poor thing.' Zara smiled, then lowered

herself so her eyes met his. 'We'll do this together. As soon as you feel the slightest twinge, tell me and I'll stop. I'm not here to hurt you.'

'I trust you.' The words spilled without thought. Ward was a man who didn't trust lightly. He trusted his team players and his parents. He was being forced to trust a man he'd met twice to cut up his body. Yet, even in his most vulnerable state, this was the easiest admittance of trust—ever.

'Good.' Zara held out her hands and he lay his palms into hers, the surge of heat made his pulse jump from the squeeze of her hands. 'Here we go.' She lowered him to the sea of positioned cushions and then rolled him onto his stomach. 'Are you okay?'

Ward lay straight and smiled into the cushion. 'I haven't been able to lie down or sleep for over a week.' He couldn't believe it.

'Wow, you'd be grouchy to live with, huh? Now, deep breaths. I'm taking off the neck brace.'

As the brace came off, he tensed all over.

Zara put a palm on his lower back and leaned down to face him. 'Hey, the cushions are positioned to support your neck. Remember, I asked you to trust me, and so now is the time. Consider this our first test. You'll find you're getting more support in that position than this brace. Now breathe and relax.' Her voice was as calm and gentle as her hands that rubbed soothing circles on his back, and he exhaled, willing his body to relax.

'*My God, Brendan's on the floor*. How did you get him there?' Shirley asked, with cups in hand.

'Oh, he bitched about it.'

'Don't take the piss out of me while I'm defenceless.' Ward smiled into the cushions. Did his mum call him Brendan—was he in trouble?

'Doubt you're the type to be defenceless. I'd bet you're a fighter.'

'My boy has always been a fighter. Here's your tea, dear.'

'Thanks.' Zara took a sip and put her mug on top of the beer fridge and gave a soft chuckle. 'You know, my dad would approve of the reclining chairs with the beer fridges. Okay, let's start, shall we?' With a clap of her palms, she rubbed them together, then placed them on his neck and shoulders, massaging his muscles.

'What is it you do, Zara?' Shirley asked, seated in Ward's chair sipping her tea.

'Reiki. It's a form of traditional massage.'

'You do training or something?' Ward needed to know. But…*man, this was good*. Her small hands shifting against his muscles had finally found some reprieve.

'Yes, six years here,' replied Zara, 'then I went to Hawaii where my mentor studied, then on to Japan before returning.'

'Do you have an official title, dear?'

'They call it Reiki Master.'

'Like a Zen Master?' Ward moaned with relief as the

tension released like waves washing the sand on an escaping tide. He wanted to cry happy tears for finding heaven, and bit his lip to stop smiling.

'No. They do a lot of meditation, perfecting the art of sitting still,' said Zara. 'Whereas, I'm the eternal fidgeter, always doing something with my hands.'

'And what good hands you have.' Ward relaxed deeper with each sliding shift of her palms. 'What about Samurai Master?'

Zara laughed. 'No. They're into warfare and swords. I can't even pillow fight, and I'm definitely no Jedi Master, either.'

Ward grinned. Her humour light, her voice calming, her temperament easy going, considering he was on the floor of his house and she wore odd pairs of brightly coloured socks. But those hands were amazing. It was hard to think straight as his body relaxed deeper.

'So, you do horses, not humans, Zara?' Shirley asked, sipping her tea as she watched on.

'I'm trained for both humans and animals, but I prefer thoroughbreds. They're tougher and never complain like people do.'

'Yeah, right. Horses aren't that tough,' Ward scoffed.

'As part of my technique of massage and Reiki, if I used the same amount of pressure on a human that I use on a horse, they'd run away. No matter how tough they think they are.'

'Are you picking on me in my delicate position?'

'Oh yeah, totally taking advantage of you in this position with your mother present.' Zara giggled as Ward chuckled into the cushion.

'It's so good to hear my boy laughing again, it's been so long. Thank you, Zara.'

'We're not done yet, Shirley. We've got a fair bit to do, if you're willing to help me?'

'Anything, dear. You name it. If you don't mind me asking questions?'

'Ask away.'

Ward lay there and tried to listen to Zara's calm soft voice. But all he felt were those warm massaging hands, working deep into his muscles in a hypnotic pattern that soon sent him into a catatonic slumber.

Five

Ward awoke face down amongst the cushions on the living room floor as the morning news played on the TV. He yawned in the fresh coffee and baked bacon aromas, then rolled over to find his two housemates in their chairs watching him.

'Morning sunshine.' Sam raised his mug in a wave from his seat closest to the kitchen.

'Is it morning?' Ward on his back, stretched out.

'Yep. How is it?' Nick asked, scooping cereal from his bowl.

Ward blinked as it dawned on him—he'd slept, stretched on the floor, and could now raise his arms above his head. 'Damn.'

'What?' Sam leaned closer, frowning with concern. 'Are you in pain?'

Ward watched his left hand make a fist. He shook his wrist, and flexed his elbow, all while lying flat on his back. 'That tingling's stopped.'

'*Oh, thank god. It worked,*' cried Shirley from the kitchen doorway.

'Mum, what are you doing here?' *How late was it?*

Amazed he could lift his head off the floor and see his toes.

Shirley sat on the man-couch and patted the dark leather. 'I stayed on your couch, dear, it's so comfy. I watched movies all night, and with your screen so big, I didn't need my glasses.'

'And your mum made us breakfast.' Sam smiled as he tapped his belly.

'I could do with a decent feed.' His stomach grumbled. Was his appetite back? Would he be able to walk properly? Ward started to sit up.

'STOP.' Shirley jumped to her feet with her hands out like stop signs.

'*What?*' All three men froze

'Zara said to take it easy. You're to roll onto your stomach then we'll help you up. No sudden movements, okay. Slowly, please?' Shirley squeezed her son's shoulders to control his pace. 'Please help him up, boys.'

Ward saw her worry and felt the fear in her voice as he rolled gently to his side, then onto his front. He propped himself onto his hands and knees. There was no tingling. No aching pains. No shooting pulse down the arm from the neck. And no neck brace.

But no doubt gravity would do its damage as soon as he stood.

Determined, Ward said, 'Okay, let's do this.' With Nick on one side and Sam on the other, they helped Ward to his feet.

'I swear you're standing taller, mate.' Nick, always a

head taller, grinned at Ward.

Ward arched his neck to face Nick. 'Oh yeah, and there's none of that damned ache.' He rolled his shoulders in slow circles where there was no more hunchback. He was whole again.

'Please go slow.'

'I am, Mum.' His muscles were tight, but not aching. 'That was the best sleep.' *Thank you, Zara.*

'You've been asleep for fourteen hours, dear.'

'Really?' Ward twisted his neck towards his mother, he twisted it back to the left, then up and down, left and right.

Nick picked up his cereal bowl and headed for the kitchen, saying, 'You were snorin' a storm when we got home.'

'I needed the sleep.' Or was this a dream, where he'd wake into a nightmare of pain any second now?

'Zara said you would. She'll be visiting after she's finished work at the racetrack this morning, dear.' Shirley gave his shoulder a squeeze.

'Was it the horse whisperer who fixed you?' Sam asked, sliding back into his seat.

'Yeah, but she's a what, Mum?' Ward raised his arms to the ceiling and stretched out his spine. To have his arms above his head he felt like doing a Mexican-wave dance.

Shirley pressed her palm against Ward's lower back. 'Slowly, *Brendan.*'

There was that warning of the first name. 'I am,

Mum.' It was as if his body had begun to thaw.

'Zara's a holistic combinated Zen master, I think?' replied Shirley.

'A what?' Sam asked.

Shirly tapped her lips in thought. 'Zara did say she uses various techniques she's been trained in, but she's a master of Remedy.'

'Reiki, now I remember.' It was unbelievable that he'd fallen asleep within five minutes of meeting Zara. 'How long was Zara here?' He asked his mother who seemed so small, now he could stand tall again.

'For hours, working on your back and shoulders. You fell into such a deep sleep and never moved. Even when we put ice and heat packs on your neck.'

Ward stretched the left arm across his chest as his stomach rumbled. 'I'm starving, Mum?' Giving his best pleading look that had regularly won him seconds of dessert when he was a child.

'Shower first. Zara said to put hot water on your neck, then stand straight and stretch slowly from side to side. But no sudden movements.' Shirley demonstrated, stretching her neck. 'Zara's predicting you'll be tender for a bit, that's why she's coming back. She certainly gave your sister what-for too. Which reminds me, I must call your aunt to find out who she saw to make a hearing appointment for your sister. Go have your shower, I'll start brekkie, dear.'

'What was this horse whisperer like?' Sam asked, folding the newspaper into quarters to start his daily crossword.

Ward picked up the neck brace that lay over the arm of his chair. He hated the thing. 'Not what I thought she'd be.' He dropped the brace and flexed his left hand into a fist. There were no pins and needles, no dull shooting aches. It felt normal.

'What did she do to your sister?' Nick asked, returning to his chair.

Ward grinned wide. 'Apparently, Zara told Tina to piss off at the racetrack for spooking the horses. But I did witness Zara telling Tina to get a hearing test, to stop shouting, and then she told Ron to take Tina home. I like her.'

Sam chuckled behind his coffee mug. 'How did your sister take that?'

'Tina looked like she'd been bitch slapped. It was brilliant. I haven't laughed like that since the fall.' He stretched his arms across his body and copped a whiff of his armpit. 'Yep, time for long shower and shave.'

'Don't rush it, young man,' Shirley called from the kitchen.

'I won't, Mum.'

'Hey, what did this horse whisperer look like?' Nick asked.

'Who?' Ward grinned at the memory of a very pretty little lady he didn't want to share.

Six

Zara stood at the door, about to knock, when her hand trembled.

It was her dad's fault she was here when she should be on her way home. She didn't do house calls. She didn't do people. Especially some famous football star who lived in the suburbs.

Zara lifted her scarf over her mouth and peered back toward her parked ute, fingering the car keys in her pocket.

But, if she didn't do this now, she'd have her dad on her back. Zara also didn't want to disappoint Ron from the track who was trying to get into the good graces of the girlfriend's family. Or worse, Ron's girlfriend might hunt her down with that voice.

Zara dropped her scarf, stabbed at the doorbell, and hoped they weren't home.

'*I'll get it.*' Shirley whipped open the front door. 'Welcome back, Zara.'

'Morning, Shirley.' Zara grinned at the unexpected hug.

'Oh you miracle worker, you.'

'It helped?'

'Come see for yourself.' Shirley hooked her arm through Zara's, dragged her inside, slamming the door behind them.

Into the lounge, the vacant trio of matching leather recliners stood alongside their bar fridges. The floor was clear of the Club-coloured cushions that were now neatly arranged on the massive couch. The walls were bare, except for the huge football flag that Zara's father would happily build a flagpole just to have it waving across his front lawn. This place was a man-cave. She was grateful Shirley was here or Zara would've never stepped inside.

Her dad owed her big time for this.

Zara followed Shirley into the open plan kitchen where coffee mugs sitting on the counter also bore the Club's logo. That team logo was everywhere. It was splashed across the stickers on the fridge. It was on the kitchen chair cushions, on the tea towels that hung over the stove, even on the glasses in the sink. The house looked like some shrine to the Club.

'Here he is.' Shirley smoothed her son's auburn hair that mother and son shared.

His bulked shoulders were square as his t-shirt stretched across his back, accentuating his muscles and strong neck—naked, without a neck brace. Zara grinned. *It worked.*

'I bet you're a meat man, huh?' Zara smiled at Ward who sat at the head of the table shovelling food into his mouth.

'Err… Morning,' he squeaked out, raking his hand to the lump of food lodged in his throat.

Zara patted his back, hard, taking a seat next to him. 'You should chew first, then swallow.'

'Thanks.' His cheeky grin offset his slightly squashed boxer's nose. With a tanned complexion that blended with his freckles, he was ruggedly handsome, in one well-built package.

She clenched her fingers to stop touching him, even if her fingertips wanted to trail down the scar that led from the right corner of his smile to his strong jawline.

Gone were the dark rings that surrounded his eyes yesterday. Today, they shone like honeyed gold under the sunlight streaming through the kitchen window.

His scent of peppered musk mixed divinely with a dark woodsy cool lime. His sports shirt clung to his sculptured chest, as biceps flexed while he worked the cutlery over his plate.

Zara licked her lips, forcing herself to breathe, to remain calm while getting lightheaded and warm at the same time. It was just like yesterday—but worse.

Not fair.

She had to remember this guy was just a client. Not even a proper client because she only worked on animals.

'So, um, big sleep, huh?' Zara asked. It was a huge improvement from yesterday. Which was good, yet distracting. Why did she volunteer to come back?

This was Dad's fault.

At least Ward's mother was here.

Shirley, seated opposite, smiled at her son. 'Fourteen hours my boy slept, right where you left him. Cup of tea, Zara?'

'No thanks. I'm caffeined out at this stage, they make the best coffee at the race track. But that bacon looks good.' She pinched a piece off Ward's plate.

'Hey?' Ward gave her a mock frown that didn't take away the gloss from his amber eyes.

'Share?' *No*, was she flirting? Her heart did some weird fluttering jig that wasn't good. *Not happening.* Not when this guy was out of her league, out of her territory, and way beyond her comfort zone.

'I can cook you some, Zara?' Shirley asked.

'No thanks, just wanted a taste.' Zara sat back, remembering why she was here and that Ward was her patient. She looked him over, aiming for that cool practitioner detachment, even though her body was burning up. 'So, any tingling sensation?'

'Nope. All gone.' Ward pushed away his empty plate, wiped his mouth, and patted his flat stomach.

'Appetite's back, huh?' *Duh.*

'Oh yeah.' Ward nodded, as his cheeky grin stretched to hide the scar on the right of his chin.

But had he recovered enough? 'Any stiffness or sore areas in your neck and shoulder region?'

'Nope.'

'Not yet.'

'What?' His grin was replaced by a worrisome frown that made her stomach drop.

Without thought, she touched his forearm to calm them both down. 'The muscles around your neck have been bunched up for a while.' She pulled her hand away because she shouldn't be touching him like that. 'It's a normal reflex reaction.' And if she kept telling herself that, she might even believe her own BS too.

'How?'

Zara held up her fist to demonstrate. She wasn't going to touch him until she had to. 'Your muscles do it to protect the nerves, and when damaged they knot up around it like a fist. Have you got physio today?'

'Yeah.'

'Good. Tell them no electric pulses and not to touch your neck region, but do ask them to show you the best ways to stretch that area. If they're any good they won't touch you. But be gentle with yourself, please?' Could rugged, professional footballers be gentle?

'What did you do to fix me?'

'We—being your mother and I—who is the best.' Zara smiled at Shirley. 'We applied hot and cold packs in between my work. That's it.'

'Sounds like the same treatment they always give me. What makes your work so different?'

'Okay, you've seen a piece a frozen steak and how it forms ice particles on the meat. Yet, when you defrost it the blood is released, and when its cooked the steak shrinks.'

'Yeah.' Ward nodded, grinning like a big kid on the verge of a never-ending summer of school holidays.

'Now, imagine that steak is a muscle that changes within its hot and cold environment. We had to trick your muscles, forcing them to react to get to that region, that was so bunched up protecting that nerve. Now they've relaxed they'll spring back into place, especially with your well-developed muscle structure.' She swallowed hard, eyeing his tight shirt and strong arms. The man was all muscle. *Hello elite sportsman.*

Shame he was a fancy footballer—and a client. Which meant she should be behaving like a professional, no matter what she felt inside.

Zara wiped her palms down her denim thighs and tried to focus. He was just a client.

But she didn't have human clients.

She rubbed her eyes with the heels of her palms to focus on the task and not the man. 'You'd relate. It's like when you've played a game and don't feel true muscle soreness until two days later?'

Rolling his shoulders, he said, 'This feels just like that.'

'Good. I'll only give you a minor rub down today and nowhere near that nerve. Your physio will show you the best techniques to stretch that area.' Zara didn't want to tread on another professional's toes—especially one of the elite crowd, the Club employed—although, she wanted to interrogate them to see if the physio was good enough to touch Ward. *Whoa.*

She sat back, flexing her fists. Was she getting protective over a client? A stranger she'd just met?

'What else do you recommend, Zara?' Ward asked.

Could she ask him to strip naked and just stand there so she could admire his body?

What was wrong with her? 'Um, well…' Removing her jacket, she retrieved a tube of ointment from her pocket. 'Continue the hot and cold treatments. I like this brand for the heat rub.' She passed him the tube. 'We used all the other ointments your mother could find lying around the house yesterday.' Who knew footballers were like walking sports-medics with enough bandages and ointments it filled a kitchen cabinet. They had a freezer full of ice packs. A medicine shelf in the fridge for aches, strains, and pains. Jars of horse-sized multivitamins kept on matching bar fridges, and a pantry filled with protein bars and other packaged nutrients to build the elite athlete.

Ward read the label. 'I've seen this at the chemist.'

'It's pricier, but worth it.' She was sure they could afford it, considering her father told her how much a professional footballer earned annually.

'What do you want me to do with this stuff?'

'Use the heat rub for ten minutes. Stretch it out, then apply cold packs for ten. Rest for a few hours and repeat.' She leaned closer and stared into those amber eyes, inhaling his delicious aroma of peppered musk and woodsy lime. 'Let me reiterate the word *slowly* because your muscles will be so pliant you may overstretch it, or worse, you could snap it. Do I make myself clear?' Even if her internals were muddled in his presence, she had to remember he was just a client who wouldn't bother remembering her after today.

*   *   *

Ward swallowed with the slightest of nods. 'Crystal.' As crystal clear as her stunning ice-blue eyes. She was the contrast of winter in those eyes and the warmth of summer with the butterscotch colour of her soft hair. Again, no makeup, no jewellery, but breathtakingly beautiful.

Zara unravelled her scarf from her delicate neck and tossed it alongside her black puff vest with her beanie sticking out of the pocket. He wanted to ask if she was wearing odd socks and what colour were they today? He wanted to talk to her, even though he still had yet to find his voice in this woman's presence.

'Good,' Zara said. 'So, have you finished pigging out?'

'Yeah.' He sighed at the lack of hero-worship he got, compared to what Sheldon received from his parade of ladies. Because Ward was just Ward.

Zara pushed up the sleeves on her grey jumper. 'Stay there, I'll work from here. Take your shirt off for me, please. You can straddle the chair and use one of those cushions to rest between your chest and the backrest.' Zara went to the sink and washed her hands.

'You're not putting me to sleep, are you?' He relished moving his arms over his head as he removed his shirt. He ran his fingers through his misbehaving hair and watched Zara. His mum was doing the same so he couldn't get busted for perving.

But now, not under any drugs, or pain, he was wide awake and watching a dream.

He followed the curve of her denim thighs, from the tops of her long boots to her cute arse. Why didn't he notice that yesterday?

She wound up her hair into a loose bun, exposing her slim waist that led to an even better set of breasts. How did he fall asleep on someone like her?

Because Ward didn't have the rock star appeal like the side-smirking Sheldon. Nope, all those women in that passing parade within his hospital room never gave Ward a second look. They were too focused balancing on their clickity-clackity heels and their shifting perfume clouds that suffocated the room. It was a shame they never gassed Sheldon in their close-up cuddles.

'Who knows if you'll go to sleep again. That'll depend on how you respond to the treatment.' Zara's smile exposed her dimples, as she dried her hands and grabbed the ointment from the table. She stood behind him, rubbed her palms together and placed them onto his shoulders.

Ward sighed under the magic of her hands. 'How did you get into this stuff?'

'My dad.'

'Does your father do this, dear?' Shirley, in her seat, sipped her tea watching all.

Zara snorted a laugh. 'God no. My father's a farmer who has RA.'

'What?' Ward mumbled.

'Rheumatoid Arthritis.'

'My sister's second husband has that in his feet and can't walk some days,' Shirley said.

'Dad's got it in his hands, and the medication he was on made him sick. But if he didn't take the medication, he couldn't move his hands, so it was one or the other. Until Mum took him to the naturopath.'

'Did it work for your father, dear?'

'Dad's great. Although, he has his moments where it flares up badly. But with exercise and diet—which is a daily argument because Dad's a complete carnivore who hates his beer fridge empty. So, you could say, it's been a long and slow process to convert him to the dark side.' Zara giggled as she rubbed Ward's shoulders.

'I can relate,' he said, on the verge of la-la-land. 'Hey, if your dad's like me, how did you convince him to try alternative medicines?'

'Are you converted, yet?' Zara said, close to his ear. Her summery scent of apricot nectar, mixed with gardenia, again reminded him of cool breezes on a warm summer evening.

'I'll need more convincing, so don't stop, please.' It

was heaven under her fingers.

'How did you convince your father?' Shirley asked. 'I know how hard it was to convince my son to see you.'

'Mum tricked Dad to get into the car, then we had to drag Dad inside while he's yelling out *that commie bastard* to the Chinese herbalist inside. It was embarrassing. Good thing Howie's got a sense of humour and relishes the challenge with his sceptical clients.'

'Like me?' He said, raising his head.

'Ah huh, head down.' Zara gently pushed his head into place.

'And he cured your dad?' Ward's eyes closed trying to get a grip on the conversation. But this massage was making his brain slow down.

'I wish you could cure RA, it's such a cruel thing. But we've put in a management plan so Dad's comfortable. Cold weather's a killer for him.'

'What did this guy do to help him?' Shirley asked.

'Howie makes this herbal tonic, Dad calls it his witch potion he takes in the morning. He has other medicines from the doctor for his bad days. We do acupuncture on the joints, and a topical ointment, if needed. Sadly, this time of the year, he wears a splint to bed so his hands don't curl into locked-claws in the morning. So, yeah, it's because of my father I learned Reiki.'

'How?' Ward asked, trying to keep up.

'Every morning before school I'd massage Dad's

hands and his knees before he had his reconstructions.'

'And now do it for a living?' Ward was seriously losing himself in the rotating motion of her hands across his skin.

'I didn't think I'd be doing this when I was a kid. But Howie gave me a part-time apprenticeship slash receptionist position, in between school and helping my parents on the farm.'

'What sort of farm, dear?'

'Horse farm, right?' Ward tried to concentrate. Her voice was so soft and calming, like yesterday, it was so easy to zone out.

'We used to do wheat, barley, and apples, but the drought was tough and Dad likes horses. Our Grandfather used to train them but we both don't ride...' Her voice faltered and she stopped rubbing. 'Not anymore.'

'Everything okay?' Ward sat up, wide awake now her hands stopped. He didn't want her to stop.

'Could I bother you for a drink? I've left my water bottle in the car,' Zara asked with a slight tremble to her voice.

'Allow me, dear.' Shirley's chair scraped across the floor, the sink's tap turned on and off and she soon passed a glass of water to Zara.

'Thanks.' Scooping up the glass in two hands she

sipped. 'So, Brendan?'

Was he in trouble, because only his family called him that? 'Yeah?' Grinning up at her with full neck movement.

'Please make sure you drink plenty of water the next few days, and not those sports drinks filling your bar fridges.'

'Why?' Zara sounded like his sister.

'Water aids in purifying the system. I'm sure, once you return to training, you'll need those other drinks to replace the salts and minerals you use. But in the meantime, please drink water and cut down on other stimulants.'

Did Zara say training?

'Like what?' Shirley poured a glass of water for everyone at the table.

'Coffee, tea, beer?'

'Great, sounds like I'm back in training.' And Ward wanted to return to training fast. He sat straighter, reached for his glass and drank it dry.

'You'd be used to doing what you're told from coaches.' Zara said.

Ward shrugged. It was true. 'Do you work at the race track?' He was delighted to see her apply more ointment onto her hands and he was so ready for more.

'Only when they need me, otherwise I'm helping out Dad on the farm.'

'Is the local racetrack the only place you've worked at?'

'Hawaii, Singapore, Japan. I've got a few trainers who'll fly me up and down the East coast and to New Zealand for the spring racing season. I don't have human patients, they can be quite demanding, whereas my equine patients never complain.' Zara's tinkling laugh travelled through her hands to his back, it made him smile with her.

'I'm not complaining.' Why would he, and with closed eyes, he was soon lost in the bliss of her healing hypnotic hands.

* * *

'That'll do you for today.' Zara stepped back and washed her hands at the sink.

'You could do that forever.' Opening his eyes, Ward sighed in a daze, lifting his head from the cushion still straddled to the chair.

Shirley got up from the couch, while a black and white movie played in the background. 'You fell asleep again.'

'I did?' Ward blinked to focus on the kitchen clock.

'You've been sitting there for an hour while Zara rubbed your shoulders.'

'No way?' Not when he'd slept for fourteen hours and had only woken a little while ago.

Zara dried her hands and reached for her jacket, wrapping her scarf around her neck. 'So, I'll see you tomorrow about the same time.'

'You're leaving?'

'Home time for me.' Zara slid into her vest, grabbed her beanie and keys from her pocket. 'Please don't forget every two hours hot, stretch, cold, relax. You can sleep in your bed tonight. Your mum's set up the pillows in the same fashion as what I'd done on the mat last night, to provide the proper support. If you find it uncomfortable try the floor again. But no chair.'

'Why not my chair?' Ward frowned as he stood. He loved his chair, it was his throne.

'Not yet,' said Zara. 'I'd rather you lay on the floor the way those cushions are set-up to support your spine. Stay on your back with feet elevated and knees bent to take the pressure off your neck. Thanks for setting it up for me, Shirley.'

'Anything to help my boy recover.'

Zara walked and talked as she headed for the door. 'Please keep that area warm.'

'Sure. So, what do I owe you?' Cold away from her touch, Ward slipped on his shirt and followed Zara's cute behind.

'The treatments aren't finished yet,' Zara said, plonking on her beanie.

He was tempted to tuck her stray hair behind her ear,

admiring the way her blonde lengths caught the sunlight.

'How much do you charge?' He grabbed his jacket, the one he'd dropped and couldn't pick up when first released from hospital. Now he could slide his arms into the sleeves as his grin grew.

'For you? The fees are a carton of beer and an autograph for my dad. He loves you guys. He's the only reason I'm doing this.' Zara shared her dimpled grin, slid on her sunglasses, and headed out into the sunshine.

Why so cheap? 'Thank you, Zara.' She was his hero. Shame she was leaving so soon.

Ward waved Zara off in her large, dusty four-wheel drive ute that stood out on this suburban street. But he was standing straight; and it was a sunny winter's day with light grey clouds on the horizon. It'd been almost two weeks since he'd stood outside and inhaled deeply while taking in the street's view.

A small rickety van that sounded like it ran on rubber bands parked in front and he frowned. '*Mum, Tina's here.* You know I'll never hear the end of this.' He walked inside leaving the front door open so Tina didn't bash it down.

'Good, Tina can take me home. Your sister means well, dear.'

'I know.' But she was a pushy pain in the process.

Shirley picked up her handbag by the couch and

stood before her son. 'Tina is just like your father, you know.'

'Doubt that.' Dad was cool—his sister was a freak.

'I saw how worried your sister was about you when we went to get Zara.'

'*Wow, look at you.*' Tina proclaimed at the front door. 'So, it worked?'

'Yeah, it worked. Just don't get a swelled head over this.' Too late. The smile on his sister's face said it all. 'But, um, thanks.'

Tina cupped her ear and leaned in closer wearing a big cheesy grin. 'Can you repeat that? The part where you said *I was right* and the *thanks* part.'

Ward frowned at the irritating killjoy. 'You heard.' Or did she?

'So, when can you play again?'

'Dunno?' Soon, he hoped. He felt good enough to attend training, but then remembered Zara said to do it slowly. The neck brace lay on his empty chair and the cushions were arranged on the floor in front of the television. 'The physio will be here soon, they'll let the coach know.' Reaching for the water bottle and the remote control it was all about setting the scene to chill.

'So, are you seeing this horse whisperer again? Even if she's a bit of a bitch.'

'Don't you dare call Zara names.' Ward pointed at his sister as she stepped back with her palms up like she was being arrested. 'You can say what you want about me, or anyone else, but don't you dare say a bad thing about Zara. Not in front of me.'

'Your brother's right, Zara's a lovely woman. And best we go now. So, bye dear, I'll call later to see if you need anything.' Shirley kissed her son on the cheek.

'Thanks for everything, Mum.' Ward hugged his mother without it hurting.

'Now, don't forget what Zara told you, it's hot, stretch, cold, relax. Dinner's in the fridge for you and the boys, and your lunch is in the microwave. I'll pop by tomorrow. Come along, Tina, your brother needs to rest for two hours. You should set a timer, dear.' She hooked her arm around Tina's and headed to the van.

'Good idea, Mum.' Ward waved, closed the door and locked it in case his sister bounced back uninvited.

He eyed his sumptuous leather reclining chair with a sigh and a low lip. Instead, he followed orders and sank onto the cushions, with feet up he flicked on the footy channel.

How soon before he could play and have his life back to normal?

Seven

The widescreen TV played the Footy Show where the expert panel of ex-players commented on the week's past games and the upcoming weekend events. Watching from their matching reclining chairs, were Sam and Nick. Their team-mate, Mills, habitually chewed his fingernails in Ward's chair, while Ward lay in a sea of cushions on the lounge room floor.

'*Coach.*' The men sang in unison as Mitchell walked through the open front door.

'How are you, Ward?' Mitchell asked, staring down at Ward.

'Great, Coach.' Ward got off the floor easier and quicker as the day progressed. Even though Zara had told him to take it slow, he was ready to run.

Mitchell stepped back, wiped a palm over his mouth as he eyeballed the standing Ward. 'No neck brace?'

'Only if I need it.'

'No pain?'

'Nope.'

'Heard it was some horse doctor? The physio told me you'd had some miraculous recovery, and the boys said the same this morning at training.'

'Sorry Coach, I know it wasn't Club approved, but my sister and mum forced me to—'

Mitchell held up his hand to silence Ward. 'What did she do?'

'Reiki.' Ward shrugged with a grin. 'Don't ask me the details, all I know it's this massage thing.'

'That puts Ward to sleep every time,' said Sam, with Nick making snoring sounds from their chairs.

'At least you're getting sleep.' With hands on hips, Mitchell squinted as he scanned over Ward's physique. 'The Physio reckons they don't need to do any more house visits.'

'Is that a good thing, Coach?'

'He reckons you're well on the way to recovery.' Mitchell stroked his chin and asked, 'So, what's this, ah, horsewoman—'

'Her name is Zara, Coach.' Ward had already copped the banter from the boys telling him they'll get him a saddle, with Mills neighing like a horse while riding the broom. Today he could laugh with them. Yesterday he would've punched them for that crap.

'Zara who?' Mitchell asked.

'Um, just Zara?' Ward was known by his surname, and he only had the surname of the surgeon willing to cut him up. How stupid was he to not know Zara's full name?

Mitchell crossed arms over his chest. 'So, what is this Zara's recommendation for a recovery plan?'

'Zara's coming back tomorrow, I'll ask her then.'

'You've got the specialist's appointment on Monday, right?'

'Yep. But I'm not having surgery. There's no need for it when I'm pain-free with full movement back. Swear it, Coach.'

'I'd rather wait for the specialist's professional opinion. As much as I'd love to put you back out there, I won't risk it if your body's not ready. Do you understand?'

'Sure, Coach.' Nope, Ward was going to tell that specialist to cancel any surgery.

'Good.' Mitchell shooed Mills off the recliner, took a seat as he asked Ward, 'What did this Zara do? And how did you get onto her? Does this woman have any formal qualifications? Where's her practice?'

Ward felt like a replaying podcast having explained it to the physio, then to the boys, then to Mills, and now the coach—who needed to be convinced most of all—because Mitchell was God in Ward's world. 'Zara's qualified, she did her training overseas and is known as a Reiki Master. She's trained for humans but prefers to treat racehorses at the racetrack. And before you say anything, it worked.'

'I see.' Mitchell raised his eyebrows like it was nonsense.

'Ward doesn't need surgery, Coach,' said Mills as his heel tapped between fingernail bites.

Mitchell's frown deepened. 'Are you a Neurosurgeon too, Mills?'

'No, Coach,' mumbled Mills, slinking back into the massive man-couch.

'Coach, I didn't believe in this crap either, and the only reason this was allowed to happen was my mum and sister blindsided me. But I'm living proof it worked. I had all this achy tingling sensation in my fingers and toes when I fell asleep last night. Then, when I woke up this morning it was gone.'

'How are the muscles?'

'Bit stiff. The physio's given me stretching exercises that help, and I'm well on my way to recovery.'

'Can't deny what I'm seeing, but...'

'Coach, Reiki's on the net, we checked it out this afternoon.' Ward still felt guilty for ever thinking bad of Zara.

Nick stopped rocking his chair and leaned toward Mitchell, to explain. 'Reiki's been around forever. It's a common practice to aide horses with their recovery for racing.'

'Hey Coach,' said Sam, with a hand in the air. 'We all checked out the many testimonies about this stuff.'

'I asked the physio about it, and he said it's a great form of massage, if you can find a decent practitioner.' And Ward had found her, with mismatched socks and butterscotch hair.

'You know,' Mills said while pausing from his usual nail-chewing, ' we're talking big bickies for those donkeys to run around in circles, so she must be alright to work regularly down the racetrack.'

'All right.' Mitchell flung up from his seat and stood in front of Ward. 'I've seen enough, but I'm still not entirely sure about this stuff either. We're playing away and won't be back until Sunday, so rest-up, then come and see me after your specialist's appointment on Monday. Until then, please, don't do anything silly.'

Damn it. Ward hated being left behind while the team flew out for Saturday night's game. 'Yes, Coach.'

'Nick, make sure Ward attends and doesn't kill Sheldon at the hospital.'

'Yes, Coach,' replied Nick, mid-chair rock.

'Have a good weekend, Ward. I'll catch the rest of you at the airport.' Mitchell gave the men a nod and headed for the front door with Ward following him outside.

'Thanks for checking up on me, Coach.' Ward waved, delighted he had full arm movement, until Mitchell's car was out of sight. He closed the door, locked it so his sister couldn't barge in and resumed his position on the carpet. 'Coach thinks it's crap.'

'Hey, I wouldn't have believed it if I didn't see it for myself,' said Mills, raking fingers through his black mullet.

Ward sank into his nest of cushions on the floor and admitted, 'I didn't believe in any of this stuff either, until— oh no, I'm gonna be stuck home alone this weekend.' Ward groaned, hiding his face in his palms.

'Sucker. Can't run and hide when Tina knows. Look out, mung-bean stew,' teased Nick, and they all gagged at the thought.

Eight

'*Hello?*' Zara called out at Ward's open front door, making another house call—when she never made house calls as a general rule.

Ward met her at the door. 'Hey, you're here.'

For the last time.

'Look at you.' *Wow.* Her heart fluttered at Ward's cheeky grin and how his amber eyes reflected the sunshine behind her. Her knees wobbled and her temperature soared. Was that from the morning sun on her back—in winter?

'Um...' *Focus.* He's a patient. A client. A human thoroughbred. Which is why she worked on horses so there was none of this other scary level of distracting emotional crap to deal with.

She inhaled deep to pull on her professional mask. She'd worked on hundreds, if not thousands of bodies in her time, and this was just another body to heal. Even if it was so near perfect it made her soul sing with its own internal choir. 'What did the physio say?'

'Wouldn't touch me, like you said.' Ward grinned as he leaned against the wall.

'Good.' The physio knew what he was doing. Yet it wasn't her business. Ward's body wasn't hers to worry about. But she did—all day yesterday. He was her final thought last night and her first thought this morning, it never switched off over this guy.

But this was her last house call, ever. To anyone.

'The physio showed me some exercises, and I did what you said. I feel good, stiff...um.' He hesitated, shuffled his socked feet and shoved his hands into his jeans' pockets. 'I mean, my shoulders and muscles were stiff. I mean...'

She tried to stop grinning at his embarrassment, it was adorable.

But she wasn't here to stroke his ego or chat niceties, she was here to do a job. So, she unwound her scarf and headed for the kitchen. 'That muscle tightness is to be expected. Let's work on that. Take a seat at the table and remove your shirt for me, please.'

She dumped her jacket and scarf on the table. Shoving up her jumper's sleeves, she washed her hands at the sink, staring out through the wide window, it faced a large backyard with nothing in it but trimmed lawn. There were no chairs, no tables, no boats, no bikes or any other big-boy's toys, not even a barbecue. Nothing. *Didn't they spend any time out there?*

She plucked a glass from the rack and got herself a drink of water. From the window's reflection, she watched Ward remove his shirt. His jeans hung dangerously low on his hips, exposing the full six pack and the torso of an elite athlete. Her drinking glass trembled against her teeth. Dry in the mouth, she drank the entire glass and was still thirsty.

'Is your mum around?' She could do with a chaperone to not be alone with this guy. But then again, why bother, she was a nobody, when Ward was this footballer who had his own fan page.

'Nah, she's at home.' Ward tossed his shirt to the side, his chair scraped across the floor tiles as he sat at the head of the table.

'Okay.' She could cope. She hoped.

From her jacket, she pulled out a small bottle and uncapped the liniment while her trembling palms itched to rub against his skin.

'What's that?' Ward asked.

'A herbal ointment that aids in muscle recovery, it's very effective.' Should she tell Ward she used this oil on horses?

She poured the dark oil, the colour of turmeric and cinnamon, into her cupped hand. Its menthol herbal scents triggered her senses to focus on the job. Palms together, she rubbed them for heated friction. Inhaled deep, exhaled slowly, and placed her palms on his skin, truly wanting to help him.

His whole body sighed and relaxed under her touch. 'Oh man, those hands are heavenly.'

She smiled. 'I'm glad you approve.'

His shoulders and neck grew limp as his breathing

deepened. 'It's like magic. You'll put me to sleep again.'

'You told me you hadn't slept for a week and might need to catch up.' He reacted well to her treatment, like a lot of her patients. But she didn't zone out for hours when she worked on the horses, not like she did with Ward.

'I don't think so. I dozed all day on the cushions.'

'Good, you're relaxed.'

'I am. Slept all night. Early to bed and everything.' He cleared his throat, tensing under her hands. 'My coach visited, yesterday.'

'Coach? Is he your boss?'

'Yep.'

'I see.' She added pressure to his muscles to work out the stress this coach was causing.

'Coach didn't believe it, even though the boys and I tried to convince him.'

'That's normal. My father's the same.' Her dad owed her big time for making her return.

'Ditto on the disbelief, and I'm sorry.' Ward's chuckle carried through to her palms making her smile. 'But this is good. You've helped me so much.' Again, he sighed deeper and relaxed.

The clock, bearing the team logo on the wall, ticked with each shift of the second hand. A car on the street tooted. The fridge hummed. Ward's breathing deepened, as she rubbed hypnotic patterns onto his skin.

Ward cleared his throat and raised his head. 'So, anyway...'

Zara grinned at Ward's attempt to keep his focus.

'Can I ask you something?'

'Sure.'

'What's your surname?'

'Phelps.' She grinned wider. Obviously, someone had asked that question. Perhaps this coach? How much star power did Ward have for the coach to visit, like she was now, performing a house call that broke her own rules? 'Speaking of names, how come no one calls you Brendan? I've only heard your mother use it.' Even Ron from the track called him Ward.

'My dad's name is Brendan too. Named after his father. Dad gets called Brian which is his middle name.'

'So, you're Brendan Junior?'

'Hated being called that. I only got called Brendan whenever I got into trouble.'

'Which must've been regularly.' She pressed her lips to suppress a giggle.

'Want me to answer that?' He peeked over his shoulder, his now familiar grin spread across his face.

'I think you just did.' She laughed, forgetting she was meant to be working. 'Sorry.' She'd never teased her clients before, but somehow, Ward was breaking through those professional and personal boundaries.

Dad's fault.

And this was her last visit.

'Coach wants to know, including me...' Again, the muscles in his neck tightened at the mention of the coach.

'What do you recommend for my recovery?'

She rubbed her thumbs in harder to fight against his muscular tension. 'You're almost there now.'

'Am I?' His amber eyes displayed hope.

She couldn't swallow and licked her dry lips. 'What you're suffering from is the after effects as your nerves and body returns to normal.' While her own body felt far from normal. She turned his head away so she could focus on the job. 'When do you see your specialist?' How soon before she could leave?

'Monday. I'll be telling him there'll be no surgery.'

'I'll bet you a carton of beer he'll tell you that too.'

'Thank you, Zara. That means a lot.'

His sincerity made her almost melt on the spot.

'Can I do stuff now?' Ward asked.

'Sure.'

'Really?' Again, his look of hope tugged at her heart.

Why was this guy so appealing to her that he effortlessly breached all her defences? 'Please don't over exert yourself and try to rest over the weekend. What's the rush?'

He sighed heavily, yet the tension tightened in his shoulders as she tried to soothe his worries. 'I hate this.'

'What?' She lifted her hands from his skin as if it was burning him. *Oh no.*

'Not you. Sorry, I didn't mean it like that.'

She exhaled, relieved to hear it.

'Please continue.'

'Sure.' *Wow, wake-up call or what.* Her eyes flicked to the clock timing this final visit. 'Let me guess, being an athlete, sitting around isn't for you.'

'I'm always training or doing something for the Club. This weekend we've got an interstate game on, otherwise I'd go to give them my support.'

'Are you ready for that yet?'

'I'm bored, trapped in this house and what's worse...' He exhaled so deep his shoulders dropped with it. 'My family know I'm home alone and I don't want to hang here all weekend in case my sister visits.'

'I see.' She grinned at his uncomfortable position. 'Your sister is unique, I have to admire her for that.'

'Really?'

'You don't?'

'Meh.' He shrugged, and his muscles were twitchy under her palms. This was definitely her last visit because he didn't need any more intense treatment.

So why was she still here? 'Don't you have any mates to hang out with so you're not tempted to overexert yourself?'

'They're all away for the game this weekend. I've lost touch with other mates because football's my way of life.

'I've seen how focused people are with their careers. Down the racetrack, the trainers all live and breathe racing, and the jockeys are consumed with their diets to keep under the scales. With you, being at the elite level, would it be the same?'

'Weight's not a worry, but fitness is a must,' replied Ward. 'My sister is dating a jockey and I know nothing about his sport.'

'Ron's a nice guy. It's good he's come back from his drug charges.'

'You know about that?'

'Sure. Bet you'd have banned substances for medicines too?'

'We do. What was Ron's deal?'

'I dunno,' she replied with a shrug. 'They're not that strict on jockeys, it's the horses that they test for steroids and stuff. Don't you get drug tested too?'

'All the time. I doubt they'd breath-test horses? Are they made to wear their sponsor's brand of clothing too?'

'On the saddle blankets and stable's uniforms they do. The jockeys are petitioning to get clearance to wear sponsorship logos on their riding breeches for race-meets. Considering they don't own the silks that belong to the horse, jockeys should be allowed to make money on the side. Is that why you have all this stuff?' Waving to the drinking glass on the table bearing the brand of the team logo.

'You should see the bathroom.'

'I have. You have more products in your bathroom than I've seen in an all-girls' boarding school bathroom.'

'Sponsors.'

'Wow. I'd never realised that.'

'Do they have sponsors in racing?'

'Race days, I only remember the beer and wine suppliers and airlines who supply the prize money. Can't miss that form of advertising. Horses don't get a wage, only winnings. But horses are owned by people paying for the privilege in these syndicates, and each horse has a team behind them to race and train.'

'We train, get a wage, suffer from sponsor restrictive choices, and have a great fan club where people pay to join. We have footy teams, not individuals, and we don't run around a track.'

'But you do run on a field just like racehorses do and that's almost oval shaped too. Both sports are televised. Spectators bet on both sports for the win. And you have signature colours to go for your team, which is the same for horses and jockeys in their co-ordinated silks that are registered to that horse like a team.'

'I'm not a horse and we don't wear silk.' He frowned at the table.

'And I'm not a horse whisperer.' She whispered into his ear that brought back his smile. 'So, what does a footballer do in his spare time?'

'Hang out with my mates. If we're not doing things for the club, we're training.'

'So, it's like working five days of the week?' With huge monetary gains, according to her father.

'Except we have games on the weekends and travel interstate. There's after-hour PR gigs and club dinners we have to attend. It's full-on during the season and we can't take holidays in winter.' He sighed under her palms as she rubbed the ointment deep into his amazing muscle tone.

'So, after playing you come home and sit in that fancy recliner chair and watch TV?'

'Yeah?' He peeked up at her sheepishly.

'That's normal. Mind you, not many people have a small bar fridge sitting next to their chairs. If my dad had one, he'd never move again.'

'Mum says the same for my dad.'

'So why not hang out with your parents this weekend? Your mother is lovely.'

'She is, but...' He hesitated. 'Don't get me wrong, I love my folks, they're the best. Yet, since this fall, they've been hanging around a fair bit. I'm not complaining, I know they do it because they care... I sound like a whingeing moron.'

'You love them but can't live with them.' She stilled her hands as he turned to face her.

'Yeah. I hope you're not getting the wrong impression of me for me saying that?'

He looked so worried about her opinion. 'It's okay, I'm the same.'

He arched an eyebrow at her. 'Really?'

'Oh, yeah. I love my dad to bits, but we can't live together.'

'Don't you live with him on the farm?'

'Sure. Dad has his house and I have mine on the same property. My dad hates being mollycoddled, which, I suspect you've been getting from your mother?'

'Yeah.'

'Which means you're better.' And her work was done.

'Am I?'

Her phone rang. 'Excuse me.' She wiped her hands on the cloth and grabbed her mobile from her jacket's pocket. 'Hey, Dad?'

'Are you still in town there, luv?'

'I'm just finishing with Brendan. Why?' She grinned at Ward's eye roll for saying his first name, but had to turn away so she didn't stare slack-jawed at his naked torso.

Her dad's baritone voice seemed gravelly over the phone. 'Listen, luv, I just gotta call from Katie. Reckon you can collect the horse float from the track?'

'Oh no.' She leaned her lower back against the sink as her stomach cringed tight. 'How bad?'

'Not good. We'll text you the address.'

'Sure, Dad.' She adored Katie, but hated it every time that woman rang.

'Gimme a call later and let me know what you're bringing in so we can prepare?'

She sighed as sorrow swirled in her lower tummy and the hairs on her forearms rose, he didn't sound too happy. 'Sure, Dad. Bye.'

'Everything okay?' Ward asked.

She didn't want to leave and face what was at the address texted to her phone. 'Um, sorry...' Yeah, she was sorry with the sour taste of dread in her mouth. 'I need to cut this visit short.'

'What's wrong?' Ward stood up, asking, 'Can I help?'

'I dunno?' The guy was a professional footballer, why would he want to get his hands dirty. 'Could I ask a tiny favour of you?'

'Name it.'

'Can you reverse a trailer?'

'Yep.'

'Have you ever done a horse float?

'No. But I can reverse my dad's caravan into his shed, which is a pretty tight squeeze.'

'I dunno.' Unfortunately, no one would be trackside this time of day.

'Let me help? I need to get out of the house, and this way you'll make sure I don't overexert myself.' He then lowered his head as his amber eyes warmed her soul. 'Please?'

'You don't want to do this stuff.' Zara didn't want to do it either.

'Come on, I can help. I promise to behave. Otherwise I'm sitting here at the mercy of my family, and you've helped me out so much already, it's the least I can do. Please.'

She couldn't refuse that pleading expression of his. 'Okay. You can come for a drive to the track because I need help putting on the horse float.'

'Really? I thought you'd be all over that horse stuff.'

'Horses, yes. Reversing a float, nope. I can't even reverse a normal trailer. Dad's given up teaching me.' Was she really agreeing to this? 'Get dressed, and warmly, please.'

'Yes, boss.' he said with a grin, slipping on his shirt.

'Don't call me that. I'm no one's boss.'

Shirt on, he tried to straighten his messy hair. 'You'd be your own boss?'

'Kind of. I don't answer to coaches, but I do have picky clients.' She wrapped her scarf around her neck and slipped on her jacket. Patting her pockets for keys, and on her phone, she Googled directions for the address while walking to the door.

'I hope I haven't put you out as a client?' Ward asked, opening the front door while slipping on his jacket and runners.

'You?' She faltered and looked at the man who was never meant to be her client in the first place. She didn't have human clients. 'You're not a client, Brendan.' Not anymore—he never was, no matter how much she'd tried to convince herself.

'Am I in trouble?' He gave her a grin as he slipped on a cap and sunglasses, palming his phone, wallet, and keys.

'As long as you don't stick your head out of the ute's window and bark at traffic, and there's to be no back-seat driving or I'll tie you onto the rear tray.' She giggled to herself, walking down the path.

His laugh echoed behind her as he closed the front door and followed, throwing a fist into the air. *'I'm free.'*

She smiled at him, unlocking her ute's passenger door. How long would their smiles last, when Katie's calls always made Zara sick to the stomach.

Nine

In the passenger seat of Zara's ute, Ward frowned at the car wrecks that were the background to half a dozen police cars parked behind a high barbed wire fence. 'What's going on, Zara?'

'We'll find out shortly.' Gravel crunched under Zara's large ute, towing a horse float as Zara steered them into an unfamiliar area of the city.

'Is this your place?' The red and blue lights reflected off broken glass where weeds grew through car carcasses. It made him uneasy.

'I've got no idea who owns this,' Zara said, slowly steering them through the wide-open gates.

'So why are we here?' A cut padlock and chain lay in pieces on the gravel driveway, where police officers waved them through. 'Give me something here, Zara. I've got to be careful of where I am because the media is always looking for dirt on us guys.'

'This is nothing to do with you or football.' She frowned at him as she stopped and turned off the engine.

Great, now he'd pissed her off. 'Sorry. I just need to know what I'm getting into.'

'I help out with the RSPCA on certain matters.'

'For horses? Is that why we brought the horse float to pick up something?'

Zara's heavy sigh filled the silence of the cab. 'That depends on its condition. Sadly, some never make it.' She gazed up at him with such sorrow in her ice-blue eyes, he shivered.

'I've never done this.'

'I don't want to do this either, but I did warn you.' She shoved on her beanie, tightened up her scarf and took a deep breath as she jumped out of her seat. 'You can stay in here if you want.' She slammed the door shut behind her.

Without hesitation, he opened his door. 'What can I do to help?' Relieved at the small smile she gave him, he rushed to her side. He wanted to hold her hand and give it an encouraging squeeze for the both of them.

'Hey Zara, thanks for coming, mate,' called a police officer the size of a bear.

'No worries, Riley. This is Brendan.'

Ward shook hands with the officer. *Woah*, she called him Brendan, was he in trouble? He caught her sly wink and grinned back at her, grateful for the slight lift in the mood, even if the cold air was heavy around them.

'Is this a social call?' Zara asked with a wince.

'I wish.' Riley adjusted his duty belt then pointed towards the lane piled with rusty cars. 'I've got a horse down there with Katie. It's in bad shape and none of us can get near it. The owner got arrested in the raid, and we were about to let the sniffer dogs loose to search all these cars when we found it.'

'That's a lot of cars to search,' mumbled Ward, the junk was everywhere.

'They'll find it. They're working up at the house at the moment, although their handlers are saying those dogs are itchin' to search the area. But I'm not letting them out here to scare that poor creature.' Riley removed his police cap and scrubbed hard at his dark crewcut and said, 'That bastard left that horse out here with no water or food amongst all this hoof-breaking junk.'

'Where is it now?' Zara asked.

'We've got it cornered.' Riley slipped on his cap and pointed down the avenue of piled cars. 'It's all skin and bone. There's cuts on its legs from dragging a coil of barbed wire, and it's spooked as hell.'

From her ute's rear tray, Zara retrieved a thick rope she looped in her hand. She pulled out a handful of carrots from a plastic bag and stuffed them into her jacket's pockets. Tossing her phone onto the dash, she left the keys in the ignition and closed the door. 'Um, you?' She faced Ward with her lips twisted to the side, squinting at him.

Ward held up his palms in surrender. 'I've gotta be straight with you, this is new to me.'

'I'm not expecting you to do anything. Turn off your phone and look out for yourself. I mean that. You're still recovering and I don't want you hurt.' She patted his arm.

'Yes, mum,' he mumbled under his breath, switching

off his mobile. He felt useless not being able to help.

'Remember, I said no back-chatting or I'll tie you to the back of the ute.' She shared a dimple-free half-grin.

'This way.' Riley led them through the maze of cars that towered above them casting shadows. The stench of choking piss-weeds, sunburnt oil, greasy fuels, and rust filled the icy air.

'Oh man.' Ward stopped and removed his sunglasses at the sight of the brown pony, its coat a saggy bag of mottled flesh, showing every single bony gap of its rib cage. Old scars and bare patches were visible as it turned towards them with ears flickering. Its front leg was wrapped in barbed wire where blood trickled to the gravel. 'Oh no, that's...' Speechless, his skin crawled, cringing at the scene.

'I looked just like you,' replied Riley, crossing arms over his broad chest. 'Sick bastards, huh.'

A woman in khaki overalls, bearing the RSPCA patches, approached them. 'Thank god, you're here,' she called out.

'Hi Katie.' Zara gave the older woman a hug.

'So, who's the dream-dish?' Katie smiled wide while her eyes walked all over Ward.

'Brendan, this is Katie, an RSPCA officer and a real saviour of all creatures.'

'The real deal, huh?' Ward shook Katie's hand, then glanced away to avoid her scrutiny.

'Yep. Do I know you from somewhere? I always

remember the cute guys,' Katie said, gripping his hand tighter.

'Um...' Ward looked to Zara for help while Riley chuckled beside him.

'He's a footballer who plays for the Saints,' replied Zara, giggling.

'Hey, you're Brendan Ward.' Riley tilted his head at Ward. 'Didn't you hurt your neck the other week when you smashed into Sheldon? I swear it looked like you'd broken your necks from the replay.'

Ward blinked at the officer. It was the first time the incident had been mentioned like that, when he'd assumed he'd just been knocked out. Now realising he couldn't remember the fall that changed his world. 'I'm good now.' Ward nodded with full neck movement, refusing to think of that tosser, Sheldon. Not today.

'Ward's getting there.' Looking to the horse, Zara hoisted the coil of rope higher onto her shoulder. 'I'm going in. My keys are in the ute and please be careful, Ward.'

'About time Zara brought the boyfriend 'round to help her,' said Riley.

'No, I mean yes—I'm helping, but I'm also Zara's patient.' Ward wasn't thinking about himself, only Zara. Not even the wind moved in this area, where the soles of her long boots crunched on the brittle weeds and gravel as she approached the four-legged bag of bones.

'Zara doesn't have human patients—except the privileged few who are lucky enough to get her help,' said

Riley. 'She fixed my back after I'd wrestled the wrong way with this drug dealer.'

'Do you normally call Zara for this?' Ward asked, not taking his eyes off Zara as she walked towards the poor distressed animal dragging a coil of barbed wire.

'Riley and his crew of bad-boys-in-blue called this one in. I just shared the love,' replied Katie. 'Zara and her dad have saved heaps of horses over the years'

'And a few dogs from our drug busts,' said Riley.

'Dogs?' Ward cocked an eyebrow, glancing sideways at the large cop.

'We get them nasty beasts that are all screwed up from their owners, Zara helps me catch them.'

'What for?' Ward didn't want gentle Zara near a snarly dog or anything that might put her in harm's way.

Huh? He liked her.

He really, really liked her.

Or was it something more, feeling that heated surge of protectiveness toward Zara build inside his chest.

'Zara tries to rehabilitate them so they can find new homes.' Katie then said with a raised chin to the cop, 'Don't you have one of Zara's dogs, Riley?'

'A big staffy, she's part of our family and I've got no worries on night shift with that dog guarding my home. Kids love her,' said Riley.

Ward thumbed the scar on his jaw and stood by helplessly and watched Zara.

Trapped in the corner of towering cars, the horse

pawed at the dirt, then kicked at the side of the rusty sedan. The animal looked dangerous.

Zara stood only a few metres away, speaking to it, but Ward couldn't hear what she was saying.

The animal stopped pawing at the broken glass amongst the gravel. The wind's whistle died through the gaps between the cars and the creaking metal against metal was silenced. No birds sang, as the sun hid behind clouds darkening this corridor of cars, while Zara and the horse stared at each other.

Then Zara held out a large orange carrot.

Its ears flickered, raising its head, nostrils flared, and after what seemed like aeons it gingerly stepped forward and the first chomp echoed in the corridor of cars. Zara slid the rope around its neck, patted the horse that kept eating and then smiled to those waiting. 'We're good.'

Ward exhaled. He hadn't realised he'd been holding his breath. *What a woman!*

'Let's get it into the horse float,' said Katie with a sigh. 'Ward, can you reverse Zara's ute in here, because we all know Zara can't back a trailer.'

'Sure.'

'I'll guide you,' said Riley, patting Ward's shoulder as they headed for the ute.

'I'll start gathering evidence for the paper trail,' said Katie as she walked toward Zara. 'I've got your boyfriend bringing up your ute.'

'Ward's not my boyfriend. Don't have one. Don't

need one.' Zara's words echoed off the automobiles.

Well, that's a shame. Ward shoved hands into his jacket's pockets and headed for the ute. No, he didn't have any of Sheldon's rock star appeal because he was just Ward.

Yet, as he glanced over the car wrecks and the state of that poor horse in this world away from football, his problems didn't matter, and he was determined to help.

∗   ∗   ∗

'Oh honey, you like the man. You can see it,' teased Katie, taking photos with her mobile phone.

'Ward's a professional footballer, a player, and just a client,' said Zara as she stroked the horse's wiry mane.

'You don't do human clients.'

'My father made me do it because Ward is from Dad's favourite team.'

'And did your father make you bring the beauty-of-brawn out here?'

'No. Ward helped me load the horse float.'

'And he's bringing it down for us now. You know, Ward's hotter in real life—he's nothing like you see on TV all hot and sweaty.'

'I didn't know you watched football?'

'How can you not? All those men's bodies in short shorts.' Katie chuckled as she stepped in closer. 'You like him.'

Zara looked at Katie, surely it wasn't that obvious.

Embarrassing if it was. Sure, they made jokes as a way to lighten a crappy situation, but she wasn't focusing on Ward right now.

'Can we not use the camera flash on this guy? I've got him, he's not going anywhere.' As she fed the pony another carrot, it leaned against her shoulder as she rubbed down its long neck. Its coat was a mess.

'What d'ya think?' Katie asked as she filmed the horse.

'It's only a small pony, three or four years old, hard to tell in its current condition. Dad would know.'

Katie crouched down to take photos of the skittish pony, zooming in on a mess of barbed wire entangled around the leg. 'Will he make it home?'

Zara heard her ute start and watched Riley guiding Ward as he reversed the horse float into position. 'We'll get him home and Dad will fix him.'

What was she going to do with Ward? This was tough for anyone to be here. Yet she was proud he took on the challenge, and grateful for his help.

The two men opened the back of the trailer and lowered the ramp. After cutting the bulk of the wire off its leg, Zara walked the small horse into the float. Once secured with food and water, Zara bandaged its wounds and then shut the horse inside.

'What's going to happen to that poor animal?' Ward asked, leaning against the side of her ute where she washed her hands from the water tank beneath the back tray.

'I'll take him home. Dad will get the rest of the barbed

wire out of his leg, then he'll be kept warm and given a decent feed.'

'Why do people do that?'

'Adults suck. The level of cruelty of some…' She chewed her bottom lip, frowning as she tried to swallow the panic rising.

'Are you okay?' Ward touched her upper arm.

'Me?' She flinched at the touch of another man's hands and stepped away from him. She couldn't even look at him.

But this wasn't Ward's fault.

She inhaled to calm her hammering chest. 'I'm just jumpy.'

'Understandable, considering the situation you've just been through.'

Did he understand? He couldn't. But to look into his amber eyes she saw his compassion and it calmed her inner-flight. 'I can get you a lift back to town later. Or you can go with Katie now, maybe, once she's finished with you.' She forced her grin to put them both at ease.

'I said I wanted a day out, even if this wasn't what I was expecting. If you don't mind me hanging around, I'd like to stay with you.' Ward stepped in closer and she drank in his peppered musk and woodsy limed aroma.

She just wanted to burrow into him to forget this horrid place.

Ward continued, 'Besides, I have a feeling if I go with Katie, I'll never see daylight again.'

She laughed, suppressing the desire to lean against his chest and admire his smile up close. 'You're a glutton for punishment if you come with me. Better warn you, my dad's gonna give you hell.'

'Why?'

'Football is his favourite topic next to beer and politics. Look, thanks for your help. You did well.' She gave him a shy smile over her shoulder as she opened her door and jumped inside the cab.

Ward scooted to the other side and into the passenger seat. 'I said I wanted to help. Didn't do much, but I'm willing to try.'

She could see he was, which only made her admire him more. Was it too late to let Riley take Ward home? 'You've helped out more than you realise.'

'I did? How?'

'I can't back a trailer, without you I'd still be at the racetrack trying. Listen, I hope you're not overdoing it?'

'Compared to that horse back there, I'm fine.' He glanced back to the horse float with a concerned expression.

'Wait and see, in a few months you won't recognise that pony. My dad's great with them, he's the true horse whisperer.' Hoping her dad could work his magic, she turned the key and gunned the engine.

'So, the horse whisperer thing is real?'

'We don't advertise it. People will then think we're weird.' She waved to Riley and Katie standing by the police cars and they were soon back on the road.

How was her father going to take this, not just the pony in its emaciated condition, but that someone like Ward was visiting their humble abode?

Ten

Ward stared out the open passenger window as they turned onto a dirt track nestled in the gentle sloping, sumptuous emerald hills. Towing the horse float, Zara steered her ute down the wide lane, on either side horses grazed in grassy paddocks dotted with large shady trees. The winter sun was warm on his face and the breeze carried a fresh sweet scent he could taste. He couldn't remember the last time he'd been in the country, where the open sky and all this space was free from stadium walls. 'Is this your place?'

'This is home.' Zara's smile widened showing off her double-dimples. It was beautiful.

'It looks like a postcard. It's pretty.' Especially the way the sun highlighted the butterscotch in her blonde hair.

'You know, whenever I turn down this lane, I lose all that city stress. There's no traffic, no dramas, and I'm home. Do you feel like that with your place?'

'Me? I sleep there.' He'd never smiled about where he lived, not like Zara did with her dreamy shine to her pretty eyes.

'Is it your house?'

'Club supplies it, it comes with a gardener and cleaner.'

'Really?'

'We pay for the privilege. I've bunked in with Sam and Nick for a while now, we're like brothers.' He spotted two houses a suburban block apart. Between them stood a large shed surrounded by smaller fenced yards. Two greyhounds greeted them with wagging tails followed by a woolly black miniature horse. 'Is that a mini horse?'

'That's Goliath, he's a Shetland pony who thinks he's a dog. Which means Dad's not far. Better brace yourself for it,' she said, sharing a slight giggle.

'Is he going to give me hell?' Unsure if he should've come along, but he'd enjoyed the drive and the conversation.

'Only in good fun.' Her brow creased as she gripped the steering wheel. 'Look, my dad's not shy to speak what's on his mind. He doesn't care what people think, especially in his own yard, so don't get offended or shocked by anything he says.'

'I won't. I deal with sledging from players and spectators during a game, I think I can handle it.' He gave her a wink and she grinned at him as the colour in her cheeks brightened. Was Zara blushing?

'Also, there's no secrets in this place, and they all love an audience. So, please don't judge those who live here.' She teethed her bottom lip, slightly wincing

'I wouldn't do that.'

'I don't think you will, or I wouldn't have brought you here.'

'Thank you for the privilege.'

'Ah huh. I'll ask you that same question later when you beg to leave.' Again, she grinned as she drove through the wide-open shed door and their eyes adjusted to the shade as she parked inside.

A deep baritone voice travelled from the rear of the horse float. 'What d'ya pick up, luv?'

Ward walked around and faced who he guessed was Zara's father. 'Hi.'

'Whoa. You're not a pony. Although, you're almost pretty enough.' He pushed up the brim of his Akubra, and amongst the deep tanned lines, he squinted the same ice-blue coloured eyes as Zara.

Did this guy just call Ward a pretty pony?

'Dad, this is—'

'Brendan Ward. Well, bugger me.' He dusted his big palm against his patched denim jeans and held it out. 'G'day mate, I'm Joe Phelps. Welcome to my backyard.'

Ward's hand was swallowed in the handshake of a strong pair of working hands. Zara's father was huge. His shoulders were as wide as two sledge-hammer handles, with a tanned face and thick neck. His flannelette shirt's sleeves were rolled up exposing faded tattoos amongst the deep tan. In stained jeans, with his dark grey Akubra and dusty working boots, yep—Ward was definitely in the country now. 'Nice to meet you, Mr. Phelps.'

'Call me Joe, I want none of that mister bull here, mate. My dad was Mr Phelps, and I'm never as old as me old man.'

'And I'm just called Ward.'

'Fair enough. Oi, I saw that fall, it looked neck breaking there, got any brains left?'

Ward didn't remember the fall. *It wasn't that bad, was it?*

'Dad, be nice!' Zara's reddening face stood out amongst the fair hair.

'So, my girl's been helping you out?'

'Zara's been brilliant. She saved me from surgery.'

'Zara's helped plenty in the nick of time. She'd send surgeons broke if we let her play on people.' Joe chuckled and opened the horse float as a younger guy approached. 'Bugger me,' Joe said. 'Them bastards.' He tore off his hat and palmed over his grey crew cut. 'Bring him out, Zara. Tim, close the shed doors, we don't want it gettin' away from us, and keep those dogs outside. Give us a hand with the ramp, Ward.'

'Sure. Happy to help.' Together they lowered the ramp as the shed's closing doors hid the sunshine.

'You'd better stand back, Ward. I don't want him to get hurt, Dad,' said Zara as she stepped inside the float.

Joe arched an eyebrow at Ward. 'The girl likes you.'

His heart swelled at the thought. But did she? 'I'm Zara's patient.' Ward stepped away from Joe's intense scrutiny.

A young guy jogged up beside Ward and held out his hand. 'Hi, I'm Tim. Are you the footballer Zara's been fixing?'

'Ward.' He shook Tim's hand that was smaller, yet just as work-hardened as Joe's.

'I'll want your autograph later,' Tim said, adjusting his worn frayed cap. The thing was ancient.

'We'll all want his autograph later,' said Joe with his beefy arms crossed, watching Zara walk the pony out of the float. 'But right now, Tim, fetch me the equine first aid kit in the tack-room.'

'Onto it, Joe.' Tim nodded his frayed cap and ran off to the far side of the shed.

Ward winced with worry for the poor creature as he watched Zara with her father, a massive man who so gentle with the horse.

'Okay, into the stall we've prepped,' Joe said, tilting his head as he watched Zara walk the pony into the stall.

Tim rushed up with the kit. 'Here, Joe.'

Joe took the bashed leather case in one hand. 'Thanks, kid. Can you make up a half-strength molasses and salt mix with some feed in a small bag like I taught you.'

'Sure.' Again, Tim nodded his frayed cap and ran off in the other direction.

'Your son?' Ward asked.

'Nah, Tim's a stray who never left.' Joe grinned as he hung his wide brimmed hat on the hook by the open stable door. 'Zara caught him trying to steal her ute, so she brought him out here to work for us.'

Ward noticed Joe's hearing aid tucked behind the left ear, which made him wonder if he'd heard right himself. 'I'm sorry, but did you say Tim tried to steal your ute?'

'Mine? No, I don't drive. I've lost my licence for drink driving. Hey Zara, how long before Tim's free from his good behaviour bond?' Joe put the case in the corner and leaned against the open doorway of the stables, surveying the horse.

'A few weeks.' Zara secured the pony to the rails as it drank from the trough.

Ward didn't know if they were joking or not. 'Hold on—a kid steals your ute and you give him a job?' Ward thumbed towards the silent vehicle parked behind him while he hovered by the wide doorway of the stall.

'I'm an old man who can't do all of this on my own, and Zara can only do so much between track-work. So yeah, we've picked up a few strays over the years to help us out.' Joe's big palm glided slowly and softly over the pony's rump. 'Tim's been here a coupla years. There's Stacey, who's our cleaner and a senior at school, her toddler's just started kindy. Adam's got his apprenticeship as a mechanic and can't wait for the courts to clear him so he can go for his licence. He'll be handy round here when he's qualified.'

'How many live here?' Ward asked.

Joe's rich baritone voice remained calm and steady, but his eyes and palm never left the pony. 'Billy, he's at school too. Pete used to live here until Zara got him a job at the racetrack as a stable hand. He's got a baby on the way and a wedding soon. Can't wait for that shindig, it should be a ripper. Then there's Phillip, he was with us for a coupla years until he got his scholarship to uni out West to be a vet.'

'You help people?' stammered Ward. 'And animals.'

'Kids and animals, we'll help. Not adults. Adults are bastards I don't bother with.' Joe crouched to check the pony's legs.

'Pardon?' Wasn't Ward considered an adult?

'Adults who do this crap. It's not kids or an animal's fault, its what adults make 'em do.' Joe examined the bad leg while Zara rubbed down the animal. 'Zara's picked up my habit of bringing home strays, where we'll give 'em a hand as long as they chip in, and they're free to leave anytime.' Joe then stood tall and looked over Ward the same way he'd inspected the pony. 'How come Zara brought you out 'ere? Do you need help?'

Ward blinked at the big man. 'Um?'

'Ward was so housebound and bored, he volunteered to help me with the horse float,' said Zara from the other side of the pony.

Joe patted Ward's shoulder. 'Good for you. God knows I've tried to teach my girl to reverse a trailer, she just can't get her head round it. You're a beefy bugger, aren't you? Won't be long and you'll be on that field again. But right now, I'd appreciate a hand with this, mate.' Joe nodded towards the pony.

'I know nothing about horses.' Ward knew nothing about animals, farming, or anything else besides football. How sheltered was he?

Joe grinned. 'Good. You won't have any bad habits then.'

Ward looked to Zara for help.

'Dad, remember Ward's still recovering.'

'Sure, he is, but Ward's not bloody useless.. Are you, mate?'

Ward was starting to doubt his masculinity and maturity as an adult in the world away from football. But useless? 'No, sir.'

Joe winked at Ward. 'I see you've been trained.' He then herded Ward deeper into the stall. 'Look, mate, all I need you to do is stand at the nose end where Zara's gonna show you how to play with the pressure points on the pony's ears. That's it.'

'Why?'

'You're gonna take its attention away from what we're doing to its leg. It's gonna be too busy eating to wanna bite, and you'll be relaxing it like Zara did with your neck.'

Ward rubbed his neck's forgotten injury. Was he up for this task?

'Isn't that what Zara did to you, took your mind off the pain while she worked on the nerve?'

'Zara put me to sleep.'

'Good. You react well to the treatment. Let's hope for the same with this pony because we'll be cutting that barbed wire out of that leg. We could do with the help on this, mate.'

Zara's nod was all the encouragement Ward needed. 'I can only try,' he said, and was rewarded with her smile.

'That's the attitude, mate. Tim, where's that tucker?'

'Here you go.' Tim passed the feed bag to Joe who led Ward to the front of the horse, there Zara showed Ward how to massage the horse's ears while it ate as they soon started to work on its leg.

It was a world away from football and his comfort zone, to be in the middle of something he'd never imagined, to rescue this one poor animal. And he was damned glad to be there too.

*   *   *

'Feels good, doesn't it?' Tim shared a lopsided grin as he handed Ward a bottle of water, then pushed open the shed's wide doors.

'What does?' Ward blinked at the sunlight as he gulped his drink, surprised how thirsty he was from standing over a horse. But they'd been at it for ages.

'Don't you think helping animals like that makes you forget your own dramas?' Tim thumbed to the stall behind them where Joe and Zara were finishing up.

'It certainly puts things into perspective.' Ward still

couldn't believe he'd been assisting in the care of an abused animal. 'Do you live here?' It was quiet. There was no traffic, no planes, with a wide-open skyline where horses grazed in lush grassy paddocks. Inhaling deeply, the scents of grasses, dry hay, and the sweet fresh air invigorated his lungs.

'You bet; this is home.' Tim straightened up and adjusted his frayed cap. Clearing his throat he said, 'Look, mate, Joe and Zara have been good to us mob who live here, so don't upset these people or we'll hunt you down. Okay?'

Ward bit his inner cheek to stop laughing at the smaller guy, but he had to admire the protectiveness. 'Why would I do that for? When I owe Zara plenty for helping me.'

Tim shoved his hands into his jean's pockets while kicking at the dirt. 'I've gotta say that, you understand.'

'I do understand.' Ward was well aware of how protective he was over Zara himself, considering he'd only known her a few days.

'You must be all right; coz Zara would've told you to piss off and never brought you out here.'

So glad she hadn't and he wasn't going to give the lady any reason to. Curious, Ward asked, 'Where's your family?'

'No idea. Haven't seen 'em since I was fifteen and I'm almost twenty. This is my family now. I'm in no hurry to leave, and they need the help more than ever.'

'Why?'

'Joe's finding this winter tough on his hands.'

'Zara said he has RA.'

'Yeah, his hands turn into clawed-fists overnight if Zara doesn't strap 'em in.'

'Joe looks healthy enough.'

'I'd love to be like Joe at his age.'

'How old is he?' Ward asked, taking another sip from his water bottle.

'Joe's seventy-one.'

Ward gagged on his mouthful and wiped his mouth. 'No way? My dad's fifty-five and acts older than Joe.'

Tim grinned, wriggling his eyebrows. 'You can see why they need the help round here.'

'I can. Where do you stay?'

'Stacey and her toddler, Toby, stay up at Joe's house with Billy—that's the big house on the right.' Tim pointed to a brick house with wide verandas. 'Adam and I camp here in the bunkhouse through that door inside the shed,' Tim said, pointing to the corridor to the right of where they stood. 'And, on that rise to the left is Zara's little bungalow.'

Ward looked at Zara's house of windows with a front veranda and rock garden. It was small compared to the big house with its wide wraparound verandas, lawn, and established rose garden.

'You'll be stayin' in the bunkhouse, there's plenty of room.'

'I was supposed to get a lift back later.' Amazed it was still daylight when so much had happened in a day.

'Those two won't be going anywhere after this, they'll be cracking a beer as soon as the delivery arrives. Stacey's only got her P's and I wouldn't trust her to drive anyone to the city yet. Here comes the rest of the mob now.' Tim nodded towards the approaching old Holden sedan that parked nearby.

A guy of Asian appearance, in a greasy blue work shirt and stained jeans, slammed the front passenger door on the tan car. '*Old women drive faster than you in their walkers.*'

'I'm agreein' with the brudder,' said the tall and slim Aboriginal lad, closing the back door.

'I've got my baby in this car, and I drive to the speed limits.' The female driver got out, opened the rear door and reached inside for the toddler in the baby seat.

Tim leaned over and explained to Ward, 'The Chinaman is Adam, the half-caste is Billy, and that's Stacey and her son Toby. Meet the rest of the family.'

Ward watched on with amusement. They argued like he did with his sister.

'We wouldn't be complaining if you drove the speed limits, not when I can run faster,' Adam said, shouldering his small backpack.

'Well, when you can get your licence you drive— Whoa, who's the smokin' piece of man-meat?' Stacey pointed and the argument stopped as they all faced Ward.

Tim announced with a wide grin, 'Everyone, this is Brendan Ward.'

'Ward's fine.' He nodded to the trio of teenagers.

Adam tilted his head and his almond-shaped eyes squinted at Ward. 'Did you come in with Zara?'

'Yes,' replied Ward, noting Adam's suspicious stare and stocky build. Billy was tall with a skinny frame, grinning a full set of white teeth against his dark skin. Stacey was blonde, and looked like any other teenager, with a small boy balanced on her hip that shared similar hair and facial features.

'Zara needed help with the horse float,' replied Tim

'Ah.' The three newcomers nodded.

'You know, sis here,' Billy said, tossing his thumb towards Stacey, 'who can't drive for peanuts going forward, can reverse a trailer. But not Zara.'

'Oi, you got home alive, didn't you.' Stacey glared at Billy.

Adam crossed his arms over his stocky chest and asked, 'So, what did Zara bring home if she had to get the horse float?' That stopped the arguing.

Tim shook his head, saying, 'A starving pony with barbed wire growing through its skin.'

'Sick mother...' Adam muttered an explosive mouthful of expletives as he headed to the stall with Stacey and Billy following.

'Are any of them related?' Ward asked, watching them.

'Nope. Except for Stacey and Toby,' replied Tim.

'But they bitch at each other like I do with my family.'

'We are family. Adam's just turned eighteen, he arrived six months after me when he got busted for stealing a cop car.'

'What?'

'Cops left the keys in it and Adam was flyin' high on an ice-ride. He didn't think, just did.'

'Crime of opportunity, is that what you're saying?' Ward arched an eyebrow at Tim who answered so casually. But Zara did warn him there was no secrets in this place and that they loved an audience.

'Yep. Adam can't drive for another twelve months coz of it. But Joe and Zara saved his flat-Chinaman's-arse from going to prison.'

'What about Billy? He's just a kid?'

'And a cheeky one too. Billy's been here for three years.'

'How did he end up here? Did Billy steal a car too?'

'Nah, we've only just taught Billy to drive.'

'So how?'

'Zara found Billy camping at the track and brought him home. Billy's got no convictions, so we just told him to shut up on that crap.'

'For what?' *Was this a house of car thieves with a chop-shop out the back?*

'Only B an' E's for food. When Billy first arrived, he couldn't read, and now he's getting good grades and is one tough little bugger too.'

'How old is he?'

'Fifteen.'

'He's tall.'

'Wait until he fills out, we reckon he'll be as big as Joe.'

'But they're not related?'

'Nah. Then there's Stacey, she's our mini-mother-hen. She's sixteen and makes sure we're all fed and does the house cleaning. Toby's her son, and he's cute.'

'Where's their family?' Blurted out Ward, surprised how open Tim was.

'Adam's family disinherited him and he was on his own for a year before he came out here. Billy's an orphan and he got lost amongst his uncle's lot of ten kids. Joe and Zara have proper foster papers for Billy, Stacey, and Toby until Stacey's ready.'

'Isn't Toby Stacey's son?'

'Yeah, Stacey looks after Toby like a mother, they had to do it for the courts.'

'Why isn't Stacey with her parents? If they're complaining about her driving, she couldn't have stolen a car too.'

'Stacey's driving is a shocker.' Tim chuckled, pulling at a strand of faded cotton from the bent brim's edge of his cap, and let the fine string go to watch it float on the breeze. 'Stacey's parents kicked her out and there was this huge uproar with welfare on account of Stacey's age. She was thirteen when she became a mother.'

Ward's jaw dropped and then shut it fast from Zara's

warning about not judging. But he had to ask, 'The boy's father?'

'Same age as Stacey, they were experimenting. No one taught them about the birds and bees.'

'Obviously not.' Why hadn't Zara warned him about this?

Hold on, she did. But he also didn't think anything of it. Ward arched an eyebrow at Tim, were they out to shock him?

Tim, again, re-adjusted his frayed cap. 'Welfare were separating Stacey from her son because of her age until Zara got the call from this copper they know.'

'That's not Riley, is it?'

'Yeah, you know him?'

'I met him today with Katie.' Ward was surprised he knew who Tim was talking about, and this entire conversation.

'We love Katie, but cringe every time that lady calls.'

'I saw that in Zara, and I now understand why.' He looked back to the stalls where the horse was being patted by the latest arrivals. 'You said Riley made the call about Stacey, why?' Was Stacey doing drugs, considering Tim said Adam had done ice?

'Stacey stole her son from the foster home and was planning to run away but got busted by Riley for shoplifting for nappies. So, Zara brought Stacey and Toby home when he was six weeks old. Joe's the doting grandfather and we're his uncles. We're re-building him a motorbike for Christmas.'

Ward watched the latest arrivals approach. 'And you all live here?'

Tim stood tall and nodded. 'We might be a bunch of misfits that nobody wanted but we're a family. Sure, we'll bitch and argue with each other, but we're tight too.'

'So...' Adam sized up Ward with a sideways glare, with Billy doing the same except with a cheesy white-toothed grin.

Tim held up his palm like a traffic warden. 'It's alright, Ward got the warning speech already.'

'Cool. So, we've got plenty of beer and pizza in the car, it's my payday.' Adam gave a nod.

Stacey asked, 'Are you staying for dinner, Ward?'

'Yeah bro, footy's on,' Billy said. 'Hey, didn't you break your neck in that wicked fall with Sheldon a few weeks back?'

How bad was that fall for everyone to keep mentioning it? 'Zara's been helping me.'

'Zara's a gem. Don't tell her I said that, wouldn't want to ruin my reputation as a bad-arse.' Billy grinned, flicking his black hair out of his dark eyes, when the smile disappeared. 'Ya know, Zara's like our big sister—'

'Already warned.' Ward chuckled at the munchkin bombardment.

'Sweet.' Billy grinned a perfect set of teeth. 'Reckon you can teach me how to kick the footy like you?'

Adam raised a finger. 'Count me in?'

'Not yet,' called out Joe coming towards them, slipping on his Akubra. 'Remember, Ward's recovering. You've gotta talk to Zara about that one. Oi, where's my beer, you lot?'

'In the car,' replied Adam.

'Not gonna get cold in there, is it. Haven't I taught you nothing about the priorities in life?'

'Yes, Joe. Never let the beer get hot.' Adam rolled his eyes, grinning with the other boys as they headed for the car and started to unload.

'They're good kids, you know,' said Joe, stopping beside Ward.

'How come you have them here?' They were a bunch of delinquent misfits.

'Like I said before, Zara and I needed a hand and they needed a home. It's not much, but there's plenty of chores to keep 'em out of trouble and it teaches 'em skills. Even if it's just driving a tractor, feeding the horses, learning to cook for themselves or do their laundry. Simple things that I'm sure you'd have learned from your folks, right?'

'Er, yeah.' Although Ward's mother still came over to cook and do his laundry, his housemates' parents were the same. How spoiled was he?

'I always wanted a big tribe of kids. Only got the two, well one.' Joe sniffed and wiped his nose then adjusted his Akubra. 'Anyway, it just happened outta the blue when Zara brought Billy home. He was our first. Now that cheeky kid's got the meanest bloody right hook I ever saw.' Joe beamed with pride at the kids carting an assortment of boxes to the house. 'Kid's an ex-street-scrapper. We got him a punching bag he practises on out back. Once a week he goes to the police gym and gets boxing lessons, where his coach reckons Billy's gonna be the next Mike Tyson.'

Ward saw the pride in Joe. 'Mike Tyson was a heavyweight.'

'Yep, that kid hasn't filled out yet, and he eats like a horse. Talkin' 'bout tucker time,' said Joe as he patted Ward's shoulder, 'let's get you a beer, mate. We all need one after that.'

'Where's Zara?' He turned to look for her.

'Putting that pony to bed. Don't worry, she won't be long and she'll be having a beer with us too. Look, you've earned your keep for what you did for us, so allow an old man to shout your dinner and a beer.'

How could he refuse when he had no better offers on this unexpected adventure. 'Beer sounds good, Joe.' It sounded damned good.

Eleven

An echoing snore woke Ward where he blinked at an unfamiliar ceiling. His neck and shoulders were stiff and sore, but he wasn't complaining, it felt like after-game soreness. It was the kind of pain he thrived on.

Ward lay back, stretched his spine and smiled. He was in the spare room in the bunkhouse at Zara and Joe's farm.

And what a household he'd been among last night. There was the brotherly banter of Tim, Billy, and Adam, with Stacey giving as good as she got. While Joe looked the part of a doting grandfather when the toddler, Toby, fell asleep in his lap.

They'd shared pizza, watching the Friday night football within a set-up that would make his team mates jealous. A big screen sat on the back veranda with a full-sized beer fridge and a fire pit.

For pre-game entertainment there was Goliath, the Shetland pony who thought it was a dog, who kept trying to open the beer fridge with its teeth.

Ward couldn't remember the last time he'd sat under the stars before a fire with a beer in hand to watch football in winter.

Yet it was this group's normal weekend activity. They'd dragged couches by the fire pit to watch the game and play couch-commentators.

Last night, he'd answered their never-ending questions of life as a footballer and scored a shoulder and neck massage from Zara sitting beside him. But before he could get any alone-time with the lady, he was escorted by Adam and Tim to this room where he'd slept solidly, until now.

What's that snoring?

Ward sat up and scratched his head, screwing his nose at the big furry blob on the floor. It was a large, cream-coloured dog, flat on its back, snoring louder than his teammates did in a group.

'What the—?' Did the boys put it here to guard him?

He stepped over the monstrosity of a snoring beast and opened the door. The dog snuffled, moaned, and blinked up at Ward. Its big head wore a face full of scars and its ears were half gone. It was ugly and scary, forcing Ward to dash through the door.

The heavy patter of paws and tapping nails on the floorboards followed.

'Easy, big fella.' Ward held up his palms with his back to the doorway that led to the stables.

Its massive bulk stopped, then shook its body, yawning a serious set of white teeth. Scars covered wide muscular shoulders, legs, and across its back. Its large butt dropped to the floor as its half-ears twitched. Sniffing with a red nose, its thick black tongue wiped the slobber from its chin.

It looked like one, big, nasty beast.

Ward gripped the door's handle to freedom. How fast could he dash outside? Did he have the speed and strength to shut the door against this beast's solid weight?

When Adam stepped out of another doorway behind them. 'Morning, Ward.'

The dog blocked the thin corridor, sitting in the centre like a solid lump. Its stumpy tail thumped on the boards and it craned its neck at Adam displaying its teeth.

Was that a smile?

'Morning.' Ward took his chance at the dog's distraction, opened the door and blinked at daylight streaming into the large shed. But the beast-of-bulk followed and sat right beside him.

'I see you've met Max.' Adam patted the big dog's head. 'I'd wondered where he got to.'

'What is he? A hellhound?'

'Pit bull. Max is cool.' Adam gave the dog a hearty pat on the chest. 'Oi, wait up you lot?' Shifting into a light jog, Adam disappeared out the main doors.

'Max, huh?' How did Max get into his room?

Doors closed and an engine started with Adam and Billy in the backseat of the Holden. Joe waved at Ward from the passenger seat as Tim drove towards the sunrise behind the hills where the car disappeared into the mist covered lane.

What was he going to do now?

Behind him, a stable door opened and Zara walked out from the stall of the horse they'd rescued. He swallowed at the vision of her hair spilling over her shoulders, wrapped in a thick woollen blanket, with her long boots peeking out below. She was beautiful.

'Morning,' he called out, hoarse in the throat.

'Hi.' She smiled a dazzling double-dimple smile, he forgot to breathe. 'Are you okay?'

Ward blinked at the mirage closing the stall. 'Um…' Scratching his head.

'How are you?' Her winter-blue eyes scrutinised his frame.

'Just woke up.' Or was he still dreaming? Rubbing palms over his ruddy face, he felt the bristles on his chin. 'I'm okay.' His mantra since the accident voiced. He stood beside her to peek at the rescued pony. 'How is he this morning?'

'Getting there. Dad says he'll recover. It's too soon to see if he'll be ridden again, but we're hopeful.'

'It's sad anyone can do that to an animal.' The brown horse's leg was bandaged and a blanket covered its bones. But it was eating, which he took as a good sign.

'Want a coffee?'

'Yes, please.'

She led them through the shed's main doors towards her house.

'How come this place has two houses and the rooms in the shed?' Ward asked.

'My brother built the bunkhouse for seasonal workers during harvests, and for his mates who used to visit regularly. This house,' Zara said, as they walked up the front wooden steps, 'it was built for my brother and his future wife.'

'Where is your brother?' He squinted at the rock garden that had painted pebbles scattered amongst the rocks. Some were pink, blue, and red painted stones with eyes on them. Was he seeing right?

'Andy was in the Army and he died in Afghanistan.'

'I'm so sorry.' Surprised, he faltered in his step onto the veranda.

'Careful.' She put a hand on his arm to steady him.

'All good. Thanks.' He stood taller and saw her genuine concern. She didn't know him yet helped so willingly. He gulped at the cool air with his heart in his throat and squeaked out, 'Your brother didn't want to stay and be a farmer?'

'The drought was rough with not much work around here, and Andy always wanted to travel, so he joined the Army and loved it. He'd planned to stay until eligible for the part pension to retire here.'

'He never got married?'

'No, they were engaged to be married until his accident.'

Her sigh made him want to hold her hand for

comfort. Instead, he shoved his hands in his jacket and found his mobile phone. He pulled it out and realised it'd been switched off since they'd rescued that pony and he hadn't missed it. Out of habit, his thumb pressed the side key and the screen came to life, as he shoved it back into his pocket. 'Do you keep in touch with your brother's fiancée?'

'Tess is married now and lives up North. She was heartbroken like we all were, but that was almost ten years ago.' She kicked off her boots showing her odd pair of socks. Today it was bubble-gum pink with white polka dots on the left, and cobalt blue with lime stripes on the right.

He grinned at the colour of her socks and liked how she didn't fuss over her dress. The woman would look good in anything, even better in nothing! 'Um, how long has your family lived here?'

'My grandfather started this place, although, we nearly lost it from his gambling addiction. My dad grew up here and said he'll die here, and my brother was planning to do that too.'

'And you?'

'I've left countless times and lived overseas for years. I returned when Mum had passed away, to help Dad and I've been here ever since.'

'Would you go back overseas?'

'Only for a holiday.' She smiled at the view from her small veranda that faced the open countryside. 'I love it here. I wouldn't want to live anywhere else. Look at the view we've got.' She pointed to the scattering of trees where white mist lingered around grazing horses. Golden reds crept across the sky as the rising sun chased shadows down the gentle sloping hills. 'There's no traffic, no smog, no sirens. It's brilliant compared to some of the overcrowded cities I've lived in. Every time I drive down that lane, all that tension lifts from my shoulders and I know I'm home. Don't you get that when you go home?'

He shrugged. 'I was glad to see my chair when I got out of hospital—that you won't let me sit in.' He grinned.

'You can sit on that one while I get your coffee.'

He collapsed onto the veranda's wicker chair, spotting more painted pebbles amongst the big rocks. Some rocks were placed in careful pyramid piles with raked gravel like a Japanese Zen garden. He relaxed into the chair to take in the view. It was peaceful here.

The pit bull trotted up the few steps and then dropped his big butt at Ward's feet.

'I see you've met Max.' Zara placed his coffee on the table beside the small pot plant of cactuses that looked a little odd to Ward.

'Woke up from his snoring in my room.'

She grinned at the dog, then blew the steam off her mug. 'That's not like Max to sleep inside. He likes you.'

'He's big.'

'Do you have a dog?'

'Nope.'

'Grow up with any pets?'

'My sister has allergies.'

'Your sister would hate this place then, huh?'

'Yep.' Ward grinned wide, then sipped his coffee. 'Why is the dog covered in so many scars?'

'Max was a fighting dog, part of an illegal betting ring. He's a red-nosed pure American pit bull who'd get thrown into a pit where he'd have to fight other dogs to the death.'

Ward frowned at the dog, as pity and disgust for what happened to the animal burned in his chest. 'Why? How?'

'They kept Max in a cage where they'd torment him to make him savage and he was.'

'And you have him here? Free.'

'It's not Max's fault. He wore a muzzle for a while, but he's good now.' She leaned down and patted the dog's big chest. 'He'd be loyal to whoever Max chose for a home.'

'Thought it was the other way around?'

'After what they've been through, we let them choose.'

'Surely he'd have a memory or a trigger to attack?'

'Took me ages to work out what Max's triggers were, which was certain foods and the bell they used to signal the fights.'

'How do you cure that?'

'We kept cooking the same foods and gave Toby the bell to ring all day long. Drove us nuts, but it worked. Max is a big sook now.' She tickled the dog's belly as he lay on his side and moaned in delight. 'Max was their Grand

Champion who'd killed over forty dogs in that pit.'

'No way?'

'Until this place, he'd never been patted, or gone for walks, or saw daylight. Where did you find him?'

'In my room. Swear I closed that door. And he snores.' Ward's phone rang, why did he bother turning it on? 'Mum, you're ringing early. What's wrong?'

'Where are you, dear? Your sister and I are at your house.'

'I'm at Zara's farm. And before you say anything, Mum, Zara and her dad have been making sure I don't overexert myself.' Ward rolled his eyes at Zara's giggle she hid behind her cup. 'Good coffee by the way,' he mouthed to Zara, taking another sip.

'When will you be home, dear?'

'Dunno?' He replied to his mother on phone while looking at Zara. Was it Zara or this place he didn't want to leave? 'When are you heading into town next, Zara?'

'I can drop you back now if you want?'

'No.' He shook his head, covering the phone with his hand and whispered, 'My mother and sister are at my place looking for me.'

She laughed at his pain. 'When do you need to be back?'

'Monday morning.' D-day at the specialist's.

'I can drop you off on my way to the race track, it'll be early.'

'Done, you've saved me.' Not only his health but

from his family. 'Mum, I won't be back until Monday.'

'Don't overdo it, dear,' urged Shirley.

'I won't, Mum. I'll talk to you then, have a good weekend.' It'd been ages since he'd had a weekend off in winter.

'Is everything okay?' Zara asked.

'I knew that'd happen. I adore my mother, but I've had them in my face all day, every day, since the fall and…' He stopped, not used to sharing and sipped his coffee.

'You need your space, I understand.'

'Are you sure you're okay about me staying?'

'Don't stress, we're used to unexpected guests.'

'Thank you.' Relieved, he sipped his coffee and rolled his shoulders.

'Are your body muscles feeling edgy yet?'

'Big time.' Ward nodded, surprised how much she'd noticed.

'Good. You can go for a run then.'

'You mean that?' He sat forward in his chair like a racehorse ready to spring through the gates.

'A slow jog, not a sprint.'

'I promise.' He bounced from his seat and the dog, Max, sat up alert.

She sipped her coffee and casually stood up. 'Okay then, the greyhounds need a run and I'll go steal Adam's shorts. Can you run in those shoes?'

'I can. Do you think I'm ready?'

'I noticed last night, your body is so used to training,

it needs it.'

'I run every morning except game day, and I've done nothing for a fortnight.' He swallowed the last of his coffee as if to swallow his uselessness and the fear spiking his heart again.

'Come on. Let's do something about it, today.' She grabbed his hand.

'You mean that?'

'If you run two and half hours in a game, how long do you run daily?'

'An hour.' Holding her small hand, he didn't want to let go.

'Good, let's start you off with an hour slow and steady.' She let go as they walked into the stables and crossed to the sleeping quarters. 'I'll find those shorts we gave Adam for Christmas. He's never worn them. He's into this macho black thing at the moment so we got him fluoro beachwear to tease him.' Zara's laugh echoed along the corridor as she disappeared into Adam's room.

'Are you sure Adam won't mind?'

'No. We all share here, and no one locks up anything. Remember, these kids came here with nothing and have nothing to hide.'

'They told me their life stories. Bit unusual, don't you think?'

'Doesn't the club share your life story on the internet for everyone to read?'

'How do you know?' Did she read it like a fan?

'Here, this should keep you going. I'll ask Stacey to find you some spare clothes up at the house to keep you warm this weekend. I'll sort the dogs out while you get changed.' She tossed the clothes at Ward.

He changed in his room, when the door handle shifted down and the door swung open where Max stood in the open doorway. 'You opened a door!'

'I saw that,' said Zara from the main walkway at the end of the corridor. 'Max likes you.'

'He won't hurt me?' Ward stepped around the dog covered in battle scars.

'If Max was still a danger, he'd be wearing a muzzle and locked in the kennel.'

'How many dogs have you got?'

'Three at the moment. Had six, but Riley's mates adopted a few. They used to belong to these drug-dealers' that are now protecting the arresting officers' families. It's a good ending, don't you think?'

'You love your job?' He could see it, the way her eyes lit up with that double-dimple smile.

'I love my whole lifestyle, don't you?'

'I do. I was…I'm worried I'll never play again.' Surprised he'd admitted it, rubbing the heel of his palm to try and loosen the tightness in his chest.

She grabbed his hand and stared at him. 'Hey, you'll play again.'

'Promise?'

'Absolutely.'

He loved the game because it's all he knew. Yet her question of a life without football plagued his mind. Who was he without the game?

*   *   *

Ward looked so worried and vulnerable to the fear of not playing, and it was a look Zara had seen in plenty of her past patients. It was the look of those on the cusp of change for the better—or for worse.

'Here, put this belt on and I'll get the dogs.' She helped him put the wide khaki belt over his fluoro shorts and long-sleeved surfer's hoodie. It was such a crude clash of colours, and certainly no team uniform or special training shoes.

'I've never walked a dog or two.'

'Something new to learn then.' On leads, she clipped the two greyhounds onto his belt. Offering a gentle smile against his worried expression, it was obvious his confidence had suffered from that fall. 'I want you to run like you normally do, or walk, until you find that stride. But just keep going one step after the other.'

'What do I do about the dogs?'

'They're trained to follow at any speed and you'll never run as fast as them.'

'Did you rescue them too?'

'Dad did. They're our first greyhounds, and they're so used to running they need it like you do. Because of them, we have no rabbits or foxes around here.'

'They hunt them?'

'Better than Dad with his shotgun and those boys spotlighting at night. Now Dad takes the greyhounds hunting on our neighbours' properties for beer money.'

'Are we talking bunnies? Don't you like the Easter bunny?'

'Rabbits are a feral pest out here,' she said, tightening the belt around his hips to give his back the proper support to balance the dogs on either side. 'I imagine our lifestyle is very different to yours?'

'I'd never realised how sheltered or spoilt I am until coming here.'

Was Ward looking down at the place? Her home?

He glanced around with squinted eyes, then grinned at her. 'Did I ever say thank you?'

'For what?' She gulped down the lump in her throat.

'For everything.'

'Huh?' She became lost in his amber eyes.

Max let out a slobbering sneeze that snapped her awake.

Zara pushed open the shed's rear doors to allow the sunshine to flood her parked ute and horse float. 'You can run down that track.'

'Are you trying to get rid of me?'

Why did she bring him here to begin with? 'Down there, it's the prettiest parts of this place. It's nice this time of year, all green from the winter rains.' She admired the rolling hills, the mist, and the gentle sway of the eucalypts.

'Do you like winter?'

'Here, all year. The end of summer's dry.'

'Like the colour of your hair.' He reached out and she pinched herself to not flinch, as he stroked a strand of her hair all the way to the end.

What was she doing? She caught herself and stepped away from him. 'Do you like winter?'

'I'm so busy in winter I rarely take notice.' He hiked up the belt on his hips and faced the misty paddock where the sun's rays filtered through the trees. 'This is my first weekend off during football season since I became a professional player.'

'Well, enjoy it.' She smiled and reached inside her ute's cab. 'Stick to the track where there's some gradual uphill and downhill slopes. This time of year, it's soft underfoot with minimal potholes. It'll be easy on your system. So please, don't push it but have fun and enjoy the view.' She put his cap on his head, slipped one water bottle into the belt's holder and another into his hand. 'I'll see you soon.' She sniggered at his outrageous outfit. 'Should I take a photo for your fan page?'

Ward looked over himself, with two dogs strapped to his belt, in fluoro shorts and some yellow surfer's hoodie. 'No way.'

'Why? Are you only allowed to wear team colours for training?' Zara grinned at him.

'Do you enjoy teasing me?'

'Keeps you real.'

'What are you going to do?'

'Get another coffee. And as my dad would say, you're wasting daylight, now get out there and run.' She slapped his tight arse like she would a pony.

'Cheeky wench.' His wide grin hid the scar on his chin. He adjusted his cap, and with a wink he began his run with the dogs on either side of him.

'You've got a shadow,' she called out, pointing to Max following.

Ward kept jogging as he called out, 'What do I do with Max? He's not gonna scrap with the greyhounds strapped to my waist, is he?'

'No. Max could do with the exercise too. Have fun, take deep breaths and enjoy the view.' She waved, leaning against the shed and watched Ward and his canine entourage jog over the hill and out of sight.

Wow, someone like Ward was staying for the weekend. Was it a good move for him?

She wanted to help him return to his prime condition like she'd done on all of her animals. Her dad said Ward was here for a reason and that was to help him.

She'd seen Ward's fear of not playing again. His confidence had been shattered from some nasty fall, where he needed to get back onto that football field fast or he may lose his nerve forever.

But that's if Ward wanted to—and if she could keep her emotions out of it.

*   *   *

Ward started his stiff and awkward jog. Out of sync, he kept going, and soon found his rhythm following the soft dirt track. Over rolling hills and into small gullies, he jogged by streams and through scattered thickets. He passed grazing horses and kangaroos that watched him from the hillside. His stride evened out and his breathing steadied, with only two panting greyhounds and one scarred pit bull for company.

Inhaling wisps of fog, the air was so crisp and clean, and with each step he ran stronger and became more fluid in movement.

Hope filled his chest that he hadn't lost too much physical condition, when it'd be a fortnight today since his fall.

If Ward was with his teammates now, he'd be in a hotel room, shared with either Sam, Mills, or Nick. They'd have a team breakfast, to then laze around under curfew until game time.

Last night, Ward enjoyed a few beers, ate pizza, pretzels and chips, and stayed out until midnight. It was none of the food types that the club's dietician would've approved of, and if his teammates saw him now, they'd give him hell for the beach gear he was wearing.

But right now, he had no one around him, no team or coaches and only had to prove this to himself.

With a burst of energy, he ran full speed to see if he

could do it. Around the curve of the track, he sprinted to the top of the hill and stopped at the impressive scene. He couldn't take his eyes off the expansive farmlands decadently spread out like a patchwork quilt. The small township lay in the distance as cars shifted like dots along hazy lines for roads. It was a wide-open world free from stadiums, airports, high rises, and congested traffic.

'This is my favourite spot on the farm,' said Zara, seated on the quad by the far side.

He jumped. 'I didn't hear you.'

'I was waiting for you.' Zara carried a few bowls and a large bottle of water that she dished out to the dogs. 'You've been running for almost an hour.' She unclipped the greyhounds from his belt, who then trotted over to the water dish.

'Didn't realise I'd run so long.' He could run more.

'Great effort for your first run.'

'I feel great.' Using a large rock on the edge of the view, he stretched out his legs as part of his daily habit. 'I thought I'd lost a lot of my fitness, I'm not one hundred percent.'

'Won't take you much to get it back.' Her head tilted and she watched him stretch, biting her lower lip.

Was she perving on him or being a professional? 'Hope so.' He needed to get back into the game. It was his life to play football, the only life he knew.

But this was surreal, scanning the scenery as the greyhounds lapped at the water. 'Those greyhounds ran so well I'd almost forgotten I was walking them.'

'Max looks buggered.' Zara's tinkling laugh echoed as the pit bull collapsed in a panting heap with his chin resting in the bowl. Too tired to lift his head, his black tongue slurped at the water.

'Don't you guys walk him?'

'Billy tries to take him for a run, but Max won't go anywhere. Yet he never left your side. Ever thought about having a dog for you and the guys to share?'

'We play away during winter.'

'You run daily, don't you?'

'Except game day, yeah.'

'And if you went away, your mum could feed him and Max would watch your house.'

'I don't want a dog, and I wouldn't know what to do, especially with a dog like Max.'

'Max is easy to look after. You feed him, take him to the vet once a year, and take him running with you. I bet Max would claim your massive couch as his bed and annoy you with his snoring.'

'Doubt our man-couch is big enough for Max.' Ward drank his water bottle dry.

'Think you can run back because I'd doubt Max will.' She laughed at the big dog huffing and puffing, almost snorting in the water from the bowl. 'The greyhounds will.'

'I'm tempted to.' Ward wanted to see where the track ended and what his body could do.

'Don't push yourself, Brendan.'

He grinned at her over his shoulder for using his first name. 'Am I in trouble?'

She shrugged.

'And, as per usual, you're right.' He stepped in beside her, admiring her warm perfume that mingled with the cool tang of rain from heavy overhanging grey clouds.

'Have you ever ridden a quad?' She tied the greyhounds to the back of the chunky four-wheeled bike.

'I've ridden a few. We hired scooters to hoon around Brisbane and I've endured the Bali madness. They're almost as bad as women drivers in that country.'

'Well go on then, smart arse, you steer this thing.'

'Do you mean that?'

'Don't flip us, because you'll be the one who'll suffer worse.'

Ward smiled wide as he climbed onto the seat. 'I won't.'

'Can you tell Max to get on the back, he's exhausted.'

'What do I do?'

'Say his name, point or tap where you want him to go and tell him to get up. Name, action, and command.'

He faced the dog waiting for him. 'Max,' he said, then tapped the back rack, 'get up.' Ward's eyes widened as the large dog jumped onto the back tray of the quad. 'He listened.'

'The only one who will, so enjoy this moment.' Zara laughed as she playfully punched his arm.

'You like taking the piss out of me.' Was she flirting

with him?

'I bet only a few people do in your world.' She collected the dishes tucking them into the pack, then sat behind him and held onto the back tray.

'Hold on.' He kangaroo-hopped the bike, hiding his grin.

'Are you sure you can ride this? Don't give yourself whiplash.'

'I won't.' He gunned the engine with a grin. All for a reason. 'I said hold on.'

'For my life.' Her hands slid around his waist and he grinned at his cunning.

'Which way?' The long way, he hoped.

'Straight ahead, not too fast because of the greyhounds.'

'I'm in no rush.' Not when he had her holding him.

* * *

After a big breakfast, Ward sat back contented in the wicker chair on Zara's veranda, watching the rain fall in a light drizzle. With Max asleep at his feet, he sipped his coffee, taking in the amazing view. It was like a holiday.

He looked at the rock garden of assorted towers and piles of different stones. There were raked gravelly stones among the few shrubs. Painted pebbles stood out amongst the grey rocks as if they were children's rock-pets. On the table was a pot plant he had to look at twice to realise they were pebbles painted as cactuses. 'Did you do the garden? You said you were in Japan, it's got that Japanesy feel to it, all you're missing is a bonsai.'

'Tried that, but I'm a plant killer,' replied Zara, walking out the front door in her bright coloured odd socks peeking out from beneath the hem of her jeans.

'A what?'

'I can't do plants; I think I kill them with kindness. Rocks seem to cope with my punishment.'

'Doubt you'd punish anyone.'

'I have my moments. Do you garden?'

'Dunno, I've never tried.' He frowned at his own reply. Did he do anything that wasn't football related?

'You said your house comes with a gardener.'

'I did.' He couldn't remember the last time he'd ventured into the backyard.

'I've prepared the massage table to give you a rub down. It'll help you recover quicker from muscle fatigue after that run.'

'Sure.' He got up eager for the treatment, then flinched. 'Oh, wow.' His muscles had stiffened and he was sore all over. 'You knew that'd happen.'

'It's my job, remember.'

'You don't have to do this, you know, but I am grateful.' He hobbled into the house after her. A large fireplace was the centrepiece of the lounge room on the left. He followed Zara to the right and through the double doorway.

'You wanted help.'

'But I don't want to impose.' She'd done so much, opened her home, saved him from surgery—and his sister.

'If you were a bother, I would've driven you back into town last night. Now please, take off your clothes and get onto the massage table. Use this towel to cover yourself and I'll give you a moment.' She closed the doors behind him.

Naked? In front of her?

Did he dare?

Did she like him?

She must do, going to all this trouble, even if her father was a fan.

He slipped off his grey matching pair of socks, rolled down his borrowed tracksuit pants, took off someone's shirt and dropped them onto the chair. 'You have an office?' Not realising he'd changed before a window that faced the countryside. *Well the horses copped a view.*

He wrapped the towel around his waist and sat on the massage table and looked at the charts of human and horse muscle structures. To one side, a clear glass cabinet displayed glass bottles. By the window, a desk stood in the corner holding a PC. Certificates and assorted framed diplomas hung on the wall, it looked like a proper medical practice.

She was the real deal, and he was just a patient.

Damn.

There'd be no hero-worship in this place.

He lay down on the table resting the back of his head

on his hands. 'I'm ready. Do you have regular business hours for patients?'

The doors slid open and she brought in her sweet scent of warm apricot nectar and gardenias. It had to be gardenias; his grandmother grew them in Queensland where he visited for summer holidays as a kid.

'Dad's my only customer, otherwise I don't do humans or practice from home. I use this office for bookkeeping our farm's accounts.'

'What am I then, if you don't treat human patients?'

'A human thoroughbred. Lie face down, please.'

He frowned and rolled over. 'I'm not a horse.'

Her laugh soon made him smile at the floor through the hole in her massage table.

'Do you work on other people?' He mumbled as his body relaxed under waves of bliss from her magical hands.

'No. But you'd be used to having rubdowns from physios?'

Why didn't she do other humans when she had the talent, the qualifications, and this set-up? 'We get rubdowns, but it's nothing like your hands.' He sighed so deep on the table, it was heaven.

'So, relax and let me take care of you.'

'Who takes care of you?' He mumbled on the verge of consciousness. Her hands faltered on his skin and he opened his eyes. 'You okay?' He raised his head to look at her.

'Sh, relax.' Pushing his head down, and again, she

soon put him fast to sleep.

*   *   *

Joe tapped on Zara's window where Ward lay stretched out on the massaging table.

She waved, then walked to her front door wiping her hands on the cloth. 'Hey, Dad.'

'How is the lad?'

'Asleep. He took the greyhounds for a run.'

'How long for?'

'Just under an hour.'

Joe thumbed back the brim of his hat and asked, 'How'd he pull-up?'

'Bit sore.'

'Hence the massage, huh?'

'Yep.' She looked back at Ward's peaceful frame. She liked watching him sleep.

'Brought the mail over,' he said, holding out a few envelopes.

'Thanks. I'll look at these later,' she replied, putting them on the side table.

'How long is Ward staying?'

'I'll take him back Monday morning. He wants to hide from his family.'

'Not the first one to do that out 'ere.'

She frowned, crossing her arms over her chest as the chill burrowed deep into her bones, pushing down a memory she'd forced to forget in her mind—yet her body remembered.

'Have you got some clothes sorted for him?'

'Stacey's already done it. Should've seen Ward in Adam's flowery surfer shorts.'

'The ones Adam wouldn't be caught dead wearin' in public?'

'I threatened to take a photo for Ward's fan club, he was good about it.' She snickered at the memory.

'Listen, luv,' Joe pulled her outside, closing her front door.

'What's wrong, Dad?'

Joe removed his hat and palmed over his greying crewcut. 'I know I said we should help Ward, but don't you get caught up with him either.'

She frowned as her voice lowered in warning, 'Dad.'

'He's a footballer who lives a different way than we do.'

'I get that.'

'They're only out for the fame and glory, chasin' the limelight.'

'What's that got to do with me?'

'Nothing. I just don't want to see you get hurt.'

'Ward's just a client.' She screwed up her face like a kid all over again.

'If Ward was just a client, you wouldn't have brought him out 'ere.'

'It wasn't planned. Besides, it was you who made me

do the house call, not once, but three times,' she said, holding her three fingers up at him. 'You made me go back.'

'I know I did, luv, only because Ward's one of my favourite players.'

'I did this for you. You knew I was at his place when you called me, where Ward offered to help me get the horse float.'

'So, why didn't you drop him back before you picked up that pony, luv?'

'I did those house calls because you made me,' she said with raised chin, needing to justify it to herself. 'I've been professional.'

'You're also a pretty girl. I know the boys all gave Ward the warning.'

'They didn't.' The heat rose in her chest unsure if it was anger mixed with embarrassment. 'I'm not Ward's type, so don't bother with the over-protective trip, okay.' She was no one's type—it was safer that way.

'It's my job as your father to embarrass you in public,' Joe said with a grin and kissed her forehead. He then slipped on his hat, adjusting his hearing aid as he started down the front steps. 'We're watching the big game tonight with the Saints playin'. After their bye last week, it'll be a test for the team to play without him and for Ward to watch.'

'I don't think Ward remembers the fall.'

Joe paused at the bottom of the steps. 'Reckon you're right. Ward gave me a curious look when I mentioned the fall, yesterday, when he'd arrived. I'm pretty sure they'll replay it on the tellie tonight. How do you think he'll react?'

'Well, that's the psychological part then.'

'True.' Sliding his hands into his jeans' pockets, Joe looked over the rock garden. 'It's a good thing Ward's here then, luv. I've already warned them boys to be themselves.'

'Good. We shouldn't change because we have company.' This was meant to be a safe zone for everyone who lived here.

'Course not, luv, it's our backyard. Anyway, the boys have promised to not get too drunk and trip over themselves.'

'That means you too, Dad,' she said, arching an eyebrow at the big man.

'I only get happy,' he replied with a cheeky grin and a wink. 'Just watch out for you, luv, I know you like that footballer, it's written all over your face.'

Oh no. She blinked at her father who was uber-observant. 'He's a client, Dad.'

'Ah huh, just be careful, luv. Don't want you gettin' hurt again.' He gave her a nod, then strolled towards the shed.

Her father was right. She didn't need to get hooked up with someone like Ward where she'd be nothing more than just a blip on his radar.

Over her shoulder, she glanced at his sleeping frame and sighed. Shame she couldn't hear her own sanity speaking, but let her emotions rule as she opened the door to resume the aide of his recovery. The quicker Ward left the quicker she'd forget him.

If she could.

Twelve

After lunch, Ward walked up to the stables where Zara was inside, working on that poor haggard creature.

He leaned against the gate and watched Zara speak in low soothing tones as she massaged its sore leg.

Zara glanced over her shoulder and gave him a soft smile.

'I'm going to call you Z.'

'Why?'

The horse lifted its head at Ward, then lay back with a sigh. Ward knew that sound, he made it himself while under the magic of her hands. 'Because every time you work on me, I catch up on the Z's, making me sleep like that horse.' That had re-closed its eyes with a deep sigh. 'I've never seen a horse lie down like that.'

'It'll do him some good to get him off that leg for a bit. He'll get up when it's feeding time.' She patted the horse, cleaned her hands and shut the gate to the small stable. 'Do you think you're ready for some upper body work?'

'Like what?'

'You'd do weights, right?'

'Yeah.'

'How often?'

'Few times a week at the Club's gym.'

'We don't have a fancy gym here, but we do have animals to feed.' She headed to the back end of the stables beside her ute that had been unhitched from the horse float. 'Think you can lift a bale of hay?' She pointed to the large pile to one side of the shed.

It was dry grass; how hard could that be? 'How many?'

'We need to deliver twenty bales to the back paddocks.' Zara slipped on a pair of gloves. She grabbed the first bale and slung it onto the back of her ute. 'There's gloves—'

'Not to be outdone by a lady.' Ward picked up a bale of hay, it was light but cumbersome. 'Ow.' He shook his hand at the piece of straw that had pierced under his fingernail.

'Straw's a killer,' she said, pulling out a pair of gloves from the back tray amongst the rope. 'Did you know it's an ancient Chinese torture technique to poke sticks under nails.'

'I thought you didn't know the ways of the Samurai master.' He shook out the sting and slipped on the thick leathery gloves, still feeling the pulse of pain beneath his nail.

'You'll live.'

'Great, make me feel useless,' he said while thumbing

the scar on his chin.

She gave his shoulder a gentle squeeze. 'Hey, you're not useless, you're just not used to it. I'll get on the back while you keep lifting, and you stop the second you feel a twinge.'

'Yeah, yeah.' Focused on the task, he'd do this for his ego's sake.

Soon he had a swinging rhythm passing hay bales to Zara. His muscles flexed in his back, shoulders, stomach, and legs, in a total body work out. She had him in training, while watching over him with a wary eye, in a gentle form of boot camp he never saw coming.

Zara jumped off the ute and smiled at him. 'That's twenty, how are you feeling?'

'Good.' He nodded, stretching his neck and his upper body. His strength was still there. To think, not even four days ago he couldn't sit or sleep. 'So now what, Coach?'

She rolled her eyes at the name. 'The distribution. I'll drive, you can ride shotgun and man the gates. Tell your shadow to get on.'

'My what?' At the side of the ute, the pit bull stared up at him. 'Max, get up.' From a standing start, the dog leaped onto the back tray in one swift movement. It was graceful, for a massive beast.

'Give him a pat for doing a good job.' Zara put a bag of carrots inside the cab. 'You give encouragement and reward for doing what you tell them. For animals it's a simple pat on the head. Does your coach do that?'

'No.' He frowned as her laughter carried. But then again… 'We get a pat on the back and a spot on the team.' Would he get his midfielder's position back?

'Good dog.' Ward patted the pit bull's large head, receiving a wide grin in return that offset the dogs scar-pitted face and torn ears. 'You're not coming home with me, no matter how much you suck up.'

The dog licked his cheek.

'Oh man.' He screwed up his face and wiped off the slobber.

Zara laughed by the driver's door. 'I said Max likes you. Come on, we've got animals to feed.' She started the engine.

'I'm coming.' He jumped into the passenger seat, happy to see what was next, because it felt like a holiday.

Zara stopped at a large set of metal railed gates that blocked the dirt track. 'Right, the rules of riding shotgun are that you get to open and close the gates.'

'I'm playing gatekeeper?' Ward asked, arching an eyebrow at the fence.

'It's the rules of the land everywhere. Not too hard is it? Besides, how many gates have you ever opened in your life?'

'Okay, okay. Can't help think there's some double meaning to that comment.' He chuckled as he jumped out of the ute.

Zara wound down her window and called out, 'But I want you to push the gates with both hands and from the chest okay.' She demonstrated from behind the wheel.

'Why?' Scratching his head at the gate, he then realised what Zara was doing. *Clever lady.* 'Yes, Coach.'

'I'm no coach.'

'Z, it is.' He grinned at her eye roll, yet impressed he'd given her a nickname. Or was it a pet name, like a guy does with his girl? He'd never done that before.

'Come on, you're causing a traffic jam here.'

'Okay, okay.' It was only a simple metal fence on a hinge, how hard could it be? He strolled up to the gate, undid the chained clip, and as instructed, he pushed with both hands. Yet the gate didn't move. It was stuck.

'The animals are gonna think we've put them on a diet at this rate.' Her tinkling laugh made him smile. *'Push.'*

He faced the gate, stiff from rust. 'I'm pushing, ya pushy thing you.' He pushed with both hands, hard. The gate swung wide on its hinge and then ricocheted straight back at him in the blink of an eye and he caught it. 'Wasn't expecting that.'

'Good, you've still got all your reflexes,' she called out while driving past.

Ward closed the gate and climbed back into the cab. 'You knew that'd happen, didn't you?'

'All our gates do it this time of year from the rain. Some stick, some don't, but they've all knocked us on our arses one time or another.' She grinned, putting the ute into gear and it rolled down the dirt track. 'Out here, you'll never know what to expect with a simple gate.'

'It's just a gate.'

'That works on your upper strength and grip you'd need to catch a ball, along with your quick reflexes. Guess what the best part was?'

Did he really do all that with one gate? 'What?'

'You didn't flinch, just reacted.' She gave him a double-dimple smile.

He wiped his mouth, staring at her as his breath stalled while his heart pumped faster. She was right. And he let his emotions take him when he leaned over and kissed her cheek. 'Thank you.'

The colour rose in her cheeks. She faced the road, cleared her throat and tightened her grip on the wheel. 'Err, um, don't thank me now, you've got a lot more gates to open and more bales of hay to off-load,' she blurted out. 'Oops.' She tugged the steering wheel to the left to get them back on the track.

Palm to the cab's roof to steady himself on the rough terrain, he smiled wide as he gave her a two-fingered scout's salute. 'Bring it on, Z.'

He pushed open countless gates and tossed hay bales off the back of the ute to feed the horses. With only a few bales left, Zara parked the ute beside another paddock fence.

'Now that's a massive horse.' Ward pointed to the tall black horse bee-lining for them. It towered over him, eager for the hay.

'That's Middy.' Zara cut the string free around the bale as the stallion tugged at the straw. 'Here you go.' She passed Ward the pocket knife, handle first.

'Thanks.' He cut the string on the last two bales and fed the other waiting horses. 'It's a stallion, right?'

'Middy is.' Patting the long neck, she smiled up at the large majestic beast.

'Middy? Strange name for a massive animal. Isn't that the name of a small beer glass or mid-strength beer?' Ward asked her.

'Midnight, and he's got one of those incredibly long racing names too.'

'Ex-racehorse?'

'Middy's won over a million dollars, and he's Dad's mate.'

'What's wrong with him? He doesn't look sick.' It was a handsome animal with a muscular gleaming coat and mane.

'Middy fractured his leg in a race and they were going to shoot him.' She pointed to the rear leg full of long scars. 'Dad and I begged them not to and brought him home in the truck. He lived in this special sling and leg-brace Dad created, while the vets put in experimental metal pins. Took six months to get him to walk, but he did.' She stroked his long black neck.

'He's massive and so placid.'

'Middy wasn't like this when he arrived.'

'How?'

'Racehorses aren't horses,' Zara said as she reached inside the cab and grabbed a handful of carrots for the pockets of her jacket.

'He's a horse, I can see that.'

'Middy was specifically bred and trained from the time he was born, where his whole life was all about preparing for the racetrack. He was trained to run at the sound of the bell. Trained to win or he'd feel the sting of the jockey's whip and ran with his heart.'

Ward played with his heart from the second the siren sounded. 'What happened to Middy?'

'The horse in front fell, Middy tripped trying to jump, and the jockey broke his collarbone.' She sighed, brushing down the stallion's glossy coat. 'When we brought him home his spirit was broken.'

'Why?'

'Middy's sole purpose was to race and then he had nothing.'

Ward thumbed the scar on his chin. Who was he away from the game?

His hands clenched into fists trying to force down that spike of icy fear tightening his chest.

The stallion's soft nose touched his fist as if sniffing at Ward's fear of the future. The warmth of Middy's breath mixed with the cool air against Ward's hand, as he peered into the big beast's black eye as if staring into his soul. 'What did you do to help him?'

'Dad showed Middy there was a life away from racing and what was in a horse's nature.'

'And now?'

'Middy lives here with his harem, and he helps us.'

'Breeding horses?'

'That, and Middy's the mob leader.'

'A what?'

'In football you've got a team captain and a coach who trains you?'

'Yes. Although you're ten times prettier than any coach I've had.' He grinned at her flush so slight to her cheeks, it was pretty.

'I'm not your coach,' she said. 'Well, Middy's kind of like the captain of the paddock, who listens to Dad who's like the coach.'

'For what? Horse games in the field? Do you have goals set up? What does your umpire look like?'

'Not like that.' Her laugh made him smile. 'When we get a tough racehorse that's big and nasty, Dad brings Middy in—'

'Who's bigger and stronger.'

'And they soon behave. Would you pick a fight with someone like Middy?'

'It'd be like taking on a ruckman. So, you rehabilitate them?'

'All Dad does is bring out that inner instinct in those we rescue to be a horse again, and hopefully, find them new homes.' She produced another carrot from her jacket's pocket. 'We showed Middy there was another way to live from a life almost stolen when he'd been staring down the barrel of a gun. And now…' Her tiny fingers wrapped around Ward's wrist as she uncurled his fist and placed the carrot into his open palm.

He hadn't realised he'd been fisting his hands so tight there were nail marks alongside the orange carrot he was holding. He thumbed the scar on his chin and looked at her. 'What are you doing?' Why was she saying these things that were slamming like a hammer into the centre of his back?

'You're going to feed him.'

'He'd chew off my hand.' Then remembered himself. He wasn't useless, she'd said he just wasn't used to it. 'How?' And her smile was enough encouragement to try.

'Hold it palm flat, like so.' She held out a carrot in her open palm as Middy pulled back his lips displaying massive teeth. The crunch echoed around them as the vegetable from her hand was soon devoured in a few loud chomps.

'How do you help them if they're trained one way all their lives to…' How could he help himself?

'It's an instinct we all have. There's also a choice on how we live. Some fight. Some curl up in the corner and let it happen, too scared to fight back.' She winced and whispered, 'Some don't get that choice.' She glanced at the pit bull seated by their feet.

'Like that pony we picked up, and Max.' She looked

so sad, almost scared. Had Zara been hurt?

Zara scratched Max's big head and the dog smiled wide with a groaning eye roll. 'Everyone wants to be treated with kindness. Some never got that. They weren't trained by affection, where their only reward was winning their race like Middy, or for Max to win his fights so he could live another day. They didn't understand there was another way to live, but they do now.'

He stared at the carrot lying in his palm, then out to the open paddock. 'I was like that,' he whispered. 'Still am. I only know football. It's all we talk about, it's everything we do… I don't know any other way.' The admittance made him heave the air as if his lungs had filled with liquidized steel burning through his chest, tasting the hot metal on the back of his tongue.

'Did you ever want to do anything else?'

'No. I was recruited while in school. Never did anything else, just football.'

'And now?'

'After that fall, it's making me think.' And her questions were doing it too. 'I've only got four years left, six if my body will let me. I know now I'm not invincible, but I'm not ready to end that part of me. I love what I do. I love playing. Yet, I'm worried I'll never get back out there.'

'You'll get there, believe it and you will. Here…' Tugging on his wrist she opened his palm that balanced the carrot. 'Let him take it.'

Velvety lips and hot breath feathered over his palm.

He braced himself as Middy plucked the carrot and used Ward's hand like a plate. Chomping on the carrot, orange bits spilled like crumbs from a cake. Again, large lips tickled his palm to scoop up the remnants. 'Is this horse gonna kiss me like Max did with his slobber?' He grinned and winced at the new sensation.

'Middy isn't a kisser, he just loves his carrots.' She gave the last carrot to Middy, patted his mane, then headed to the ute's driver's side. 'Come on, I think I'll let you play with Billy. Don't forget about Max.'

'Billy, why?' Ward asked while wiping his hands free of horse-slobber on the rag in the back of the ute. 'Max, up.' Patting the back tray, he was amazed the dog listened to his commands and patted the big head as a reward. 'Good dog.'

'Good boy, Brendan.' She ruffled his hair with a giggle as she passed by.

He smiled at her double-dimple grin she shared from across the ute's rear tray and climbed into the passenger seat. 'Okay Z, how many gates do I have to open and close, now?'

'One.' She replied, starting the engine. 'I took you the long way around.'

'Okay then, so why do I have a feeling it's not simple playtime with Billy?'

'Ever boxed?'

'We've done it for training.' He sat up and looked at her hopeful. Was she suggesting more farm training?

'Have you ever sparred with a fifteen-year-old street scrapper?'

'I wouldn't want to hurt the kid.' He liked Billy and his cheeky grin.

'I'm not worried about Billy, I'm worried about you.'

'Me?'

'Don't underestimate Billy, he's got a killer instinct. Do you?' She gave him a side-glance as she drove homeward.

Ward never had to fight for anything, except for a football in a game. Everything was handed to him and all he had to do was follow instructions, to eat this and drink that, to wear this while you train on that. Go to practice and listen to the trainers. Go to the airport, catch the team bus, and play the game. Get patted on the back for every goal and rubbed down after every game. Then go home and do nothing.

He was so spoiled compared to these people who'd opened their home to him.

'You have that instinct, it's there when you fight for that ball in every game.'

He had a backbone somewhere, but where was it now?

'The reflex training will be good for you and Billy,' Zara said. 'But I'd better warn you, Billy's got a longer reach than you, so I doubt you'll get near that kid.'

'But?' He rubbed the back of his neck and shoulders. This emotional ride was draining, asking questions he'd never dared ask himself.

'Your neck will be fine and I'll be there to watch, but you shout the second it twinges. Which I doubt it will.'

'Do you mean that?'

'Why would I lie to you?' She gave a half shrug as she steered downhill towards the shed.

Again, that feeling of breathlessness filled his chest. But it wasn't fear. It was a warmth that radiated from his heart, bringing a weightlessness to his body when he looked at her. Was he floating, with this mixed sensation of wanting to jump, to leap, to run, and to hug her all at the same time. 'You told me to trust you when we first met, remember that?'

'I did. Do you?' Her eyes on him, she gnawed her bottom lip as if scared of his answer.

'I do.' His palm reached out and gave her shoulder a slight squeeze. What he really wanted to do was pull her into his arms to kiss her and hold her tight. He trusted her. 'And I believe you.' Because what he also saw was that Zara believed in him too, which filled him full of hope.

Thirteen

The fire pit crackled and a log shifted, sending sparks to the stars that shone like silent witnesses. Ward crossed his boots at the ankles, enjoying the warmth of the fire and the miss-matched family surrounding him. He settled back into the curve of the couch, with the best view of the large television on the veranda.

Joe sat like a proud grandfather with the toddler, Toby, cradled in his lap, while Zara massaged his large hands. Tim, Adam, Stacey, and Billy bantered with each other on the rest of the couches. They talked, laughed, shared, and joked about anything and everything but football.

So unlike his own family, where he'd be arguing with his sister who'd be complaining about something. His mother would try to keep the peace, while his dad typically zoned-out, ignoring all.

Yet, these strangers had let him into their home, shared their food and clothes with him. They'd teased him, made him laugh, and treated him like normal.

Ward rubbed his jaw's twinging-ache from Billy's lightning fast punches, having copped a few in the face. Grateful his neck survived from that part of Zara's training regime, proving she was right, his neck and nerves were securely back where they belonged.

After that, it'd been playtime, showing the boys, Adam, Tim, Billy, and the tiny Toby, how to kick a football in a paddock. He'd taught them how to push and weave from the opponent in play. He even got Joe and Stacey involved with their simple backyard game. Ward had coaxed Zara to join in and took every opportunity he could to get his arms around her while playfully tackling her for the ball.

Ward grinned at the Shetland pony, Goliath, repeating his escapades with the beer fridge. The pit bull, Max, who hadn't left his side all day, was now asleep at his feet alongside the greyhounds stretched out before the warming fire pit.

Earlier, Tim had walked Ward through feeding the dogs, then Joe taught him to cook dinner on an open flame. They never rubbed his nose in it. Never made him feel out of sort. They'd all been where he was; someone who wasn't useless—just not used to it.

'Game's on.' Billy rushed to the TV on the veranda and turned on the outdoor speakers.

'Get us a beer while you're up,' called Joe.

'Yeah, yeah. Move, Goliath.' Billy shouldered the Shetland pony from the fridge, opened the door and gave the horse a carrot. Goliath clip-clopped away with an orange carrot hanging out of his mouth like a cigar while

Billy handed out drinks and they soon settled in for the game.

Near half-time, Ward shook his head in frustration at his team losing on the live telecast. He could see why. His teammates were trying to fill his position in the midfield that was being overrun by the opposition. The coach had rotated the one position—the spot Ward thought he owned—that was now in the hands of six other teammates. He'd been so easily replaced, yet horrified at how bad they were performing.

'What's it like watching something you're a part of?' Zara asked, seated beside him.

'Frustrating. I can read the play the ruckman's going to make, but my teammates aren't following through.' It was a series of plays they'd practised all the time.

'Don't you guys man-up?' Billy asked with his cheeky signature grin.

'You stick with your opposition when you need to defend,' said Ward, 'but you're always wary of the others around you. Sometimes you can predict the play.'

'Like an instinct?' Tim asked, pulling another stray cotton strand from the brim of his decrepit cap.

'Yep.' His team should know this, yet they were getting hammered with plays he could easily read from his benched position.

'What would you do there?' Adam pointed his beer towards the TV.

'Watch their ruckman. Hassle my opposition. Try

and lose my tag. And right before the bounce, I'd move to steal that ball, barge through and pass it to my teammate. If not, I'll either kick clear toward the goal-end or duck and hope the umpire sees it.'

'For the freebie?' Billy asked.

'It's called crumbing. A few of us in the game do it, where we get low on the ankles and keep our head over the ball. Sheldon's one of them.' Ward scowled, thumbing the scar on his chin.

'You can see your team's missing you tonight. They're not doing very well, mate,' called out Joe. 'And that's my team, remember?'

Ward wanted to smile and joke with them, but it hurt to watch when he should've been there.

With the game over to a dismal loss, he couldn't bear to watch the highlights being replayed. Tim, Adam, and Billy started shifting furniture undercover and Ward was about to help when Coach Mitchell came on-screen for his after-game interview, and Ward returned to his seat.

'It's obvious your team was missing Ward out there today,' stated the reporter. Aiming a microphone at a stony-faced Mitchell, with his arms crossed, standing in the playing field near the dressing room's entrance.

'We're still filling that gap,' replied Mitchell without any positive-speech spin on *lessons to learn from this game for a better future*. Nothing. Just short and sharp.

'Is there any news on Ward's injuries?'

'We'll be deciding on Monday with an update of his

condition,' replied Mitchell bluntly, not even giving an inkling of hope for Ward.

'Will Ward play again soon?'

Mitchell looked over his shoulder to his team leaving the grounds with their heads down, dragging their feet at the depressing defeat. 'We won't make a decision until we have the reports from the medical team.'

Was Ward being replaced?

With the coach's interview over at the stadium, they crossed to the studio where a panel of three men spoke. They were ex-footy players who'd interviewed Ward a few times. Ward and his housemates had made many jibes about this panel's so-called words of wisdom, and how much these guys loved the sound of their voice in Tv-land.

But tonight, Ward listened and watched with interest.

'It was obvious the Saints lacked that skill in their midfield, missing their player Ward,' said the sports commentator who looked to his offsider on the panel in the television studio.

'That's obvious. And with that horrendous fall Ward and Sheldon shared, not only do they have to recover physically, there's the psychological impact to consider too.'

Ward frowned at the words *psychological impact*. What was the big deal? He fell and all was good again. Were they going to start calling him Humpty Dumpty?

'For those who don't remember, we'll show you a replay of the spectacular fall between Ward and Sheldon,' announced the TV commentator.

Ward sat forward eagerly, he'd never seen the fall. Couldn't remember it. Yet, there it was in front of him in a slow-motion replay.

There was the leap for the ball. The players slipping in the mud beneath him. His fingers reaching in the rain for the ball that twirled under the flash of lightning.

But then he winced, watching his skull collide against Sheldon's in mid-air, then their crash, spearing headfirst into the ground. His eyes widened in horror at the dead-drop his neck took from the impact, as his body twitched in an epileptic fit in the mud. He stared at the other players who stood around him and Sheldon as they both lay unconscious under the rain.

It looked like he'd *broken his neck!*

Zara gasped and grabbed his hand. Max put his large head on Ward's knee, while Ward stared at his unconscious self in front of a silenced stadium full of people.

It didn't look real.

How come he'd forgotten that accident?

Yet, he remembered it now.

'Max senses what you're going through,' whispered Zara

Incapable of speaking, still reeling at what he'd seen. He could've been a paraplegic.

'Animals have instincts.' She reached across and patted Max's head that rested on his knee. 'They might not speak, but they can offer a nudge, or just offer their silent company to keep all your secrets like a best friend.'

He patted Max's big head where worry was worn in the animal who'd been through so much. 'Who's your best friend?'

'What?' Zara pulled her hand away.

'Who keeps all your secrets?' Ward turned to Zara.

'I have none,' she whispered.

'Everyone has secrets?'

'Not in this family,' she said with a half grin, but her dimples didn't show. 'Hey, you'll get through this.'

Why was she helping him? Why was this group of strangers so willing to open their home to him?

'Excuse me.' Ward got up from his seat.

He didn't want to be here.

He wanted to be home, not here among strangers.

Staggering from the house and onto the long driveway, gravel crunched under his shoes as he allowed the blackness of the night to swallow him. His eyes adjusted to the dimness, as stars blinked between clouds like a holey blanket in the sky. The wintery night bit at his skin as he heaved in lungs-full of icy air. He reached the fence where the wooden rail was coarse under his grip.

Again, flashbacks whirled in a never-ending replay in his mind's eye. The scent of rain, mud, and clipped grass. He could hear the thunder and the blood roaring in his ears as he leaped for that ball. He gasped at the falling sensation, and winced at the blinding pain from his head, neck and spine.

He relived it all.

Ward gripped the cold, wooden rail tighter at the memory of waking in the corridor of the stadium. He'd been strapped to a gurney, kept helpless against the stabbing pain of every wheel roll toward the waiting ambulance. There was the excruciating journey to the hospital, and then the look on his parents' faces where his mother had aged overnight.

No wonder his sister was hanging around, and his teammates were so willing to put up with his crap.

No wonder Sheldon had all those women flock to his hospital bed.

They could've broken their necks.

The game he loved… could've killed him!

* * *

Zara stood, intending to follow Ward with her heart aching for the man in pain.

'Don't.' Joe captured her wrist from his chair. 'That boy needs some time to clear his head.'

'I didn't know it was that bad. How could they replay that on TV?'

'Hadn't you seen it before?'

'No. I never knew who Ward was until you told me to go to his house.'

'I thought you did.'

'There's over two dozen men on that field, I don't remember who's who. I'm flat out remembering the horses' names down at the racetrack.'

'Racehorses have ten names that no one is expected to remember.'

'It's obvious Ward never remembered his fall until tonight. Poor guy.'

'Why would they hide that from him? He could've looked it up on the internet anytime.'

'I don't think Ward realised how bad it was. Neither did I.' It was horrible to watch, let alone live it.

'He knows now.'

'And he's out there, alone.' She pulled her arm free from her father's grip and said, 'If I'd known it was that bad, I wouldn't have let him watch it in front of a crowd.'

'You can't protect him, luv, he's a grown man.'

'But I can be his friend.' She wrapped her blanket tightly around her shoulders like a shawl and headed into the dark to search for Ward.

By faint moonlight, she found him by the front drive with his head down, his breathing laboured, and she approached with caution.

Would he take a swing at her and yell at her for the intrusion?

What was she was doing out here, alone, with a man in the dark?

She was about to walk away when he sighed so deep, she heard his pain. 'Hi.'

'What the?' He whirled around, his face fierce in its fight with his inner demons.

She winced, hating that she'd scared him—and was scared of him. Should she run now?

But then the moon's glow exposed his pained expression, and like the first time they'd met, her heart melted to see him looking like he did.

Did she stay… or go?

This was her home, she was safe here. It was time to start facing her own fears if she expected Ward to do the same. Removing her blanket, she put it across his shoulders.

'What are you doing?' He said.

'If you're going to stay outside at least be warm.'

'Why are you doing this? You don't know me.'

'So? You don't know me either.'

He shook his head, his eyes glassy, removing her

blanket. 'Take this back. I don't want you getting cold either.'

'I'm going up to my place to make a hot chocolate.' She glanced at the grey clouds hiding the moon, smelling the rain. 'Up to you if you want to join me? You can stand out here with that blanket and I'll leave you alone, or I've got a nice fire going.' The rain started to fall in light drops.

'I don't want to put you out.' He lifted the blanket to shield them from the rain.

'How many times do I have to tell you, I wouldn't offer if it was a bother. Should I make a tape recording, or put it in a rulebook to give to guests who cross the front boundary line?'

'You are in a mood.' The rain fell harder.

In a mood? Hell yeah, on the verge of running for cover, or rushing forward to kiss him. It'd be a rain-kiss just like they had in movies that made girls everywhere sigh. But if he didn't look so hurt, and if she wasn't so scared and… 'It's raining, it's dark, it's late, and it's winter.' *I'm such a* chicken! 'Max can come too.'

'Okay, you've convinced me.'

Thank god.

They dashed through the rain to the house. Shucking their boots off at the veranda, they bustled through the front door.

'Get comfortable in front of the fire,' she said from inside her kitchen where she made the drinks with shaky hands. What was she doing with a man in her house after dark? *A man.*

But he was hurting.

'Is it okay for Max to be inside?' Ward called out by the front door.

'Max normally hides in the shed and goes nowhere. He likes you.' It'd be nice if Ward did too.

'I don't want a dog'

'I'm not saying that, I just said Max likes you.' She found him still standing by the front door. 'Here you go.' She handed him a mug then headed to the fireplace and added another log. 'Make yourself comfortable. Sorry, don't own reclining chairs with matching beer fridges.'

'You're right about your dad, I can see Joe having a recliner by the fire pit.'

'He'd never leave that spot if he did.' Zara sat on the floor amongst a pile of cushions. Max stretched out with a groan and grumble before the fireplace, while Ward hovered by the door.

'I see the dog found the best spot.' Ward hesitated, then stepped around the couch and lowered himself onto the large cushions. Leaning back against the couch, he aimed his socked feet at the fireplace, and sipped his hot chocolate. 'Hey, this is like a nutty chocolate.'

'My mum's recipe, she loved her hazelnut chocolate with a dash of Dad's rum.'

'How did she die?'

She sighed, staring at the flames. 'Horse accident.'

'I didn't mean to pry, sorry.'

'That's okay, it's no secret. Mum was out riding and something spooked her horse. She fell and broke her neck.'

He winced, rubbing his own neck. 'Is that why you don't ride?'

'What?' How did he know?

'You mentioned it massaging my shoulders in the kitchen with my mother.'

She lowered her head and stared at the flames. 'Dad and I never wanted to ride after mum's accident. It wasn't the horse's fault. Wasn't anyone's fault. Mum was doing what she loved when she fell.'

Again, he winced, thumbing the scar on his chin.

'Dad was grief stricken and stopped everything. He'd even stopped caring for the thing he loved the most—besides Mum—and that was looking after the horses.'

'He stopped? He works them now. What happened?'

'Middy.'

'How?'

'I was over it.'

'You got mad? I can't imagine you mad.'

She frowned at him. 'I was pissed off.'

'Because your father was grieving?'

'Because Dad gave up and left me to run this place on my own. I'd be down the racetrack in the mornings, then here at night, while Dad just sat in his house. He'd removed all our horse photos, all our riding ribbons, and all of his horse trophies he used to be so proud of. We'd shout at each other daily, because I was tired and he was just cranky, refusing to take his medication for his arthritis so he couldn't walk or use his hands. He gave up,' she said, frowning at the dancing flames in the fireplace.

'Joe doesn't seem the type of bloke to give up.'

She leaned towards him with chin raised and said, 'He did.'

Ward put his palms up in surrender. 'Okay, I believe you.'

'Thank you.' She sniffed, gripping her mug tighter.

'What did you do to get Joe working again?'

'I moved into this place, herded the horses closer to make it easier for me, and then…' She hesitated and sipped her mug of hot chocolate that deliciously coated her throat.

Ward's eyes narrowed at her. 'What did you do?'

'I got mad.'

He gave her a sly side grin. 'I'm seeing a whole new side to you, Z.'

She rolled her eyes at her new nickname.

'And?' He nudged her with his elbow.

'I grabbed Middy, walked the horse into the lounge room, closed the door and left them to it. I was so mad at Dad.'

Ward tilted his head back and laughed, she smiled with relief to see it.

'That horse is massive,' Ward said, 'his head would've touched the ceiling.'

'Mum would've killed me for that, but I was over it and wasn't going to let Dad give up.' She wasn't going to let Ward give up either. 'You see, it was Dad's dream to rescue and care for these animals who were depending on us. I couldn't do it on my own, so I brought in his best mate, Middy.'

'So what happened then?'

'I could hear Dad calling for me.' She winced, cradling her cup tighter with two hands. 'Hardest thing I did was to ignore Dad and not rush inside to help him, he was so upset. I knew each step would be painful for him, but I'd hoped Middy would get to him.'

'What made him move?'

She grinned wide and said, 'Middy's tail swiped books off the bookcase. He knocked over chairs, tipped over the table, totally trashing the place.' They both laughed.

Ward faced her with head tilted and a shine to his amber eyes. 'But it worked?'

'Yep. Dad got up and walked his best mate out of that house and into the sunshine. That first step was all Dad needed. You see, Dad's greatest fear is being alone. Mum was his best friend and they'd been together since school and he couldn't cope without Mum.'

'But he had you?'

'Dad knew that. But I was also determined he should be independent too. You see, Dad relied so heavily on Mum for everything, he'd never washed his clothes or made his own bed before.'

Ward cringed, squirming in his seat on the floor.

'What?'

'My mum still comes over and does my laundry.'

'Are you kidding me? Does she cook for you too?' She said, narrowing her eyes at him.

'Um, yeah,' he replied with his shoulders up to his ears.

'You're spoilt.'

'I know.'

'My Dad was spoilt too, but I wasn't going to do it for him.'

'You're a tough crowd.' Ward rolled his eyes at her as he sipped from his mug.

'I was busy running this place and working at the track too. But I made Dad learn.'

'Must've been a shock at that age to learn.'

'But he did. It's why we teach those other boys who come here, so they don't get to Dad's age and realise they're not able to take care of themselves. It works. Dad's never alone and has help by helping those kids doing what he loves.' It was a win for everyone.

*   *   *

'I... I can't get that vision out of my head,' whispered Ward, staring at Max sprawled before the fireplace where the glow from the flickering flames highlighted the dog's scars. The wind howled, forcing the rain to pelt harder against the house. It was as if he was in the centre of the storm swirling around him, as the words clawed at his throat for freedom. 'I'd never seen it until tonight. Didn't know what the fuss was all about, but I remember it all now. The look on Coach's face, my teammates, my parents, even my sister, I couldn't understand why they were all overreacting until I watched that footage tonight. I must have blocked it out to not remember.'

'If I'd known,' Zara said, 'I wouldn't have let you watch that in front of everyone, or at least warned you how bad it was.'

'Hadn't you seen it before?'

'It was my first time, sitting next to you. I'm so sorry.'

Why was she sorry? He didn't want her pity. Yet he couldn't stop speaking. Was it the rum and chocolate combined with the few beers earlier that was loosening his tongue? 'Now that I remember, it keeps playing over and over in my head. It's like a nightmare, re-living the pain and that falling sensation of never landing again.' He sighed watching the flames. 'I remember and wish I didn't.'

The flames danced as tiny sparks disappeared up the chimney. The dog breathed deep in his sleep. The rain hit against the roof as the wind howled in the darkness outside. Inside, he was warm and safe, and a whole world away from the one he knew.

'When I play, I don't feel the knocks or the punches until after the game. Sure, we're meant to be tough guys who put up with it, sledging each other on the field, giving each other hell—for what?' He scowled at the flames in the fireplace that matched the burn in his chest. 'To chase a bloody ball on the field, risking another injury to my body—or my life. I don't know if I can do it again... play?' He looked at the pain reflected in her ice-blue eyes.

Hesitant, like a timid bird she touched his arm. He reached for her small fingers and held them.

'It scares the absolute crap out of me.' His confession whispered as he traced the lines in her small palm resting in his hand. 'I'm scared I'll never play again. Scared I'll let the team down. I'm scared because I don't know anything else but the game I've lived for, that could've killed me.' He fisted his chest, and she winced, pulling away.

He'd scared her.

How could he be such an idiot to do that to her? 'Sorry, I didn't mean to.' But again, the unfiltered words tumbled. 'I've never feared anything in my life. I've never had to fight for anything except for a ball on a field. I've always been a part of a team, part of some club, always belonging somewhere, doing my bit for my side. Now, I might be alone, so easily replaced, and I don't know what to do or what to say.'

'Hey, it'll be okay.' She slid her palm across his upper back and he lowered his head onto her shoulder. Her soft hair was like silk against his cheek and he wrapped his arms around her slender frame, inhaling her soothing aroma.

'One step at a time, Brendan.'

And he knew he was in trouble.

Fourteen

Ward woke amongst a sea of cushions, snuggled deep under a warm thick doona. Ever since the stupid fall he'd slept in different places: stadium corridors, the hospital, his lounge room floor, his reclining chair, his bed—once. Then in the bunkhouse at Zara and Joe's farm, and now in Zara's living room. But two days in a row he woke up to Max's snoring, and no Zara.

Damn. He'd fallen asleep on Zara again, after confessing in ways he'd never done to a living soul in his life.

What the hell had he become to admit he was scared?

He didn't even recognise himself.

Ward got up and stretched, facing the bright daylight through the wide bay windows. In the glossy emerald paddocks, horses grazed in the distance, it was so serene. He understood what Zara meant; it seemed to take all his troubles away—if he didn't think too hard.

Ward rubbed his jaw's coarse bristles, feeling just as rough on the inside. He hadn't shaved in days and wasn't even wearing his own clothes.

But it was warm inside by the fire, and the aroma of

rich coffee was inviting.

'Morning, lad,' called out Joe from Zara's kitchen.

'Um, morning.' Unsure if to call it a good morning, when he was tempted to burrow back under the blankets. But he was stuck here until tomorrow morning, and right now he missed his chair and widescreen to zone out on and not think.

Ward cleared his throat and winced at Zara and her father, both seated at her kitchen table. How was Joe going to react at finding some guy asleep on his daughter's floor?

But nothing had happened between him and Zara.

Pity.

Ward slothed around in his borrowed tracksuit pants and socks into the kitchen. At least his socks matched, unlike Zara's where one was the colour of marmalade, the other had iris blue checks. It almost cheered him up.

'Coffee?' Zara asked, fetching him a cup.

Ward nodded, dumbfounded. Her ice-blue eyes warmed him. Her hair, loose around her shoulders, shone like a halo in the kitchen's sunlight.

He dropped into a seat and blinked at the table's decorative bowl of glossy strawberries. It took a moment to realise it was filled with painted pebbles to look like strawberries.

Soon he sipped his coffee, and over the cup's rim he saw fine needles in Joe's right hand, resting on the table. 'Sore hand?' He'd seen Zara rub Joe's hands at night, seated around the fire pit, to then strap them into braces. But what was the deal with turning Joe's large hand into a pin cushion?

'RA's givin' me a bit of grief this time of the year, mind you only the one today. And I come here for the coffee.' Joe picked up his mug, as his eyebrow arched at Ward. 'So, you did the hot chocolate last night, huh?'

Ward nodded. Was he going to cop a lecture? He doubted his brain could cope and searched for strength in the coffee. 'Coffee's good.' Receiving a shy smile from Zara that defrosted him some more.

'I agree, mate. I've gotta stick to the decaf muck on this dumb diet.'

'Dad?' Zara frowned at her father.

Joe rolled his eyes, the same colour as Zara's. His weather-worn face crinkled with his lopsided grin. 'Yeah, yeah. She's torturing me coz she cares. The bonus is I get a coffee while I get this done.'

'What is that?' Ward asked, nodding at Joe's hand.

'Acupuncture,' replied Zara, sipping her coffee.

'You're an acupuncturist too?'

'I do it for Dad.'

'Zara's been doin' this since she was seven, helping her old man. Good thing that Chinese doctor I called a commie bastard gave her a job.'

'Dad, I only started doing acupuncture when I was eighteen.' A small alarm rang on the mobile on the table. She turned it off, washed her hands at the sink, removed the pins from Joe's hand, dropped them into a dish and carried it down the small corridor. 'Flex it, Dad.'

'Yeah, yeah.' Joe shook his hand, held it by the wrist, and opened and closed his fist. 'Are you carrying the country on your shoulders there, mate?'

Ward now understood the term emotionally drained, feeling confused and numb, but he wasn't into oversharing his story either. Instead, he sipped more coffee.

'You should go for a run. It's a beautiful morning after last night's rain. Get that fresh air into your lungs and that sun on your face.' Joe stood and patted Ward's shoulder and said, 'Take a tip from an old bloke who's bin 'round the block a few times. One step at a time, mate, that's all you can do.' Joe slid on his Akubra, drained his cup, put it on the sink, and headed for the front door. 'Oi luv, we doin' this bull-dance?'

'Yes, Dad.' Zara returned to the kitchen and finished her coffee. 'Are you going for a run?'

Ward wanted to lie down before the fireplace and hide his head under the cushions. 'Do you need me to run the greyhounds?'

'Billy's got 'em with Toby this morning on the quad,' said Joe, opening the front door. 'We let Stacey catch up on her study. It'll be good to see that girl graduate.'

'Yeah, I'll go for a run,' Ward said with as much enthusiasm as a kid lining up for his vaccination jabs at the doctor. He stepped into the sunshine, trying to remember where his sunglasses were.

Zara closed the front door behind them and slid her

mismatched socks into her long boots. 'Don't push yourself, Brendan.'

'I won't, Z.' At least he got a single dimpled smile from the woman who'd put him to sleep last night, *again*.

'I'm sure the man's old enough to know what his body can and can't do. Not like I do, at my age, when you're restricted like a newborn,' complained Joe as he walked down the front steps.

'You whine like a big baby, Dad.'

'Ward's fine, let him be. Run as long as you need, lad.'

Ward sat on the veranda's wicker chair with coffee in hand. He didn't want to run at all. He didn't know what he wanted. His brain was foggy like the mist entwined within the thicket that led to the small gully.

'For you.' Zara put a water bottle on the table beside him. 'We'll be on the other side of the stables in the orchard by the plum trees, if you need us.'

Ward didn't know the difference between an apricot or apple tree. How was he expected to find a plum tree?

'Come on, luv, I'll be late for church.'

'Yeah, yeah.' Zara skipped down the steps in her long boots and hooked her arm through her father's.

Ward sipped his coffee, with Max sitting in front of him. 'You ready to do this, Max?'

The dog's entire lower body wagged as his stumpy tail thumped on the floor.

Did Ward have the energy?

Shoes laced, he stood and faced the scenery where

sunrays filtered through the canopy of trees that dotted the open paddocks. The clear air was fresh and alive from last night's storm. 'One step at a time.' And began his run with his canine companion beside him.

* * *

He ran until his muscles burned, his lungs pumped fire through his system, and when he thought he couldn't run anymore, he pushed on. Into the main yard, through the shed's open doors and up to the industrial-sized sinks. There, Ward caught his breath as he stretched out his legs.

Max, with black tongue lolling limp from his panting mouth, staggered in behind Ward.

Joe was right, the run helped Ward clear his head. He grinned at the puffed-out pit bull that collapsed into a heap in front of the water bowl.

At the large sink, Ward put his head under the tap and gulped mouthfuls of the sweet rainwater. The ice cool water trickled down his back, contrasting against the hot sweat of his skin. He felt great. Pleased with his normal recovery time.

But the dog wasn't doing too good, puffing dust clear from his spot on the concrete. 'You're out of condition, you could've stayed, Max.'

Max's black tongue lapped up the water from his sprawled position, its chewed ears and scars caught the sunlight.

'No, you're still not coming home with me.'

The dog's brow creased as if it understood.

'You've got all this space, why go to the city?' Why was he talking to a dog? Ward chuckled, refilled his water bottle at the tap and drank more. He liked the water here, even his sister would approve.

Adam looked up from his work at the bench by the bunkhouse doors and said, 'Did you know Max lived in a cage before he came here?'

Ward gave Adam a morning nod. 'How big a cage are we talking about?' Considering Max's massive bulk.

'Small. About the size of a coffee table. Max couldn't stand in it but he thought it was his home.' Adam bent down and patted the dog who raised his head between panting snorted slurps of water. 'When Zara brought Max here and opened that cage, he wouldn't get out.'

'Wouldn't the dog want his freedom?'

'Nope. This was all new to him.'

Ward looked around the large farm shed. 'It's all new to me too.'

'I'm hearin' ya, mate,' Adam said with a nod. 'But you see, Max was snatched from his mum and thrown into a cage, stuck in a shed in the middle of this noisy industrial block. He never saw the sun inside that hot tin-shed, where he got poked and beaten as part of his training. Then he'd get let out of that cage to fight for his life in front of all these screaming men.'

'No way.' Ward's heart dropped, staring at Max

sprawled across the concrete.

'It took ages for Max to walk ten paces away from that cage, he never let it out of his sight. Now, it's over there in the shadows.' Adam pointed to the far corner near the tack room entrance. 'He doesn't go near it anymore, but for about six months he'd stick close to it. We tried to get him up to the house and stuff, but he does his own thing, always inside the shed in the shadows like he grew up.'

'How could anyone do that to a dog and keep them in an undersized cage to fight?' Ward craned his neck at the shed's height. Hay was stacked in the far-left corner, wooden horse stalls ran along the entire right side. Zara's ute and horse-float were parked in the centre facing the rear doors. The tack room, with the bunkhouse was on the left within this shed with plenty of shadows for a dog to hide.

'People think big dogs need big yards, Max doesn't. He only needs food, water, and somewhere to lie down, even if it's the corner of a shed. But he likes you,' Adam said, sharing a lopsided grin.

'I'm too busy to look after a dog.'

'What's to look after? You eat, he eats. You can tip some food out of a can, can't you? You run, he'll run, and then sleep all day. Max doesn't want much.'

Why were they putting the hard-sell on him to adopt Max? 'Why does Zara bring animals and people out here to help them?'

'Zara only does it for the few, so consider yourself privileged there, mate, coz she'll bring home more animals than humans.'

'Why?'

'Animals don't hurt her.' Adam sighed, facing Zara's small house. 'Zara can relate to those hurt, the abused, and the defenceless. She can relate to all of us kids' coz she's been there, mate.'

'No way. Joe's a top bloke.'

Adam scowled. 'Not Joe. He'd kill anyone who'd hurt Zara. We all would.'

'But you just claimed Zara was abused?' A fire churned in his guts stirring towards a white rage. 'Who? Why?' He felt sick, and pissed, towering over Adam for answers.

'I… ah.' Shirking back, Adam raised his palms in surrender.

'Don't start and not finish. Who?'

'Zara had this bloke, who was one of her patients.'

'Zara doesn't do human patients.' Was this kid lying to get Ward to bite?

'She used to work in this practice in the city, that's where she met this idiot.'

'Zara works at a racetrack.'

'She does now.'

'Go on.' Ward stepped back to give the kid space, and to control his fiery temper.

'Zara used to work in a city practice. She only worked on people back then, and was the best too, booked out months in advance. That's where she met and fell in love with this dickhead who they all thought was Mr. Nice-guy. It turned out he was abusing Zara behind closed doors.'

'Why didn't someone notice?'

Adam shrugged.

Ward remembered Zara flinching like a timid wild bird. The fear in her eyes and that haunted look when she'd said *some didn't have the strength or courage to fight*. 'Zara didn't have the courage to tell anyone she was being abused, did she?' He scrubbed palms over his face, as his shoulders stooped, and the rage dimmed.

'Zara told no one.'

'How did they find out?'

'Joe got the call and found her in hospital all banged up, punctured lung, broken collarbone.'

Ward held his stomach, ill to the core. 'What happened to that bastard?'

'Got his arse arrested, went to prison for a bit. And oi,'—Adam pointed at Ward— 'no one knows where he is now because we've all gone searching for him ever since we'd found out, because we'd kill him, just like you wanna do now.'

Adam was right, Ward was angry enough to want to hurt that sick bastard. Taking a deep breath, he uncurled his fists and wiped his palms across his chest. 'I can see now why you're all so protective over her.'

'Yeah, we are mate, Zara gave us all a second go.'

'When did this happen to her?' Not Zara, it couldn't be true.

'Before my time. Joe said Zara took ages to recover because her spirit got broken. She still flinches if you raise your voice.'

Ward had seen her flinch at him, now horrified he'd done that to her.

'Joe and his wife put Zara on a plane to Hawaii where that Chinese herbalist recommended she continue her training. Howie said Zara's gifted as a healer, and they'd all hoped she'd heal herself in the process. Then, that mentor in Hawaii sent her onto some fancy smancy place in Japan.'

'Then back home after her mother died,' Ward murmured as he stared at the shed's concrete floor. 'Is that why Joe calls adults' bastards?'

Adam nodded. 'It's also why Zara will only work on animals. People ring here all the time begging Zara to go back to work on people in the city, but she won't do it. Until you.'

'Zara did that as a favour for her father.'

'We know that. You should've heard Zara and Joe arguing over it too.' Adam chuckled.

'Over me?'

'Yeah. Zara didn't have a clue who you were, mate. She didn't want to touch you and was going to give your mum someone else's number until Joe found out.'

'But Zara came to my house.' He'd argued with his sister about not wanting to see Zara in the first place.

'We know,' said Adam, crossing his arms over his stocky chest. 'And Joe's been made to suffer for it ever since.'

'How?'

'Zara's got him on a diet. She took all his rum to her place, and she's making him do Thai Chi in the mornings when she's not at the track.'

'For his health?'

Adam grinned. 'We know it's for Joe's benefit, but you should hear him bitch too. Decaf coffee in the mornings, rabbit food, and white meat fit for toothless newborns. Only allowed his full-strength beer on weekends, and no more cigars on Sunday, except at Church.'

Ward assumed his mother had talked Zara into visiting, and that somehow his charm had convinced Zara into spending time with him too. 'So, all this time Zara has been helping me, was as a favour for Joe.'

'Come on, we all know it's more than that.' Adam shared a cheeky grin and said, 'Zara likes you. We can all see that.'

It took everything inside to not smile like the day he'd signed his first player's contract and happy-danced along the corridors of the clubhouse. 'Zara's helping me.' Hoping that sounded calm.

'She's helped us all, mate. No matter what demons you've got dancing within your head, body and soul, she'll help you. Like she's done for me, for all of us, even Max.' Adam patted the panting dog on the back.

'Do you think Zara does it to distract herself from her

own troubles?'

'Yep. She gets us all involved with the animals, because it makes us realise there's worse out there.' Adam smiled towards the farm's long driveway. 'This place is our refuge, it's helped us all, and it'll help you too.'

'I'm okay.' A mantra that kept rolling in his head with each step he took this morning along the track. 'I'm spoiled compared to you lot.' Zara was right. So why would she bother with someone as selfish as he was?

'You can afford to be, on your wage.' Adam then cleared his throat and straightened his stance. 'Hey mate, I know the others have warned you already, but you play nice with Zara or you'll have hell to pay.'

His eyes narrowed at the kid and he said in a low voice, 'I'm not an animal who'd hurt a woman—ever. *Especially Zara.*'

'Nah, I reckon you wouldn't.' Adam grinned as he walked backwards with palms up and read the watch-face on his wrist. 'Bugger, I've gotta get the car ready for Joe or he'll be late for Church. Catch ya later, Ward. You know, you should take Max home, then you'll earn points with everyone, especially Joe and Zara if you did.' Adam spun on his boots and jogged towards the main farmhouse.

'I'm not taking the dog.' Ward glanced at Max still recovering on the floor.

Ward thumbed the scar on his chin, musing over Adam's conversation. Was it all true?

He headed for the bunkhouse showers when he

spotted Joe, Stacey, and Zara amongst the straight corridors of trees that followed the field's slope. The last of the morning mist tangled above the trunks' skeletal bare limbs like cotton candy for leaves. It was another side to the property he hadn't seen that was pretty and peaceful. Was that the plum orchard, where the trio were doing a martial art stretching thing that Joe looked rather awkward at?

'Okay, that's it,' called out Zara. 'You did well, Dad.'

'New-fangled bulldust,' Joe mumbled, snatching up his hat from a nearby tree branch. 'G'day mate, have a good run?'

'Ah, yeah, thanks,' Ward replied with a nod.

'You look better for it too. Well, I'm off to Church, be back in time to cook the roast.' He put on his Akubra and headed towards the waiting car where Adam, Tim, Billy, and little Toby waited.

'Church?' Ward asked.

'Nah, it's the pub,' replied Stacey, waving at Toby in his baby seat in the back of the passing sedan. 'It's the only place Joe can smoke his Sunday cigar now Zara's banned them from the property.'

'Because of me?'

'Zara's been trying to get Joe to stop smoking for years, we all have, since I've been here. You were the bartering tool Zara was looking for.'

Which did wonders for his ego—*not.* 'Glad it worked out for everyone then.'

'Let's hope it works for you too. I've got an

assignment to finish. Later.' Stacey waved and headed to the house.

Ward turned to face Zara approaching him. 'Don't you go to church, Zara?'

'Used to when I was younger. Mum went to church and Dad went to the pub to wait for her. I had a choice, I could try to sit still as the eternal fidgeter, or get a lemonade and an education in the wise ways of men.' She rolled her eyes, sharing her double-dimple smile. It was beautiful.

'What were you doing with your dad?'

'Thai chi. Your mum should try it, she was telling me about her hip and knee problem. It's a gentle exercise and it helps Dad with his knees, I've got him doing it a few times a week, finally.'

'I heard it was because of me he's doing these things, for his health?'

She grinned, hiccupping a laugh. 'That's true.'

'I see.' At least someone was benefitting from his fall.

But did she like him as a man, like Adam said, or was she being professional only seeing him as a patient for Joe's sake?

'So, how are you feeling?'

Professional—damn. 'Good.'

'No soreness?'

'Nope. I had a good run, stretched, then I alternated between sprinting and walking and my recovery time's normal.' He felt his normal self again. Almost.

'Good to hear. Although, Max is worn out.'

Ward chuckled at the dog sprawled out on its side next to the water dish.

'Have you ever ridden a horse?'

'Me, no.' He shook his head while screwing up his nose.

'Come on, then.' She grabbed his hand and led them to the side door of the shed and into a small fenced yard.

'What are we doing?' Not that he was complaining about holding her hand.

'This is Bob.' She pointed to the biggest white and grey horse Ward had ever seen.

He'd thought Middy was big, but this thing was even bigger and stockier. 'What is that?'

The horse lifted its huge head from the water trough.

'I told you, that's Bob. The most amazing gentle giant you'll ever meet.'

Ward hesitated. 'Is that a Clydesdale?'

'Yes.'

'I'm not riding that.'

'*We're* not going anywhere.' Dragging him behind her, they approached Bob. 'Unless you want to?'

'Don't you need a saddle? And a ladder or a crane to get on his back?'

'The fence will do. We'll only be here for a minute.' Somehow, without any rope or bridles, she walked the horse to the side of the fence. 'Come on, you can't go to a horse farm and not get on a horse. Chicken.' She giggled as she climbed the railings.

'Oh man.' He scaled the fence beside her, but the horse was so far away.

'He's good for this.' She had the horse stop close to them.

'Who?'

'Bob. Now swing your leg over.'

'Um?'

The horse stood still, chewing like a cow, peering through his thick lashes and a long mane.

'Like this,' Zara said as she effortlessly climbed onto the horse's wide back. 'See, you could put a bomb under Bob and he won't move, he's deaf.'

'He's big.'

'Leg over, cowboy. Or is this your first rodeo?'

'If I do, will I get a cowboy hat, and you'll pin a gold star to my chest and call me Sheriff?' He mumbled. Then he looked at Zara, biting her bottom lip, sitting on a horse. She hadn't been on a horse since her mum died. 'Are you okay?'

'Um, you?' She swallowed with a wince.

'All right, if you can do it, so can I.' He clambered onto Bob's broad back. 'Damn, he's tall, and wide.'

'Yeah,' she whispered, holding the horse's mane in a tight grip.

'What do I hold onto?' Seated bareback on a horse.

'Me.'

He didn't even blink as he slid his palms around her slender waist. 'I guess there's some benefit to sitting here.'

He shunted close to her back. The soft silky stray stands from her plait tickled against his cheek. 'Now what?'

'Would this distance be as high as what it was when you fell?'

Ward peered at the ground and frowned, holding her tighter. *Damn.* Everything she did was to help him. 'Why are we here, Zara?' Was he ready for this? Was she?

Her forehead creased, displaying fear in her eyes, licking her lips. 'This, um… This was the horse my mum fell off,' she said in a near whisper.

'We don't have to do this, Z.' He'd forgotten his own fear as he held her back against his chest. She peeked at him through her fringe he tucked behind her ear. 'But I'm right here with you.'

'Good, we'll do this together. Hold on.' She nudged the Clydesdale, and it clomped around the pen.

'Woah, horsey.' Ward hugged Zara tighter.

'We're not stopping yet.'

'Are you sure you're okay to do this?' He wasn't.

'If you can, so can I. We'll both face our fears, and if we fall we'll pick ourselves up again. But don't tell my dad, he'll kill me, huh. But we're doing it.' Her forced laugh gave him the confidence to at least try.

'I've never been on a horse.'

'Nothing to it, it's like riding a quad.'

'Where are the pedals, hand grips, and brakes?' Although cuddling her was nice. Inhaling her soft warm floral fragrance, it mingled with the scents of horse, hay, and his own sweat from running—or was that from fear?

The earth moved beneath him in a whole new way, as Bob clomped his big hoofs around the holding yard for a few slow laps, then stopped.

'How do we get off?'

'You jump.' Zara swung her leg over the horse's long neck and jumped to the ground.

'Hey?' Stuck on a horse in the middle of the yard and nowhere near the fence. 'Are you okay?'

Her double-dimple smile was his answer. 'Your turn.'

Heights had never bothered him before, but the distance worried him now. He'd fallen that far to land on his head that put him in hospital. He licked his lips. The pulse pounded in his neck and his breath became shallow. He wiped his sweaty palms on borrowed sweatpants.

'Deep breath, and jump. You can do this.'

Could he? Or was he frozen by his fear?

He thumbed the scar on his chin and eyed the distance to the fence.

When the horse shifted beneath him, without thought he leaped off and landed on both feet. 'I did it.'

'I knew you would.' Her palms squeezed his upper arms and her eyes shone bright.

'You did it too.' A rush of pride washed over him because together they'd both faced their fears.

'One small leap for woman, one giant leap for mankind,' she called out in mock humour with her arms in the air.

'I didn't land on the moon. Although, I feel like an alien in this place.'

'Don't be,' she said with concern. She opened the gate into the shed leaving Bob to clomp over to the feeding trough to resume his cow-chewing.

'I didn't mean it like that, I'm…' *What was that mantra of hers?* 'I'm not useless—just not used to it.'

She shared a huge smile that warmed his soul. It was beautiful, and he was so gone for this girl.

'So, what do we do now, Z? Do you have your own church to chill on Sundays?' He gave her a gentle nudge on the arm as they walked side by side through the shed's main thoroughfare.

'I veg out.'

'How does a horse-whispering, self-confessed eternal fidgeter, veg out? Are you going to make me do chai tea too?'

Her laugh echoed like music on Christmas morning. 'Thai Chi. Chai is a tea.'

'I know it is, my housemate, Nick, drinks it,' he said, grinning sideways at her. 'What do you do as a side venture for fun, besides rescuing strangers?'

'I paint pebbles as a form of gardening.'

'You've already admitted to killing plants with kindness.'

'And you've never tried to garden.' She playfully poked at his chest.

Trapping her hand over his heart, they stood in the centre of the wide-open doorway. 'True, but I am a master of chilling. Remember, reclining chair, widescreen, drinks fridge to not move. Hint, hint.'

'Movies?' Zara asked with an arched eyebrow.

He cupped a palm to his ear. 'I think you're singing my tune, sweetheart.'

Her laugh sung to his soul. 'You're so predictable.'

Was he? 'I'm trained to be unpredictable in a game so the opposition can't pick my next move.' What was his next move in life? *Nope, no deep thinking, not today.* 'You're not going to make me watch some historical chick flick, or some artsy foreign film with subtitles. Unless you want me to go to sleep again, Z?'

'I'm sure Adam's got some movies you'd like. Only after you've showered, mate.' Holding her nose she skipped ahead through the main doors.

'I was on my way to shower before I got distracted.' In the best possible way. 'I'll meet you shortly for another one of your coffees?'

'And brunch.'

'Done. It's a date.' He grinned as she peeked shyly over her shoulder, skipping up the path towards her house. It was a great view of those long legs and cute arse in her riding pants. At the veranda she kicked off her boots and stepped through the door, her odd pair of colourful socks were so bright against her black riding pants, grey hoodie and black puff vest. He liked that colour-surprise hint of her hidden personality that seemed so conservative on the outside. So, what was on the inside?

With a sigh and smile, in his horsehair covered sweaty clothes he'd never wear in public, he strolled past Max towards the bathroom. The dog gave a half thump of his stumpy tail without bothering to lift his chin from the floor. 'You should stay there and veg out too, Max. I don't need a chaperone on this one.' And was looking forward to it.

Fifteen

Sprawled out on the couch, Ward watched the movie, snacking on popcorn with feet up, and chilling. This is exactly what he'd be doing at home, and looked to Zara seated beside him.

'What?' She grinned as she threw a piece of popcorn into her mouth.

'Where did you learn to do the painted rock thing?' He blurted out, instead of what he really wanted to say.

She had a rock with painted penguins on it that she used as a doorstop. A stout rock sporting a silhouette of a saxophone player, rested in the corner, surrounded by smaller pebbles painted as sheets of music. They were everywhere, like inverted cobwebs in corners, unseen— until you saw one, then you saw all.

'Oh, I learned it in Japan. I'm the ever-eternal fidgeter,' she said, rubbing her thumb and fingertips together. 'I had trouble trying to meditate, so they gave me a pebble to hold.'

'Did it work?'

'Sure, and from there it began this thing, a hobby, or as Dad calls it a rock-dreamer's obsession.'

'That's a lot of meditating considering you have an entire rock garden out front.'

Her head tilted back as she laughed, it made him smile. 'Not like that. You see, I'll find a pebble in my travels like people collect shells at the sea. Some I'll paint or add to the pile out front and make another cairn. I've started collecting for a moon gate like the ones I've seen in traditional Chinese gardens, but that's a long way off.' From the side table she picked up a ceramic plate with more pebbles and said, 'These are my bonsais.'

He plucked a cold, smooth, grey pebble from the ceramic plate, turned it over and inspected the face where she'd painted a bonsai tree. Astounded at the intricate details of the bark, branches, and even leaves. 'I'm not an arty person, but these are pretty cool.'

'Keep it.'

'I couldn't.'

'Yeah, you can. I have a whole yard full.'

'Never thought I'd say this, but I like your rock art. But why rocks, what's wrong with paper?'

'Some carry stones for luck, for wishes, or to carry a memory of a place they've been to. Some are used for massage, and some for grounding.' She grinned at Ward rolling his eyes, as she put down the plate. 'You're like my dad.'

'Here.' He reached across her to put the pebble back, inhaling her warm fragrance.

'Nope, you've picked that one, it's yours now.' She

closed his fingers over the stone and pushed his fist into his chest. 'You have to, consider it a gift.'

She was a gift. 'What do I do with a pebble?'

'You can toss it if you want.'

'I won't.' He gripped it tighter in his palm, it fit—solid as a rock. 'Thank you. And thank you for everything.'

'I didn't do much.'

'Yeah you did, you listened last night, and today you made me jump, and let me chill.'

'You needed it, and I did too.' Her shrug appeared casual, but her forehead crinkled as she chewed her bottom lip.

'Why did you make me climb that massive mountain of a horse?'

'Seemed like a good idea at the time.' Again, she shrugged. 'You needed to know you could land on your feet, and I couldn't get on a horse by myself so you helped me, too.'

'Are you going to ride again?'

'I'm in no hurry, and Dad would freak.'

'He's protective over you, they all are.' How could anyone hurt Zara?

'That's family. Aren't you protective over your sister?'

He screwed his nose up. 'I suppose, in our own weird

twisted way.' He chuckled, running his thumb over the pebble in his palm. 'You help so many; what do you want for yourself?'

'I have all I want.' She smiled with shiny eyes at her living room and out to the amazing view of the open countryside.

'I'd believe it.' He could see it, she lived in a great place and did what she loved.

'Have you worked out what you want?'

'To play football again. But that's not what I want right now.'

'What's that?'

He inhaled deep. It was now or never. 'I want to kiss you.'

Her eyes widened and she froze on the spot.

His fingertips stroked her cheek, admiring the few fine freckles scattered across her dainty nose. She held her breath as he leaned towards her. Was he forcing her to face her fears too?

This might be his only shot, because tomorrow he was returning to his own world.

Right now, he didn't want to think of tomorrow. He'd been overthinking and just wanted to feel and follow his instincts by pressing his lips to hers. And did.

Her plump lips were soft and warm as he grazed her

top lip, then her bottom lip. Tasting the salt from the popcorn and the sweet heat of her skin, the spark inside his chest magnified and threatened to blaze like wildfire.

He pulled back, swallowing hard, unsure if to go further, and held her hand, toying with her delicate fingers. With his other hand, her traced the outline of her beautiful face and stared into her eyes. 'I won't do anything you don't want, but I want to kiss you again.' *And never stop.*

But would she let him?

*　　*　　*

The fire crackled where sparks flew from the log that shifted in the fireplace as the TV carried on in the background that neither watched nor listened to, focusing on each other.

Her chest heaved as she licked her lips, trapped under his amber stare. She shivered at the tickled pleasure from his fingertips that traced along her cheek. Tasting him on her tongue, it'd been so long since anyone had kissed her. And somehow, his presence and this moment were pushing away the loneliness she'd nurtured for so long—right out the door.

But was she truly ready?

There was only one way to find out.

She pressed her lips against his. Her lips parted and his mouth meshed with hers, giving into the temptation to be in his arms was too great to resist. Tongues tangoed as his hands slid around her body, sending pleasure-prickles across her skin. She wanted his skin against hers and trembled with an overwhelming desire.

Ward's kiss plundered deeper. He brushed his fingers through her hair, cocooning her in his heat, igniting her passion. She rose to her knees, clutching his shirt in her fists. It was her reality's dream to be with someone again, to be with him. Just once. Just today. And now.

Their kiss deepened as her hands skimmed over his strong arms to his shoulders. Her fingernails scraped through his thick auburn hair. Chest to chest, the press of their clothes was like a canyon between them.

He lay her down on the couch, their lips not leaving each other's as if he was her oxygen. She moaned as his palms slid over her waist and cupped her breast. His thumb stroked her hardening nipples that only heightened her flame.

She couldn't take this distance and pulled off her shirt. Undoing the buttons of his shirt, he ripped it off his back as if reading her mind. Her nails dragged across his strong chest, where she wanted to discover the muscular twists and folds of his skin. She licked down and around his nipple, nibbling his skin as he sighed.

He pulled her back, and she gulped at the heat in his darkening amber eyes. It made her surrender her back to the couch and he followed, kissing her lips, her jaw, her throat, pressing his hardness between her legs where only denim separated them now.

Her eyes closed with his mouth against hers. There, it was as if he'd pierced her veil of fear, and froze all her thoughts of time, except to truly indulge in this present.

*   *   *

His lips drank her sweet skin like nectar along her soft slender throat. His fingers shook and his body trembled the lower his lips travelled towards her plump breasts. There, he discovered the delicious landscaping swell of her breasts.

He needed this, to not be broken, but to be whole again. To be a man.

'Tell me to stop,' he whispered in a hunger to take her, to hold her, to paint her skin with his scent. He was on that last ladder rung before the animal inside was unleashed beyond the brink of insatiable insanity.

Zara's eyes trailed her fingertips down his chest as his muscles tightened beneath her touch. The tip of her pink tongue licked her swollen lips, cupping his face she whispered, 'I don't want you to stop.'

He rested his forehead against hers, pressing his arousal shamelessly against her. He had to be sure.

'You're so beautiful.' The words spilled. Captivated by her fragility, he wanted to be strong to protect her, to be that man for her.

'You're beautiful too.' Her smile matched her eyes

that opened his soul like a flood without pain but only passion. She was his sustenance and his light, as the chains of lust bound him to her where her scent and taste were a celebration of life.

He lay her down. Her breasts swelled beneath swirling licks from his tongue. Her hips pushed to meet his groin, rock hard and hungry to discover untold secrets between her thighs.

He kissed her stomach, his tongue trailed around her belly button as his fumbling fingers undid the buttons on her jeans. She helped push them down, along with her lace underwear. His heart soared, the pulse pounded in his ears, and his hardness strained to be inside her. He kissed her deep, with the thirst of an alcoholic filling up on her flavour. His fingers slid into her heat and explored a whole new realm as her back arched and her moan made his mind roll. He rushed to free himself from his jeans, and between her legs his teary tip ached at the edge of no return.

He stopped and stared down at her, his entire body length lay against hers. Her hair fanned over the cushions, her soft bare breasts shifting with each breath that matched his.

Craving to mesh his mouth against hers, he paused with his body poised above hers. Had fortune's wheel turned in his favour?

He waited for a sign to know it was okay—for her.

Her reply was her hand pressing against his backside as her pelvis lifted and he pushed past her soft silky folds and into the gates of heaven. Her hips met his and her body shuddered with him, as he surged deeper into the tightness of nirvana. Eyes locked on hers, he retracted and pushed inside her again, as the sensation tilted his world and he moaned.

Teeth gritted, bodies and bones bent to the weave of flesh as his lips collided against hers. Her hips rocked as he plunged deeper. His chest strained against ribs that rattled for air amid wet breaths and slickened skin, as the momentum increased its hypnotic rhythm of furious friction, striving for a higher heaven.

Her back arched, her neck stretched, her arms and legs wrapped around him, she squeezed and cried out like a stadium's siren that echoed in his ear for the final quarter. His body pistoned to meet her intense heated rush, where a rumbling roar started from deep within his soul. Muscles bunched. Veins bulged. His life force twisted and unfolded, catapulting him beyond time zones to where only angels dared travel.

Only then he surrendered to gravity and gasped for air.

Blinded, he collapsed on top of her, pulsing inside her, and could only breathe her in. Her skin against his, their bodies knitted, as her heart raced against his. He held her close and never wanted to let go.

He was raw. Alive. Healed.

He was a man.

And once again, he believed he was king of his world.

Sixteen

Out front of Ward's house, at four in the morning, Zara pulled up her ute with the empty horse float in tow. 'Well, here we are.'

With his face highlighted by the dashboard's lights, Ward toyed with a stray lock at her nape. 'Do you do that drive every day?'

'Depends on my clients, who are all at the racetrack, which is fifty minutes for me on the other side of the city.' The streetlights beamed like yellow spotlights among dark houses that followed the curve of the long road. So different from the open farm that slept under moonlight. 'I don't deal with peak-hour traffic with my work hours and the drive allows me time to think. Or I sing really badly at the top of my lungs to some random radio tune.'

'No one sings as bad as me. No, wait, you haven't heard my sister's screech—it creates voice-quakes.'

She smiled at the playfulness shared between them. All morning on the drive into town they'd talked, sang, and joked around. After an intense day yesterday with Ward on her couch, then in her bed, it was time to say goodbye.

His amber eyes focused on her as he raised the back

of her hand to his lips. She almost melted in her seat.

'When can I see you again?'

'Um…' She swallowed her heart that was wedged in her throat. *He didn't mean that, did he?* 'You've recovered now, and you've got your appointment with the specialist today.' And her job was done.

'Are you still betting on a carton of beer he'll give me the all clear?' He grinned wide with chin up and chest out.

She giggled at his infectious cocky confidence. 'I should double my bet.'

'I had an amazing time with you this weekend and I want to do it again, Z.'

It'd been incredible, but she couldn't let it go on. 'At the moment, you need to focus on you.'

'Yeah, but—'

'You've got the doctors and the coach to talk to today, and soon you'll be back in training. You'll be so busy getting yourself ready to play your next game, you'll need to focus on you.' Not her. She was prepared to be a blip on his radar, where she'd watch him from afar. He would then become her secret story to keep for decades to come.

'But…' His frown faltered, brushing her fringe to the side. 'I want to see you again. Don't you?'

With everything inside her, she did. But she also wanted to avoid the risk of heartache. 'Brendan—'

He winced. 'I'm not in trouble am I, Z?'

'No.' Zara was the one in trouble, falling for a guy she couldn't have. 'You're better now. How do you know what you're feeling isn't part of the treatments?'

'Was sex part of the deal?'

'*No.*' Zara sat back horrified.

He slapped his forehead with the heel of his palm. 'Sorry. I'm so sorry I said that. Please forgive me, we both know I'm an idiot.'

'It's okay.'

He sat back wiping his mouth. 'No, it's not. I should never have said that. I don't want to ruin the memory of our time together—which was brilliant— and it's why I don't want you driving away from me.'

She rubbed his shoulders hoping to comfort him. 'Hey, you've been through a lot, both physically and mentally, you've come out the other side. Now you need to settle back into your routine' —*back into your world of football fame.*

He sandwiched her small hands in his. 'I get that, still, I want to see you again.'

Why was this so hard? She wanted to give in and throw herself into his arms and say, *yes, take me.* But there was too much at risk. 'Have you ever heard of the Florence Nightingale Syndrome?'

'No?' The dim light of the early morning shadowed his frown.

'It's when a patient or wounded soldier falls for their nurse that helped them recover.'

'Is that what you think this is?' His face screwed up, shaking his head.

'Look, find your own feet again, and well...' She winced at the hurt in his eyes. 'I want to thank you too.' She opened his fingers, lifting his hands by the wrist she kissed the base of his palms. 'It's been a while for me.'

'I'm such an inconsiderate—' He paused with his lips pressed into a thin line that highlighted the scar on his chin. 'I'm sorry for thinking only of me.'

Oh no. Did he know?

Ward shifted in his seat, facing her while still holding her hands. 'I'd never hurt you, Z.'

Oh crap—he knew. She needed to leave, *now*. 'Get back out there and play football, which is your passion, first.' Where he could face his crowds of fans and she'd disappear back into her cocooned comfort zone.

'Can I call you, please?' He lowered his head, meeting her eyes and waited with that pleading face.

'If you want?' Surrendering to his expression.

'Are you going to answer?' He grinned as hope displayed in his eyes.

But before she could reply he leaned across and kissed her.

It was the kiss of clichés, of summer strolls, of candlelight and wine-song, and of the thawing from winter to the rebirth of spring. She wanted to laugh, sing, dance, and cry out to murder her darkest memories that shackled her heart.

Yet here, now, she was defenceless in his embrace that shielded her from the outside world. Safe in his warm aroma, his strong arms, broad chest and powering heartbeat, she never wanted to leave his arms, which scared her more.

She'd trusted once.

And once was enough.

She pushed against his chest, pulling back from his kiss. 'Sorry, um, I'm late for work.'

'I'll call.' He feathered a kiss on her nose, her eyelids and her forehead, where each kiss splintered her suffocating soul. 'And you'd better answer when I do.' He jumped from the cab, closed the door, and held his hand up in a wave.

She waved back and started to drive away. She looked through the cab's side mirror and wanted to cry as his silhouette was lost at the bend in the road. Ward wouldn't call because he'd forget all about her in a week, like she wished she'd forget him too.

*   *   *

Ward stood on the street until the lights of the horse float disappeared. He sighed, shoving hands into his jeans pockets. He got no hero-worship from Zara and didn't want it. He wanted her, as is, right down to her odd socks and painted pebbles. Yet, it was as if his heart was torn from his chest, following that ute's driver.

Did Zara just give him the brush-off?

In his pocket, he fingered the stone she'd given him.

He'd never let a tag get away from him in a game and he wasn't going to let her do the same.

'Damn.' He didn't get her phone number. 'Dickhead,' he spat out in the dark. But he'd find it, even if he had to talk to his sister to hassle her boyfriend, Ron, at the racetrack. So there was hope.

Ward unlocked the front door, flicked on the inside light and turned to close it. 'Max?'

The great lump of a pale pit bull sat on the front mat, thumping his stumpy tail. A chewed rope dangled from his collar, as his black tongue flickered to lick his chin, crinkling his scarred brow.

'Are you stalking me?' Zara had tied Max up in the stables while Ward hitched the horse float onto her ute this morning.

'You stowaway.' Ward picked up the rope and inspected the chewed end. 'So, I'm guessing, you jumped into the back of the ute while I was busy with Zara.' He ducked from that long black slobbering tongue swipe. 'Bit early for dog kisses, mate, when I only want to kiss Zara.'

He stood with arms crossed as Max dropped his massive head onto his paws, his half-chewed ears flattened, giving a pleading look.

'What am I going to do with you? Can't leave you out here, you'll scare the neighbourhood. But?' His smile widened. 'I'll have to hunt down Zara's number now. Well done, mate.' He gave Max a pat. 'Come on in and make yourself at home.'

The dog pranced into the house with stumpy tail up and soon began sniffing the new surrounds.

Ward laughed as he closed the door. 'Don't get too comfortable, Max, I'll take you for a run, as long as you don't eat the children.' How were his housemates going to handle waking to the massive, mean-looking mutt?

Ward needed to go for a run because he wouldn't be able to sit still and clock watch. It was D-day. Today he'd get the official results to find out how soon he could play again, and he was praying for the right result.

Seventeen

'Will Sam be okay, home alone with that dog?' Nick asked, walking beside Ward through the hospital corridors.

They'd left the beast asleep on the massive man-couch that Max had made it look small. 'Are you scared of Max?'

'Well, I mean…' Nick hesitated, screwing up his nose.

'Didn't you have dogs as a kid? We couldn't because of my sister's allergies.'

'We got them as a puppy, not as some full-on ex-fighting dog.'

'Hey, I was the same when I found out that dog's history. Don't worry, Max won't be around for long, which gives me a good excuse to call Zara.' He grinned wide, so light on his feet, he was tempted to slide down the wide corridor—because he could.

'So, you and this Zara, huh?' Nick said, with a cheesy grin and eyebrows bobbing up and down.

'I hope so.'

Nick stopped and his jaw dropped. 'For real?'

Ward kept on walking, he didn't want to share, even

if Nick was one of his best mates. Yet he just couldn't help himself—he wanted to shout it to the world. 'Zara's not like the others.' She was unlike any woman he'd ever met.

Nick jogged to catch up. 'She's not dazzled by our prowess and football fame?'

'Nope.' Ward had no rock-star appeal and got no hero-worship. He didn't want it.

Frowning to himself, he walked down the corridor. As a kid, he had the spotlight put on him as young player, winning Rookie of the year. He'd won best and fairest with his club a few years in a row. He thought he'd wanted the adoration of thousands, but now, he just wanted to play the game, play it well and then go do other things. When did that change?

Deep in thought, he pushed through the double doors with Nick beside him. He stopped and shook his head at the waiting room entrance. 'Talk about star power.'

The television on the wall played the morning news. Last decade's magazines were scattered on rows of plastic chairs. On the right, front and centre, sat Sheldon, with two different women as his escorts, this time a brunette and a sandy blonde.

'What happened to the twins?' Whispered Nick.

'Tell me you didn't come just to check out the twins?'

Nick shrugged. 'And to stop you killing Sheldon. How does he get the babes to go in pairs like that?'

'Don't know and I don't care.' Ward glanced at the women that had Nick drooling. Nope, they weren't Ward's type.

Noooo. Ward plonked down into the nearest seat. Normally, he'd covertly check out the beauties while scowling at Sheldon with jealousy. But now he just stared at the two females in their short skirts, low cleavage, the teased hair, the perfume clouds, makeup, and jewellery. They were pretty, but he felt nothing.

Had he totally fallen for Zara?

Zara in her denim jeans, odd pairs of coloured socks and baggy jumpers. He pictured her hair spilling from her plait, with no makeup, no jewellery, and her warm soft scent that reminded him of a floral summer rain.

A nurse exited a room and Ward watched her walk down the corridor. Was he suffering from this so-called Florence Nightingale Syndrome?

'What the hell, Ward, what did you do?' Sheldon said, scowling in his neck brace. Sheldon wore no signature side-smirk that Ward always wanted to wipe off with his fists. Still wearing his fancy designer labels, but they lacked that tailored fit Sheldon's wardrobe always had.

Ward paused his hate at public enemy number one, who was stuck in the cumbersome neck brace. Sheldon bore dark rings under his dull eyes and was unshaven, pale, and for once, the fancy superstar of football looked like crap. 'How are you, Sheldon?'

'Wrecked. What did you do?'

'Me?' Ward rolled his shoulders and stretched his arms across the back of the chairs. Crossed his boot over his knee. Rolled his neck from side to side, up and down, and looked at everything in all directions of the waiting room. Yep, he no longer suffered under the old-man soft-shoe shuffle with a carrot up his arse. 'I'm great,' he said, and let rip his winning smile.

Nick chuckled next to him. 'Yeah, our man's all fixed.'

Sheldon winced as he shifted in his seat. 'Are you doing physio?'

'Not for five days. You?'

'Twice a day, hot and cold packs, you?'

'Nope. Don't need it'

Sheldon's face broke out in a sweat as he shunted to the seat's edge. 'What painkillers are you on?'

'None. I'm healed, brother.' Ward shook his head from side to side with a shoulder roll.

'*Sheldon and Ward,*' called out the nurse in the hallway.

'Here.' Ward jumped to his feet while Sheldon groaned and moaned to stand with the two women helping him. Ward felt no guilt or sympathy towards Sheldon—who was, and will always be, a wanker. 'After you.'

Sheldon scuffed his boot soles across the floor, gripping the corridor's side rail like a lifeline. Each breath rattled. Sweat beaded on his forehead and dripped off the tip of his nose. Head still from the neck brace, his eyes tried to see the floor, with hunched back, his shoes slid to match the hand-rail shuffle and groan as Sheldon shifted towards the door.

Ward opened the door wider smiling at his nemesis. Why wasn't he feeling some form of pity for this idiot?

Because Sheldon was the type to slam the door in Ward's face and spill oil on the floor to make Ward fall. Except Ward just let the old-man shuffle inside.

Ward strolled past the nurse and into the examination room. Stripped off his hoodie and t-shirt, tossed the stupid blue paper gown over his shoulder, and sat on the chair beside the examination table.

On the other side of the room, Sheldon struggled to undo the buttons on his shirt, and the nurse—like all females—ran to Sheldon's aide.

'Here, let me help you with that,' said the nurse, lowering Sheldon's shirt down his arms, then held out the gown.

'Thanks,' mumbled Sheldon, trying to slide his arms into the paper gown. His torso of tight muscles he'd flash any chance he got on the field for the fans, had faded.

Ward wasn't a hundred percent, but close to it with his physical condition and was catching up fast.

Sheldon winced with sweat trickling down his cheek as he shuffled to face the room to allow the nurse to slide the paper gown over his shoulders. 'What did you do, Ward?'

'Nothing.' Nope, he wasn't sharing with this dickhead. 'Excuse me, nurse, can I ask you something?'

The nurse tied up the back of Sheldon's gown, saying,

'That depends on that question?'

'Have you ever heard of the Florence Nightingale Syndrome?'

The nurse sniggered. 'Yes. You aren't going to fall in love with me, are you?'

Ward shook his head at the middle-aged woman. 'Err, no. So, this Florence thing is real?'

'Yes.' She nodded.

'Exactly what is it?' Ward didn't care if this conversation was happening in front of Sheldon. The guy wasn't listening, breathing heavily while slowly lowering himself to sit.

To think Ward was like that only just last week.

'The Nightingale Effect is the inappropriate romantic relationship between a patient and their nurse, or vice versa,' said the nurse.

'Some fall in love, right? Don't they make chick flicks of soldiers falling in love with nurses in the war?'

'That true.'

'So, it's common?'

'Some have fallen in love with those who've helped them. But it's a breach of medical ethics and considered unprofessional if they do.'

'Who, the patient or the nurse?'

'For the caregiver.'

'So, the caregiver or healer can get attracted to their patient too?'

'It happens. But the thing is—'

'Careful.' Sheldon winced slightly at the nurse taking off Sheldon's boots.

'Sorry,' said the nurse, who then stood and faced Ward. 'Once a patient has recovered and returns to their normal lives, that attraction they had for their nurse disappears and we're soon forgotten. We're warned in medical school about it, and I've seen it happen many times.'

'How come it's a thing?' Ward asked.

'Because we show compassion and empathy that's easily misinterpreted as affection, when we're only doing our jobs to aid in a patient's recovery.'

'I wished you'd aid in my recovery,' muttered Sheldon, glaring at the nurse with pinched lips.

'But that only matters with human patients, if this Nightingale thing is real?' Ward rested his elbow on the examination bed beside him and thumbed over the scar on his chin.

'The Nightingale Effect is real,' said the nurse. 'We get asked out all the time.'

'What's wrong with that?'

'Besides being unethical and unprofessional, we tell the patients to ask us in a week and they never do.'

'Why not?'

'Because when patients return to their normal lifestyle routines, they'd rather forget about their ill health and the time spent in hospital,' replied the nurse at the door. 'I'll tell the Doctor you're ready to see him.'

Ward rested his forearms on his denim thighs and stared at his palms pressed together. Zara told him to focus on himself this week and get back out there. A week. So, was this intense attraction for Zara part of this Nightingale Effect?

'What treatment did you have, Ward?'

'Huh?' Breaking from his thoughts, he looked up. *Bugger, it was Sheldon.*

'Come on man, give me something.'

'Morning, gentleman.' The specialist strolled into the room, reading glasses in one hand, charts tucked under his other arm, as the nurse shut the door behind him. 'Any change, Sheldon?'

'I'm over it!' Sheldon barked out, then he glared at Ward. *'And he's normal.'*

'Ward?' The specialist whirled around and faced Ward with an arched eyebrow. 'Is this true?'

Ward stood up, nodding, as he crossed his arms over his chest. 'I've got a bet going for a carton of beer you'll give me the all clear.' Should he hold his breath now?

'Let's take a look.' The specialist began his examination of Ward's neck. 'What treatment have you been having?'

'Massage.'

'Bit more than massage, young man. Your nerves have returned to normal, and you have full movement back.'

'Said I was fine.'

'I can see that. How?'

Ward hesitated and then mumbled a secret he didn't want to share. 'Reiki. Heard of it?'

The specialist slid on his spectacles, clicked his pen, and scribbled on the chart. 'Yes. I've had quite a few patients who swear by it, and for some, nothing. It depends on the practitioner and the severity of the matter. But Ward…' The specialist peered over his glasses that balanced on the bridge of his nose.

'Yes?' Now he was holding his breath, tempted to chew his nails like his teammate Mills.

'You've won your bet,' said the specialist with an amused expression. 'I'll be cancelling your surgery and giving you a full medical clearance to play.'

'YES.' Ward wanted to high five the ceiling.

'Good luck out there.'

'Thank you.' Ward shook the specialist's hand, then snatched up his shirt and hoodie. 'Catch-ya-never, Sheldon.' Slipping his shirt over his head, he opened the door to freedom where Nick waited for him. 'I've got my clearance.' He gave a thumbs-up to Nick.

'Well done, mate,' said Nick, heartily patting Ward on the shoulder. 'Great to have you back.'

Yep, Ward was back.

'*I want a name, Ward!*' Sheldon shouted from the room as the nurse closed the door.

No way was Ward going to share. Besides, Zara's practice wasn't open to any human patients, and that thought made him smile.

Eighteen

Ward walked through the front door with Nick following, both dumping their training bags by the wall.

'Hello, chair.' Ward smiled at his most sacred spot in the world. He gripped the cool leather armrests, dropped into its cradling sumptuous shell that moulded to his frame and revelled without fear of pain but one of pure chill-ax-indulgence.

Ward snatched a drink from his chairside bar fridge, flicked the handle on the recliner, put his feet on the inbuilt footrest, gazed at the wide-screen, and let his first-class throne do its magic. 'I'm exhausted.'

'Coach was tough on you today,' Nick said, sitting in his recliner that rocked.

'It was expected.' Ward grinned at Max, flat on his back on the man-couch, where the pit bull barely lifted his head as he gave a thump of his stumpy tail. 'Please, don't get up, Max. You look too comfortable.' Ward chuckled as Max yawned wide and did as told and lay his head back down.

'Perfect timing, it's T-bone steak, fellas.' Sam dished

out the plates and asked, 'Did Coach say when you can play again, Ward?'

'He wouldn't say.' Ward cut into the prime beef, took a bite of his juicy steak, and chewed thoughtfully. He'd received a hero's welcome from his teammates but copped the cold squinty-eyed stare with the permanent scowl from Mitchell. 'The coach has the specialist's paperwork, the team doctor's medical clearance to play, and I know I kicked arse in the physical tests too.' He was fitter than he thought.

'We both saw how much you were trying, especially with the coach pushing you so hard,' said Sam, stabbing his piece of steak with a fork.

'I expected that. I didn't even flinch in the contact paces they put me through, I know the coach was looking for any psychological impact.'

'Is there?' Sam asked.

'No. The team doctor checked for that with his questions. I don't have mummy and daddy issues, but I may have mung-bean-stewing-sister issues.'

Thump-thump-thump.

The three men turned to their right where Max lay, drooling, with tail thumping on the couch.

'Oh man, there's a dog in the house,' murmured Nick. 'That beast won't attack me for the bone, will he?'

Ward arched an eyebrow at the massive dog. 'Hope not.'

'That's comforting, when I'm sitting the closest.'

Sam cut up the steak on his plate and said, 'Max has been fed. I bought a bag of dog biscuits when I picked up dinner. The butcher gave me some big bones, and you should've heard Max crunch them like ice cubes. They were the size of my knee and he disintegrated them into splinters.'

'No?' Nick's brow wrinkled, running a shaky hand through his hair as he looked at the dog then back at Ward.

'Max's dog dish is that salad bowl we never use,' said Sam, inspecting the piece of steak poised on the end of his fork.

'Max is only visiting. Which reminds me.' Ward took a bite of his dinner, jumped from his chair, and grabbed his mobile from his training bag.

'What are you doing?' Nick asked, taking teeny bites of his steak while eyeing off the dog that watched Ward's every move.

'Looking for Zara's number.' Ward scrolled the online directory as he returned to his seat.

'Zara, huh?' Nick leaned toward Sam and said, 'I reckon those two got it on.'

Sam matched Nick's grin. 'So that's why his head's so high in the clouds, dude.'

Ward couldn't wipe the smile off his face if he tried.

Tap-Tap-Tap and the front door swung open. 'Hey, you're home.' Mills waltzed straight through, stopped, and pointed to the couch. 'Is that a bear?'

'That's Max,' said Sam. 'The Underworld's

Heavyweight Grand Champion.'

'Ya full of it,' spat out Mills.

'It's true,' said Nick. 'Can't you see his battle scars, the half ears torn, and that stump for a tail?'

Mills screwed his nose at Max lying flat on its back. 'He's a bloody big dog.'

'Max, get off the man-couch,' ordered Ward.

Max grizzled and groaned as he rolled over and slinked onto the floor to sit in front of Mills.

'He's scary looking with all those scars.' Mills stepped around Max and sat on the man-couch. 'Can he hear with those ears?'

'Dog's as big as you, Mills,' teased Nick.

'Full of it. How come he's here?' Mills asked.

'Max ran away, or is that stowed-away?' Ward kept scrolling for Zara's number through the directory. He'd searched for Reiki businesses in her area but found nothing. In the white pages he pressed a number he'd hoped was for Zara Phelps.

'Hello?' said the young male voice over the phone.

'Billy?' Asked Ward, it sounded like the cheeky fifteen-year-old.

'Who-dat?'

'Ward.' He grinned at the teenage wannabe gangsta with a mean right hook.

'Hey bro, what's up?'

'Is Zara around?'

'Nah, she's still in town.'

'Have you got Zara's mobile number, because Max is here?'

'How did he end up there?'

'Chewed through his rope and must've jumped on the back of Zara's ute this morning. I didn't know he was here until I walked inside.'

'How's he coping?'

'Good, went for a run and he's been fed,' Ward said, as Nick tossed his bone to Max who caught it mid-air and crunched on it loudly. 'He's still being fed.' Ward grinned as he spoke over the phone.

'Max will eat anything, easy as,' said Billy.

'Sorry, but Max can't stay here.'

Sam frowned as he tossed his bone to Max, while Nick looked relieved, and Mills chewed his nails watching Max eat.

'Why not keep him?' Billy asked over the phone. 'If Max has run away to be with you it's obvious where he wants to be.'

'I don't think the house lease allows for pets?' Nick and Sam shrugged, but it was Ward's excuse among the many. 'So, have you got Zara's number to come and collect the dog?' Ward tossed his bone to Max and Sam stole his plate with a frown to the kitchen.

'Sure, but it won't do you any good,' Billy said, chuckling over the phone.

'Why not?' His dinner lumped like concrete setting in his guts. Didn't Zara want to see him?

'Zara left it charging in the stable, heard she was running late this morning?'

Ward grinned. That was his fault because he didn't want to let her out of her bed. 'Can you give me the number anyway?' Ward reached over to Sam's bar fridge for the pen and half-finished crossword and wrote down the numbers dictated by Billy.

'If you want to earn points with Zara,' Billy said, 'keep Max and she'll come over and check on him. And, when you go away Zara can bring Max out here, then you two can see each other.'

'Are you playing matchmaker, Billy?'

'It's obvious there were sparks happening, and Zara's shy with that stuff. Hey, we like you, if we didn't, we'd tell you to piss off, bro.'

'Thanks for the vote of confidence.'

'Only coz you play for the Saints or we'd tell you to lose our number. Are you playing this weekend?'

'Hope so. Listen, can you tell Zara I called? Tell her she won her bet because the specialist gave me the all clear.'

'Joe's gonna be stoked to hear that. We're all gunnin' for you, bro.'

Ward was touched to have the family of misfits behind him, it was nice. 'Thanks, Billy. Hey, how does Zara advertise her business? I couldn't find it in the directory.'

'Sis doesn't advertise.'

'How does Zara get her work then?'

'Because she's the best in the biz. It's all word of

mouth.'

'Racing community must be small then?'

'It'd be the same as your footy kingdom, right?'

'Guess so.' If one club tried something new the rest soon followed. Another similarity between both sports that Ward shook his head over.

'Hey, don't worry about Max, he's easy to look after, and he's house trained. I'll tell Zara you called and want to keep the dog, bye.' Billy then hung up.

'What the?' Ward stared at his phone, he couldn't keep Max.

'Hoolloooooo,' shouted Tina with her rustling layers of skirts bursting through the front door. 'Oh, I see all the Neanderthals are sitting like monkeys in a row.'

'ARRUUUUUUGGGG.' Max stood in front of Tina, howling.

Tina jumped back with hands tucked under her chin like a mouse. '*What is that?*'

'Did that dog just howl when Tina hollered?' Nick asked.

'I think he did.' Ward's laugh led the rest of them.

'*AH-Choo.*' Tina sneezed, holding a hand over her nose. 'You have a dog? Get it out. *Out dog.*'

Max sat down with his back to Tina and snubbed his nose in the air.

'Did that dog ignore me? Ah-Choo.'

'Hello boys,' said Shirley, walking in with Brian through the open doorway where they both stopped and stared. 'Is that a dog?'

'*Ah-Choo.*' Tina sneezed, digging through her many skirt-layers for a pocket to find a tissue. 'It's a great big lump is what. *Out Dog*'

'Max, stay.' Ward grinned at Max who'd laid down, as ordered. 'Good dog.' Leaning over, he patted the dog as a reward.

'Oh, your allergies, dear,' said Shirley, patting Tina's back.

'I can't stay here—*Ah-Choo.*' Tina gasped for air with her face all screwed up with watery eyes. '*Ah-Choo.* I've—*Ah-Choo*—gotta go. *Ah-Choo.*' She slammed the front door behind her.

'We're keeping that dog,' exclaimed Nick, leaning towards Ward.

'Dude, you've got to keep Max now, that's the quickest your sister has ever visited,' said Sam on Ward's other side.

'I vote we keep the dog,' said Mills, chewing his fingernails on the couch.

'You don't live here, Mills,' said Ward.

'Near enough, I'll share couch-surfing duties with Max.'

'Hi, Mum, Dad.' Ward stood to kiss his mother on the cheek.

'Thought we'd see how you're doing, son.' Brian patted Ward's shoulder then stepped around Max and sat beside Mills. 'That's a big dog.'

Mills nodded while chewing his fingernails.

'You look well,' Shirley said to Ward.

Ward slid back into his chair, cranked back the handle, and grinned up at his mother. 'I am. I got my medical clearance to play and went to practice today.'

'Did Zara say it was okay? I know she didn't want you to overdo it, dear.'

'I was with Zara, and she had me running with the greyhounds, lifting bales of hay, and boxing with young Billy.' Ward explained the horse rescue, and his time at Zara's and the family she lived with. It seemed so surreal now he was home. Most of all, he missed Zara and wanted to share his good news with her.

'Whose dog?' Brian asked.

'*Ward's*,' announced the three boys.

'No, he's not,' said Ward. 'Max is a runaway from Zara's place.'

'Is this Maximus?' Shirley asked as she crouched towards Max who sniffed up at her.

'Mum, meet Max.' Who knew a dog would be centre of attention in this place?

'Oh, you poor thing.' Shirley patted Max's big head, who lapped it up. 'I heard about you, getting shot by the police when they raided the illegal dog fights where they arrested eighty people that night.'

'They shot the dog?' Nick's eyes widened at Max.

'They had to, with a tranquiliser gun, apparently he was covered in blood finishing a fight. He was their Grand

Champion, people bet thousands on him to win. Oh, you're just a big teddy bear, aren't you?' Max rolled over and had his belly scratched.

'How do you know Max's story, Mum?'

'Zara told me while she worked on your neck. You were asleep then, dear.'

Ward did that a lot on Zara, but he liked sleeping with her most of all.

Shirley smiled as she scratched the dog's tummy. 'Aw, he's such a placid thing. Wouldn't believe he's such a dangerous dog with his own police record.'

'Dude, you've got a bad-arse for a dog. I vote you keep him,' said Mills, gnawing on his fingernails.

'Max needs a good home after the torture he's been through.' Shirley sat between Brian and Mills. 'Stop chewing your nails, dear,' Shirley said, pulling on Mill's wrist and he tucked his hands under his thighs. 'Unfortunately, if you kept Max, Tina wouldn't be able to visit, not with her allergies.'

'We're keeping that dog,' said Sam and Nick in unison.

'Oh brother,' mumbled Ward, feeling the peer pressure, even from his own mother. But it was his excuse to see Zara again. He tapped on his smartphone's screen and sent her a text, hoping she'd answer soon.

* * *

'How come I lied my skinny, little arse off for you, sis?' Billy returned the phone to its cradle and stared at Zara standing on the other side of Joe's kitchen counter.

'I told you *not* to give Ward my number.'

'I did because I like the guy.'

'Me too,' replied Zara, couldn't help it but she did.

'So why are you avoiding him then?'

Zara shrugged. Avoidance was good.

'Because he's a fancy footballer who has hundreds of women to pick from,' said Adam, leaning against the pantry cupboard, drinking milk straight from the carton.

'And he's choosing you, sis, out of the thousands of hopefuls.' Billy grinned. 'I thought you liked the guy, Adam?'

With the back of his hand, Adam swiped at his milk-lip. 'I do. I just don't think he's good enough for Zara.'

'No one's good enough for sis.'

'Hello, I'm standing right here!' With hands on her hips, she stood in the centre of the kitchen, shaking her head at both boys. 'Use a glass to drink the milk, Adam.'

'Grouchy, huh? Zara likes the guy too much to admit it.' Adam grinned, taking a mouthful of milk before slipping the carton back into the fridge.

'That's why I gave Ward the number. And hey, Max is there.'

'Are you for real?' Zara asked Billy, who nodded at

234

her.

'Max never went anywhere out of the shed,' said Adam, 'except to follow Ward.'

'Yep, Max ran away to be with the footballer. So why can't you give this guy a chance if Max has, sis?'

'Because… Because…' Zara sat hard on the stool. Resting her elbows on the bench, she held her head in her hands and sighed. 'He's a professional player, and he's busy.'

'You didn't do the Nightingale BS brush-off did you?' Asked Adam.

Zara shrugged.

'It's sneaky, but it works,' said Billy with a wide grin, but it faltered as he faced Zara. 'But that's bull, right? Ward's not like that, he likes you.'

'I can see why Zara did it,' said Adam, leaning back against the pantry, crossing arms over his chest and nodding at Zara.

'You do?' If it had been the right thing to do, why did it feel so wrong to her?

'Well fill me in, because I don't get it. You like Ward. He likes you. Hello, there were fireworks. So, what's the problem?' Billy shrugged his skinny shoulders.

'Because Ward's a footballer,' replied Adam.

'So? It's a job in a sport that's not forever. I'm gonna be a boxer and Ward's a footballer, so what's the big deal?'

'Ward's famous, on the tellie, and he earns big bucks, lives in the city and we live here,' replied Adam.

'We're only an hour out of town. Some people commute two hours to get to work when they live in the city. Besides, Zara drives in nearly every day as it is, so I'm still not getting it.'

'Adam's right,' said Stacey, walking into the kitchen with a washing basket on her hip and dropped it onto the kitchen table. 'Don't mind me, I overheard from the laundry. But if you want my opinion—'

'Oh please, go ahead, join the party.' Zara rolled her eyes at this entire conversation.

Billy raised his hand in the air like he was in school. 'I still don't get it.'

Zara sat up on the stool and knew they'd badger her for a reason. 'It's simple. Ward lives in a different world to us. He's all about football. The training. The playing. The team. The club functions. Where their lives are so controlled in what they eat, drink and do, all governed by a coach. Ward lives a life on display and has to be careful where he goes in case of media digging for dirt. Come on, you guys showed me his fan page.' So why would he bother with someone like her?

'So what, Ward's a down-to-earth guy,' said Billy. 'If he wasn't, you would've told him to piss off, so would've Joe. In fact, we all could've, but didn't because we liked the guy.'

'Why do I bother,' Zara mumbled under her breath.

'I reckon it's because Zara cares about Ward in such a huge way it scares the crap out of her,' said Stacey, facing

Zara. 'You can see it.'

'Woah?' The two boys stared at Zara with widening eyes.

'Yep, Zara's fallen so deep for the guy she doesn't want to go there. I'm right, aren't I?' Stacey stood with hands on her hips and chin out. 'I dare you to call me a liar.'

'I'm not discussing this with you guys.' Zara turned on her boots' heels and headed for the safety of the back door.

'I reckon you're right, Stacey,' said Adam, as Zara walked past him.

'Wow, sis, you're in love with a footballer,' said Billy with a big cheesy grin.

'And I bet Ward doesn't even know it,' Stacey called out.

'Or he'll get all caught up and forget her,' said Adam. 'I guess that's why Zara's cuttin' her losses now to protect herself.'

'Ward's loss,' said Billy.

Zara pushed through the screen door. Yes, it was her loss too because Ward would soon forget her.

Gravel crunched under her boots as she headed for the shed. Her mobile beeped in her back pocket, alerting her to an incoming text message that read:

Hi Z, Max stowed away to my place & you won your bet. Call me to work how & when you want delivery of beer and canine?
Talk soon, Ward.

Zara turned off her phone and tried to forget Ward's message. It was better this way. It was safer.

Nineteen

The room was full of men in various stages of undress, the scents of sweat and differing deodorants mingled with steam from the showers. One of the men shouted out, 'Hey Ward, are you playing this weekend?'

Ward closed the door to his locker and zipped up his bag. 'I hope so.' He'd done his best to prove himself and felt fit enough to play. 'Won't know until the coach picks the team.' Which was BS. Ward hadn't worried before, not since he'd secured his position five years ago. 'What do you know, Greg?' Hoping his team captain had inside information.

Greg closed his locker opposite and turned to face Ward. 'Maybe Coach doesn't want to risk it, after what you've been through.'

'But I'm good, back to normal.'

'Everyone can see that, mate,' said Greg, patting Ward's shoulder. 'Hey, did you hear, Sheldon's scheduled for surgery?'

'Couldn't happen to a nicer wanker,' mumbled Sam, in front of his locker on the other side of Ward. A few surrounding players also murmured their agreement, who obviously weren't a part of Sheldon's cheer squad.

Greg slipped on his jacket and palmed his keys and phone. 'What did you have done, Ward, considering you and Sheldon had the same injury? Weren't you treated by a horse doctor?'

'Zara's not a horse doctor.' Ward frowned at that comment, checking his mobile for the umpteenth time. He'd rung Zara twice, left her a few text messages, and got zilch in replies.

Greg crossed arms over his chest, with head tilted, he eyed over Ward's physique. 'What did she do?'

'Zara's a Reiki Master. She used to work on people in this large practice, but now only does racehorses that are worth a fortune.' Middy had been worth a million, retired to his harem in the back paddock. Zara was right about the stallion's long pedigree horse-name, because Mills googled it for them while sharing the man-couch with Max.

'You know, some of 'em donkeys live better than kings,' muttered Mills, slamming his locker shut, brushing down his black glossy mullet. 'But you're keeping Max, right?'

'Nope.' Even if Max had settled into the place these past couple of days, it meant no visits from his sister, which was a bonus.

'Does Zara advertise her practice?' Greg asked.

Ward slipped on his boots, lowered the hem of his jeans, tucked in his shirt and did up his matching leather belt. Careful of his appearance, that was part of Club grooming like the rest of the men around him, because it wasn't unusual for members of the media to be waiting outside for scandal days. 'Zara doesn't need to advertise when she's the best in the business, and only works on animals.'

'How come?'

Why was the captain so interested? 'Because they don't backchat grizzle and complain like humans do.'

'So, she's legit?'

Ward slid on his jacket and ran his fingers through his misbehaving hair. 'Zara's got lots of diplomas and gets flown around the country by horse owners for the spring racing carnivals. And hey, I'm living proof she knows her stuff, when I didn't think it'd work and had it done against my will.' Grateful no one listened to him then.

'Have you got her number?'

Ward picked up his training bag, then narrowed his eyes at his captain. 'Why?'

'I'll be blunt with you.' Greg stepped closer and lowered his voice as he said, 'The coach and the doctor want to talk to her to find out what she did.'

'Why didn't they ask me themselves?'

Greg shrugged. 'All I know is, Sheldon's coach has called our coach, hoping to share this lady's number.'

Ward frowned, as Sam and Nick mumbled their complaints. His housemates knew their history and so did his captain. 'No.'

'I know none of us like Sheldon, but I got asked to do

it.'

Why didn't Mitchell ask himself? 'Are you feathering your nest with the opposition—who can afford to find their own Reiki Master? Leave Zara alone. I said she doesn't do humans and worked on me as a favour for her dad who's a fan of our club, otherwise she wouldn't have touched me.' No way would he let Zara touch that douche-bag, Sheldon. Not his Zara.

Greg held his palms up. 'Okay, Ward, I get it. But if I was looking at surgery, unable to play for a year, I'd be looking for alternatives too—especially when you've been cured of the same injury as Sheldon.'

'Yeah, man, you couldn't walk or sleep and was grouchy after a week,' mumbled Sam, as Nick nodded at Ward.

Ward remembered the pain all too well. He shoved his hand into his pockets and rubbed his thumb over Zara's painted pebble that nestled into his palm. He headed for the door with his housemates following. 'All I can do is ask.' He didn't want to.

'So, how much did she charge for these treatments?' called out Greg.

Ward grinned at Greg over his shoulder. 'An autograph and a carton of beer for her dad.' Which he hadn't paid Zara yet, because she hadn't returned his calls. But he wasn't going to give up trying.

Twenty

'Heard from Ward?' Stacey asked, seated at the table flicking through a magazine in Zara's bright kitchen.

'He's called a few times,' replied Zara, dabbing her paintbrush into the small tin of white paint.

'Have you actually talked to him, or are you still screening his calls?'

'I can't believe Billy gave out my number in the first place.'

'I'd do the same you know, Ward's nice.'

'He is.' Zara tried to hide her smile and picked up a flat grey stone.

'See, you like him. So, what's the big deal?'

Zara shrugged, applying a base coat to the pebble in hand. She let it rest beside a few dozen similar shaped stones drying on sheets of newspaper spread across her kitchen table.

'What's your painting theme this time?' Stacey asked, sipping from her cup.

'Little houses. I'll pile them up on this piece of driftwood like a suburb.' The inspiration came from dropping off Ward, the last time she saw him, standing beneath the suburban streetlight on the winding road.

'Are you avoiding him because you're scared you're gonna get hurt?'

Zara's paintbrush paused in the air. There were a few reasons why.

'You know, the boys warned him off.'

'Why?' Zara frowned.

'Because they care.' Stacey put her hand on Zara's and said, 'Didn't you tell us to let go of our past.'

'Why cling to the bad?'

'Isn't that what you're doing to yourself?'

Zara narrowed her eyes at Stacey, only sixteen, and a mother wise beyond her years.

'We don't think Ward is the type to hurt you like your ex did.'

'No one thought Paul was like that either.' Zara hated saying his name, even after all this time. 'Besides, in a few days, Ward will forget all about me. He'll be too busy doing his thing, and I'm busy doing my thing,' Zara said, stabbing paint onto the pebble.

Her mobile rang and she checked the caller. 'Were his ears burning?' She dropped the phone face down and let it ring.

'Who is it?' Stacey turned it over. Her eyes widened as she snatched the phone and answered it. 'Hello?' Stacey grinned and ducked from Zara.

'I'm not here,' whispered Zara, waving her hands like

a traffic cop in a no-go zone.

'Hi Ward, it's Stacey. You wanna talk to Zara, huh?'

Zara bolted for the door, but Stacey grabbed the back of her shirt.

'Hold on, I'll get her.' Stacey shoved the phone into Zara's hand. 'Talk to him.'

'Biatch.' Zara wanted to drop the phone like it was a burning brick.

'Enjoy.' Stacey laughed, closing the front door behind her.

Zara cleared her throat and winced at the phone as the heat crept up her neck. 'Hello?'

'Hey, is this really your phone number?' called out Ward.

'Yeah, why?'

'I was beginning to think Billy gave me the wrong one.'

'You're lucky to have this number.'

'Why?'

'Because we don't give it to anyone.'

'You don't share your number for work?'

'No. The only people who have my mobile is the family, and now you, so please don't give it to anyone.'

'Wow, I'm privileged to be part of that inner circle — that's a racing term, right?'

'Winner's circle.' She nervously giggled, fidgeting with the paintbrush in the jar, where the white paint clouded the water.

'So how come no one at the racetrack has your number? How do you get bookings for work?'

'They ring the house and the family takes a message.'

'Why? Are you screening calls?'

'Yes. I pick my clients.' Just like she'd screened his too. *Oops. Obvious much?* 'I might squeeze in the odd request when I'm trackside. Otherwise, I've got a regular weekly schedule from racehorse trainers and I'm already booked-out for the oncoming spring racing carnival.'

'What racing carnival?'

'Everyone knows the race that stops a nation.' She paused.

But Ward said nothing.

'I'm talking about *The Melbourne Cup*.' How could he not know Australia's most famous horse race!

'Oh, yeah. Forgot.' He cleared his throat, sharing an embarrassed chuckle. 'So, I'm guessing the Melbourne Cup for you would be like the AFL Premiership Cup for me. They're both going for gold in a cup.'

'I never thought of it like that.' She giggled at the comparison.

'So, if another person wanted your help what do you guys do?'

'They'll tell them I don't do people and to look in the phone book, we have a list of names to try.'

'And if they wanted to book you in for a house call?'

'I don't do house calls, except for you.' Her shoulders hunched up as she pursed her lips at the admittance. *Why was this so hard?*

'I'm so glad you made those house calls.' His chuckle made her smile so wide, her heart warmed, picturing his smile that hid the scar on his chin.

'So how are you feeling? No pain?' Trying to steer this conversation to a strictly patient-carer call. Even if it was nice he rang, she had to give him points for persistence.

'I'm great. I'm back in training and owe you a carton from the specialist cancelling my surgery.'

'I'm so glad to hear that.' Relief swamped her in bucket-loads. 'Are you playing this weekend?'

'I dunno?' He sighed so deep, she frowned with concern. 'Wish I did, because this waiting sucks.'

Her heart squeezed for his sorrow, finding it hard to keep this call professional.

'I've passed the medical, the physical, yet, for the first time, I had to ask the coach if I'm playing and he won't give me an answer. I hate this, not knowing which position I'll play—when I've played in the same position for years. Or if I'll play at all. It's like he's not convinced of my recovery. I bet he'll put me in the lower grades.'

Her shoulders sagged as if carrying the weight of Ward's disappointment. 'It's understandable.'

'How? Greg, our captain, said the coach doesn't want to put me in any danger. I wouldn't risk myself, and I hate being left out when I can prove I'm ready to play.'

'Why prove it to this coach?'

'He's God.'

'Brendan—'

'Am I in trouble?'

'No.' She gave a short laugh at his boyish charm, which made it harder to distance herself from him. 'Why do you need this coach's approval so much?'

'To play again.'

'Do you believe you can do it?'

'Yes.'

'And that's all you need to hear. End of story.'

'Um?'

'If you believe in yourself, you don't need the approval from anyone else. If this coach doesn't think so, that's his problem, not yours. You only need to have faith in you.'

'If I don't have the coach's approval I'll be dropped to the lower grade.'

'Where you'll kick arse proving to this coach he was wrong.'

'Mmm.'

There was silence on the phone.

'Are you okay, does it hurt to think?' Zara asked, giggling.

'Did you hear the gears clunk?'

'Is that what that rusty noise was?' She could hear the sounds of the TV and men's voices in the background.

'You'll keep.'

'How's Max?'

'He's claimed the man-couch just like you said,

playing couch-tag with Mills, who regularly crashes on the thing.'

'Is the dog keeping it warm for Mills?'

'More like the other way around. Max is spoilt, and my housemates keep feeding him. When are you coming to collect Max?'

'I'm not.'

'Why not?' Ward whined.

'Its obvious Max is where he wants to be.'

'I didn't ask for this.'

'Is Max destroying your garden? Is he chewing up your shoes, peeing on the carpet, or slobbering on your television? Oh no, don't tell me he's taken over your reclining chair. Or are you having trouble getting team logo doggy-designer dishes to match the décor of your man-cave?'

Ward laughed 'No. Max eats from the salad bowl we never use.'

'Don't tell my dad that, he's still fighting me with his food choices.'

'We blend all our daily nutrients into one bullet for the morning.'

'You also run a daily mini-marathon and you're not in your seventies.'

'True.'

'So, do your housemates hate Max?'

'They want Max to stay and brag about him all the time. Sam's even bought Max this fancy big studded collar.'

'To go with the bad boy image, right?' Zara laughed, imagining it.

'Yep, they've butched his bling, and Nick's brought him this fancy organic dog wash too. I haven't had to do anything.'

'Is Max scaring your visitors away?'

'Mum loves Max, although we've only seen Tina once when her allergies acted up, so that part's bliss.'

'Well, what's the problem with having Max around?' Zara paced her kitchen floor, unsure of this whole conversation. She didn't talk to men unless it was for work or for family.

On the other end of the phone, it sounded like a door was being closed shutting out all background noises, except for Ward's sigh. 'I've never looked after a dog, and I'm worried I'll mess up.'

Her heart fell as fast as it took for her to sit.

'I've never been responsible for anything in my life. Which is stupid for a guy my age.'

'How can you say that? You play a part in a team.'

'It's because everything else is taken care of. This is a club house, we've got a gardener and a cleaner. Our mothers cook us meals for the freezer, or we get fed at the Clubhouse.'

Ward sounded ashamed of himself. 'You can afford not to worry about those things. We pay Stacey to do our cleaning and I live on my own.'

'I've never had to take care of anything but myself my

entire life. Sounds selfish, but it's true, Zara. Max has been through hell and I don't want to ruin it for him by stuffing up when I've never owned a pet.'

Why was this man single? He was almost perfect. 'Perhaps Max recognizes you won't take him for granted, and that you'll be someone who'd treat him like a mate and not as a pet.'

Again, there was a silent pause on his end.

'Remember when my dad asked you to help us with that pony we rescued, you said you didn't know anything about horses? What did Dad say to you?'

'That I had no bad habits.'

'You're not useless—'

'Just not used to it,' he finished. 'But—'

'Why not try it for a week. If it's not working out, call me and I'll come and get him. Until then I won't go near your place.' *If ever.*

'Are you avoiding me?'

She chewed her bottom lip and tried to think of a gentle response to a question she didn't want to answer. She *did* want to see him—but didn't, which confused her on all levels.

'Hey, I asked a nurse about that Florence Nightingale syndrome?'

'You didn't?' Zara covered her mouth to stop her laugh, impressed with his inquisitive mind and bravado.

'I did,' he said with smile to his voice. 'I'm not shy about asking, which might be the only thing my sister and

I have in common.'

'Not her cooking?'

'I don't do peppered mud,' Ward said, chuckling. 'Anyway, the nurse explained the Nightingale thing and I understand your point too.'

'I want you to focus on yourself.' How could Ward be so sure it wasn't just a passing phase? She lived in the country and liked to keep to herself. He was a city boy living in a bachelor pad with a hectic social life.

Zara stared out her kitchen window that framed the farm. She loved this place. She smiled as Tim rode the quad with the toddler, Toby, in his lap while the greyhounds raced behind them. Joe and Adam worked under the bonnet of the old Holden sedan. Billy was practising at the punching bag in the shade of the shed. Stacey hung out the washing at her dad's house, feeding her prized pet hens picking at the lawn beneath her. Why would Ward be bothered with her?

She shook her head, pacing the floor in her odd socks. Nope, Ward was a client. Maybe a friend, too. Sure, it'd been an intense few days with the guy to get him back on his feet, and she'd done that. Job done.

'I want to focus on my game, but it doesn't mean I have to forget about everything else. Like you, Z.'

She melted on the spot. Why was he making this so hard?

Ward broke the awkward silence. 'How's that horse you rescued?'

'You helped me.'

'I did not.'

'Yes, you did. It's something to be proud of.' She wanted him to be proud, because she liked him—too much.

'Have you got a name for him?'

'Norm.'

'That fits. Did Toby choose it?'

'He did, and Norm answers to it too.' She finally relented and sat at the kitchen table where they spoke for ages, not about football, but everything else that went on in their lives. Yet, they lived in two different worlds that she couldn't see blending together.

Twenty-One

The shouts of men competed with the thumping kick of leather as the egg-shaped footballs were kicked, handballed, and punched in various groups on the oval. The team practised with kicking coaches, running coaches, and handball coaches. Team drills were played as individual skills were tested. Ward gave it everything because this was it—decision day.

Was the coach going to let him play or bench him? Was he going to lose his spot and get rotated with other team members to never play his position permanently again?

Ward knew the second Coach Mitchell stood on the edge of the oval as the cool down session began. The coach lifted his clipboard and read from the list as everyone listened for their name. 'Adler, Benson, Edice…' Mitchell made his way through the list of players, Ward prayed the coach was calling the team players in alphabetical order. With only a few left standing, Mitchell called, 'WARD.'

Ward grimaced as he snatched a water bottle with sweaty palms and jogged towards the man who ruled his world. 'Coach?' *Please don't cut me. Please don't cut me.*

'How are you feeling?'

'Great.' *Oh no.* Mitchell wore a familiar frown, carrying a huge responsibility that rested on one set of shoulders for an entire club's future. Yet Ward still couldn't handle a dog like Max

'Listen, son…'

Oh no. Not the *listen son* as the start to the speech that life was now over.

'I've been thinking…'

Ward wiped his mouth on his sleeve to stop swearing and held his breath. *Here it comes.*

'I'm putting you into the lower grade for this weekend's game,' said Mitchell.

Crap! Ward frowned so hard at the ground, water spurted from the bottle he'd squeezed.

But then he paused, remembering that Zara told him to expect this.

It was time to man-up.

Chin up, chest out, Ward said, 'Sure, Coach, whatever you think's best for the team, I know you're looking out for me.' Even if it was a pile of steaming horse-crap.

'Huh?' Mitchell screwed up his nose as he scratched his head. 'Where's the dummy spit.'

Oh, he wanted to—but Zara was right. 'Because I'm going to prove to you I'm back, Coach, by kicking arse in that VFL game.'

Mitchell stared at Ward for a moment as practice

finished and the rest of the men headed for the change rooms. 'Okay then, I'll call their coach to slot you in for the weekend.'

'Sure, and I'll be here to support the team after my game.' Ward hoped he seemed calm on the outside while ticked off on the inside. Although, it'd be an easy early game on Saturday that'd leave him the rest of the weekend free. Maybe he'd call Zara. He headed for the showers, formulating a plan.

'Ward?' Mitchell called out and half-jogged to catch up to him. 'Do you believe you're ready to get back out there?'

'Absolutely.'

Mitchell smoothed over his hair and looked out over the empty field, then back at Ward. 'Okay, you've convinced me.'

Ward didn't even breathe, daring to hope.

'You're in. Same position as always, on Saturday.'

'Who was replacing me?' He didn't want to screw over a mate either.

'From the A grade. I hadn't told him yet, because I wasn't quite convinced in replacing you either.' Mitchell crossed off a name on his list and wrote down Ward's.

'You ripper.' Ward wanted to high-five the clouds. 'I won't let you down.' He had a game on Saturday, and it felt better than the first time he'd gotten a game as a fresh-faced seventeen-year-old, standing amongst a field of tough men. Men who were once his idols, now long gone. So where were they now?

'Hey Ward, I forgot to ask you something,' called out Mitchell.

'Yeah?' Ward spun around to face his coach again.

Mitchell frowned, wiping his thumb and forefinger down either side of his mouth as if grooming an invisible handle-bar moustache. 'The Magpie's doctor has asked for this horse-person's number who, err, provided something to help you, to help Sheldon?'

Ward frowned as the protectiveness burred up like flames in an over-fuelled fire pit in his chest. He wasn't going to let that smancy prick near Zara. Ever. 'Coach, Zara doesn't do that.'

'Why not? She did, whatever it was, to you—'

'Only as a favour to her dad, who's a fan. Don't ask me for her number because Zara doesn't give it out.' So glad he had her number and the time spent talking with her last night.

'How does she run a business without sharing her number? ESP?'

'Zara doesn't advertise and chooses who she deals with which is only animals. She doesn't do humans.'

'Okay, I get it, I don't like sharing anything with the Magpies either, they are the opposition,' said Mitchell, giving Ward a crooked grin. 'You did ask her about Sheldon, though?'

'Yes. Kind of.' *Not really.* 'She'll say no.'

Mitchell cocked an eyebrow at Ward. 'What's her

name?'

Ward scowled at Mitchell, protective over Zara. His Zara.

Mitchell patted Ward's shoulder. 'Please, Ward, just a name to get them off my back. Let this lady make that decision, it's her business.'

Ward hated this. 'Zara Phelps. They can find the number themselves.' He hoped Zara's family played damned good gatekeepers, and headed for the showers.

'Are you in, Ward?' Greg, their team captain, asked with a towel wrapped around his waist.

'I'm in.' Ward grinned wide, entering the changeroom from the showers.

'You bloody ripper, mate,' shouted Mills, patting Ward's shoulder, which led the hero's welcome of back slaps and cheers as he passed his teammates on the way to his locker.

Mills slid on his inside-out, pre-buttoned shirt, flapping the twisted sleeves as he tried to get his head through the gap. 'Hey, are you gonna keep Max, or what?'

Ward shrugged at his locker, reaching for his deodorant.

'Zara told Ward he had a week to decide,' said Sam at his locker on Ward's right. 'I vote we keep him. We're allowed pets with the lease, I checked.'

'I vote yes for Max,' said Nick, pulling up his jeans. 'I

know Max scared me at first, but he's cool.'

'What breed?' Greg asked, doing up the buttons of his collared shirt.

'Pit bull,' replied Sam.

'Don't you need permits for that breed of dog?' Greg asked, tucking in his shirt.

'Dunno.' Ward shrugged and grabbed his socks. He sat down and stared at the perfect pair of black socks, unlike Zara and her odd socks of many colours. A week seemed a long time.

'I'm sure you do,' said Greg. 'Aren't pit bulls on some dangerous dogs list?'

'I'm pretty sure Max would be on that list when he's got a police record,' replied Sam.

'The cops shot him, so of course they'd know all about the Grand Champion of the underworld,' said Nick.

Ward chuckled to himself as he slid on his boots. His housemates still bragged about the dog.

'Is Max registered to you, Ward?' asked Mills.

'Max stowed away to my place,' replied Ward. Although, registration sounded like official adoption papers.

'Max has made himself at home,' said Mills.

'Just like you.' Ward arched an eyebrow at their semi-permanent houseguest.

'I said I don't mind sharing the man-couch surf-turf with Max.'

'I'll talk to Zara about Max's registration.' Ward

smiled at another excuse to speak to the lady.

Greg stepped in closer and asked, 'Did you give the coach Zara's number for Sheldon?'

Ward scowled at his captain. Why was everyone on his case to help Sheldon, who wouldn't help anyone but himself?

'We all agree he's a wanker, but…'

'I've spoken to the coach, it's up to them now. See you on game day.' Ward picked up his sports bag and headed for the door. He didn't want Greg or anyone else trying to talk him into sharing that phone number.

In the club carpark, Ward threw his training bag into the boot of his car beside a large manila envelope containing his x-rays from the fall.

Dammit.

He slammed the boot with two hands and leaned against it, with head down he breathed deep as guilt slammed heavily between his shoulders. Only a week ago he was in Sheldon's shoes doing the old-man shuffle of no sleep.

There was only one way to fix this.

Even if he couldn't stand Sheldon, Ward couldn't believe what he was about to do.

Twenty-Two

Ward parked his car behind Zara's ute and headed towards the racetrack's stables. He'd only been here with Zara when it was deserted, yet today there were people everywhere. There were men wandering around in shorts and thongs through to those in full three-piece suits. Some women wore designer labels, teetering in heels that disappeared into grass like spikes, while other ladies were barefoot in frocks and feathered hats, carting champagne bottles like trophies. On the edge of the busy stables, bookies shouted out odds, as the day-punters and gamblers chased numbers away from the shadows of the grandstands.

Ward spotted a familiar face. 'Hey, Ron?'

Ron cringed over his shoulder, then started to walk away. Fast.

Ward dashed forward and gripped the cool shiny silk sleeve of Ron's jockey uniform. 'What are you running for?' As if Ron could out-run Ward.

'Please don't hit me?' Ron held his hands up to his face.

'Why would I want to hit you?' It'd be like hitting a

twelve-year-old kid.

'You're not here to hassle me?'

'No.'

'Why are you here then?'

'I'm looking for Zara. Do you know where I can find her?' Ward asked, looking at the rabbit warren of stables, horses, and people.

'She's over there, I'll show you,' Ron said, leading the way. 'So, you're not here to hit me then?'

'Why would I want to do that for?'

'Haven't you seen Tina?'

Not if he could help it. 'For a fleeting five seconds when Max arrived.' Ward grinned at the memory worth keeping. 'Why?'

'We broke up.'

'It happens, and that's between you and my sister.'

'But, I… I love her.'

'Why?' Ward screwed his nose up. 'Nope, don't tell me.'

'I only broke up with her because Tina won't take that hearing test, and then she got jealous over Zara, saying I liked Zara.'

Ward stopped and frowned down at the smaller Ron. 'Do you?'

'Zara's just a mate, I keep telling Tina that, but she wouldn't believe me.'

Ward was relieved to hear it.

They wound through the stables filled with big

horses doted on by handlers and trainers. They dodged piles of steaming horse poo that didn't bother most except the women wearing fancy hats and heels. The PA system announced the next race creating an urgency in the bookies' shouts. In the background excited voices from the crowd competed with the neighing horses and the clip-clop of hooves on hard surfaces.

He'd been here before when this place was nothing more than a ghost town of silence. Reminding him of the difference between the calm of practise on the oval, compared to the electrified tension felt in a game before a stadium filled with fans.

'So, you're saying you only split up with my sister because of a hearing test?' Ward asked Ron.

'Yes. I offered to take her because I think Tina might be part deaf.'

'Since Zara mentioned it, I agree.' The woman caused voice-quakes and Ward agreed with Zara on lots of things—but not the nursing syndrome. Or did he?

He'd know for sure when he saw her.

Ron trotted to keep up with Ward's long-legged stride. 'Tina's having trouble at work, not hearing customers when the music's on.'

'That isn't music.' Tina played wailing voodoo-chants as background atmosphere for her hippy-dippy-love store. All that incense, crystals, and tie-dyed clothes made him dizzy if he stayed in there for too long.

'Not my taste either, but I admire her passion. The

only problem we've had is over her stubbornness to get her ears tested.'

Ward could give Ron a list of Tina's problems, if he wanted it.

'The thing is, Tina reckons if she gets a hearing aid, I'll dump her.'

'Zara's father has one and you'd never notice it. Hold on, you're saying you dumped my sister because she *didn't* want to go for her hearing test?'

'I did. I adore your sister and don't care what she wears, bells and all.'

'Those bells on her ankles are irritating,' said Ward. 'Are you sure there's nothing you don't like about Tina?'

'Tina's cooking,' replied Ron. 'I offered to take cooking classes with her when she got upset after I told her that mung-bean stew was crap.'

'We all hate that stew, it tastes like peppered dirt.' Ward screwed his nose up. Even the smell of horse manure and hay was better than Tina's mung-bean stew.

'I thought you guys liked that stew?'

'Can't stand it. I've wanted to tell Tina, but Mum said we can't hurt her feelings.' Even his whole household was in on the act. Maybe, somewhere, deep down, Ward did care about his sister's feelings.

'Tina called me a liar because you all love that stew. Its why she's making it all the time.'

'Wish Mum would let me tell Tina the truth. Mum's pretty protective over Tina's delicate ego.'

'Tina reckons if she fell off the planet nobody would notice. But if you did, they'd drop everything and run.'

Ward never admitted in public that Tina was his sister. 'We care about her.' In some weird blood-related way. Although his family did drop everything to be by his side at the hospital, and his parents were at every home game too. 'Do you think Tina's jealous of me?'

'Yeah mate, sorry.'

'Not your fault.' It bothered him, which was unusual to be bothered by anything when it came to his sister. 'Tell you what,' Ward said, patting Ron's small shoulder, 'I'll call Tina and have a chat?'

'You'd do that?' Ron widened his eyes up at Ward.

'I'll have to ask Mum for Tina's number because I've never had it.' Surprised he was volunteering. 'Even though Tina will probably just shout at me for interfering, all I can do is try. I'll even back you up and tell Tina that the hearing test will only help, and that her mung-bean stew smells like dirt.'

'Really?' Ron asked, hopeful.

'You told the truth and so will I.' *This might be fun.* 'I'll warn Mum first, she is the family peacekeeper.'

'Thanks, Ward. I appreciate it. I miss her.'

Sick. Yet, each to their own. When he spotted another familiar face standing at the side gate, plucking a stray strand of cotton from a faded baseball cap's visor. 'Tim?'

'Oi Ward, you lost? This is a race track for thoroughbreds, not a football field for humans treated like thoroughbreds.' Tim grinned as he re-adjusted his battered cap.

Ward chuckled. 'You'll keep. Tim, this is Ron, my sister's boyfriend, well sort of, don't ask.'

'Aren't you with Zara?' Ron asked.

'Yeah, she's family, but Ward's the one with Zara.' Tim waved his thumb at Ward.

Ward tried to act cool when he wanted to smile wide. 'Where is Z?' His lady, his nickname. *If* she wanted to see him, and *if* he wasn't suffering from some stupid syndrome.

Tim pointed to the left. 'She's in that stable.'

'Well, I've gotta get ready for my race. Thanks for the chat, Ward,' said Ron, holding out his hand.

'No worries. Hey, I can't promise anything with Tina, but I'll try.' Ward shook Ron's hand, their grips matching. 'Good luck with your race.'

'Ta. Good luck with your game this weekend.'

Ward watched Ron leave. He didn't mind the guy, making it the first time he actually liked any of Tina's men.

'Does that mean you're playing, Ward?' Tim asked.

Hands in pockets, smile on face, and with a swagger to his step, Ward said, 'Oh yeah, I'm playing.'

'Well done, mate. Joe and the crew will be stoked to hear,' said Tim, patting Ward on the shoulder. 'Zara's almost finished, this way.'

'How come you're in town?'

'I had to see my parole officer. In a few weeks, I'll be cleared. I told 'em I'm staying on with Joe and Zara at the farm, going for my truck license in a month. Joe reckons there's plenty of work hauling harvests, if I wanted it.' Tim smiled with his chin up and chest out, as they strolled across the wide walkway with stables full of horses on either side.

'Congratulations.'

'Thanks, it's seasonal stuff, but it's a start. Well, there she is, turn off your phone,' warned Tim in a whisper, checking his own mobile. They entered a quiet area with no crowds, through the double doors and into a large open stable with soft sand on the floor. 'This is the VIP section for that one horse they reckon it's worth twenty million.'

'Really?'

'Them two big-chested blokes over there, own it.' Tim pointed to the men in suits and said, 'They're worth gazillions. One owns a few mines, and the other guy owns TV stations.'

They looked familiar to Ward. 'Are they the ones who fly Zara around?'

'Yeah. When they win big, they'll dump a load of cash to Zara to help with the horses back home.'

'Good to hear.' Ward peeked over the wooden rail to the large stall. And there she was… Zara.

His heart felt like it was about to burst, as he gripped the gate as his world tilted.

He'd missed her. Tempted to jump the rail and hug her tight, to kiss her dimples, to rub his cheek against her hair in a loose plait. He wanted to know what colour her odd socks were under her long boots, and to just hold her against his chest and breathe in her aroma.

His eyes followed the curve of her riding pants, hugging her toned legs, the customary grey hoodie and black puff jacket with pockets she used like a purse. For someone who'd made such a powerful impact on him, she seemed so small and delicate compared to the massive dark brown horse she was working on.

All noise around him ceased to exist, and like tunnel vision, his focus narrowed on one thing—Zara.

It wasn't any Florence Nightingale Syndrome, it was more. He didn't understand what, but could only watch her with pride, awe, and pure adoration.

Was Ward in love?

* * *

'Oh man,' Zara muttered, finding Ward standing beside Tim on the other side of the stall's gate. She smiled at Ward, as a delicious lick of heat swirled with a fluttering in her tummy. 'Hi?'

'Hi.' Ward's shine in his amber eyes warmed her all over.

How did he do that?

'Have you finished, Zara?' Tim asked, making faces at her as he opened the stall's gate.

'Yes.' She headed for the sinks, tempted to dunk her heated face under the cold tap. Why was Ward here? She couldn't even look at him as she dried her trembling hands.

'I'll pack up the gear so you two can chat.' Tim hooked his arm through hers and guided her to face Ward. 'Here you go, Ward, the lady is all yours.'

'Hey?' She didn't want to be alone with Ward, who shouldn't even be here.

'All good then, Zara?' called out the horse's owner.

'He's good to travel,' said Zara, pointing to the horse shaking his gleaming coat and mane as if waking from a deep slumber.

'Excellent, I'll tell the trainer. Until next time.' The men waved and looked over the horse, returning to their conversation.

'All yours, Pip.' Zara nodded to the stable-hand who closed up the stall. Tim headed off with her work bag towards the ute, where she should be, and not stand around with a footballer amongst the stables. 'Are you lost?'

Ward chuckled. 'Can't I say hello?'

'Sure, but I thought you'd be busy.' He should've forgotten about her by now.

'I'd just finished training and guess what? I made the team.' His smile widened and his stance was so tall and proud, it sucked he looked so good.

'Congratulations. That's great news, knew you'd do it.' She smiled, squeezing her hands together to stop herself from hugging the guy.

'Do you want to get a coffee, heard this was the best place for one?'

'It is. Sure, this way.' She needed a drink for her dry throat.

She led him to the small canteen where tables were scattered beneath a large leaf-barren tree that allowed the winter sun to shine through. They grabbed their coffees and found an empty table. He sat so close beside her, the hair on her forearms rose like he was her magnet.

'How's Max?' She was so nervous, hiding her lips under her scarf, gripping her cup, scared she'd spill her coffee everywhere.

'Good. Hey, does Max need a permit? Like a dangerous dog thing?'

'Definitely. Are you thinking of keeping him?'

'Well, you are right in saying Max is easy to look after, but I haven't decided yet.' His forehead creased as he sipped his coffee.

'I'm glad you're taking the time to consider your options, you'll know at the end of the week. Although, it sounds like Max has settled in already.' She'd missed the big dog, who deserved a good home. But she also noticed the way Ward's tone had shifted about Max. Was that beautiful big dog winning over the footballer?

'Max likes the man-couch, and the boys brag about having some underworld Grand Champion in the house.'

She giggled nervously and wiped her sweaty palms across her denim thighs.

'Can anyone have a dog like Max in the city?' Ward asked, grabbing her hand and toyed with her fingers, making her eyes follow as he brought her hand to his lips.

The heat rose inside and out, it was hard to swallow, all from the way he looked at her and how gentle he was with her hand. She blurted out, 'If you're thinking of keeping Max, Katie and Riley would need to do an inspection. They both know Max, and you've got a big backyard with a tall fence to keep Max contained, not that he'd go anywhere.' She was rambling—when she never rambled.

'When did you see my backyard?'

'Through your kitchen window while you were asleep.'

'That's why I call you Z.' His shoulder playfully nudged hers, she grinned, relaxing a little more.

'You needed it, considering you hadn't slept for a week.' She was so out of practice with this stuff—because it wasn't meant to happen.

'At that stage, I hadn't.' He then frowned at the table as if in pain.

She forgot her fear as her heart gripped with worry for him. 'What's wrong?'

'Dunno how you'll take this?' He stroked over the scar on his chin.

'What?'

'You know my fall?'

'Yes. You're not suffering any nightmares or flashbacks?'

'Nope, only dreams of you though,' he whispered

into her ear, sending prickles across her skin. 'Mushy, huh? But I can't help it with you.' He shuffled closer and put his arm around her shoulders. 'Have you gone shy on me?'

She was speechless, shy, awkward and dumb. This was so foreign to her, yet it felt so good to be near him too.

'I won't rush you, I promise.' He gently stroked the back of her hand.

'Thank you,' she whispered and tried to smile. She tucked her ratty hair behind her ear and picked a strand of horsehair from her sleeve. Why would he choose her?

But then she saw his smile falter. 'What's wrong? Why did you mention the fall?'

'There were two of us who were hurt in that fall.'

'That other guy from the Magpies. Dad hates that team.'

'Me too. Do you know him?'

'Who?'

'The other guy I hit? Sheldon.' His eyes darkened, frowning, he again swiped his thumb over that scar on his chin with a vicious swipe as he said the name, 'Thomas Anthony Sheldon.'

She shrugged. 'No idea who you're talking about.'

'Thank you.' His smile ripped wide as the amber shone in his eyes. 'Guess footballers aren't known much in the horseracing world.' He picked up his coffee and sipped.

'So, who is this Sheldon?'

'Dickhead,' he spat.

She winced.

'Hey?' Squeezing his arm around her shoulders, it was comforting. 'I didn't scare you, did I?'

'No.' She had to stop flinching. 'So, you don't like this guy.' Did she dare ask why?

Ward sighed, resting his elbow on the table and rubbed his forehead. 'No.' Then he looked at her. 'Did you know we both suffered the same injuries?'

'That's rare.'

'I hate having anything in common with Sheldon.' He reached for her hand again and watched his thumb stroke gently across her knuckles. 'Unlike me, because I found you,'—he smiled at her and she wanted to melt into his arms and revel in his aroma— 'Sheldon's scheduled for surgery and their coach asked my coach to ask you if you'd—'

'No. You were a one-off. I don't do people.' She shook her head. She'd never meant to work on Ward in the first place.

'Cool. I asked, and that's the end of that topic.' He smiled, then kissed her temple, causing her heated blush to rise to a whole new level. 'What are you doing tonight?'

'Home, and I'm not going near your place while Max is there.'

'Why?' Ward whined with widening eyes.

'Because if Max sees me, he may fret, which may influence your decision. We agreed a week.'

'For me or Max?'

Oh brother! 'Max,' she whispered, finding it hard to

fight her attraction to the guy.

'Do you want me to keep Max?'

'That's for you and Max to decide, not me.'

'Week's up tomorrow.'

'It hasn't been seven days.'

'A working week is five days which ends tomorrow.'

'That's sneaky.'

'Max showed up uninvited.'

'Max wanted to be with you.' Did she?

'Would you hate me if I didn't take Max in?'

'No.' Zara gave Ward what she hoped was a gentle smile to put him at ease.

'So, you wouldn't think I'm spineless or…'

'No.' She gripped his hand with both of hers and faced him squarely. 'It's a big decision because if you keep Max, he'll be part of your family for the next ten years.'

'That's a long-term commitment.'

'I wouldn't judge you if you didn't take Max. I'd respect your decision, no matter which way you went, because you're taking the time to get to know each other first. Don't let anyone talk you into something you may regret later.'

He brushed her fringe to the side, tucking it behind her ear, sending a shiver down her spine. 'You're very understanding. Can I take you to dinner?'

'When?' She blinked at him, not expecting that at all.

'Are you working in the morning at the track?'

'Yes.'

'Saturday morning?'

'No. I try to avoid the tracks when they're at their busiest.' Noisy crowds bothered her.

'Good. I'll take you out Friday night.'

'You'd drive all the way out there to pick me up for dinner?'

'It's not that far once you hit the highway. Are there any good restaurants in your area?'

'We've only got the pub.'

'Nope, you deserve better. I'll come up with something, and I'll call you later for a time to be ready.'

She chewed her bottom lip hidden behind her scarf.

Ward lowered himself to meet her eyes. 'Hey, what I feel for you isn't a Nightingale deal, Z. Please have dinner with me?'

'Okay,' she whispered. Did she just agree to a date?

'Great, you won't regret it.'

She hoped not.

Twenty-Three

'Hey, Mum?' Ward walked through the back door of his childhood home, carting an assortment of shopping bags.

'This is nice surprise, dear.' Shirley walked around the kitchen bench and kissed his cheek.

'Brought those dishes back.' He put the shopping bags on the bench. It was a sweet deal, readymade homemade meals for the freezer when no one at home felt like cooking. 'I've put the money inside.' He pulled out a chair and took his usual seat at the round kitchen table.

'You gave me too much last time.'

'So, what. Go get a haircut or buy a new dress with the change.' He liked spoiling his mother, who spoiled him.

'Thank you.' She patted down his unruly hair, making him feel like a little boy all over again. 'I've made a special dog stew for Max. Saw it on the tellie the other day, it's to help with his digestion with the roughage needed for such big dogs.'

'You're cooking for the dog now?'

Shirley removed a large bag from her freezer to show him. 'They're portion-controlled on what that tellie-vet recommended for a dog that size.'

Everyone else did something for Max, except Ward, who only let the dog follow for a run in the mornings. 'I haven't decided if I'm keeping him, Mum.'

'It'd be a shame if you didn't. I've always wanted a dog, and Max is such a lovely big bear.' She put the food back in the freezer, flicked on the kettle, and dished out a plate of cake.

'Why not get one, now Tina doesn't live here.'

'It's not just Tina, your father has allergies too, dear.' She put a plate of sliced cake on the table, then started on the tea cups.

'Dad seemed fine patting Max.' Not like his sister who'd ran out the door sneezing.

'He's fine in small doses. We're okay to look after the neighbour's dog for a week.'

'Where is Dad?' Ward asked, plucking a slice of homemade carrot cake from the plate.

'Work. Remember, it's only Thursday, dear.' The tea bag's tag fluttered on the side of the mugs she carried to the table and sat next to Ward. 'Tell me, did you make the team?'

Ward dunked his tea bag and grinned up his mum. 'Yep, I'm playing on Saturday.'

'We'll be there.' Shirley smiled wide with pride.

'Mum, do you think you could babysit Max for a night? Or do they call it dog-sitting?

'Why?'

'I want to take Zara out.'

'Didn't Zara say you and Max were to stay together for a week?'

'Yeah. It's not a full week, and I haven't made up my mind. The boys are keen, and Zara's fine if I say yes or no.' Which had been a huge relief, because Ward never wanted to disappoint Zara. 'But with my lifestyle, and if Dad's got allergies I'd need someone to look after Max when we play away.'

'Oh, honey.' Shirley pressed her hands against her heart.

'Don't get too far ahead, Mum.' Guessing it was too late if his mother was already cooking for the pit bull.

'We'd be happy to have Max here, but only in small doses to not upset your father's allergies.'

'Cool, so how about tomorrow night?'

'No.'

'Why not?'

'The deal was you had to spend a week with Max.'

'But I want to go out on a date with Zara and—'

'*Helloooo*.' Tina's nail-scratching screech caused the glass cabinet doors in the kitchen to rattle.

'Oh no, voice-quake.' Ward reached over and stilled the glass doors. He then rubbed his forehead at the headache strolling through the back door with a rustle of many skirts.

'Mum, I brought that gluten-free bread for you and Dad to try, it'll help with your digestion.' The shift of clothes and bell ringing stopped. 'Ward, I didn't know you were visiting?'

'Didn't you recognise my car in the drive? You walked right past it to get inside.'

'No.' Tina's bells jingled while she placed her groceries on the counter.

Did his sister need glasses too?

Shirley got up from her seat and unpacked the groceries. 'Did you fetch more of that yummy fruit?'

'Told you that organic fruit tastes better.' Tina passed a bunch of bananas to Shirley, giving her brother a side-glance. 'You'd notice the difference in taste too if you Neanderthals cooked something besides meat.'

'They make the best banana cake,' said Shirley, giving Ward her peacekeeper's look.

Ward shrugged eating his mum's carrot cake. 'Have you had your hearing test yet, Tina?'

'The appointment is for tomorrow,' Shirley said to Tina across the kitchen counter.

'Are you going?' Ward asked his sister.

Tina shrugged. Shirley raised an eyebrow, pursing her lips together.

'Wouldn't hurt. Even if it's to tell you there's nothing wrong with you.' Even if his sister was beyond help.

The bells on Tina's ankles rang as she swivelled to face her brother. 'Hey, I got that same lecture from Ron— which I don't need from you—especially when you couldn't care what happens to me.'

'I do.' Ward brushed the crumbs off his palms and leaned back in his seat. 'I'll admit, you are a pain in the arse, but if you were in hospital I'd visit. I'd even get you some flowers.' He'd prefer to send them, if he could get away with it. 'But this is your health and lifestyle, and hey, hearing aids are so small you'd hardly notice them.'

'How would you know?'

'Zara's dad wears one.'

Shirley closed the cupboard as she flicked on the kettle, putting a tea bag into another cup. 'Zara did tell me her father had one, can't sneak past him anymore.'

'That's *her* business, not mine.' Tina jutted out her chin.

Ward watched his sister over the rim of his mug. 'I saw Ron today.'

'We broke up.' Tina blinked as if forcing herself to not cry, while their mother stroked Tina's shoulder.

Wow, Tina really liked the jockey. His heart tugged at her pain. Huh, he did care about his big sister who, most of the time, was painful. 'Ron told me why he broke up with you.' Surprised he was talking to his sister—and doing it for Ron.

'What did that little bugger tell you? Of course, you'd side with him.'

'I do.' Ward nodded, sipping his tea. 'Which is the first time I've agreed with one of your boyfriends.'

'Typical,' scoffed Tina, crossing arms over her chest, screwing up her nose.

'Now, dear, your brother's only teasing.' Shirley rubbed Tina's upper back while glaring at Ward with wide eyes in a warning to stop.

But Ward didn't want to stop. 'Ron told me the reason he broke up with you was because he wants you to take that hearing test. He said you refused to go believing he won't like you if you had to wear a hearing aid. Which is BS. Ron doesn't care what you wear.' Waving his hand over her tie-dyed-sunbeam trip she wore today. '*And* he said he loves you.'

'Really?' Shirley smiled wide, gripping Tina's arm. 'I like Ron too, dear.'

'Ward's making it up, Mum.'

'No, I'm not,' Ward said, reaching for another piece of cake.

Tina re-crossed her arms in a huff, the bells rang, and her clothes rustled like paper being screwed up by a class full of kindergarten kids. 'Are you keeping that monstrosity of a beast at your place?'

'Haven't decided yet.'

'Shouldn't have a creature like that in society, he should've been put down.' Tina threw her hands in the air, rolling her eyes, and huffing like an outdated steam train.

Ward scowled at his sister. 'Max is a good dog. It's not his fault he was made to fight for his life.'

'I like Max too,' Shirley said, pouring hot water into the teacup that she left it on the counter beside Tina and returned to her seat at the table.

'Dangerous, is what that dog is,' scoffed Tina, picking up her cup.

'Aren't we all? Or are you faking your need to save all creatures big and small? I met a real one of those saviours from the RSPCA last week. You've got to respect them for what they do.' Ward was glad to know the pony he'd helped rescue was recovering well, according to Zara's update earlier.

'Sounds like you're keeping him, huh?' mumbled Tina, taking a sip of her tea, leaning her hip against the kitchen bench. 'I bet it eats like a horse.'

'Mum's made Max a stew.'

'With all these vegetables too, dear,' said Shirley proudly. 'You must tell me if Max likes it.'

'Will do, Mum.' Ward grinned at his sister's scowl that he was about to make worse. 'Hey, talking about food, I agree with Ron. Your mung-bean stew smells like peppered dirt, it tastes like mud, and I hate it.'

'What?' Tina's jaw dropped as her forehead crinkled.

'We weren't allowed to tell you because we didn't want to hurt your feelings. So Ron isn't a liar. In fact, he's the only one with the courage to tell you the truth.' Ward popped more cake into his mouth and watched his sister's reaction.

'But—but—' Tina stuttered as her eyes darted between her mother and brother. 'Is that true, Mum?'

'Well...' Shirley wiped her palms down her skirt, took a deep breath and swivelled in her seat to face her daughter by the bench. 'To be honest, dear, I don't like it either. I tried. But it does taste gritty. Now, I do love that pumpkin risotto you make, that's nice. Your father loves it, too.'

Tina pressed her lips together, staring at her mother.

'Ron told me he wants to do some cooking lessons with you.' Ward did say he'd go bat for the little man, even if his sister hated him more than ever. He had nothing to lose. 'Why don't you go? You like cooking and Ron said he didn't mind trying new things with you because he loves you. You can see it.'

Tina flopped into the chair next to their mother, plonking her cup onto the table. 'Did Ron really say that?'

'Yeah.' Ward nodded. 'Now, that's your deal. Said I'd have a word, and I did it.' Should he bolt for the door to dodge the gooey state of his sister? But he didn't doubt Ron would be getting that gushy call shortly. *Ugh—where's the bucket.* 'So, are you going to take that hearing test? Ron said he'd take you.'

'I...' Tina's shoulders sagged as she fidgeted with her fingers on the table.

'You made me see Zara against my will,' said Ward.

Tina stuck her chin out, head high, and looked down her nose at him. 'And you're better now.'

'You'll never know if this might work for you, too, if you don't try?'

'Your brother's right. Remember all that fuss Brendan made, refusing to see Zara that first time—and now they're seeing each other.' Shirley reached over and patted her son's hand. 'I like Zara, and you two would make such a lovely couple, dear.'

'What?' Tina screwed her nose up at her brother. 'You and Zara?'

'Yes. So stop thinking Ron's got the hots for Zara when he doesn't.' But he was glad he saw Zara today, even though she got all shy on him. But he did get a kiss and cuddle in the carpark. Then she drove away from him again, with Tim making faces at him out the ute's passenger window. But he had tomorrow. 'So come on, Mum, please look after Max so I can take Zara out for dinner.'

'Not for the first week.'

'Where are you going?' Tina asked, reaching for some cake.

'Dunno, they've only got a pub out there. But I want to do something special, the lady deserves it.'

'Really?' Mother and daughter grinned at each other and then at Ward.

'Early days, you two,' he said, hiding his smile behind his cup. 'Hey, Tina, you must have an idea of what's good for a first date, right?'

'You're asking me?' Tina stabbed her thumb at her chest.

'I know, it's shocking for me too, but you've been on more first dates than anyone I know.' That included his whole team combined. 'You must have an opinion. Please.'

'Wow.' Tina rested her elbows on the table, her palms

covered her mouth, and stared at her brother.

'Oh, my boy.' Shirley covered her mouth same as Tina's, with tears in her eyes. 'We'll help you.' She reached across and patted his hand, then nudged Tina with her elbow. 'Won't we, Tina?'

'No weird stuff. I don't do that, and Zara doesn't either.'

Tina kangaroo-hopped her seat closer to the table asking, 'Do you want something romantic?'

'Yeah.'

'A candlelight dinner,' said Shirley.

'Yeah.'

'With flowers and music,' said Tina.

'Okay?' *O-oh.* He grimaced at the spark in their eyes that was about to become a bushfire. It didn't hurt to ask, and he was never shy about asking. But the weirdest part was he'd asked his sister for help and listened to her ideas. And that never happened. Ever.

Until now.

Twenty-Four

'Yo, I bring food,' shouted Mills, walking through Ward's front door with a large tray in hand. Sam and Nick were setting up the table for their poker game in the lounge, while Max sulked on the floor.

'What did you bring?' Nick asked, shuffling the chairs around the table.

'Mum's lasagne and more cake-of-the-day.' Mills put the dishes on the kitchen bench.

'Nice,' chorused the boys.

'What's with Max? Has he got couch-surfing sickness?' Mills asked, patting the sulky dog.

'Max is going home.' Nick gave a half-hearted shrug, carrying another chair from the kitchen to the card table.

'When?' Mills asked.

'This afternoon,' replied Sam, sorting out the playing cards and coloured chips.

'That blows. Hey, Ward?' called out Mills.

Ward had overheard all while making his bed. He blinked at the made-up bed with dirty clothes in hand he actually tossed into the empty wash basket because he'd done a load earlier while he'd cleaned his room. *What's going on?*

Ward picked up his duffel and closed the door to his tidy room. 'Yes, Mills.'

'How come you're taking Max home? You said a week, and Max's week doesn't end until Monday. You haven't had enough time to bond yet.'

Ward held up his palm to calm the passionate Mills, hoping to avoid a repeat of what he'd been through earlier with Sam and Nick. 'Sorry, decision's been made. I'm going back out there tonight.'

'You're going out? Tonight? You can't. You're meant to be resting for tomorrow's game, dude. We all know how hard you've worked to get back on the team.'

'I'm not ruining my chances when I've just got back. I'm not that stupid,' Ward said, grabbing his car keys and sunglasses from his shelf on the bookcase.

Mills crossed his beefy arms over his chest and asked, 'Where are you going?'

'Ward's got a hot date with Zara,' Nick said, shuffling out beer coasters across the table with a big grin.

'Full of it, when we all know Ward doesn't bother dating,' said Mills, jabbing at the air between himself and Ward.

'I do too.'

'No, you don't.'

'Okay, I do now.'

Sam put a stack of drinking glasses on the table and said, 'You should hear what lover-boy has got planned for tonight.'

'Oi, leave off.' Ward shouldn't have said anything to his mates, yet, hoped it was worth it.

'I think it's a good idea. If I found a worthy lady, I'd make the effort,' Nick said.

'Zara is worth it,' Ward admitted more to himself. But still…

'Didn't Zara say you were suffering some nurses love thing?' Mills asked with his nose screwed up at Ward.

'Florence Nightingale Syndrome, dufus.' Ward ruffled up Mills' mullet. He might not be too bright but he was passionate about everything.

Swiping Ward's hands away, Mills tidied his glossy mop of hair. 'Yeah, that. Didn't she tell you to cool it?'

'But our main man didn't,' said Sam, snatching a handful of peanuts he placed on the table. 'When are we gonna meet her?'

'Why, no rush?' Ward shrugged.

'So we can check her out,' Mills said, lifting his chin as he hitched up his jeans and puffed out his barrel chest. 'Or, are you scared our good looks and charm are gonna steal her away from you?'

'No.' Ward frowned as he turned away and picked up his bag.

Nick said in a lowered tone, 'We wouldn't do that to you, Ward.'

'We'd never let a woman ruin a friendship, mate,' said Sam with a nod.

'I know.' Ward trusted the men in this house. He'd never do it to them either, it was part of the mates' code. Well, it was supposed to be.

But there were some things he didn't need to share with the team.

Ward frowned, staring at his keys. It was the first time he'd thought like that and believed it too. 'I'm outta here. Say goodbye to Max.' Max stood at the sound of his name.

'Oh man, that blows big time. My mum was gonna start baking biscuits for Max.' Mills patted the pit bull and said, 'Max, your ugliness makes me look pretty, and I'll gladly share man-couch duties with you, anytime.'

Sam passed a bag to Ward. 'Max's bowl, dry food, and leads are in there.' Sam then crouched down and gave Max a good pat. 'See ya, mate, you can come back anytime. Shame Ward said no.'

'In the bag is Max's organic oatmeal dog wash, and that bamboo massaging bristle brush he loves.' Nick sighed as he gave Max the farewell pat. 'Sorry I didn't think much of you in the beginning, Max, but you're a good dog. Our door is open anytime you want to run away.'

'Come on, Max.' Ward opened the door and Max followed slowly with head down and tucked under tail.

'Bye Max, hope you find a good home you deserve, dude,' cried out Mills, waving.

'You're a champion in our eyes, Max,' said Sam, standing beside Mills.

Nick joined the group and waved alongside them. 'You're a real winner, Max. We'll never forget you, mate.'

Ward blinked, open-mouthed at his housemates. The three men looked like they were about to cry over a dog that hadn't been in the house for a week. A dog who'd never been invited.

Ward opened his car's passenger door. 'Come on, Max, get in.'

The dog clambered into his seat and faced Ward with crinkled furry brow and pleading eyes.

'I don't know how to look after you, Max, and I haven't been doing that because everyone else has been looking after you for me. I'm sorry, mate, but you deserve better than me, being stuck in a house in suburbia with a view of a fence. Out there you have a large yard and soil that's soft to run on. It's paradise, mate. And…' It was more than he could give a dog who deserved so much better.

Ward closed the car door. His mates still stood by the front door waving Max off, as Ward drove away feeling like the arsehole of the year.

Twenty-Five

'**A**re you nervous?' Stacey asked, seated on Zara's reading chair beside the dressing table. The cupboard doors were wide-open exposing a half empty closet, while assorted dresses covered Zara's bed.

'No.' Zara pulled on her woollen dress and her hands trembled doing up the zip. 'Yes.'

'I think it's sweet. I've never been on a date before.' Stacey started returning the dresses to the closet and pulled out a light blue silk scarf. 'Here, wear this scarf, it's the same colour as your eyes. You look nice. Sexy.'

'Thanks.' Zara didn't feel sexy, she felt fake, wrapping the scarf around her throat like she did with all her scarves.

'Not like that.' Stacey stylishly re-knotted it around Zara's neck. 'You need to accessorise accordingly, yep, Ward's eyes are gonna pop seeing you like this.'

'Doubt it.'

'I can't remember the last time I saw you all dressed

up,' said Stacey, scooping up the remaining dresses off the bed and returned them to the closet.

Putting her shoes back in the cupboard, Zara closed the door. She'd never been into fashion, they never had the money, and living on a farm working before dawn, social lives didn't exist much. 'It's been a while.' Almost half a decade. 'Thanks for your help.' She'd be wearing her jeans and sock-drawer-surprise if she'd been left to her own devices.

'This is the first date I've seen you go on since I've moved in. Hair down.' Stacey plucked the hair clip that unravelled Zara's bun. 'When was your last date?'

Zara shrugged, fidgeting with her scarf.

'Not with your ex, right?'

'I need a beer.' Zara headed for her bright kitchen.

'How come you won't talk about it?'

'Nothing to talk about.' She'd never discussed what happened with anyone. It was no one's business. 'Do I crack open a beer now?' Noting the time on her kitchen clock. Could she fake a sickness and hide with the dust bunnies under her bed?

'You can wait.' Stacey closed the fridge on Zara. 'Tim said Ward's totally into you.'

'Okay, and Tim would know, how?' Her own laugh

didn't sound true. Why was she so nervous?

Because it was a first date.

A date with Ward.

But she knew Ward, who was a client. *Was.*

'Tim said when Ward first saw you working on that horse yesterday, it was like the guy went into some la-la dreamland.'

'What?' Zara arched an eyebrow at Stacey.

'That's what Tim called it. He swears Ward zoned out while gawking at you and didn't hear a word Tim was saying, and they were standing right next to each other.'

'Come on, we all know the boys like to exaggerate their stories. Don't make it more than what it is.'

'Well, what is it then?'

'A first date.' Zara wiped her sweaty palms on her dress. They'd all teased her about her date, yet her dad said nothing. For a man who loved a chat, it was rare for her father to be silent. She'd never dated when living at home, because in a small town everyone knew each other, making this her first date at home. Ever.

Was it too late to hide?

The greyhounds barked and Stacey peered through the front windows. 'Ward's here.' She grabbed Zara's hand and started dragging her towards the door. 'Come on, I wanna see his face when he gets a load of you.'

'This is embarrassing.' Why did she agree to do this?

* * *

Ward parked his car behind Joe's Holden. Getting out, he waved at Adam and Tim setting up the television on the back veranda. Goliath, the Shetland pony, stood staring at the beer fridge door. Horses grazed in paddocks, lifting their heads at all the fuss, while the greyhounds sniffed around his car's tyres. It was such a different world compared to his place.

'Hey man, you're all spiffed-up,' called out Tim with Adam making their way over.

'Oi, whose fancy wheels?' Billy asked, carrying Toby on his shoulders, on his way back from the shed.

'Mine.' Ward opened the passenger door and Max clambered out of the car.

'MAX,' called out Toby with tiny fingers reaching for the big dog.

'No, bro, tell me you did not bring the dog back,' said Billy, lowering the toddler from his shoulders who rushed to hug the dog.

'He's here, isn't he?' Adam said, pointing at the dog being patted by Toby.

'Dammit, I've lost the bet,' whined Billy.

'What bet?' Ward asked.

'The one I had with Joe. I was gunning for you, bro.'

Billy shook his head, sliding his palms into the back pockets of his jeans as he kicked at a stone in the dirt.

'What were you betting on?'

'My fault on that one,' said Joe, coming from the shed. 'How you doin', mate? You look better than your last visit.' He held out his hand.

Ward shook Joe's large callused palm. 'Fine, sir.' Zara's father was betting against him? He was used to people doing footy-tippings in the office like his own father did. Gamblers bet on the win, or for the first goal and who'd get best player, it happened every game. So what was Joe's bet about?

'Heard you've got a game tomorrow. Same possie?'

'Yes.' Ward smiled wide. He loved his job and was looking forward to it.

'Good. We'll win for sure.'

'Hope so.' Ward opened his car boot. 'I come bearing gifts this time. There's two cartons of beer for letting me stay over.' He passed the boxes to Adam and Tim. 'And this is for all of you.' He lifted a large duffel bearing the Club's logo, dropped it on the lawn, and opened the zip wide to reveal a mash of material. 'Find what fits. Help yourselves.' He pulled out scarves, beanies, shirts, coolers, towels, cushions, all sorts of Saint's memorabilia from the fan club's store. 'Tim, there might be a new cap in there for you, I've put in every style they had for you to choose.'

Tim tapped the brim of his frayed cap and grinned. 'Dunno, mate, not when I've only just broken this hat in.'

'Check this out.' Billy grabbed a scarf and wrapped it around his neck.

'There's an outfit in there for Toby too.' Ward needed to impress one more male in this household and from the back seat he pulled out a large, heavy, wrapped parcel. 'Joe, this is for you.' He hoped this worked.

'You brought beer, mate, that's enough. It's not Christmas,' said Joe, holding the wide thin package with two hands.

'Me open?' Toby reached up with little fingers and Joe bent down to the toddler who tore at the simple brown paper. 'What is it?' The boy looked at the picture.

'That's my game-day Guernsey, signed by the team and the coach, with our last club photo. It's a collector's item, Joe.' His teammates had willingly signed it when he'd explained to them it was for Joe who'd made Zara visit Ward in the first place.

'The whole team?' Joe held up the frame in the light and the boys all crowded around. Joe's jaw opened and closed but nothing was said as his glassy eyes widened.

'The entire team.' Ward was proud he'd made the effort. 'That envelope stuck on the side, that's a seasonal family pass to watch us play our home games. Even if the season's started, there's still enough home games to play yet.'

'Bloody hell,' muttered Adam as his almond-shaped eyes widened.

Tim gripped his frayed cap with two hands as if it

was going to blow away. 'Season pass, no way.'

Billy snatched the envelope and opened it. 'Hello, golden tickets, brothers.' He waved them in the air.

Joe looked at the picture, the clothes, and the tickets Billy was using as a fan. 'This—it's too much. The beer was enough, mate.'

'Zara told me her fee was to give you a carton of beer and an autograph.'

'I'd meant a simple signature on a beer coaster.' Joe held up the picture like a priceless trophy. 'I dunno what to say there, mate.'

'How about thank you, Dad?' Zara stood behind them; hands tucked under her chin with tears in her eyes.

'Ah, thank you,' mumbled Joe.

'Wow.' Ward swallowed as he stared at Zara. Not wearing her jeans, but in a dress that kissed the curves he wanted to follow with his palm. Her makeup accentuated her eyes and plump lips he wanted to kiss, and now. 'You're gorgeous.' He was drawn to her, inhaling her floral perfume, sliding a palm across the soft fabric on her lower back.

'Thank you,' replied Zara as the colour rose in her cheek.

'That's so sweet,' gushed out Stacey beside them.

Zara rolled her eyes and mumbled, 'They're all watching, it's embarrassing.'

'Don't care. You're beautiful,' whispered Ward, as he kissed her cheek. 'Stunning.'

'Aww, he's whispering sweet nothings. Why can't I have a date like that,' cried out Stacey, hugging herself.

'Stacey?' Zara blushed brighter as the boys laughed.

'Come on, let me rescue you then.' Ward grabbed Zara's soft hand and led her to the passenger seat. 'Has Zara got a curfew, Joe?'

'What?' Joe looked up at Ward, with large frame in hand, blinking at his daughter.

'No,' snapped out Zara getting into the passenger seat. 'Have a good night, Dad.'

'You look pretty, luv.' Joe watched with stern face and arms full.

'What are we doing with Max?' Billy pointed to the sulking dog that lay on the grass watching Ward's every move.

Ward opened the back door. 'Get in, Max.' The pit bull leaped into the back and his stumpy tail thump-thump-thumped on the seat.

'Bet's still on, Joe,' said Billy, wearing three scarves, two beanies, a cap, a team flag over his shoulders and a beach towel wrapped around his waist. Beside him, Toby wore a footy guernsey like a long dress, footy socks covered his arms like gloves, playing peek-a-boo from beneath a beanie that covered his entire head.

'What bet?' Asked Zara from the front seat.

'Never you mind, have a good night, luv,' Joe said, giving her a short nod of his Akubra.

'We will.' Ward closed Zara's door and jogged

around to the driver's seat. Phase one had the family happy, who stood in a row and waved Ward's car off as they headed down the long driveway.

Now he hoped phase two would go just as smoothly.

*　*　*

Zara clutched her fingers tight in her lap, while Ward steered onto the road that ran along the front of the farm. 'Are we going to the pub?'

'Nope.' He gave her a side-grin.

'So where, if you've brought Max.' She turned around and gave Max a pat on the head, she'd missed him. 'Max, you look good, your coat is so shiny. Have you been stealing the boys' locker room deodorants? Coz, honey, you smell so nice.'

Ward laughed. 'I didn't buy the dog deodorant, Nick got him stuff. Didn't know they had dog deodorant.'

'You could create one and market it to your sponsors.' Teasing the man as she patted Max's glossy coat, noticing the strong muscular tone in the pit bull's chest and shoulders. 'Couldn't you find anyone to babysit Max tonight?'

'Mum wouldn't, but my housemates would've, that's for sure.' He sighed as he gripped the steering wheel.

Was Ward ready to give up the dog?

They drove along the road and turned left down a dirt track and through an open gate.

'Hey, we're still on the property?' Zara sat forwards as they reached the top of the hill. She frowned at the view of farmlands with the town in the distance. 'Why are we here?'

'You said this was your favourite place on the property.'

'It is, I love this lookout, but I thought you said dinner?' Considering she'd gotten all dressed up for the occasion.

'I did.' He parked the car, let Max out, jogged around and opened her door, holding out his hand. 'Come on.'

She slid her hand into Ward's as if it was the most natural thing to do. Yet her skin bristled from his touch that squirrelled a lick of delicious heat along her arm to her scalp.

He led her to the edge. Thumbing over the scar on his chin, he watched her, waiting for her reaction. 'I hope you like this?'

Zara stopped and blinked as if clearing her vision. 'I don't believe it?'

A table had been set with bright yellow and purple flowers as the crackle of burning wood came from a chimenea that warmed the area. Assorted Moroccan lamps dotted the edge of the plush rugs that lay beneath the table, set before the view of the countryside with its various crops in blocks of colour like a patchwork quilt. Behind it all was the sunset that stretched a fiery red glow across the horizon, chased by a mauve line leading the night.

'You did this?' Her palms covered her mouth as she took in all the incredible details. The table was set with colourful crockery and beautiful chunky glasses that were stylish art pieces themselves. It complimented large teak chairs and stout candles ready to light for their dinner under the stars.

'Do you like it?' Ward pulled out her chair that held sumptuous colourful cushions.

'I do. This is amazing. This chair is like a lounge chair. How? When.' *Why*. She'd never met a man who'd done this for her.

How many women had he done this for in the past?

'I had help.'

'Who, how? I'm sorry I'm repeating myself, but...' She watched him pour a cocktail from a bottle he had in an esky.

'This is a non-alcoholic mojito. I like it to go with the heat on some of these dishes. I've got some beer and a batch of margaritas, if you want?' Grabbing some smaller dishes that were on the Mexican heater's grill, he put them onto the one serving dish in the centre of their table.

'I'll try this, thanks.' Her stomach grumbled with hunger at the brown bag containing corn chips artfully arranged amongst assorted dips and salsas. There were melted cheese-covered potato skins, mouth-watering pinwheels, and delicate lettuce cups displaying vibrantly coloured foods matching the cocktail's cool green.

Ward uncovered the pre-prepared dog bowl and

placed it next to the water dish. 'Here, Max, I didn't forget you.' The dog shadowed him with that stumpy tail wagging as he sniffed at the tasty treats.

Ward patted the dog, then approached the table with rolled towels. 'Dinner is cutlery optional and since we've both been patting the dog.'

Zara grabbed the rolled wet towel and cleaned her hands, amazed in the details. Flames flickered at the open mouth of the cast iron chimenea, where on one side sat a tray covered with foil. Ward was very prepared.

She sipped her drink where the lime was invigorating against her dry throat. She put down the heavy goblet with trembling hands, scared she was going to spill it. 'These glasses are gorgeous. The cutlery, the plates, I love the colours. How?'

'Not what you're expecting?' Ward sat in his seat and reached for his glass.

'Dinner, yes. Candles, maybe. But this? It's amazing.' The large coloured lanterns of stained glass glinted against the dying sunlight, she couldn't wait for darkness to see them shine.

'Here, try this,' he said, holding out the platter. 'Max even got a special feed too. Mum's been cooking for the dog.'

'I can picture your mum doing that too.' She took one of the small lettuce cups and bit into it, releasing a flavour explosion on her tongue. The spice of chilli, beans, and zest of lime married superbly with the smooth creamy guacamole and the crisp crunch of lettuce. 'This is brilliant.'

'I like Mexican food.'

'I only know tacos and nachos. What is this? It's fabulous,' she asked, taking another flavoursome bite.

'There's nachos in various dipping sauces—I love my nachos,' he said, coating a nacho chip in chunky, rich, red sauce, topping it with guacamole. 'In the lettuce cups you have the Mexican street black bean and corn, the other is shrimp and guacamole. That's the coriander lime chicken tortilla pinwheels—my favourite.'

'This is the entrée?' *The man was a foodie?*

'For mains we have slow cooked Mexican beef burritos.'

'You like Mexican?' Zara was so glad she'd been too nervous to eat all day. The Mexican setting was fun, vibrant, and romantic too.

'I like the food and drink, and these colours are pretty cool.'

'You wouldn't know you liked bright colours.' The plates were like a fiesta for the eyes.

'Why do you say that?'

'Your place is this masculine black and brown theme, with a bit of red on that huge team flag on your living room wall.'

'True. Not like yours. Open and colourful. I thought you might like Mexican from your painted cactus pebbles on the veranda, and your colourful socks.'

'I do like it. I haven't indulged or looked in-depth at

that culture or food yet, but this is sensational.' She picked a corn chip and scooped up some dip. 'I like these plates, and these goblets too, are they yours?' Now she was rambling.

'They are now. I'm almost a grown-up.' He grinned, flicking the napkin open and putting it on his lap. 'I now own a set of plates, cutlery and glasses.'

'You don't, in that house?'

'Its Club supplied, fully furnished. I only own my clothes, bed, car, the chair, and now cutlery.' He chuckled, lifting up the fork he polished on the sleeve of his shirt. 'These plates are chunky enough for my big hands, I'm not scared to break them.'

'It feels like a summer party in the middle of winter. It's brilliant. Did you cook too?'

'Nah, I wish. Dinner is from my favourite Mexican restaurant and this is the chef's selection.'

'Wow, you went all out. How many times have you done this?' Biting on the burst of spicy shrimp against the cool of guacamole and the crunch of lettuce. Each bite was a dance on her tongue, even though she wanted to hold her breath for Ward's answer to her question.

'Never.' He shrugged his shoulders and popped the loaded corn chip into his mouth. 'I wanted you to be comfortable, and you said this was your favourite place.'

'It is. I'm honoured.' Overwhelmed and hungry, trying to not stuff her face silly. *But come on*, the guy was a good-looking footballer who could have anyone. Why her?

'You date, don't you?' Bugger her mouth speaking first, and filled it with more food. She didn't need to know his past love life, because she didn't want to speak about hers.

'I've done the restaurant thing twice with this one other girl...' He winced and gulped his drink down, focusing his amber eyes on her. 'I don't date.'

So why was he doing this now? Ward didn't owe her anything, he'd paid her fees with all the gifts for her family.

It also confirmed he was a player. 'I see.' She sat straighter, fidgeting with her goblet's thick stem. Confused at the effort he'd put into tonight. Why bother, when he had his own fan club for hookups. He didn't need to date. So what was this?

He leaned back in his chair and grinned at the outdoor dinner setting. 'If my mates could see me now, they wouldn't believe it.'

She could hardly believe it herself. 'How long did it take to organise this?'

'We planned it yesterday and did the running around today, and we rushed setting-up before I picked you up.'

She reached for another crunchy chip. 'We?'

He shuffled in his chair and grinned at her across the table. 'You won't believe this—'

'I'm still amazed by all of this, so bring it on.'

'I like this side of you.'

She covered her mouth to stop her snort-laugh while trying to swallow her food. 'I like this.' Waving her hand at the setting, the food, the effort he'd made was incredible.

'Well, after you agreed to dinner, I visited my mum, when my sister showed up.'

'Has Tina had her hearing test?'

'Yeah, Mum and I took her this morning, and you were right.'

'I didn't want to be. I shouldn't have said anything.'

'Hey…' He reached for her hand. 'I'm glad you did because Tina's getting hearing aids, and you'd be pleased to know we didn't kill each other.'

'No way. Don't you two argue?' She couldn't stop smiling if she tried. The food warmed her and the setting was amazing. This was her first date—would it be her last?

* * *

'I'll admit, my sister and I argue all the time. Tina and I are so different and Mum's always playing peacemaker.'

'Saw that.'

'I doubt you'd miss much.' He grinned at her as he sipped his mocktail. 'But when I asked my sister—who's been on more first dates than anyone I know—and with the help of Mum and her classic carrot cake, we came up with this idea.' It'd been the first time he'd actually had a conversation with Tina in decades. 'I rang Tim and got him to unlock the gate for me, said he'd keep it a secret.' With a promise of a carton and new cap.

'Tim said nothing.' Her eyes shone at the surprise.

'Good.' Ward felt his heart expand in his chest at the sight of her double-dimple smile. Zara's expression was worth enduring his sister's chalkboard-screeching voice and incense cloud. He'd do it all again just for that smile. 'The plates, glasses, and these chairs are from my sister's shop.'

'Your sister has a store?'

'I thought it was all incense and tie-dyed stuff, I avoided it because that's not my scene. Today was the first time I'd visited in a long time and it's packed with all sorts of stuff from all these exotic countries. Tina picked all this gear out.' He'd been surprised his sister understood his taste and style, considering her lack of wardrobe ethics. 'Tina drove out with Mum to help me set up, and they loaned me their lanterns, chair and the rugs. The chimenea is Dad's. I'd bought it for him one year, he uses it when they go away, kind of like camping in style.'

'You go camping much?'

'It's rare. During summer holidays as a kid, where Dad's idea of camping is going to caravan parks near the sea.' The entire journey involved the siblings bickering in the back seat with his mum playing peacekeeper while his dad zoned out, driving.

'That'd be nice.' She took a bite of the salsa, her eyes rolled, her pink tongue flickered on her plump, lickable lips. 'This food is amazing.'

He sat taller, proud of the effort he'd made. 'My favourite food.' Yeah, he'd already said that. *Duh*. At least he didn't have to worry about table manners because Mexican food was messy and fun to eat. He watched as she tried more dishes and her eyes glistened with the last of the sunset. He had a blanket for later where they might cuddle-up next to the heater under the stars. And he had to admit, Tina was a genius at her tips and tricks for *First Date Do and Dont's*.

'I told Mum how you've got Joe doing Tai Chi, she's going to look into that with Tina.'

'Really?'

'Oh yeah, and...' They chatted over their meal, watching the sunset with Max stretched out before the flickering flames of the Mexican heater under a cloudless night where the sky soon filled with stars. It was perfect.

Twenty-Six

'**A**re you nervous?' Zara asked.

Ward, with his arm wrapped around her shoulders, he held her close to his side as she escorted him to his car.

In six hours, he would be standing in the middle of a stadium full of screaming fans. Yet here he stood in the serenity of the countryside where horses grazed in emerald fields beneath clouds that floated like overfull marshmallows. A dog barked, a horse neighed, and chickens clucked. But there was no one else, except the most amazing woman before him. Wrapping his arms around her slender waist, he admired her hair that was the colour of summer. It contrasted with her eyes that matched this morning's winter sky.

'I don't get nervous before games anymore. Used to in the beginning.' He'd been nervous about last night's dinner, scared of her reaction—which went better than expected. Would he be nervous today?

He'd been so distracted by her, he hadn't thought about the game until now. How was that possible?

'When did you get nervous before playing? On the

first whistle thingy?'

'Siren.' He grinned at her lack of game knowledge. 'I dunno, it's been a while.' Stroking the soft strands of her fringe from her eyes, he tucked them behind her dainty ear. 'It used to be just before we ran onto the field, that's when it'd hit me the most. The rest of it's the waiting, keeping occupied, stretching, and prepping before I play. I know how to keep busy.' Nuzzling below her earlobe and delicate neck, he watched the prickles rush across her skin.

She squirmed as the blush glowed softly on her cheeks. 'Have you got the energy for today?'

'If I didn't have to go, we'd still be in bed.' He brought her close, chest to chest, kissing her lips he just couldn't stop kissing.

'You don't want to be late.' She pressed her palms against his chest, breaking from his embrace and stepped back.

He frowned at the distance, now cold away from her.

Zara wrapped the blanket around herself like a shawl, covering last night's dress. 'If you get nervous and feel it's all too much—'

'I won't.' *The woman cared, awesome.* Unable to help himself, he pulled her back to his chest. He liked her close, especially when he knew she was naked under that dress.

'Just in case, feel free to call me, okay?'

'Will you answer?' His eyebrow arched, resting his forehead against hers.

'I will today.'

'And every other day I call.'

'Pushy, huh?'

Yet it was her palms pressing against his chest trying to push him away, again.

'I go after what I like. If you hadn't realised, Z, you're my favourite.'

Her eyes narrowed at him. 'Like a favourite brand of chocolate or TV-show-of-the-moment?'

'Not like that. More than that.' He pressed his lips against hers to stop his mouth from making more of a mess. Holding her body close, he didn't want to let go of her at all.

'Wow.' Her beautiful eyes were glazed, blinking up at him as if to regain her focus.

'See you soon.' He winked at her and turned to his car where Max sat waiting by the door with head low. He wiped his mouth, looking at the dog's pleading eyes.

Ward opened his car door and the dog whimpered.
Damn.

Ward slid his thumbs into his jeans' pockets, tilting his head at the dog. 'Max...' He paused his prepared speech—but he couldn't say it. 'Get in.'

The dog leaped inside before Ward had finished speaking. His huge fawn rump filled the passenger window until he found the perfect spot to sit. With a wide gummy smile, his black tongue flicked across his furry face, and the thump-thump-thumping tail tap-danced against the leather seat.

'You're taking Max home, huh?' Zara wrapped her arms around herself as she smiled into her blanketed arms as if covering her lips from the cold. But her eyes shone brightly with joy that warmed his own heart.

He couldn't be a prick. Not now. But still…

'You have until Monday, focus on the game first, please.'

It was as if the woman had read his mind.

'Good luck today, you'll do well.'

'Thank you.' The belief she showed him made him hug her more. 'I'll talk to you soon.'

He drove along the long gravel driveway, watching Zara wave him off through the rear-view mirror. He was going to come back soon. Very soon.

Onto the main road, he glanced at the massive hulking frame of the dog in the front seat. 'Do you think Zara will want to do this as a permanent thing with me?' He looked at the dog who sniffed at him. 'She's special, and you're just ugly, you know that.' He chuckled at Max with his half-chewed ears, covered in scars.

Yet there was an increase in the muscle tone and strength to Max. All that running was paying off and the light tanned coat had a shine to it. 'My housemates will be glad to see you. Not sure if I'll share my new crockery with them though.' Ward laughed. He owned crockery and cutlery, all for one dinner date. Did that make him domesticated?

'Just so we're clear, this is until Monday.' He had his

excuse to return when he had Monday off and knew Zara did too. 'I'll make my decision then, okay? Can't believe I'm talking to a dog.' Which was starting to become a regular thing.

Max gave him that sad, puppy-dog stare as if he understood.

Ward dodged a black-tongue flick. 'Don't do doggy kisses.' Not when he had Zara to kiss. 'You did well last night. You're a good dog.' He patted the dog's big head, bringing on another round of thump-thump-thumping taps of the tail.

But Ward had other things to focus on as he drove towards town. Today was game day, where he'd prove to the coach and those sceptics that he'd recovered. He was fit enough to play, but knew they were waiting to see if he was mentally fit too.

'I'll show them all.' Ward drove back to the city to get ready for the game. He loved the game. He loved his job. Did he love Zara too?

Twenty-Seven

Ten minutes before game time, all the players were in the changeroom beneath the stadium. Physio's strapped up limbs while assistant coaches shared their re-spun speeches. Twenty-two men wore the Club's game-day black, red and white uniform. Some sat and did deep breathing, as if meditating. Some bounced a ball against the wall. Others paced the floor like wildcats. While others leaned against the walls, heads down with earbuds in, listening to music or motivational podcasts.

Seated in front of his locker, Ward watched them prance about with the jitters, jumping and flexing before the siren.

'Well, what d'ya know?' Zara was right about footballers being two-legged thoroughbreds. All that attention to muscle strength, reflexes, agility training, and cardio, all for this one moment. The more he looked, the more similarities he found between the two sports.

Ward glanced at his game-day uniform, the shirt, the shorts, the long socks, and the footy boots. It felt foreign, not having worn it in his three weeks away from the game.

He blinked as the internal visions hurtled through

him from the last time he'd worn this uniform. The wet rain, the cold wind, the salty sweat stinging his eyes as he leaped for the ball, clambering over teammate's backs. The lightning flashed and thunder rumbled, as his fingertips reached for that ball spinning in the dark skies, then it all came crashing down.

He winced, bracing himself, slapping palms over his ears as he lowered his head between his knees. He panted as muscles tensed, trembling with fear that led a fine sheen of perspiration across his skin. The pain of plummeting to earth spiked like a spear ramming along his spine and into his neck. It hit in a massive wave so deep, so heavy, his heart boomed in his ears with each pound of his pulse. His lungs squeezed. It hurt to breathe. Hands fisted with whitening knuckles against his scalp, he shivered in a mass of tight muscle.

Lost, he turned away from his teammates and spotted his mobile that lay beside Zara's painted pebble in the pocket of his sports-bag. Fear gripped him hard as he clutched the cold stone in his hand and forced himself to breathe. With the other hand, his thumb stabbed a number in his phone. 'Pick up. Pick up.' His head dropped as he squeezed his eyes shut tight. The pumping blood pounded in his ears, competing with his phone's dial tone. 'Pick up. Pick up. Please, pick up.'

'Hi,' said Zara's soft voice over the phone and he sighed at the sound.

'Thank god.'

'Nervous, huh?'

Was this a panic attack? He sniffed at the stale sweaty locker room air that tasted like a bad acidic medicine at the back of his throat. 'Just hit me.' Whatever this was, it was like he'd been trampled by an entire team of players attacking him for the ball.

'Keep deep breathing and roll those shoulders for me.'

He croaked out, 'Okay.' Used to taking orders he did as instructed. 'Just keep talking, please.' The sound of her voice was soothing and the pebble in his hand was warming. He filled his lungs and exhaled, hoping to release the stress gripping his shoulders. How did she know his shoulders would be like this?

'I'm guessing your uniform might've been a trigger.'

'I've never been like this, Z.' Where was his backbone now? Had he regressed to the fears of a boy playing his first game?

'You have.'

Frowning, he sat straighter facing the locker with his back to the room. 'No, I haven't.'

'Yes, you have. When you first saw your fall on the TV it must've sparked the nightmares you suffered that night.'

'I don't remember having any nightmares.' Then he remembered he'd woken before her fireplace on the stormy night his memory had returned and kept reliving the fall. 'I remember you were there.' She'd rubbed his back and her voice soothed him back to sleep. *Was that real?*

'I didn't leave your side that night.'

Again, he sighed with relief, and the icy grip around his soul was exchanged with a warmth that flooded through his chest.

'You've been through this before. You've faced your demons and worked through them yourself. You jumped off a horse the same height you fell and landed squarely on your feet.'

'But you were there to catch me.'

'I didn't need to catch you because I believed you'd do it. You got yourself there. It was you who had the courage to face your fears, and you did it.'

'You helped me.'

'But you had to want to do it for yourself first. It's you who has always had that belief in yourself.'

'Me?'

'You were the one willing to take that chance and let me work on you. It was you who went running in the mornings, not me. It was you who lifted hay bales and pushed and pulled gates and continued training. You climbed onto that horse, not me. All I did was guide you because you had that courage to try.'

He opened his palm and stared at the intricate details of the tree she'd painted onto the flat pebble. It was so small and delicate in his hand, comforting him like the lady herself. 'You've been there for me, Z.'

'I'm here now.'

'Where?' He sat up, looking over his shoulder to the other men performing their own pre-game preps.

'Here at the game.'

He felt that warmth in his chest spread through his limbs as his grin grew with hope. 'Here at the stadium?'

'Yep, the whole family is here.'

'For real?' From the open doorway the echo of the roaring crowd filtered into the room like unseen ghosts crawling across the ceiling.

'You gave us season passes for home games, so there's no way we'd miss your return game. We even raided Toby's paints and used old bedsheets to make homemade banners with your name all over them. It's like we're your personal cheer squad.' Her giggle chipped away the last of the fear.

With relief and pride, he covered his mouth with the fingers that clutched the pebble. She was here. His Zara was here, he could almost cry with joy.

What was wrong with him to be so emotional?

'Now don't you disappoint us, okay? We didn't put up with Stacey's driving for nothing, you know.'

Ward smiled, wiping the fine layer of sweat from his face, as he chuckled at her comment. 'I'll admit, Stacey is a shocker behind the wheel.' A teenager who drove so slowly he'd jogged right past her on the farm's track, beating her home. *Home?*

He sat taller, rolling his shoulders, wriggling his toes in his shoes, as the spike of adrenalin coursed through his veins. 'Where in the stadium are you, Z?'

'On the left side of where you guys run out of the change rooms. We're a few rows back from the fence line, Dad says they're great seats. We've got *Ward rules* as our banners, so I'm apologising upfront because they're embarrassing. The boys are decked out in every bit of Club gear you gave them, and I'm the one ducking for cover, just like you do with your sister, pretending they don't belong to me.'

Her laugh made him laugh with her, picturing her double-dimple smile.

'So, are you okay now?' Zara asked.

Ward gave a slow grin, there was no more fear as his focus returned. 'I'm good, knowing you're here.' It was the truth. He gripped the pebble as if feeling her strength and held it to his heart.

'You bet we're here. Have you ever tried to get four men, two women, and a toddler into one car—its chaos. So please, have a great game, we'll be cheering you on.'

'Thank you, Z, I appreciate that and I'm glad you answered my call.'

'Said I would.'

'*One Minute,*' came the cry from the assistant coach and the surrounding men moved to their feet.

'Can you stay for after the game?' It was game time, and he should be focusing on the game now. But here he was planning for after the game—he'd never done that before.

'Um?'

'Please?' If it wasn't so close to game time, he'd run out there and look for her.

'Okay.' Her reply was so quiet amongst the crowd.

'Great. I'll tell the steward; they'll come and see you with a pass.'

'Don't go to any trouble.'

It was no trouble, he'd do anything for her. He'd done everything she'd asked that got him to this moment—to play.

Locker doors slammed and the soles of footy boots clacked along the concrete floors. Liniments and last-minute bandage strappings were applied as players gathered by the closed door waiting to run through the tunnel and out onto the field. It reminded him of the thoroughbreds milling around the back of the chutes on the racetrack, prior to getting locked behind the starter gates—another similarity between the two sports.

'Z, I've gotta go.'

'About time you got out there and looked busy.'

'I will.' He smiled wide at the phone.

'And take no prisoners.'

'Where did that come from?' He chuckled, not expecting that out of Zara.

'That's Billy's war-cry before he fights. Works for him, it might work for you too?'

'I'll remember that, thanks. I'll see you soon.' Ward smiled at the pebble in his palm and kissed it as if for luck from the lady herself.

He could do this now.

With a deep breath, he slid his mobile and pebble into his bag. He rolled his neck and shoulders, flexing his fingers to pump the adrenalin through his veins.

Yeah, he was back.

This is what he was trained to do.

It's all he knew and what he loved to do.

It was game time.

*   *   *

Amongst the aroma of coffee, beer, and meat pies, the many fans gathered in the stadium's stands to soak up the winter sunshine. Zara sat with her family, wearing the Saints' colours that Ward supplied. She laughed at their homemade banners, waving like limp flags stolen from some ancient sailing ship stranded without a breeze. The disjointed lettering read: *WARD's our Hero; for WARD's the man; he's the WARD against evil*. It was nice that they'd done this and hoped it boosted Ward's confidence.

But today she was nervous. This was her first live game of AFL. The big leagues.

'Was that Ward calling?' Joe asked, seated beside her.

'Yeah.' Zara smiled at the phone as she slipped it into her pocket, hoping Ward was okay.

'Nervous, huh?'

She shrugged. She didn't want Ward upset, yet glad

he'd called her. Was she getting too attached to him?

'You're like your mother, she always knew what to say.' Joe patted his daughter's shoulder and faced the field. 'Should be a good game, luv.'

'I hope so.' The pristine grass looked like carpet, about to be churned under footballers' boots. Would the players run along the fence like thoroughbreds on a track with grass flying behind them? Would they snort for air as they raced for the ball first or to get ahead of the pack? Would the crowd be just as loud vying for their spots to watch for the photo-finish?

But the sheer size of the stadium was unexpected. It blocked the outside world where she had to crane her neck back to stare up at the window view of the sky. An electrified air swirled around as the seats began to fill, she hadn't expected this many people.

'Oh, it'll be a pearler of a game, luv. Our boys are gonna kick career goals havin' Ward back, that's a massive boost, along with a home ground advantage. You wait 'til you hear this crowd roar. I'd better turn off my hearing aid before it erupts.' Joe fiddled with the aide behind his ear. Readjusted his Akubra, and with a new team scarf around his neck, he grinned wide, soaking up the atmosphere.

It began like a storm rolling in off the ocean that travelled through Zara's boot soles as it raced to her chest and deafened her ears. She flinched and reached for her father as the crowd roared. He patted her hand that gripped his arm, giving her an encouraging grin, cheering along with the tens of thousands of excited fans as the players ran onto the field.

The fans screamed louder as Ward came out onto the grass like some superstar, and not just a face on the television. She could feel it, see it, and even smell the anticipation that spread like an invisible electric current saturating the crowd as the excitement built.

She gaped up at Ward, larger than life on the big screen, proclaiming his return like a rock star. It was so surreal. She knew a man who was on television screens shown across the country. This world of fame was nothing like her slow-paced cocooned lifestyle on the farm. This was the world of elite football and Ward was at the centre of it.

'*Ward. Ward. Ward.*' The crowds chanted, while Ward shouldered opposition players jostling on the field as he positioned himself in the centre, waiting and watching like a warrior about to begin the battle.

Why was Ward bothering with her? She was just a face amongst a sea of faces, when he was a superstar who had the world cheering his name.

*   *   *

The crowd cheered as the final siren blew and the Saints were victorious.

Ward stood in the centre of the stadium and took in the moment. He'd missed this. The game, the crowd behind him spurring the adrenalin that still sizzled within his bones.

He shook hands with the opposition players and headed for his teammates gathering by the changeroom's tunnel to sing the team's song. It was all part of their post-game routine.

'*Ward?*' shouted the sports reporter, waving the microphone at him.

'Oh, man.' Ward searched for an escape, trying to walk around them.

'Hey Ward, just a few words, mate?' The reporter jogged towards him with camera crew in tow.

Too late.

The late afternoon chill nipped against his hot skin in a sweat-soaked shirt and shorts. But he had to do this and took a drink from a team runner as the camera crew got ready. Not that he had any idea of what to say when he had yet to catch his breath.

It'd been a tough game. His focus had only been on the game from the first siren where it was all about getting that damned ball. Pass it to his teammates. And kick some goals.

And he'd done just that.

All he'd seen were his teammates, the opposition, the umpires, and the goal posts. All he'd heard was the whistle. But now he could hear thousands of voices singing their team's song to a footy field now void of players.

'We roll in thirty seconds,' called out the reporter. He was an ex-premiership captain, and one of the few who'd made it into media after retiring from the game.

What happened to the rest of the ex-superstars of the game?

Ward ran fingers through his sweaty hair to tame his cockatoo crest. He'd done live interviews a few times over the years and used to love it. But today he wanted to get it over with, and fast.

He wiped at the sweat still trickling around his eyes and took another swig of the sports drink. He spotted the banners waving his name, where Zara's family of misfits waited. That's where he wanted to be. Not here.

Yet, Ward used to love being a part of the media parade, but now, he didn't want a bar of it—*oh man, what's going on?*

The cameraman signalled with palm up, counting down with his fingers. 'Five, four, three, two…'

Showtime.

The sports reporter started the interview holding the microphone between them. 'Ward, you were a powerhouse out there today, mate. How are you feeling?'

'Good.' His voice was hoarse from shouting during the game, he cleared his throat and took another drink.

'You've recovered from that spectacular fall a few weeks back?'

'Yep.' Ward grinned with a hell yeah. Then remembered to act cool in front of the camera or he'd get hassled by teammates later, and took a calming breath and allowed the media training to kick in.

'The team missed you and you led the charge today by making the most in possessions. You also beat your personal best for kicking the most goals in one game.'

Ward arched an eyebrow in surprise. 'We did it together, as a team. Even when I wasn't well, the team supported me both on and off the field. Now I'm back and I'm bringing my best.' Ward answered the interviewer's questions keeping it as brief as possible. He had other things to do, and one of them was to get warm.

The reporter said, 'It's great to see you back in action today.'

'Thanks, it's great to be back.' Ward loved playing.

'And you were back with a vengeance.' The reporter patted Ward's shoulder and spoke to the camera for a moment and then the interview was over.

Ward met his teammates who'd gathered by the exit to their change rooms. A team-runner handed him a small football and marker for Ward to gift to someone in the crowd. It's what they did after winning and that was to hand out either an autographed flag or banner.

They only played eighty minutes of actual game time stretched into an average of two and a half hours. The rest of the time was practising and promoting the club. This part he didn't mind and knew who he'd give this ball to.

He jogged to the oval's edge to find Billy squeezed amongst the crowd along the fence line with Toby in his arms. Ward held out the ball to the boy.

'WARD.' Toby clutched the ball in his small hands as

Ward beamed with pride at the delight on Toby's face.

Other people jostled and called to Ward for his attention. He got in a few photos and slapped out a few high-fives to fans. Signed a few shirts and scarves, waved at the crowds, and then he saw her. Her black beanie crowned her butterscotch locks that spilled down her shoulders, while her scarf covered her lips to keep them from the cold. He raised his hand in a wave, her eyes shone as she smiled, and he no longer felt the cold.

'Let's go, Ward,' called Nick, by the gate.

'Coming.' He gave Zara a sly wink, tempted to climb the fence to be with her. But he had to go change and celebrate with his teammates. The fans' cheers followed him as he ran down the concrete corridor.

As a prince in a world of kings, he'd missed this and was so glad to be back.

*   *   *

'Ward's like this superstar,' said Stacey beside Zara and Joe at their seats, as the crowd spilled through the exits.

'Ward's a legend, who played a top game,' Adam said, climbing over the chairs to the vacated row in front of them.

Billy walked up carrying Toby who hugged his little ball. 'I've never been to a proper professional live game before.'

'Better switch this back on,' mumbled Joe, fiddling

with his hearing aid. 'So, what did you mob think of the live game?'

'I'm hooked,' said Tim with a wide smile. Gone was the crusty brandless cap, now replaced by the new Saints' cap he was busily bending to perfection.

'I thought boxing was tough,' said Billy, 'but we've got gloves and only one person to contend with. Not like Ward, he had nothing to protect him when he had those two guys on him. They mustn't show the punches and knocks on TV, coz Ward got thumped heaps out there. He's tougher than I thought.'

Adam nodded and grinned, looking over at the field. 'True dat. Ward gave as good as he got in that battle zone.'

With scarf covering her lips from the cold, Zara watched the greenkeepers inspect the oval's turf like it was precious carpet. The stands that had once been full of people were emptying fast, replaced by cleaners. It was so quiet and calm now. It'd taken until the second quarter to stop flinching at the screaming men around her. They weren't yelling at her but at the game.

She'd never seen a game like it. Sure, they'd watched the local country games and the weekend TV games, but not this. Live in action, the entertainment was borderline-brutal, with crowds screaming for blood and where the players were like gladiators in the arena.

It wasn't what she'd expected.

She caught her father observing her. 'Dad?' He was a clever man who saw all. Yet she read her father like he read her and knew why he wanted her to witness the world Ward belonged to. Which she did, while clinging onto her father's arm.

Didn't her father trust Ward?

'Ward played well.' She'd seen a different side to Ward today. Should she fear him too?

'Ward's recovered now. He's always been a tough player, and now he's back where he belongs.' Joe placed a palm on her shoulder and leaned in closer, saying, 'I know you're caught up with him, luv, but how long will it be before this footballer gets all caught up in his world and leaves you behind?'

'Dad!' She glared at him for interfering, even if he was right.

'Hey Zara, are you going to use your backstage pass and catch up with Ward?' Asked Stacey.

'Give it to me if you don't want it,' Adam said, holding out his hand.

'Nope, that's for Zara.' Stacey faced Zara and asked, 'Are you going?'

'What are you guys doing now?' Zara fingered the yellow pass in her pocket, wishing she hadn't promised to wait for Ward. She sniffed at the cool air with its scents of cold concrete and clipped lawn, the place was so different now. It was almost ghost-town empty.

'Let's go to that pizza place we all love,' Joe suggested and the crew cheered their approval.

'Yum, I'm hungry,' said Zara.

'Don't you dare?' Stacey said, grabbing Zara's arm.

'Don't what?' Zara grinned at Stacey's stern expression.

'You're wearing that same look when you tried to back out of your mystery date with Ward, and you had a good time then.'

'I did.' Zara hid her smile in her scarf. It'd been brilliant and Ward's effort had been amazing. 'But…' She hesitated and looked at her father.

'Listen, luv, if you get stuck call us and we'll come and collect you.'

Zara nodded at her father who could read her mind. It was scary when he did that.

'With Sister Stacey's snail's pace driving we should be just leaving the carpark 'bout sunrise,' said Billy with a wide white-toothed smile, as Tim and Adam sniggered beside him.

With hands on her hips, Stacey glared at the boys who were like her brothers. 'Hey, I'm a careful driver.'

'You are, luv, and you'll get quicker when you're more confident,' said Joe. 'Don't go too fast, though, don't think my ol' Holden would handle it.'

'See,' said Stacey with her nose in the air. 'So go, Zara.'

Zara rolled her eyes as her only defence against the peer pressure. 'Yeah, okay, I'll go.' She couldn't disappoint Ward. 'Tell you what, I'll definitely catch up. There's taxis in the city.'

Stacey screwed up her nose, whining, 'But what about Ward?'

'It's rare we all go out to dinner together, so I'll meet you there.'

Joe gave a nod of his Akubra. 'Good idea, luv, it might take us a while to get there.'

Stacey's jaw dropped as her brow crinkled. 'That's not coz of my driving, is it?'

'No, luv, we've gotta wrestle this crowd to the car, then we've gotta compete with all of 'em other parked cars through the car park, that'll take time. Zara, why not ring when you're on your way and we'll start them cookin' your order,' said Joe, looking pleased with her decision.

'You bet, thanks, Dad.' She had her escape plan, with room for Ward to join them if he wanted to. If not, she'd go on her own. No dramas and no commitment.

She lipped her scarf, shoved hands into her pockets, nodded at her father, and took the steps down into the lion's cave. How soon before she could escape?

* * *

Showered and changed, Ward searched the corridor where some fans had gathered. His heart grew as big as his smile to find Zara leaning against the wall at the back of the group.

'You came.' Ward hugged her, inhaling her warm aroma. 'Thank you.' He tucked her fringe behind her ear.

She had to be the only woman he knew who looked sexy in a beanie and scarf.

'For what?'

'For the phone call and for waiting for me.'

She gave a shy shrug, lowering her eyes.

'So, what did you think of the game?'

'Good. I've never seen a live AFL game before. How are you feeling?' Her eyes followed her palms that slid over his shoulders and arms. He recognised that look, it was her practitioner to client look.

But he wasn't her client. 'I'm good, I won't feel anything until tomorrow. Come on.' Giving her hand a tender squeeze, he led her back down the corridor.

'Where are we going?' Her heeled boots echoed behind him, but he wasn't letting go.

'To get my bag. Unfortunately, we can't leave yet.'

'Why not, game's over isn't it?'

'We have to hang around and talk to some of the members for half an hour, less if we sneak out.' He grinned at her, but only one dimple showed in her smile and her eyes didn't shine. Was she nervous?

He led her through the double doors and into the main room where his teammates and their families mingled with members in the typical post-game victory celebration. Her hand squeezed his tighter. Was this too much for her? 'What do you want to do after this?'

Her forehead crinkled as she licked her lips. 'I'm meeting the crew for pizza at this great place for dinner.'

'Really?' Didn't she want to hang out with him?

'It's got great food, nothing fancy. You can come if you want?'

That made him grin, again, while he rubbed his thumb over the back of her hand that clutched onto him like a vice. 'Could do with a feed. Do they do pasta too?'

'Yes, it's an Italian restaurant. The boys vote it the best place.' She stepped closer and whispered, 'Can you go out after a game?'

'I don't want a late one when I've got a light practice tomorrow, then a few days off to do our own thing. Hey Sam, Nick?'

Zara squeezed his hand tighter as her eyes darted around the room, biting her lower lip.

'Relax, Z, they're my housemates. I won't leave you alone for a second.' Not with his teammates checking Zara out, and they should, the lady was gorgeous.

It was also new to his team because Ward didn't date, and he'd never brought a girl to the changerooms before. Did that make Zara his girlfriend?

Sam nudged Nick in the ribs. 'Check it out.'

Nick turned and raised his eyebrows at Ward's approach.

'Hey fellas, this is Zara,' introduced Ward, his chest filled with pride to have her at his side.

'Zara?' Nick scratched his head then his eyes lit up. 'Hey, we heard about you and what you did with our mate.'

Sam nodded in recognition. 'We want Ward to keep

Max. Can't you talk him into it?'

Zara grinned and her grip on Ward's hand loosened a little. 'That's Ward's choice about Max, no pressure from me.'

No, she never pressured him into anything. He gave her a sly wink because the woman was his hero.

'What are you up to after this, Ward?' Sam asked.

'We're going for pizza and pasta with Zara's crew.'

'They can come, the more the merrier,' Zara said, shrugging at Ward.

He was pleased she included his mates. 'Yeah, you guys should join us?'

'Did someone say pizza?' called out Mills, stepping to their small group. 'Hey, who are you?'

'That's Zara,' said Sam with a wide-eyed nod.

'No way.' Mills' eyes bugged out.

'Oi? Manners, mate.' Ward gave a warning frown to Mills.

'She's proper pretty.' Mills wiped his mouth as his eyes walked over her, when Nick gave him a sharp elbow in the rib. 'What? Did I say that out loud?'

'You did, dickhead.' Nick shook his head while Sam chuckled.

'This is Mills, he's harmless and honest, and our unofficial housemate. Mills shares the man-couch with Max,' explained Ward.

'That couch is big enough for four people,' said Zara.

'Max makes it look small.'

Mills screwed his face up, giving a half shoulder shrug apology. 'So, you're the one who cured Ward?'

'No, I didn't.'

'Yes, you did.' Mills nodded, sending ripples to flow down his glossy black mullet. 'I now understand how that whole Florence Nightingale deal can be a real problem.'

'Hey!' Ward punched Mills in the arm.

'You told them?' Zara arched an eyebrow at Ward, her eyes shining with amusement as her handgrip loosened even more.

'Well, they are my best mates, and it's like your lot at home where we have no secrets.' *Home*? Whose home, his, hers, theirs?

Mitchell approached and patted Ward's shoulder. 'Good game, Ward.'

'Thanks, Coach. Zara, this is Mitchell.'

'Zara?' Mitchell shook her hand, then stepped back blinking, tilting his head. 'Are you that, ah, Reiki stuff?'

Zara nodded with a tight-lipped dimple-free expression. 'I do stuff, yes, although my official title is Reiki Master.'

Mitchell crossed his arms over his chest with eyes narrowing at Zara. 'You do horses, right?'

Ward cleared his throat, annoyed at how Mitchell spoke to Zara.

'Horses are my specialty.' Zara seemed calm as if used to this questioning from sceptics, when he'd been one himself.

'So how come you did Ward then?' Asked Nick.

'My father is a huge fan of you guys.'

'So, is it true you're like a horse whisperer and stuff?' Mills asked, as Mitchell screwed up his nose.

Ward frowned at Mitchell and said, 'Zara works on horses worth more than this whole team, Coach, I've seen it. Her clients are billionaires who fly her around the country for race meets.'

Zara squeezed his hand as the colour dusted her cheeks. 'Ward, please, no one needs to hear that.'

'You should be proud of what you do, Z.' He was proud of her, yet she was so humble. His arm wrapped around her shoulders pulling her close to his side. She fit there.

'Zara, did Ward ask you about Sheldon?' Mitchell asked.

Ward sneered at the name—*why were they doing this?* 'I asked and Zara said no.'

'Why not? It's the same injury,' Mitchell said to Zara.

'I only work on animals.'

'Aren't you're qualified for humans?' Sam asked.

'Yes, but I prefer to treat animals.'

'Would you consider doing some side-work for our team,' said Mitchell, 'should they require a one-off treatment?'

Zara stepped back, and Ward squeezed her shoulders to stop her in case she ran. *What the hell was Mitchell thinking?* His eyes narrowed and his voice lowered in warning, 'Zara only does horses, Coach.' With teeth clenched, he glared at the man he called god. But right now, that gloss melted like thin wax covering a false idol in the sun to reveal Mitchell as only a mere man.

'Are you saying our mate's an animal?' Mills blurted out with a cheesy grin as Sam and Nick chuckled and the mood was defused.

'The boys at home call Ward a two-legged thoroughbred,' Zara said with tongue in cheek to Ward.

'Well, Zara, whatever you did,' Mitchell said, patting Ward's shoulders like a father to son, 'I can't thank you enough for your help in fixing our boy.'

'Glad I could help.'

'Me too.' Ward watched Mitchell walk away, no longer hero-worshipping the man, but someone Ward respected. When did that change?

'That's a man carrying a lot of responsibility and pressure, huh?' Zara said.

'Yeah.' Ward never wanted Mitchell's job. As coach, Mitchell carried the team, the club, and all the fans across the country on his back. Yet, Ward had trouble committing to a dog.

Ward hadn't expected that from Mitchell. He didn't want to share Zara with anyone, or have her touching their bodies. Thankfully, she only worked on animals. Sure, he liked his teammates, and some were like brothers, but he was protective of the lady who had yet to agree to be his girl. He couldn't rush her, considering what she'd been through, and knew he'd have to earn her trust. 'Come on, let's run away.'

Through the crowded room that was suddenly too loud and stuffy, he dodged conversations, avoided eye contact, and aimed for the exit. Leading Zara by the hand, through the double doorway and out into the vacant corridor, where his arm slid over her shoulders and she fit perfectly at his side. He collected his duffel from the bench, and for the first time in his career, Ward was the first to leave the club rooms during a victory celebration. Glad to get-gone, he never looked back.

Twenty-Eight

Ward approached the clubhouse, with Zara tucked under his arm on one side, on the other side was Max trotting along on the lead. 'Because we won, there'll be no this-is-where-we-stuffed-up speeches and it'll be a light training session today. Are you sure you don't want to hang out at my place before I take you home?' Why didn't he call his place home?

'This'll be good for Max,' she said.

'Are you trying to con me into keeping the dog?' Max adored Zara, the way the pit bull carried on last night like a kid needing attention, when he'd brought the lady home with him after dinner.

'No, but you didn't take him for a run this morning.'

'We were busy.' They'd both slept in and lazed around in his bed that neither of them had wanted to leave.

'His week's almost up, huh?'

Tomorrow he'd decide about Max. 'Is Max going to be okay with all these people?' He nodded towards the scattered fans who'd arrived to watch their training sessions.

'If he wasn't, I wouldn't bring him. Remember, Max

used to walk into a shed full of screaming men like crowds at a football match and not hear it, same as you.' Zara pointed to the oval where the assistant coaches were putting out orange cones in a pattern across the grass. 'This is calm compared to what you feel in the game.'

'No way.' Ward stopped and stared at the dog realising the common link.

'There's a reason Max likes you, you both go to battle in your own way.'

The scarred pit bull sat at his side without instruction. 'I've never played with him and stuff, all I do is feed him and run him, that's it.' His housemates played with him, fed him, and bathed him.

'You've taken Max for a drive and on dinner dates too.'

'I haven't said yes or no.' He walked them to the side gate that led to the stands.

'That's your decision to make. Either way, Max has a place at home as long as he likes, and this could be his idea of a holiday.' She gave a meek grin that accompanied her shrug.

'Yeah, no pressure.' Although, it sure felt like it. 'How come Max chose me and not someone else?'

'How come you're closer to Sam, Nick, and Mills, than the other men on this team?'

'I dunno, we just get on well,' replied Ward, as he nodded to the gatekeeper to allow Zara and Max through to the practise field.

'And yet you and your sister don't?'

'Tina's a pain.' Even if they'd shared a few adult conversations these past few days, they'd never be besties who braided each other's hair and swap recipes. Nope, he couldn't see his vegan-loving sister arm wrestle him for the next round of beer and beef burgers either. But at least they were talking, which made his mum happy. 'Max won't burr-up out here?'

'Not unless he's challenged or doing it to protect those he cares about,' said Zara.

'Has he? You've said he's done it with Toby?' Toby was a cute kid, not that Ward knew about kids.

'In the past, when I've brought out a few dogs that carried on, Max would show up and do this low guttural growl, and they soon behaved. Come on, who'd tussle with Max when he's so scary looking.'

'Mills says Max's ugliness makes him look good.' Mills and his unfiltered mouth had made for entertaining dinner conversation last night with Zara's family of misfits.

'I like Mills,' Zara said with a laugh.

'Don't let him hear you say that or he'll climb into your ute and go home with you like some stray.' Ward grinned at his stowaway who waddled calmly alongside as people gave him a wide berth, like he was some traffic controlling mini-bouncer who cleared the path. 'Does Max help you with the dogs the way Middy helps your dad with other horses you rehabilitate?' It sounded like a prison farm, but it wasn't.

'It's Max's choice to be involved like he chose to run away and be with you.'

'P-p-p-pressure. I'm sure they made a song I should download.'

'Max listens to you, and he's never attacked except fight in self-defence, it's his protective nature of being part of a pack. You might not get on with your sister, but if someone was to say—' She winced and licked her lips. 'If Tina got hurt, you'd help her, right?'

'Yeah.' He stopped and held her hand and said, 'I'd never hurt you, Z. I know it's none of my business, but Adam told me what happened to you.'

The colour rose in her cheeks and her lips tightened into flat line. 'No secrets in our family. I want no pity.'

He leaned his forehead against hers. 'Hey, I'd be the same as your family, I'd destroy anyone who'd ever hurt you like that.' On their date night, he'd kissed each scar on her back and ribs, as if trying to heal her and to show her how much he cared. What kind of bastard would do that to her!

'We all have our own battle scars from the past. But you have to pick yourself up and keep moving forward.'

She tried to step away from him, but he refused to let go of her hand. 'Come on, you've got practice. I've got a paper to read, a coffee to drink, and time to work on my winter tan.'

'Sure. I'll show you a great spot to watch me, which is also the best place for me to watch you.' He slid his arm over her shoulders keeping her close where she fit so well at his side. She might tell him the story, but would he have the strength to hear it?

*   *   *

With practice over, Mills strolled into the locker rooms with a towel around his waist, using another towel to dry his mullet that he'd blow-dry to perfection over the next two hours. He approached his locker next to Sam, and began his grooming routine. 'Hey Ward, my mum wants to bake a cake for Zara and her people. Is that okay?'

Seated two lockers down, Ward slid on his boots. 'Can't see why not, Zara's got a household to feed.' Mills' mother baked a cake a day for the team and all the boys loved it.

'Do they foster those kids out there?' Sam asked, slipping on his jeans.

'Billy, Stacey, and Toby are fostered to the Phelps,' replied Ward. 'Tim and Adam aren't.'

On the other side of Ward, Nick rolled up his towel like a yoga mat and asked, 'How many others have they helped out?'

'Ten, I think? All boys, except Stacey. One's studying to be a vet out west, another one's a fisherman up north, and there's a stable-hand at the track. I'm not sure about the rest.'

'Tim was telling me he's got a few weeks left on parole and Adam's got another year to go. You wouldn't pick it with that pair,' said Mills, re-wrapping his mullet-mop in a towel. 'Billy's a funny kid too.'

'I like Billy,' said Sam.

'Everyone likes Billy.' The kid had that type of personality that matched his cheeky grin.

'What's a Billy?' asked Greg, their captain, at his locker opposite Ward.

'A fifteen-year-old kid they're predicting to be a champion boxer,' replied Nick.

Ward stamped the soles of his boots as he stood up and tucked in his shirt. 'Billy will be. The kid's got me a few times, and he's quick, with a long reach.'

Greg slapped on the deodorant and picked up his collared shirt. 'Hey, I saw that dog of yours, man. Scary.'

'Max isn't mine, he's just having a holiday,' Ward said as he slid on his jacket and spotted Nick, Mills, and Sam's frowning faces. 'Zara said if I didn't take Max, he'd keep helping her rehabilitate other dogs. He's useful out there.' Why would the dog want to stay stuck in suburbia staring at a fence when he had acres of countryside as his daily view?

Sam sighed as he sat before his locker slipping on his socks and shoes and said, 'If Max listened to me like he does with you, I'd take him, but it's obvious he likes you.'

Greg tucked his shirt into his slacks. 'By the way, Ward…'

Ward ran fingers through his wayward hair and zipped shut his duffel.

'Your girlfriend's Zara, right?'

He hoped so. 'Why?' Slinging his bag over his shoulder he faced his captain.

'The Magpies' coach is here,'—all those nearby stopped and stared at Greg—'and he's outside talking to your lady. Reckon they're trying to convince her to do her thing on Sheldon.'

'*He'd better not!*' Ward dashed for the door.

'Zara's already said no,' said Sam, closing his locker.

'What's the drama if she's fixed Ward?' Mills asked. 'If Ward asked Zara, I bet she'd do it for Ward.'

'Not when it comes to Sheldon,' said Greg, looking to Nick and Sam.

Their words echoed behind him as Ward dashed outside and found Zara in the stands with Max beside her on the bench. Three men stood before her, his team's doctor, then recognising the opposition's coach and their team doctor. 'What's going on?'

'Ward,' said the Doc, 'do you know Mark, he's the coach of the Magpies.'

'There'd only be a rare few who wouldn't know who

Mark is.' This man was *the* coach in the league, a living legend. The God of Gods.

'We've never met, but I know all about you, young man. You're a helluva midfielder.' Mark shook Ward's hand as his black eyes scanned over him the same way Mitchell checked out a player's physique.

'Thank you.' Normally he'd be doing some back-patting-revel-in-the-moment, but not today. 'Are you here to see me?'

'We're trying to talk Zara into helping Sheldon like she did with you.'

'That's Zara's choice. Ready to go, Z?' He didn't like Zara surrounded by these men. Ward then noticed Max had positioned his bulk in front Zara as if protecting her from the other men. *Good dog.*

Zara tucked her newspaper into her bag and shared a polite smile. 'Nice to meet you, gentleman.'

'Look, Zara, here's my card. All my numbers are on the back and I'll double your normal fee, whatever you want. I don't want to see Sheldon in the pain he's in,' Mark said, holding out his business card. 'I'm aware you only practice on horses, but Ward's proof of what you can do. From our research, you're the best in your field of expertise, and my men deserve nothing but the best.'

Aaand let's add another thick, wadded, lumpy layer of glue to the hard-spun sales-pitchy plea that Ward wasn't buying into. Instead, he grabbed Zara's hand, ready to escape.

She looked at Ward a little confused and slid the card into her pocket. 'Can I think about it?'

Mark sighed with relief as if he'd held his breath. 'Sure. Call me anytime, day or night. Just say when, where, anything, and we'll set it up for you. Thanks for hearing me out and, hopefully, I'll hear from you soon.' He nodded, and with the doctors flanking him, they headed down the concrete steps of the stands.

'She didn't say yes,' mumbled Ward under his breath, watching them leave with squinting eyes.

Ward led Zara and Max to his car, and they were soon on the road. 'What was that all about, with Mark and the Doc?' Ward asked.

'Your team doctor just asked me what I did on you. He seems nice.' She smiled, but Ward turned away and gripped the steering wheel so tight his knuckles went white.

'What else?' His breath sharpened and pulse quickened.

. 'He asked if I'd be available to help out on the odd occasion with your teammates.'

'And Mark?' He gritted his teeth, bracing himself for it as he steered through the minimal Sunday traffic.

Zara stared at her fingers clutched in her lap. 'Mark asked if I could help this guy, Sheldon.'

'You've already said no a few times, so there's no problem is there?' His eyes narrowed at the road ahead, pursing his lips, he stopped at the intersection. He swiped viciously at the scar on his chin and waited for the lights to change.

'What if I agreed to help this Sheldon?'

'*What*? NO.'

Her eyes widened, pressing herself against the passenger door.

In the blink of an eye, she'd unclipped her seatbelt and was out the door running across the road.

'ZARA?'

He could run after her and catch her, but the car behind him tooted its horn as the traffic lights changed green. He reached across and closed the passenger door as she sprinted down the alley way. He drove around the corner, but she was nowhere in sight.

Oh no. What had he done?

* * *

Zara ran in blind fear like a rabbit dodging a fox. She turned right down one alley, left down the next, and then right into another. Until she went around a corner and found herself at a dead end.

Her palms slapped the wall in anger as hot tears trickled down her face. She hated how the fear had filled her so fast that her heart threatened to jump straight out of her chest.

She bent over, hands on knees and gulped for air, unsure if to cry, scream, or throw up in the alley that stank of rotten vegetables, piss, and decades of black sooty mould. Too scared to leave the shadows, her legs trembled as she heaved air, swallowing the acidic taste of fear, forcing it back where it belonged.

Her mobile rang in the back pocket of her jeans, and she shut her eyes tight trying to deafen the sound.

But still the phone rang.

The skyline was blocked by tall buildings offering window views of grimy brick walls. She tried to lean against the wall but her legs trembled so much she crouched to the floor where the vile stench of rotten vegetables floated from the gutter.

Silly girl, always running into a blind corner.

But at least this time she'd run.

Forcing a slow exhale through her rounded lips, she focused on relaxing her toes hidden in her shoes, to her feet, ankles, shins, calves, knees and then all over.

All while her phone rang. Again.

She swiped at the sweat mingled with unrealised tears, snatched up her phone and blinked at the screen flashing one name. Ward.

Switching it to vibrate, she dumped the mobile and watched it vibrate along the ground.

She'd seen Ward's expression darken. His white-knuckle grip on the steering wheel. The clear precise words as he spoke. The sharp breathing. The white flat lips. All the signs of anger building, and she wasn't sticking around for a backhander across her face like she'd done in the past.

At least this time she'd run.

Not like before.

Again, her phone vibrated on the concreted lip where the road met the pavement where she sat on the gutter's edge staring at Ward's name.

But Ward was different.

Ward also had the ability to harm another person. On the field shouldering other men, elbowing them, charging for a ball, he didn't care who blocked him for what he was after. If he reacted like that to a ball in a game, what was he like with people in his life?

A text message flashed on her phone's screen from Ward: *I'm so sorry, Z, I never wanted to scare you. I'm sorry.*

They were always sorry *after.*

She hugged her knees and lowered her cheek to the denim of her jeans. She'd left her bag and jacket in his car—*stupid girl.*

Now she shivered. Was it the adrenalin passing or the coolness of the shade?

Then she heard the tap-tap-tap on concrete accompanied by some heavy panting that approached the blind corner. Where could she hide?

Nowhere.

With her back to the wall, she held her breath and waited for what was coming.

'Max?'

The scarred pit bull rushed around the corner. his black tongue lolling out of his mouth, dragging Ward who'd released his lead as the dog rushed towards her.

'Good boy, Max, you found her.' Ward stopped and watched the pit bull rush to Zara and she hugged him.

'You brute, Max.' She found comfort in the dog's short coarse fur and through her fringe she watched Ward stand in the centre of the walkway with a water bottle in hand. At least he kept his distance.

But he also had her trapped.

* * *

'I'm sorry, Zara.' Ward crouched down, his heart squeezing to see her like a timid bird that had fallen from the nest with a broken wing. This was his Zara, sitting on the edge of the gutter at the end of a dark alley, who'd fled from him in fear.

He hated himself for doing that to her.

'I'm so, so, sorry, Z, I didn't mean to scare you.' He wanted to rush up and hug her but forced himself to stay. Crushed that she could only peek at him through her long fringe while hiding behind the dog. 'I'm sorry, Z. I'm jealous, that's all.'

But she said nothing.

'Please don't ever be scared of me. I'm such an idiot.' He scrubbed palms hard over his face. 'I didn't mean that, and...' He sighed heavily and readjusted his footing in his crouched position. But she didn't flinch, which he took as a good sign.

'Do you know I get tongue-tied with you?' He wiped his mouth that refused to work when it came to talking about life away from the game. 'I have no idea what to say, or how to say it, except I'm sorry I reacted like that. Believe me, Zara, I'd never hurt you. I swear it.'

But he'd stuffed-up, never seeing her look so fragile.

'Please believe me, because it'd kill me if I ever hurt you. I've never ever raised a hand to a woman, and, come on, we all know how annoying my sister is. She's an expert at stabbing my angry button, but even as a kid I never thumped her. Sure, there were times I wanted to, but I never did.' *Was that the right thing to say?*

If only she could give him another sign, instead of using Max as a shield.

'Did you know, for years we've lied about Tina's mung-bean stew that tastes like peppered dirt because we didn't want to hurt her feelings. And if I do that for my sister—who I clash with consistently—there's no way I'd ever do anything to hurt you.'

She raised her eyes to meet his and it filled him with more hope.

'You know, through our first date, it made me have an actual adult conversation with Tina. Sure, we argued, or as Mum says, we debated. Although we sounded like bickering kids again—but we had you.'

'Me?' Her voice so soft and frail it hurt, yet she'd spoken while Max lay on the road before her, relaxing. Another good sign.

'Yes, you, Z. Tina's going to apologise when she sees you next.'

'Why?'

'For being judgemental and rude to you, especially when you're the only reason I bothered talking to Tina at all. You see, I wanted to impress you so much with our first date, I got my sister to help me and she knows all about dating because…'

Her head rose and her eyes narrowed at him as she said, 'You. Don't. Date.'

That was cold.

He sighed and his shoulders drooped as his soul dropped lower than the crappy concrete he was crouched upon.

'It's true, I don't date, and you deserve to know why.' His thumb wiped down the scar on his chin. 'The reason I overreacted like that, is because…' He let out a deep breath trying to halt his frown, not at Zara, but at his own past.

'Because?' Her head tilted and those ice-blue eyes were watching.

But he wanted her eyes to shine and to see her double-dimple smile again, no matter what it cost him or how much it hurt to say.

He licked his lips and began. 'Sheldon and I were once housemates. We'd started the same time together with the Saints and we were best of mates for years.' He wiped his sweaty palms on his jeans and looked at her as he continued. 'And, well, Sheldon has always had the women flock to him. I'll admit it, like most blokes, I wanted that too, but not now, no way.' He shook his head, catching her sceptic expression he raised his palms in surrender. 'Honestly, Zara, since I've met you, I've haven't looked at another woman because I've never felt this way with anyone but you. This,' —patting his heart that hurt for her— 'scares the crap out of me.'

'How?'

'I haven't experienced this before, and I'm worried you'll reject me.' Now suffering his biggest rejection with her fleeing from him.

But he couldn't let her go. Not without her hearing his heart speak first.

'I know I'm an idiot, and I know you tried to push me away in the beginning with that Florence Nightingale thing, which I'm not suffering from when it comes to you. I'd thought about it too. You see, I felt like this from the first time you walked through my front door. Believe me, I had visions of some old weatherworn, haggard-looking horse doctor with these yellow gnarly fingernails strong enough to tear horseshoes straight off of horse's hooves.'

She gave a slight smile, *thank god for that.*

'You tilted my world from the first time I saw you standing in my doorway. You made me smile and laugh when I was in pain and hadn't slept in a week. Yet, every time I saw you, this feeling intensified where I forget everything except you. You'd become my number one priority and— Damn it.' The words wanted to spill from his chest like melted metal pouring from the bowl hanging above an inferno. 'I'm gonna say it and it might be the wrong place,' he said, glancing at the scummy alley. 'Wrong time…' With her huddled behind a dog because he'd scared her. But he had to, and with a deep breath he said, 'I love you, Zara.'

Her gasp echoed in his ears, making it his turn to flinch.

'I've never said that to anyone before, but it's true, I fell in love with you, and I'm in love with you, Zara.'

'Oh god.' Her palm covered her mouth, and she flicked her fringe to reveal the vulnerability in her eyes.

He shifted a little closer in his crouched position, just a little, with palms out front. He didn't want to scare her any more than he'd done. He wanted to gain her trust, even if it was the steps of a baby bug, he'd take it. 'You don't have to say anything. I understand you've been hurt in ways I can't comprehend. I just don't know how anyone would do that to you.'

'Not your problem.' She sat taller, her chin jutted out and her pride was on show. Another good sign.

'But it is, Z.'

'How?'

'Your problems are my problems and I want to help you anyway I can. If you're hurting, I'm hurting.' He clutched his heart that squeezed at the sight of her pain. 'I've scared you over something that isn't your issue, it's mine. It's my past that's now biting me.'

'Really?'

He nodded at her, again shifting that little closer towards her. 'You see, I liked this girl, a lot. She was the first one I'd ever taken on a dinner date in this restaurant where the waiter asked me for ID to check if I could legally drink the cocktails I'd ordered.'

That brought a limp twinge of a smile to her lips, but it wasn't enough.

'I'd never even slept with her and we were dating, proper dating for a month. I was this awkward nineteen-year-old, I mean no virgin, but I liked her a lot.' He blinked at the alley's stained tarmac and couldn't remember the woman's face. She was a brunette, that he remembered, but not much else.

'What happened?' Her voice was so soft and timid, but he was relieved she'd asked.

And he'd answer her to the best of his ability. 'I was meeting her at home for dinner, and that's when I found her on the couch being screwed by Sheldon. That bastard didn't even stop when I'd showed up,' he said with a scowl.

'Oh no.' Her palm slapped over her mouth and her empathy shone like a star. 'What did you do?'

'I kicked his naked butt and punched the crap out of him. We destroyed the house trying to kill each other, until the cops showed up because the neighbours heard us fighting, and they arrested us to keep us apart. We didn't press charges against each other so they couldn't book us for anything.' Ward, again, thumbed the scar that ran down the left of his chin.

'Did Sheldon give you that scar on your chin?' She mirrored his movement.

'Yeah.' Under his thumb the scar burned. It was his weak spot, an ugly reminder of why he didn't date and why he hated Sheldon. 'They had to stitch it three times.'

'Why?'

'After the first lot of stitches, Sheldon and I crossed paths in the corridor at the hospital, where we brawled again. The same cops pulled us apart along with hospital security. We got banned from that hospital, so I had to go to another hospital to get the second set of stitches.'

'And the third time?'

'Next day at the clubhouse, where we'd been hauled in to explain ourselves. Greg, our team captain, Sam, and Nick had to stop us, and after that we were split up.'

'Over a girl?'

'I thought she was special,' he admitted with a shrug. 'But you know what? I can't even remember what she looked like. But I remember the spiteful things Sheldon said about her, and I know he'd seduced her on purpose because of how I'd felt about her.'

'Why?'

'It's just a game to that bastard. The women don't really matter to him, and somehow, he's got this gift with them. Whether it's because he's rich or good looking, I don't know. But ever since then, all I want to do is wipe that smug side-smirk off his face with my fists.'

'That bad?'

'Oh yeah. We had to pay fifteen grand each for the damage to the house. It ruined my rental history, which is why I rent a room off of Nick and Sam through the club because I can't lease through a real estate again.'

'I thought you were equal tenants.'

'We are, but not on paper because the lease is in their name. I've been saving for my own place but I've always liked living with the boys. Until now.'

'What changed?'

He shrugged with a slight grin and said, 'I bought crockery.'

She hid a shy smile beneath her scarf. Her nervous habit, and the one and only thing he'd want her to change because he adored her smile.

In his crouched position, he shifted to his other leg and got one step closer. 'Anyway, that summer, Sheldon transferred to the Magpies and I stayed with the Saints. Only a few people know why we hate each other, which is Greg, Nick, Sam, and Mitchell, who was an assistant coach back then. It happened out of season and, thankfully, we were still considered a nobody as far as the AFL and the media were concerned. Since then, they haven't put Sheldon and me in the same room, except at the hospital in this special spinal unit where we were in traction and couldn't move. But he irritated me the entire time.' He ran his fingers through his misbehaving hair, curbing his anger over Sheldon. 'You know, if the coach asked you to work on my housemates, even Mills, I wouldn't worry, but with Sheldon I do.'

'Don't you trust me?'

'I don't trust Sheldon. I could never work out how or why, but he sucks females in and uses them. He can have all of them, when I only want one—and that's you, Zara. I don't want to lose you.' Even if he was on that knife's edge of never having her commitment. 'I want you in my life, permanently. I'd give up everything else, but not you, I can't let you go—that doesn't mean I want to own you either, ugh.' His bloody mouth and mind couldn't get it together and he clutched fingers through his hair. 'There's nothing I want more than for you to be happy, to share in your happiness by having you in my life because I'm a better person with you.'

'It's only been a few weeks.'

'It's been life-changing for me, Z.'

'You'd suffered a serious fall.'

'Which woke me up.'

'In what way?'

'I've started to take more responsibility for myself.' He looked at the dog he had yet to decide upon. 'I've had my mum teach me how to do my laundry because of you.'

'You didn't?'

'I did, and I make my bed daily, which all started after you told me how your Dad couldn't look after himself. Guess what? I'm the same, I'm spoilt.'

'I said you can afford not to bother with that stuff.'

'But it doesn't mean I shouldn't learn how, I'm not ashamed to.'

And there it was, a smile. A small one—but it gave him hope.

'Before I met you, Z, football was my entire world. I was living in some AFL bubble where my coach was God, and I followed all their rules like a good little boy. But since I've met you, I've seen a bigger world.'

'The world's always been there.'

'Not how you've shown it to me. Wherever I go, it's all about football. All we talk about is football. But with you, conversation topics are endless and I have something new to talk about, experiencing new things with you. We rescued a pony. I'm babysitting a runaway pit bull that has a criminal record. I've checked out the staff entrance of a racetrack. I rode bareback on a Clydesdale and ran with greyhounds. I'm tempted to mess up my sock drawer to wear odd pairs like you do, and I've never looked at pebbles the same.' He pulled the painted pebble from his pocket and held it out in his open palm. 'You make me want to be more than just a footballer.'

'But you are a footballer.'

'You know, my biggest fear when I woke up after that fall was never playing football again, and I love the game, I do. But I'll only be a footballer at this level for a few more years. After that, all I see is you.'

'Me?'

'Yeah. This stage of my life will only last as long as my body holds out. If I'm lucky, I'll play past thirty, but after that, I have no idea. Yet, I've found hope. I have hope that whatever my life will be after I retire from the game…' He crouched on the other leg, taking another step closer. 'My future will always include you.'

Her hands covered the scarf that shielded her lips while her eyes searched for an answer he didn't know how to give.

'Remember when we met, I was at my most vulnerable,' he said.

'You were in pain.'

'I was at the weakest point of my life, Z. My sister was taking charge of things and I was powerless to stop her, and that mung-bean stew, from entering the house.'

Was that a giggle she hid beneath her scarf?

'At that first introduction, you held out your hands to me.' He stretched open his palm that hovered above the dog that lay between them. 'You asked me then to trust that you wouldn't hurt me. I'd just met you and I was hurting. Yet for the first time I took a risk on something that was outside the club's rules and realm, and put my trust in you.' He lowered himself to gaze at her with hope. 'Now, I'm asking you to trust me.'

* * *

She'd stopped breathing, letting the trapped air roll around her stilted lungs, staring at his open hand.

Her palm itched, and she rubbed her fingertips together. Did she dare?

On the verge of tears, so dry in the throat that it hurt to swallow, she bit her bottom lip as her fingers uncurled and slowly reached out. She touched his palm and his hand enveloped hers, where the warmth travelled up her arm to the top of her head.

But he didn't rush her. Didn't push her. Didn't pull her. Just held her hand and shared a soft smile that hid the scar on his chin.

'I'll try to trust you,' she whispered.

'And I'm honoured you're willing to do so.' He pressed his lips against the back of her hand and another chink of her inner wall fell, causing her to blink back tears.

'Hey, don't cry, Z, I'm sorry.'

'I'm okay.' *Stupid tears,* trying to swipe them away.

'Are you sure?' He sat next to her, as his thumb stroked the back of her hand sending liquid warmth through her veins.

She shrugged. He held out the water bottle. 'Thanks.' She drunk thirstily, watching a newspaper page float like a magic carpet on the wind. It somersaulted across the pavement and disappeared around the corner.

It was like a page of someone's story, gone, but never

truly forgotten.

She screwed the lid onto the bottle and handed it back, hugging her knees. 'Do you know why I only work on animals?'

'Because they don't back-chat and respond better to your treatments?' His grin warmed her soul and the care in his amber eyes made her want to share. He'd shared with her and she now understood him better. How else was she going to get over this if she didn't share with Ward? But would he understand?

Only one way to find out.

'I only worked on animals at the farm as a favour to Dad. Other than that, I'd only ever treated people at Howie's surgery and in the city practice.' She hugged her knees tighter and whispered, 'It was there, a man walked in named… Paul.'

Ward grabbed her hand, giving it a comforting squeeze. 'You don't have to tell me, Z, if you don't want to.'

But for the first time she wanted to.

'Paul was this high-flying businessman, who dazzled me. He was strictly a patient only; and then he wasn't my patient anymore. We caught up in town while I was out with some of my girlfriends in the city, partying like any other single girl.' How simple life was back then, so free of horrors.

'You dated him?'

'Yes. Although, I'm useless at dating too.'

'No way! You're gorgeous.'

She lowered her head as the heat rose from her neck to her face. 'It's true. I didn't have a boyfriend all through school.'

'How come?'

'The boys in town were more like brothers and my dad can scare the crap out of anyone, when he wants to.'

'I'll admit,' he said with a grin, 'I took a step back when I met your father, he's a big man.'

'My older brother was bigger.'

'So that must've changed when you moved out of home?'

'It did. But I was hopeless at it. I didn't know fancy restaurants. My dress sense sucked, lacking that city-chic I wanted back then. People didn't take me seriously when I told them what I did for a living, expecting me to have dreadlocks and wear tie-dyed clothes.'

'Like my sister.'

'Yeah,' she said, sharing a grin with him. 'Paul didn't care about that. He taught me about the restaurants, fine dining, the best shops, as if giving me an education of city living. It was fun too. I even learned to speak clearer and not do the nasal lazy twang.'

'To change who you were?'

'Experimenting. I was trying to find who I wanted to be. At that stage I was saving to go overseas because I'd received an exclusive invitation to study at this place in Japan. But then, I deferred it.'

'Why?' Ward asked.

She gave a half shrug pressing her lips to her shoulder.

'Did Paul know?'

'Paul asked me to move in with him and not go away.'

Ward lowered himself down to meet her eyes and said, 'I would've let you go, Z, and I would've tried to visit when I could.'

'You would?'

'Yeah. If it's something you wanted, and if it makes you happy, I'd help you get there. Of course, we'd have to learn how to Skype nightly and you'd have to answer your phone more.' He picked up her mobile where the screen displayed his ten missed calls, giving her a cheeky grin.

Oops. She shrugged, tucking her phone into the pocket of her jeans. She had to admit Ward was adorable. So different to Paul—or was he? 'Paul got jealous of me with my work too.'

Ward sat straighter and his brow flickered into a frown for only a second. 'I see.'

Did he?

'When Paul picked me up after work, he'd see the patients I'd treat and would complain about my male clients. I told him it was my job, and I didn't think anything of it. I'd never realised how jealous Paul was. He hated me touching another man's bare skin, and I honestly didn't see that when I worked on a client. I just saw the body, the muscles. Nothing more.'

'But he did?'

'I worked on this plumber who was having regular weekly sessions for a back injury. Every week I walked him out of the treatment room on a Thursday night, he asked me out and I said no and told him I don't date clients. And that was that. He'd re-book for the next week, and I'd walk him out. Locked the door. Turned around to clean up and found Paul in the waiting room.' She frowned at the asphalt that spread like a cracked black carpet beneath her boots. It was the background screen for another replay of her recurring nightmare. 'Paul shouted at me, accusing me of having an affair with this guy. He pulled me by the hair and dragged me into my treatment room and…'

'God no.' Ward wrapped his arms around her and held her to his chest. She breathed in his aroma, feeling his steady heartbeat, and with his arms surrounding her like armour it gave her strength.

'He beat me,' she whispered, not scared, but angry at what Paul had done. After all these years the memory was still vivid. 'Before that he'd shouted at me, called me names, and slapped me around for over a year. He was always sorry after, but that time, he beat me. My boss found me the next morning, and I woke up in hospital.' Her palm pressed on his heart and she wanted to push away. It was her habit to push away. To remain on the edge. To never get involved or hurt again.

Instead she looked up at Ward, with his messy auburn hair the same colour as his eyebrows. The tan blended with his freckles that surrounded his amber eyes that clearly displayed his worry and fear. Was she also seeing his love for her?

'It was Dad who got me to work on the animals because I didn't want to leave the farm. I couldn't talk to anyone or touch another person. It was that comfortable silence of an animal, and how they looked at me as I worked on them, it also gave me a lever of comfort, too. My parents accepted the invitation on my behalf and sent me overseas to do some soul searching.' But back then, it never stopped the nightmares that woke her with a scream frozen in her throat.

'Since I've returned, I'll treat animals and charge a regular fee. As for the very few people I agree to work on, I'll charge a carton of beer for Dad to keep it casual. No appointment, no human clients.'

'That's why you never put a money price on me?'

'It keeps you from being a client, because I don't and won't have human clients again.'

'I get it. Do you miss working on people?'

'No. I get more personal satisfaction helping an animal than I ever did with another human being.' Her head lowered and she whispered, '…except with you.'

'Did your world tilt when you first saw me too?'

'No.' She giggled up at him.

'It did for me. I had to grip my chair worried I'd fall. You sure you didn't get that with me?'

'No. First time we met I felt sorry for you.'

'But we shared sparks when we first touched. You blamed the carpet and took off your boots and I copped a gander at your odd socks. That was all us, Z, *electric*.' His nose nudged against the edge of her jaw below her ear and his warm breath sent prickles across her skin.

'I tried to resist you.'

'You're still resisting, and now I understand why. I don't want you to be scared of me, ever, Z. I'd never ever hurt you, and I'll swear on that with everything I have.'

She tried to smile, but her jaw ached from clenching her teeth. Yet, she whispered, 'I believe you.'

His eyes lit up brighter than a sunset reflecting off the ocean. 'Thank you,' he said, and kissed the tip of her nose.

'Did you know, you've helped me too?' She admitted.

'How?'

'Besides getting on a horse together, like we did,' she said with their grins mirroring each other, 'you helped me want to get past what Paul did, by challenging me to look at my own fears. I had all these gurus overseas who tried to help me, but I wasn't ready then. I'd pushed it aside, buried it so deep and never let anyone in, until you came along. We've been helping each other the whole way through, Brendan.'

'Am I in trouble?' He lowered his head sharing a cheeky smirk.

Finally, she grinned wide. 'No, quite the opposite.'

'Good.' He kissed her lips and held her, as the world

around them became silent and still. 'If you ever want to get back into working on people, I won't get jealous.'

'Nah, people are pricks, especially adults,' she said, repeating her father's mantra.

'Even if I asked you to as a one-off favour for one of my teammates?'

'Dunno,' she murmured with a shrug. 'I might, only casual though. I sort of give in if put under pressure because I want to help those in pain.'

'It's your nature, which is what I love about you.' With his arms around her, he gave her a tender squeeze.

He loved her. *Wow.*

'If I said it was okay for you to work on Sheldon, would you?'

'Would you want me to, considering your history together?'

He screwed up his nose. 'Not sure.'

At least he was telling the truth, and she respected that.

'Right now, I think we deserve some sort of celebration feast where we can talk some more.' He stood up and held out his hands.

She slid her hands into his. 'Food sounds good.'

He pulled her to her feet. 'There's this great place near the sea where we can let Max go for a swim.'

'I don't know if Max has ever seen the ocean.'

Max sat up and whimpered at the mention of his name.

'That's where I was planning to tell you, a bit more romantically than this place, how much you mean to me.'

'Huh?' She looked around the stinky dark alley. 'Sorry.'

'Don't be, as long as you got the message that's all that matters.'

'Message received.' Was she ready to say it back?

Yet the way Ward looked at her, he wasn't pressuring her to rush it either.

'I can't believe you used Max to track me down?'

'Like a blood hound,' said Ward with a grin. 'Max almost reefed my arm out of my shoulder chasing you.' He slipped his arm over her shoulders and tucked her into his side. 'You know, you fit perfectly right there at my side.'

And she liked it there. She felt safe there.

Ward picked up Max's lead and took their Sunday stroll away from the alley where they'd confessed all of their dark pasts. It was a step in the right direction where they headed into the light.

Twenty-Nine

The smell of roast beef wafted through the air around the farmhouse where Ward sat back watching football with Max splayed out on the dirt alongside the greyhounds. Beside him, Joe was perched in his worn armchair. Tim and Adam shared the couch opposite, with Toby tucked between them, while the Shetland pony, Goliath, guarded the beer fridge on the veranda.

In the background, a phone rang inside the house. Outside they remained glued to their seats watching the Sunday game with the cold fire pit between them.

Billy kicked open the screen door and stepped onto the veranda, saying, 'Aaaaaaand that was another guy from the Magpies' footy club asking for Zara. Move Goliath, I need the sauce for dinner.' Billy shouldered his way past the petite pony to get into the fridge.

'They're keen to bother us on a Sunday,' mumbled Adam, slouched low on the couch.

'It's the opposition, why bother,' muttered Tim, adjusting the brim's bend on his Saints' cap against the afternoon sun.

'Didn't that Sheldon have the same injury as you,

Ward?' Joe asked, resting a beer glass on the worn leather armrest.

'Yeah.' Ward thumbed over his scar, squinting at Billy, annoyed that even out here Sheldon was reaching them. 'The Magpies' coach visited the clubhouse this morning and spoke with Zara.'

Joe cocked a grey eyebrow, tipping up his hat's brim and leaned in closer. 'Are we talkin', coaching gold, Magpies coach, the Marks-Master?'

'Yeah. Should I have asked for his autograph for you?' Ward chuckled, and Max sat up as if picking up on Joe's excitement. Or was he confusing Mark with Max?

'Nah. He's the bloody opposition.' Joe leaned back in his seat and sipped his beer. 'What did he want with my girl?'

Ward tried to stop the scowl and licked his lips. 'To ask if Zara would work on Sheldon.'

Max plonked his big boof-head onto Ward's knee. Did the dog pick up on the hatred still smouldering beneath Ward's skin?

'Mm,' mused Joe over the rim of his glass as he took another mouthful.

'Hey Ward,' called out Tim, 'you're doing the same ear-tip trick with Max like you did for that pony, Norm.'

Ward hadn't realised it and stopped rubbing the pit bull's ears. Max's eyes opened and looked at him with pure relief as if to say *why stop*. 'You're getting under my skin, dog.'

'You gonna keep him, bro?' Billy asked.

'I'll make my decision tomorrow.' Ward was still unsure which way to go. 'Hey, what's that bet of yours, Billy?' Was Zara's father betting against him?

Billy gave his infectious, signature, white-toothed grin. 'It's simple. You keep Max and I get a new pair of boxing gloves.'

'Now you're giving him inside information,' said Adam, shifting in his slouched position. 'Aren't there rules with footballers and gambling?'

'People are always betting on the game. Won't influence me.' Normally, he didn't care, but Joe was Zara's father.

'Didn't think it'd bother you, lad,' said Joe and drank his glass dry. 'Billy, it's still Sunday. Couldn't fetch us another coldie while you're dancin' with that pony, could ya?'

'More like wrestling.' Billy rolled his eyes, reaching for the beer fridge while squeezing past Goliath.

'What's your prize in the bet, Joe?' Ward asked the big man beside him.

'If Billy was eighteen, it'd be a carton of beer.' Joe grinned at Billy who topped up Joe's glass. 'Thanks, lad, much appreciated.' He took a mouthful of the amber liquid and wiped the froth from his top lip. 'Augh, gotta love Sundays and full-strength beer. Just missin' my Sunday cigar.' He patted his empty shirt pocket.

'Ya had one at church, earlier, Joe,' Billy said, passing

the bottle to Tim. 'Wouldn't want Zara on your case for breaking her deal, Joe.'

Joe grumbled under his breath as he took another sip of his beer.

Is that why Joe seemed standoffish toward Ward, because his lifestyle had been restricted when Zara had helped Ward? 'Billy, what happens if you lose the bet?'

'I've gotta clean out the chicken coop and the stables for a month. So, bro, I hope you win coz that's a lot of dung to ditch.' Billy's grin had them all chuckling.

'Hey you lot,' sung out Stacey, opening the kitchen's screen door. 'I need a hand with setting the table, and can someone get the washing in? Toby, you need to wash-up for dinner, and Billy, where's that sauce?'

'The little mother has spoken, boys,' said Joe.

'Dinner, dinner, dinner,' said Toby, the awkward toddler who rolled off the couch between Adam and Tim. He clambered up the steps with the boys following, leaving Joe and Ward behind.

'You don't think I'll take Max?' Ward blurted out as he stared at the dog.

Joe shrugged. 'It's your choice, mate. I'm aware you've never had a pet before, and it's a big decision. Besides, there's no hassles in Max stayin' round here.'

'And what do you think of me seeing your daughter?' He had to ask because Joe had seemed quiet around him all afternoon. 'I won't hurt her.'

The wrinkles on Joe's suntanned brow deepened.

'How can you be so sure?'

Why not clear the air? 'I'll never do what that Paul did to her. Can't understand what sort of animal would do that to someone like Zara.'

Joe tilted his head and frowned. 'Did Zara tell you her story?'

'Yes.'

'How much?'

'All of it. What he did to her before he put her in hospital, everything.' Zara's household policy was a place of no secrets, and he'd asked her to share. 'We're working it out, Joe, so I don't accidentally trigger any past pain.' So she'd never run from him again.

'Then you'll be the first because Zara's never told a soul.' Joe squinted his eyes at Ward. 'I don't think you'd hurt Zara the way that wanker did.'

'But you still think I'm not good enough for her?' Ward wasn't scared of Joe, especially when he'd done nothing wrong.

'Would you take Zara from here?'

'Why take her away when this is her home? She feels safe here.' It felt like home. 'I also said if Zara wanted to work on people, I wouldn't restrict her. Zara's free to do what she wants, I respect what she does.'

'What about you and your life of an elite footballer?'

Ward brushed fingers through his misbehaving hair. 'What do you mean by that?'

'Zara's a private person.'

'I see,' mumbled Ward, realising Joe was just being a father. 'Zara doesn't have to do anything she doesn't want, especially if it makes her uncomfortable with any of my Club events. Besides, I'm over the media intrusion myself.' Which had only happened recently. 'Until I met Zara, I was all about football. Don't get me wrong, it's a job I love that pays good money, but since that fall I've come to realise I've only got a few years left.'

'What are you gonna do when you retire from the big leagues?'

'No idea. But Zara's shown me I'm not too old to learn new stuff.'

'I tried baking my first cake the other day. Mind you, it was half cooked, so the chooks ate most of it. Should've seen young Stacey chuckin' a fit at the state of the kitchen and finding Toby covered in chocolate. But the dogs licked him clean. Shh, wouldn't want welfare to hear 'bout that.' Joe snort-laughed and Ward chuckled.

'Bet Toby laughed.'

'You bet, that toddler's got the kind of laugh that makes you wanna laugh with him. Kids do that.' Joe sipped his beer and then sat forward. 'Can I be blunt here?'

'Sure.'

'I tried to warn Zara off of you, and I know the boys did too.'

Ward was so glad Zara hadn't listened to her father. 'I understand why, but I've never hit a woman, and I've got the most annoying sister in the world and I've never hit her.'

'Heard about your sister. Zara told her to piss off for scaring the horses, huh?'

Ward still wished he'd been there to see that. 'Tina's getting a hearing aid now because of Zara.'

'Did you have to trick your sister into going to the appointment too?'

'No, but I made her go with me and Mum.' It was the first time his sister had been in his car, and the first time she'd been quiet in any of their car rides for the entire trip.

'Sometimes family make you do things when you don't want to.' Again, he patted his empty pocket. 'Like giving up my Sunday cigars.'

'Only because they care.'

'True.' Joe's frown deepened as he rested his boot on bent knee. 'With what happened with Paul and my little girl, I didn't see it comin'. Usually I pick up things with people, but I didn't. And when I saw what that bastard had done to her it broke my bloody heart. I blamed myself.'

'Why?'

'I'd let my little girl down. Couldn't protect her from the world and hadn't done my job. Zara's like her mother, they've got that gentle nurturing nature. But what that bastard did to her just broke me,' Joe said with a frown, and he sipped his beer as if to wash away the bad flavour of the past. 'Zara cares about you, and you've helped her too.'

'How?'

'I dunno, but she's smiling again. Got that proper

smile with the double-dimples I haven't seen in years.'

'I like her double-dimple smile.'

'Me too. And she's only been doing that since you showed up.'

Well, didn't that make Ward want to high-five the sky. 'All I want to do is make Zara happy.' She was his personal brand of happy pills he wanted to overdose on.

'Me too. So, my guts are tellin' me you won't hurt her either, but can you trust yourself?'

'I do.'

'Paul loved Zara, an' that was the truth, he did. But he got jealous of her doin' her work like he didn't trust her. Would you trust Zara with her work?'

'I already told Zara I did, and I will.'

'How? When you won't let Zara work on that Sheldon.' Joe stood, hitching up his patched jeans. 'It's obvious there's some bad blood between you two.'

'How do you know?'

'I've seen your expression darken every time Sheldon's mentioned.'

'If you can pick that, how come you don't trust me with Zara then?' Ward stood and faced Joe for answers.

'That's me, not you. You seem like a good lad, and it's obvious how you feel about her. You'll try to do what's right for her.' He gazed down at the pit bull sitting between them. 'And, well, mate, if you weren't any good, Max wouldn't have bothered with you. Animals can sense stuff about people, or I wouldn't have bought those boxing gloves hidin' in the shed for Billy either.' He tapped the tip of his wide-brimmed hat and, with a grin, he headed for the house. 'Can you tell Zara dinner's ready, mate?'

'Sure.' Ward watched Joe saunter off to the back door. He'd expected the protective father speech but hadn't expected Joe's last comment. Was Joe backing him to keep Max?

Talk about pressure.

Ward headed for the stables with Max shadowing. He peered over the stall's gate where inside, Zara brushed down the bony frame of Norm. The pony's motley coat had a slight shine and his stomach seemed fuller, yet he still wore a bandage on its leg.

'Hey?' Zara looked up and there was the double-dimple smile that made him sigh.

'How's Norm doing?' Ward asked, pointing to the pony.

'Good. Tomorrow we'll put him into the holding pen out the back. Then when his bandage comes off, we'll put him in the paddocks.'

'He still looks scrawny.'

'That'll take time.'

'Will he ever be ridden?'

'Dad's confident Norm will be good for Toby when he outgrows Goliath. By that stage, they'll both be ready.' Zara put down the brush on the shelf and closed the stable door behind her. 'Is dinner ready?'

'Yep. I had a chat with your dad, I've never had the

don't-mess-with-my-daughter speech before.'

'I don't think my Dad's ever given that speech, either.' Raising an eyebrow at him, she asked, 'Issues?'

'I trust you. You know that, right?'

Her reply was a teeny quarter tilt of her head, that couldn't really count as a nod. But it was a nod. Wasn't it?

Damn. 'Well, I may have an idea for both of us to break this whole trust factor barrier we've got. Hopefully, it'll be a drama-free miracle cure.' He chuckled, shaking his head at his oversell, but at least she smiled.

'How?'

With his palm on her hip, he pulled her closer, sliding arms around her slender frame. He liked her close. 'I want to prove to the both of us that I trust you, and this may help you.' She hadn't said she loved him, and he understood it'd take time. It was like getting to the grand final where you started with the first quarter in the first game of the season and moved on from there. And he was in this for the long haul. 'Would you be willing to try?'

She gazed up at him as if searching for an answer in his eyes.

Would she be willing to take that risk?

'Um, what's the plan?'

'Let's discuss it over dinner, and we'll need to make a few calls. But I'm giving you the option to say no at any time, okay? No pressure from me.'

'We should find that *Pressure* song you mentioned.' With matching smiles, they looked like some corny couple in a chick flick about to skip off into the sunset, hand in hand.

He didn't care what it looked like, the woman had his soul. Was this what it was like to be soulmates?

'They say it's always the hard stuff first and then it gets easier,' he said.

'Now you're playing coach?'

'I'm sure I've picked up a thing or two over the past couple of decades. There's no way I'd want the constant pressure Mitchell's under.'

'Me neither.'

'So, are you game?'

Her lips twisted to the side.

The pony neighed in his stable and some chickens clucked nearby. The scent of hay and horses from the stables mingled with her fruity floral perfume as he waited for her answer.

'Okay, Brendan, I'm in.'

'Am I in trouble?'

'Depends on what you're proposing.'

'Now I don't want to do it, in case it doesn't work.' Or risk how far they've come in such a short amount of time.

'Come on, let's discuss it over dinner. Are you still hungry after the amazing brunch we had?'

'I think all that sea air made me hungry.' After lunch, they'd strolled along the shore, collecting pebbles while Max frolicked in the sea—no way, *frolicked*—he was living some dream.

But with dreams you woke up to reality.

He sniffed, trying to control his worried frown. 'Maybe I'm comfort-eating from all of these heavy emotional conversations.'

'I eat ice cream for that.'

'Sweeeet,' he said with a grin, mimicking Billy.

'So, what's the plan?'

'I'm open to suggestions you might have with this, Z.'

'Sure. But I want to know why first?'

'Well...' Did he dare? He grappled for words of wisdom from the ether of his brain, that didn't sound like regurgitated baby food. 'Let's hit the target while the defences are down and the wounds are still raw and exposed.' *What, were they going to war?* 'I mean, I think we should do this before there's a regrouping where our walls start going back up. Did that make sense? Did I sound like the coach?'

Her double-dimple smile shone. 'Yes, you made sense.'

'Okay, then.' He hooked his arm over her shoulders and headed to the house, their strides falling into a natural rhythm where she fit perfectly at his side.

He hoped this plan wouldn't be the bullet to end what they'd only just begun.

Thirty

Ward pressed the doorbell to an inner-city apartment, holding Zara's hand, while Max sat at their feet. 'We can still back out, you know?'

'Nope. We're doing this.' She squeezed his hand, glancing down the windowless hallway. 'I don't miss city living.'

'It's the only way I've ever lived.'

The door opened revealing a guy with a roasted chicken leg hanging out of his mouth. 'Ward! What the fu —
'

'Stephen, watch the mouth, mate, there's a lady present.'

'Sorry.' Stephen swallowed and nodded apologetically to Zara, still gripping his half-eaten chicken leg.

Ward led Zara and Max inside without waiting for an invitation.

'What the hell, Ward?' Sheldon hobbled by the couch near the wide window view of the city lights that spread out below as the backdrop.

'Do you want Zara to help you or not, Sheldon?'

Ward's anger simmered but the squeeze of Zara's hand made him exhale the hate. They were doing this for a reason. 'You look like crap.' Worse than the last specialist's appointment that seemed like decades ago.

'And don't you look *peachy*,' snarled Sheldon.

Where was that smart-arse's signature smug side-smirk?

'Best I've felt.' Chin raised, Ward smiled wide. Still amazed at what he was doing for love. 'Mark came to our clubhouse this morning. He told us about your surgery.'

Sheldon squinted at Ward. 'As if my coach would lower himself to visit the Saints' clubhouse?'

'He was there to talk Zara into fixing the pain in the neck you' —*are, and always will be*— 'have.' Ward grinned, shifting his neck from side to side, up and down. He winced at the white on white décor, betting he'd need sunglasses to sit in this room in the daylight.

The lift dinged and footsteps echoed down the corridor.

'Wow, this is a flash dog-house,' said Mills, with Nick and Sam in tow as they strolled through the open door.

Stephen stepped back from the doorway at the uninvited new arrivals. 'What are you lot doing here? This isn't a Saints reunion is it?'

'We're here to make sure Ward and Sheldon don't destroy the place when Sheldon gets that carrot out of his arse,' Sam said with a grin as he nudged Nick in the ribs.

'My bet goes on the dog doing that first,' Nick said.

Mills nodded, sending ripples down his glossy black mullet. 'Yeah man, you touch Zara or Ward and that dog will rip your throat out.'

'What is going on?' called out another tall male coming from the kitchen.

'G'day Angus,' said Mills, craning his neck right back to stare up at Angus's sheer height. 'Nice of you to join the party.'

'What party?' Angus scratched his head and turned to Stephen who only shrugged by the front door, taking another bite of his chicken leg.

'Zara's here to fix Sheldon,' said Ward, amused at their last-minute surprise visit.

Mills peeked around Angus's bulk and into the kitchen. 'We've brought a deck of cards and popcorn.'

'Bit unusual don't you think?' Angus said. 'It's Sunday night.'

'What matters most is that we're here.' Ward then faced his long-time enemy. The man who'd equalled him on the field and bested him off-field, who was now hunched over and broken.

Sheldon's eyes were bloodshot with black rings and bags that highlighted his pale ruddy skin. His hair was scraggly and oily, wearing a tacky, stained tracksuit. Gone was the superstar gloss, replaced by the appearance of a homeless guy who'd aged decades in days.

'Do you want this or not, Sheldon?' Ward asked.

'Yeah.' Sheldon winced, trying to nod in the

restricted collar.

'I don't miss that neck brace.'

'Hate the bloody thing.' Sheldon scowled and shifted his hollow gaze to Max. 'Why did you bring a dog?'

'Meet Maximus,' proclaimed Mills, puffing out his chest,' he's the underworld's undefeated Grand Champion. Complete with his own criminal record, and one dangerous brudder you don't wanna dance in the dark with.'

'Great, it's a circus,' mumbled Ward, shaking his head, as Zara quietly laughed beside him. 'You lot, go look busy.'

'We'll be in here checking out their fridge stash,' said Nick, herding the others into the kitchen. Soon chairs scraped along the floor. Cupboards opened and closed. Glasses clinked. The microwave's whirl released a buttery popcorn aroma, as the television clicked through channels like a mismatched rap tune.

That left Zara, Ward, Sheldon, and Max, alone in the spacious and silent lounge room.

'Hi, I'm Zara.' She stepped forward.

'Sheldon.' His eyes walked all over her and Ward frowned, but it was Max who growled and placed his beefy bulk between Sheldon and Zara.

'Good dog, Max,' Ward said, patting the dog's beautiful big boof-head.

Sheldon swallowed and hobbled backward. 'Whose dog?'

'Mine,' said Ward and for the first time he believed it.

And it was Zara's double-dimple smile that did it for him. He loved that smile. 'Max belongs to Zara and me, he's part of our family.' *Decision made.* If he wanted to commit to Zara, he'd commit to Max. It was a done deal, signed and sealed with a smile.

'Finally, he's come to his senses,' called out Mills from the kitchen doorway.

'Knew he'd do it,' said Sam, as he peeked over Mills' shoulder. 'Come on, Mills, you can show them how badly you cheat at cards.'

'Right, let's do this.' Zara fetched some cushions from the couch and placed them on the rug.

Sheldon stood still in the centre of the room, while Ward flopped onto the couch with Max jumping up beside him.

'Hey, that's a nine-thousand-dollar white couch, Ward.'

Ward plonked his boots on the pristine white coffee table. 'You were ripped off, mate. It's not that comfortable, and Max should know, he is a couch expert.' Ward grinned at Max doing circles on the white princess-couch to find the perfect position. Would those dog nails pierce the material, and how much hair would Max shed?

Max finally found the right spot and lay his head beside Ward's thigh, facing Zara. With a grizzling groan of relief, the pit bull's scarred body sagged with a sigh.

'Don't you snore, Max, you're on the clock here.' Ward patted the big head of *his* dog. He had a dog! Did he get a cigar, a pat on the back, and a round of drinks for this moment?

Zara sorted out the cushions on the floor, while Sheldon stood and blinked as if lost in space without an astronaut suit. It would've suited this place that appeared to be allergic to colour.

Ward liked colour in his life, which all started from a lady wearing odd socks and her painted pebbles. Maybe he always did, and the woman just brought it out of him. He truly was a better man with Zara.

But some habits were hard to break. 'Did your mother decorate this place?'

Sheldon scowled at Ward.

Zara wiped her palms on her denim thighs and held them palm open to Sheldon. 'Can you give me your hands, please?'

'What are you going to do?'

'I'd like to get you onto the floor where I'll remove your neck brace, then massage the area to see what I can do. I'm not promising anything, but at the least you might get some sleep.'

Sheldon remained still.

'I won't hurt you.'

'I'm not worried about you, it's Ward and that mutt.' Sheldon sneered, squinting his eyes to the right at Ward, while his body remained rigid in the middle of the room.

'Don't worry,' said Ward, 'I don't kick anyone while

they're down, Sheldon. Besides, I'm here to assist and to see what Zara does. I slept when she worked on me.' Still did, hence the nickname, Z. 'My mum assisted Zara when they worked on me.'

'My mother's overseas.'

'Huh?' Ward cocked an eyebrow at Sheldon. In the hospital, Ward's entire team had visited along with his parents. For Sheldon, only a few teammates had visited, but there were lots of women, but no family.

So where was Sheldon's nameless passing parade of women now?

Ward scanned Sheldon's showroom apartment where there were no family photos. Not like Joe's house, covered in childhood images of Zara and her brother, and Joe's wedding photos. His own parents' place showed off their times as a family, and Ward had photos of personal milestones shared with his best mates on the bookshelf. Yet there was nothing here to show it was a home.

Home? That four-letter word that had rolled around in his mind for weeks.

Then it clicked. A home was a place that shared the history of the people inside. It was a place that sheltered a family, not this box view of city lights. He missed the open view from Zara's windows. Waking up to the whip-crackers and magpies' birdsong, where early morning mist hugged the trees that gave grazing horses a mystical appearance. It was a great scene to wake up to, and even better with Zara beside him.

'Don't you normally do this in a surgery during office hours?' Sheldon asked Zara.

'I don't normally do this at all. I work on horses and don't have regular office hours, nor do I make house calls,' replied Zara with a shrug.

'So why are you doing this then?'

'As a favour to me.' Ward grinned at the stunned expression on Sheldon's face. Ward actually felt sorry for the wanker. 'Trust me, Zara won't hurt you, and you'll get a decent sleep out of it too. I know I did when I was in your shoes.' To think, almost a month ago he was a cripple living in fear of a life without football.

But he wasn't scared now.

Or should he be? If this didn't work...

'Okay, okay. Be gentle with me.' Sheldon placed his hands in Zara's.

For a nano-second Ward wanted to leap from the chair and punch Sheldon for daring to touch his girl.

'I want you to put your weight on me and lower yourself with your knees,' Zara said in a calm business-like tone.

Ward recognised that tone, she'd used it when they'd first met. It was her work tone—and this was her job. It wasn't personal.

Ward exhaled heavily. Leaning back against the white over-priced princess-couch, he patted Max's back as if to calm them both down.

Zara guided Sheldon to lie face down on the cushions

and removed his neck brace. 'Now, all I'm going to do is massage your shoulders and see if we can help you.'

We. She'd said we, and that made Ward smile like he was a part of her team. After all, he was a fine-tuned team player, and always would be, now hoping for a permanent spot in a close-knit team of two with Zara.

She rubbed her palms together and looked at Ward. 'Are you okay?'

'I am, if you are.' He was okay about this too. He trusted Zara to do her job, and pitied Sheldon who really didn't have it all. But Ward wasn't going to leave her alone for a second with that guy.

'Let's begin.' Her hands touched Sheldon's shoulders and massaged them and he soon shared the snoring sounds of someone in a deep sleep.

✳ ✳ ✳

Zara zoned out on the feel of the skin, flesh, and muscular structure of Sheldon's shoulders and neck region. The muscle tone wasn't there like Ward's, and Sheldon's skin was pale and freckle-free.

She was doing this for Ward, and to see if she wanted to work on people again. Two separate personal hurdles by two people over the one body.

She had to give Ward credit for this plan. It was a drama-free solution, with his teammates supporting in case Ward and Sheldon overreacted.

In the beginning, the tension between the two feuding men was like a spark smouldering beneath a fuel-soaked rag that threatened to explode. Then something had shifted in Ward and the tension had disappeared like fine fumes on the breeze.

Beneath her palms and fingertips that kneaded into the muscle, the flesh shifted as the bones lined up straight like keys on a piano. 'There.' She nodded with a deep breath and sat back on her haunches, grabbing the cloth she wiped her hands. 'It's done.'

She was pleased she hadn't lost her touch, and washed her hands in the bathroom.

'Did you fix it?' Ward asked, handing her a towel.

She re-wiped her hands and shook them, flexing fingers that had been working for almost an hour. 'Hope so. I've released the pinched nerve, but he'll have a longer recovery period than you.'

'Because you did me sooner and gave me the best recovery programme on the planet.'

She grinned. Crouching down beside the sleeping Sheldon, she gathered her ointments and dropped them into her bag. 'You could say that.'

'Is that the same treatment you gave me?' Ward asked, returning to his seat on the couch beside Max, sharing a yawn.

'Similar. With you, it took a lot longer to find the area. With Sheldon, I knew where to look straight away. I needed more hot and cold packs for you, because your muscle structure is so dense. Sheldon doesn't have your tone.'

'I can see how much he's lost since the fall.'

'Are you okay?' Ward had asked lots of questions while assisting her the same way his mother had helped her work on him.

Ward narrowed his eyes at Sheldon's back that rose and fell with each deep snore. 'Yeah, Z, I'm good.'

'Really?'

His eyes met hers. 'Yeah. I'm not bothered with him anymore. In fact, I feel sorry for the guy.'

'You do?'

'Yep, he hasn't got what I have.'

'What's that?'

'You.'

She stopped breathing as the world tilted, glad to be on her knees.

'I trust you, Z. If you want to work on someone, go for it. If it makes you happy, I'll support you, because what you do is amazing.'

Her throat thickened as tears threatened to cloud her vision that only saw Ward. 'I'm so proud of you.' She'd meant to say something else.

'Aww, honey.' He got onto his knees and leaned across to kiss her as Sheldon lay face down, asleep, between them on the floor. 'Is this where I say I love you, again?'

He'd been saying it all day. First time in the alley this morning, then in the car, at lunch, while sharing a romantic beach stroll collecting pebbles. Now, this. Would she get sick of hearing it?

Not while it spread pleasure tingles up her spine every time he did say it.

'Are you okay, Z?'

She looked down at the body that lay between them. The guy who'd hurt Ward. So harmless now, snoring. A patient, a stranger she'd worked on who'd be fine. She knew what she wanted. 'Can I tell you something?'

'Sure, anything.'

'First, I want to say thank you.'

'You're thanking me?' Ward thumbed his chest.

He could be such a smart-arse, but he was her smart-arse who made her smile so much her cheeks ached.

'Wow, I must've done something right to see that double-dimple smile.'

'Can I tell you a secret?' Beckoning him with crooked finger.

Ward leaned in closer, she admired his aroma of peppered musk and woodsy lime. She wanted to catch that aroma in a jar to inhale whenever he wasn't around.

And she wanted him around.

'Sure, Z, your secret's safe with me.'

Safe with him?

It was time to let go.

She licked her lips and her heart raced, not from fear but a warmth as her stomach went giddy. Her voice was husky as she trembled the whispered words, 'I. Love. You. Too.'

'You do?' His eyes widened.

She nodded, biting her bottom lip. Did she say the wrong thing?

But then he smiled so wide it hid the scar on his chin, he then cradled her face in two hands and rested his forehead against hers. 'That's the most perfect thing anyone's ever said to me, Z.' He kissed her, and she kissed him back, savouring his flavour. Her fingers brushed through his messy hair as his strong arms wrapped around her body, and she loved him.

It was perfect—except for the snoring body that lay stretched out between them in a stranger's living room.

Stephen cleared his throat from the kitchen doorway. 'Err, so, all good?'

'Yes, he's good.' Zara smiled at Ward, who kissed her forehead.

'Come on,' said Ward, 'let's go find a cosy place that involves ice cream and coffee, without sleeping bodies and snoring for background music.' Ward helped her to her feet while Max shook himself on the couch as the rest of the men filtered in from the kitchen.

'So, what's the go?' Stephen asked, pointing to the sleeping body stretched out on the lounge room floor.

'Sheldon should sleep through until morning. Please tell him to make no sudden movements when he wakes up. I'd recommend he takes a hot shower and slowly stretch from side to side.' Zara demonstrated the type of neck stretches and then picked up her bag.

'You might need to help him up off the floor. One on each side when he first wakes up, like we did with Ward,' said Nick, with Sam nodding beside him.

'Tell your physio to come and show Sheldon some stretching exercises in the morning, about ten-ish. But then I had you, Z,' Ward said, putting his arm around her shoulders.

'Are you going to come back and treat Sheldon?' Stephen asked Zara.

'Um?' She glanced at Ward.

'I'll be okay with it, I'll support whatever you decide, Z.'

'You were an exception to my rules.' Ward had broken all her barriers that she felt so much lighter. It was a gift to be in love and to have that love returned. And with love there was trust, and she trusted him, like he did with her. 'I'm sorry, I don't take on human clients anymore, I specialise in racehorses.' She preferred animals, they gave her much more personal satisfaction. It was her path and truly believed it.

She dug into her bag and pulled out a business card. 'Here's the number for my mentor. I'll call Howie and tell him what I did to Sheldon. He'll need to attend Howie's practice during business hours.' She handed the card to Stephen and caught the wink from Ward. She was that giddy with joy, she wanted to twirl on her tippy toes.

Stephen looked at the card and placed it on the white sideboard. 'What does Sheldon owe you for this?'

Ward stared at the snoring body on the floor. 'Tell sleeping-ugly we want a keg of beer dropped off at the Saints' clubhouse, and one carton for us. Then the team can have a drink together and I can have a beer with Zara and her dad.'

Stephen and Angus both raised their eyebrows at Zara. 'That's your fee?' Angus asked.

Zara nodded. 'Sorry, we don't want any Magpies' paraphernalia.' The boys would burn anything from the opposition, with her father leading the sacrificial charge.

It was like Ward read her mind, laughing to himself, as he picked up Max's lead. 'See ya on the field, fellas.'

'Thanks for coming.' Stephen opened the door, leaving the sleeping Sheldon sprawled out on the mat amongst a sea of cushions.

Angus called out from the open doorway, 'Our guys appreciate what you did for us, Zara.'

Ward put his arm around Zara and kissed her cheek leading them to the lifts. 'Zara didn't do it for you guys.'

No, she'd done it for Ward and for herself. He was a clever man under that cheeky guise. A guy who cared, and someone she loved.

Epilogue

With his sports bag over his shoulder, Ward strolled down the corridors of the MCG at the end of the final game of the season. When he spotted Sheldon walking out of one of the many doorways.

'Sheldon,' he muttered and kept walking. Ward didn't want to waste his breath conversing with the wanker. With Sheldon recovering in the lower leagues, it'd been a year since they'd seen each other.

Today they'd battled on the field where the Saints had won their final game of the season. Sadly, it wasn't the Premiership, but there was always next year to go for glory.

'Ward.' Sheldon stopped and turned. 'Hey, are you coming to watch the Grand Final next weekend?'

'We're having a Grand Final party at home.' With a full bunkhouse of guests.

'I heard you moved out of Nick and Sam's place,' said Sheldon.

Ward smiled wide. 'I live,'—yes, he lived—'in the

country, on a couple hundred hectares with Zara and her family.' Yep, that same night he'd left Sheldon's, Ward collected his colourful crockery and favourite reclining chair (that got christened at home with Zara in front of the fireplace), and that was the start of his family life, complete with Max.

Mills had moved into Ward's old room and upgraded from part-time man-couch duties to buying his own special chair to join the ranks of Sam and Nick, playing princes of their suburban castle. Sam had adopted one of Zara's rehabilitated dogs, who became the man-cave's new mascot. And the awesome foursome regularly crashed in the farm's bunkhouse like it'd become their second home.

'Didn't think you'd be the type to live in the country,' Sheldon said.

'Me neither.' Ward doubted he'd live any other way now.

'Long drive to the clubhouse, isn't it?'

'It's not that far if you avoid peak times.' Ward was used to car-pooling with Zara. During the week he'd study trackside drinking the best coffee, hanging around until he had to go to practice. On weekends, the whole family made the journey if he was playing at home. On the away-games his best homecoming was meeting Zara at the airport where his feelings for her only intensified on his return.

'Nice place?'

'Yeah, it's,' —*let's not brag about nirvana*—'good. We're currently working on making this circular moon gate from stones for Zara's latest rock garden. It'll be a great sculpture to view from our bedroom window.' Yeah, he was learning to landscape while playing with some big toys, like tractors that came with gadgets better than any TV remote control.

'Huh?' Sheldon stepped back, scratching his head. 'So, I never said thanks for bringing Zara over.'

'Don't need to. You dropped the beer off, that's enough.' A keg, which the team consumed in a team bonding session, that'd been a hell of a good night.

The carton went home to Joe, where they booed at the Magpies game on the TV. It was a night under the stars with the fire pit warming them and the sleeping dogs, while Goliath tried to raid the beer fridge.

But that was ancient news, considering all that'd been happening in his life.

'So, what are you doing in the off-season?' Sheldon asked.

'Hanging at home, plenty to do there.' Yep, he was becoming a farmer! If someone told him a year ago that he'd study for an agricultural degree, he'd never have believed it. But it'd proven to be both a physically and mentally challenging lifestyle. He didn't mind doing the fencing and working the fields for crops. He enjoyed picking his own organic produce that even had his sister giving her bell-ringing nod of approval.

He had Joe as his mentor, Tim was his off-sider, and he helped Zara with the animals, and they shared horse riding lessons together. All while Ward was learning a trade that was an entire world away from football. He still ran in the mornings with Max and the greyhounds, worked on the farm, and attended his scheduled practices. Ward was in prime physical condition.

He'd even helped the local school do a few football training sessions. The Principal and the local country football club asked if he'd assist coaching when he could, so there was a future that still included the game he loved.

'That's it, not taking a holiday over the summer?' Asked Sheldon.

'Well, once the racing spring carnival is over, I'm taking Zara to Bali for a few weeks. My sister's getting married over there. I'm the best man.' Ron would become the brother-in-law, slash, good friend Ward saw regularly at the track. Ron had convinced Tina to take a cooking class together, which started their Balinese love affair, and, thankfully, that dirt smelling mung-bean stew was long gone history.

'So, you're still with Zara then?'

'Absolutely.' There was no life without her.

'Why did you bring the dog that night when Zara helped me?'

'Didn't trust you or me back then.' It'd helped Ward and Zara crush one major hurdle that was the catalyst of their relationship—trust.

'Is that because of what I did with that chick, right?'

Ward doubted Sheldon even remembered her name. Funny thing was, Ward couldn't either. 'Things happen for a reason, mate. You can have all those worshipping women because none of them mean jack to me.'

'You're really into this lady?'

'We're married. Twice.' Ward showed off the gold band he wore on his finger with pride, still living the honeymoon.

Sheldon's eyes widened as he stepped backward. 'C-c-congratulations.'

'Thanks.' Not that Ward needed Sheldon's approval when he was the happiest he'd ever been. Ward and Zara had gone to Mexico for a holiday and bought all sorts of crap to fill his sister's shop. There, while dancing after a fabulous fiesta and indulging in tequila under the full moon, he'd proposed and they were married within days. It was perfect.

But they hadn't expected the upset families on their return. Joe wanted to give Zara away, his best-mates wanted a bachelor party, and his mother wanted family photos. Under the combined families' pressure, they re-swore their vows at their favourite look-out on the farm where they'd shared their first date. They then shared a feast under the orchard's blossoms on a fine spring day. It was even better, wearing their wedding outfits again, this time with a photographer to display the magical memory, for not only their home, but their families and friends who'd all been there to celebrate.

Max even got his mugshot upgraded for the walk down the aisle, that soon made him a star on Instagram! As the face for their not-for-profit rehabilitation group for rescue dogs, Max still followed Ward like a shadow for their morning runs and then slept all day. Still a major part of their family, Max now had his own group of puppies on the way.

But there was only one woman who did it for him, one he'd do anything for, and he smiled at Zara approaching. Even with Sheldon at his side, she looked only at him with her shining eyes and double-dimpled smile.

'Hey beautiful,' said Ward, kissing her warmly.

'Hey yourself. It was a great game.'

'It's over for a while.' Ward smiled at her, happy for the holidays. 'Do you remember Sheldon?' *Douche-bag number one.*

'Hi.' Zara held out her hand.

Sheldon shook her small hand. 'Hey, I never got to say thanks for what you did for me.'

'That's okay.' She turned her attention back to Ward. 'So, are you ready? The gang's all at that Italian restaurant.'

'Mum and Dad, too?'

'Yeah, even your sister and Ron are joining us. Dad said Christmas this year is going to be huge. Pete's coming in from out west with his baby too.'

'Yeah, and ours for the New Year.' He patted Zara's baby bump, delighted. He was going to be a family man, for real. 'Take care of yourself, Sheldon.'

Sheldon's jaw dropped, as he blinked at Zara's

tummy then up at Ward. 'Err, yeah, you too.'

'We will, because I've got my best mate to take care of, who takes care of me. Maybe I'll let you read all about it when I release my best-selling player's memoir—*not*.' He put his arm around Zara's shoulder where she fit perfectly at his side and headed for the car. 'He's still a dickhead,' Ward whispered. 'I think he's jealous of me now.'

'No way.'

'Oh yeah. I bragged about living the good life.' He glanced over his shoulder where Sheldon remained staring at them with a stunned expression and no smug side-smirk.

'You're not.'

'I am, Z. I'm living a dream.' Living a life he'd never expected, as the winner of his own personal Premiership Cup, that just kept on filling with a future that worked wonders for Ward.

The End

Did you like the story?

If so, *your opinion* matters to me!

I'd love to read your review on

GOODREADS, BOOKBUB.

Or share a cover of this book on social media so I can see

how far this story has travelled!

Please add *#Escape2HEA* for me to find you.

With much gratitude,

mel

A . R O W E

And now, read an extract from…

THE ART OF

DUST

MEL A ROWE

One

It's a strange sensation being weighed down by guilt. It made Kat grip the steering wheel tighter while her internals stirred with the giddy sensation she'd once loved as a child. All from the faded road sign that read, *Welcome to Elsie Creek.*

'Did you live here, Mummy?' Kaytlyn asked, brushing away the auburn strands freeing themselves from her pigtails. Her sparkling, lapis lazuli blue eyes, took in the passing view.

'Only for the summers.'

'When?' Kaytlyn asked, straining her neck to see while her finger marked the page of the colouring book nestled within her purple tutu.

'Before you were born.' Back when life was so much simpler.

'How come you've never told me about this place?'

Kat never wanted to. She didn't even want to make this trip.

'Is that a tractor? And, it's…*moving*.' Kaytlyn waved energetically at the farmer like he was a famous movie star, driving a slow tractor as they passed him on the road. 'This is the country, isn't it? Like real milk-making country?'

'Not that kind of cow, sweetheart. They're beef cattle.'

Their hire van, with the U-Haul trailer rattling behind

them, slowed as they approached the herd spilling over the sides of the road. Men in sweat-stained Akubra's steered their quads around the cattle with horns bigger than the handlebars on their bikes. Stocky Blue and Red Heelers yapped at the Brahman's heels, while more stockmen on horseback whistled as the odd stockwhip crack rang in the air.

'Mum, they're cowboys rounding up the herd!'

'Don't call them that. This is Australia and they're cattlemen, stockmen, ringers or drovers, and they're mustering the mob or they're droving. *I think*—it's been a while.'

She drove through the herd and continued along the open highway that stretched like a never-ending black carpet. It sliced through the centre of red dirt scrublands, with the railway line running alongside. All heading for the tiny Northern Territory town, dead ahead.

They passed rolling fields of drying grass waving in the breeze like a huge green sea. Tall gum trees crested hills that kissed the cerulean skyline where wallabies lazed in their shade. Nestled amongst its bark-peeling branches were flocks of white cockatoos, hiding from the late afternoon sun. The familiar countryside generated an electrical hum beneath Kat's skin. She was glad this long drive was almost over.

Then the hard part would begin.

Again, the weight of dread slammed heavily across her shoulder blades.

'Can't wait to go bushwalking with you, Mummy.' Kaytlyn clicked the heels of her new hiking boots, peeking out from the edge of her tutu.

Kat hadn't hiked in years. 'Tell me again, please, what are the rules of walking anywhere out here?'

'Always take a hat, a water bottle, sunscreen, snacks for the trail, and tell someone where you're going. Carry a big stick to smack the ground to scare snakes and goannas getting suntans across the tracks. Don't use the stick to poke down holes, coz the scorpions and spiders can kill you. Don't climb trees that don't have green ants on 'em coz they'll have white ants that eat trees inside out, so they'll break. Don't play near fruit bats coz they can make you very, very sick. Don't pat the cattle coz of their horns…um, am I missing something?'

'Water. What did I tell you about the water? It's the most important,' —*and terrifying*— 'part.'

'Oh, I'm never ever allowed to go swimming in any of the water holes, billabongs, rivers, lakes, streams or seas, and I have to stay back from the water's edge coz the man-eating crocodiles like to eat children for lunch.'

The place didn't sound like fun at all. 'Are you okay with all that?' Kat wasn't.

'I can't wait. How come you know all this when you grew up in the city, like me?' Kaytlyn sat taller, her fingertips reaching for the dashboard, causing her crayons to spill out of her tutu and onto the floor of their rental van.

'I used to stay with Uncle Frank and Aunty Bea for school holidays.' A time she once lived for.

'Bee, like a black and yellow stripy bee that stings? I can spell that—B.E.E.'

'Brilliant. Although, the native bees here don't sting, but the wasps do.' Was there anything good she could share without scaring her daughter back to the more civilized southern states of Australia. 'Oh, and you spell Aunty Bea, B.E.A. It's short for Beatrice.'

Kaytlyn sat back mouthing the letters, committing the new spelling word to her fast-growing vocabulary.

'How come they don't visit us?'

'How many days has it taken us to get here?'

'Five. It's the longest road trip of my life!'

Kat laughed at the seriousness of the six-year-old wearing a tutu and hiking boots.

'Do Aunty Bea and Uncle...' Kaytlyn waved her crayon like a wand.

'Frank, short for Franklin.' Everyone's name was shortened, including her own of Kathryn to Kat.

'Yeah, him. Do they have any children I can play with?'

'No.' *They would've loved some.* 'I'm sure there are plenty of new friends to make in your new school, honey.' Kat hoped she sounded excited when she'd rather be back in their studio apartment. All this space was daunting compared to the comforting claustrophobic cocoon of a capital city.

She sat higher behind the steering wheel as they entered the town's main street, with its row of shops on either side. There was the hardware-feedstore, the small supermarket, and the mighty pub that stood proud as the centre of this small country town. There was a park with signs pointing to the train station's Tea Room.

Even though she hadn't seen the place in seven years, the town was the same, as if stuck in some weird time warp, except now it had a set of pedestrian lights guarding a zebra crossing.

'What's that?' Kaytlyn asked, pointing to the road ahead.

Kat slammed on the brakes and stared over the steering wheel with wide eyes. 'I think it's a water buffalo.'

A short, black, shiny-nosed water buffalo stood smack in the middle of the road, in the centre of town. It stared at them through long black lashes, chewing like a cow, with red ribbons waving on the breeze from its curved horns.

Was it going to charge their hire van?

'It's got ribbons on it, Mummy, so it must be someone's pet, huh?'

A ute across the road tooted its horn, and the driver shouted out of his window. *'Get off the road, Cecil.'*

The buffalo kept chewing as he ever so casually strolled in front of Kat's car. Red ribbons waved off its horns and tail, and on its sides were large letters written in bright red chalk.

'What does that writing say, Mummy?'

'Um…Choose your movie for the marathon today.' *Weird.*

As the buffalo ambled along the sidewalk, they continued down the main street in silence. At the outer edge of town, they turned onto a bitumen road, where properties extended into acreage.

A group of children played in the street while push bikes lay in the grass on the side of the road.

Déjà vu hit Kat like she'd woken inside a dream, slowing down for the game of street-cricket where the children stopped and stared as they drove past.

'Mummy, how come they're playing on the road?'

'They do that in the country.' Just like she used to.

'There are more children on this street than in our whole building. Will they all be going to my new school?'

'I assume so.' There was only one local bush school, with the nearest boarding school over four hours away by bus. It was a ride Kat knew well.

They approached the road's dead-end before an expansive field of golden grasses that rippled in the breeze.

At the sight of the two-storey weather-worn house, her heart hitched a lump into her throat. 'We're here.'

Find the rest of the story
at your favourite online bookstore...

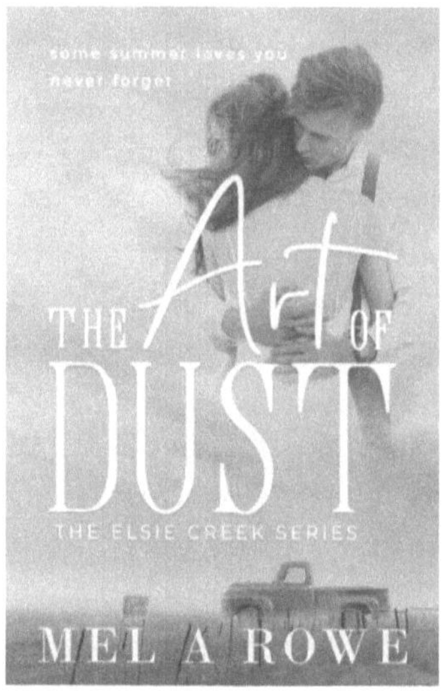

Acknowledgements

Thank you

Thank you for reading this story.

Thank you to the amazing *Handbrake* for not disowning me. Thank you to my sister, Jackie, for always supporting me while sharing your fabulous in-depth knowledge of AFL as a life-long fan of the sport.

Thank you to my writer friend, Renee Conoulty for sticking with me and giving me that prod when needed most.

Thank you to my fabulously patient critique partner, Suzi Frewin, for your amazing honesty and support.

To Nik Eveleigh, the Englishman who popped out for bread and milk and ended up in Africa with a wife and two kids, your bravery is respected for daring to read my work!

Lastly, to you, dear reader, thank you for taking the time to read this story, where I look forward to sharing more with you in that *Escape to Happily Ever After. (#Escape2HEA)*

Thank you, because I can, because I did, and because I continue to do so …

Until next time,

mel

A. ROWE

About the Author

Australian Bestselling Author, Mel A ROWE, creates escapes for you to enjoy from the comfort of home.

Delivered with a dash of drama, witty humour and quirky family units, Mel is known for reinventing romantic versions of *home*, taking her common characters on uncommon journeys that lead from boardrooms to billabongs as they try to find their own HAPPILY EVER AFTER.

Living in Northern Australia, Mel enjoys random outback road trips, fumbling with her camera, annoying her family with her bad singing, and making new friends in the middle of nowhere—except for water buffalos. She's been chased by a few.

Feel free to contact Mel as her word journey continues at…

MelAROWE.com

For Further Reading

& for finding so much more
go to...

MelAROWE.com

Be sure to join Mel's vibrant email group for insights, updates and exclusive offers on NEW RELEASES.

You wouldn't want to miss out...do you?

Also by Mel A ROWE

Avoiding the Pity Party

Unplanned Party

Winter's Walk

THE ELSIE CREEK SERIES

The ART of DUST

DIAMOND in the DUST

CAKED in DUST

Xmas DUST